THE TURNING OF THE BONES

A KI KHANGA TALE
BY
BALOGUN OJETADE

MVmedia, LLC
Fayetteville, GA

MVmedia, LLC
PO Box 143052
Fayetteville, GA 30214
www.mvmediaatl.ocm

Ordering Information:
Quantity sales. Special discounts are available on quantity purchases by corporations, associations, and others. For details, contact the "Special Sales Department" at the address above.

The Turning of the Bones/ Balogun Ojetade. -- 1st ed.
ISBN 979-8-9905121-0-8

Contents

I dedicate this book to my wife, Iyalogun. For over twenty years you have tolerated the late nights and weekends with my typing away at the computer, writing yet another novel. I am forever thankful, grateful, to have a wife as patient, understanding and supportive as you.

CHAPTER ONE

"Etse! Where the hell are you, man?" Kwadwo was astride his kwapawnkah, waiting for the boy yet again. It was intolerable. An accident of birth made the spoiled sprat an obirempon's son. That didn't give him the right to keep others waiting all day long. Bad enough to have to play nursemaid for him, but worse by far to put up with his tardiness. Among other rampant flaws.

The other men were already mounted up, ready to go. Their kwapawnkah held their place in the keep's courtyard, but little shifts in their legs and ears showed they were picking up on their riders' impatience. A standard patrol of six, plus Kwadwo and, of course, Etse. If he ever showed up. The other men were quietly whispering to one another and chuckling a little. Kwadwo ignored the cowries he saw passing from hand to hand. Etse had something of a reputation, and not a good one. If he wanted to ruin any faith these men might have in him as a leader, then he was well on his way.

And if he was rolling in the hay with some little gbolo (*whore*) again today, Kwadwo rather thought at least one of the patrolmen was about to make some money.

"Etse...!" he started to call out again but heard the clopping of hooves behind him. He gently kneed his mount around, and it pivoted gracefully in place.

"I'm here, Kwadwo," Etse said. And he seemed to have actually taken care in his preparation this time, thank God. His hair was tucked neatly inside a helmet. He was wearing a full mail shirt, the same linked-ring protection most of them wore when they bore arms. A spatha was belted at his side – the longsword of Kiswala. Kiswala might have abandoned this far off outpost, Kwadwo thought with some bitterness. But Asanteman had not yet abandoned Kiswala, or civilization. And it would not, while strength remained in his bones and sinew.

Sometimes he despaired being able to pass that on to the youth, though. And then sometimes – like this moment, seeing Etse astride his kwapawnkah (*antelope*), resplendent in white beaded armor with shining silver bracers and greaves and a sword belted at his side – sometimes, he could see a future that filled him with hope. If only he could find a way to pass the banner on, to get the beardless young man to live up to the potential Kwadwo saw in him.

"Well, now that we're all here," Kwadwo said, "Let's begin. We're to patrol along the Pra River. We look for any signs of scouts – tracks, campfires, anything you see that looks out of place."

"Perhaps we'll catch raiders in the act," Etse said.

"The Gbawmehi Fawji rarely raid this far west, but they could. The Abonsa Hii from Kongo are a greater risk, though. Remember: if we see one boat, we investigate. More than that, and we retreat for reinforcement. We're too few to stand in the way of a large raid," Kwadwo added, with a pointed look at Etse. Who still looked hopeful, damn him. Trust an untested boy to want bloody battle. He knew the other men in this patrol. They were career soldiers, and like Kwadwo, preferred peace to war.

Peace was less likely to make you dead.

Kwadwo took his kwapawnkah up to a canter, and the rest of the men fell in behind him. The gates stood open, as always during the day. With a lookout in the towers, it was simple to spot any danger coming at them across the open moor, so the gates were only shut at nightfall. Takoradi wasn't the port city Nicran was, but when Gbawmehi Fawji raids around the larger city had increased tenfold, Asantehene (*King*) Kwesi decided it was more prudent to move his government West, away from the invaders. Takoradi was far from impregnable, but it had stood since long before Kwadwo was alive to see it, and he imagined it would still be there long after he was gone.

Outside the walls, the straight road from the city to the seaport was cluttered on either side now. Batches of small huts, tents, and other dwellings stood where a few years ago there had been nothing. Hundreds had gathered there, forming a small town of temporary houses outside the gates. There was another proper town down by the shipping docks, but it had been overwhelmed by the number of refugees coming toward them from the East.

The Gbawmehi Fawji were coming, working their inexorable way across Asanteman. It was just raids now, but it would be war before long. Kwadwo could see it like storm clouds on the horizon.

He led them off the main road, down a path that took them away from the port, and out over the moors. There on the open land, he gave his kwapawnkah a nudge, and she obliged with more speed. They shot toward a distant point of shoreline with long, graceful strides.

It was beautiful country here. Some trees – enough for shade, enough to break up the line of the fields. Rolling low hills, covered with tall grasses. The scent of the sea in his nostrils, blowing in from the west. The sky was blue, the wind in his hair, the ocean beckoning... Sometimes, on days like this, Kwadwo remembered what it was like to be young and without care. He loved this time, with just the wind and the steady beat of hooves to keep him company in his thoughts.

"A sail!" Etse called.

Kwadwo reined in his kwapawnkah, slowing her to a stop. The patrol fell in around him, Etse pointing a hand toward the river, which had already become quite wide here. From their vantage, he could observe a good chunk of the banks, and there was indeed a small boat headed into a sandy beach.

"Something odd about that boat," Kwadwo muttered. His eyes were not as young as they once were, and he couldn't make out the details at this range, but something looked wrong to him about the way the sail flapped and fluttered in the wind.

"We should investigate, right?" Etse said. "One boat – we investigate."

"Aane," Kwadwo said. "Etse, your eyes are young. Can you see the man on their tiller?"

The boy raised his hand to shield his eyes from the sun and squinted. "I can see the tiller, but I don't see anyone manning it."

That was what had caught Kwadwo's eye. The ship wasn't being steered. He could see that even more clearly now. It drifted in toward shore, washed by waves and a light breeze, but the prow of the boat wobbled back and forth like an unsteady drunk trying to find his way home while the sail snapped wildly back and forth at the whim of the breeze.

"We'll go check it out. Something has happened to them, and we should find out what. There could be survivors," Kwadwo said. Then he had a thought and added "Or it could be a ruse. Stay alert, swords and wits sharp." He hadn't lived this long by being incautious.

Etse kept his disappointment in check as they wound their way down the hillside toward the shore. Old Kwadwo seemed relieved that the boat was adrift, but more than anything else Etse wanted something to happen. Life had to be about more than just studies in the morning, patrols and sword work in the afternoon, and then more studies in the evening – didn't it? Was it any wonder that he slipped away when he got the occasional chance? If it was up to men like Kwadwo and his father, he'd never do anything worth anything.

He'd been wearing a sword since he was eight. Even before that he'd carried a knife as long as he could remember. But he'd never once drawn in actual combat, and he knew every man riding with him had. It burned him that they knew he was still raw, untested. Etse had confidence in his skill – he'd disarmed Kwadwo himself in practice just last week. But how could the men ever truly trust him until he'd seen actual battle?

He knew they would not. Oh, they'd follow him, because they were ordered to. But he wouldn't really be one of them. Couldn't be, while things remained as they were – boring.

They were careful as they approached, moving slowly enough that the boat had almost reached the shore before their kwapawnkah hit the beach. The boat wallowed there, bobbing in the shallows. It was a small craft, only about twenty feet long or so. The sail was slack now, luffing a bit in the wind, and Etse could see from here that it was torn, tattered.

"Dismount," Kwadwo ordered.

Etse swung a leg down from his kwapawnkah, carefully holding the reins in one hand. Something had spooked her, but at first, he couldn't see what was bothering her.

Then he still couldn't see it. But he could smell it.

The wind blew the scent from the boat, and Etse's stomach turned. Decay, he smelled, and rot. Something long dead and left to sit in the sun. His stomach roiled as his mind envisioned what they were about to find. He swallowed hard and stepped into the water with the other men around him. Their confidence gave him courage.

"Dosseh, Amuzu, grab the prow and bring her closer to shore," Kwadwo said. The two men took a line dangling from the front of the boat and hauled it closer to the beach. A minute later, sand was grating on the bottom of the boat.

Etse stepped closer, but Dosseh came between him and the vessel.

"Not yet, Etse," he said, stepping up and grasping the side of the boat. Etse saw his nose wrinkle at the smell, much worse this close to the source. He peeked over the guardsman's shoulder.

The boat was small, a tiny sailboat. A fishing boat, perhaps, with no cabin or cargo area. At first, he thought the bottom of the boat was covered with debris. But then he realized what he thought was debris was human remains.

Tattered cloth. Bits of broken bone. Chunks of flesh and other bits left rotting in the sun. *Odd that the birds hadn't been working on this mess*, he thought, his mind racing as it tried to make sense of the scene. Then he saw movement.

"Look there, Dosseh!" he said.

"God, one of them is still alive!" Dosseh said. He reached into the boat, holding his hand out. "Here, take my hand. We'll help you."

The hairs on the back of Etse's neck raised as an arm rose slowly from under the human remains. It was slender, emaciated. Almost skeletal in appearance. The movement struck him as wrong, somehow, and he reached to Dosseh's shoulder to pull the man away.

"Dosseh, I don't think..."

That was all Etse managed to say.

The thing in the boat became a blur of motion, pushing itself up from the deck of the boat and latching itself to Dosseh's arm. It wore nothing but tattered rags, and its skin was covered in what looked like infected bite marks… and it moved faster than anything Etse had ever seen.

Its jaws locked onto Dosseh's flesh just below the elbow, below where the studded shirt would perhaps have warded off its teeth. Blood spurted. Dosseh let out a yell, and tried to pull his arm away, but it held him fast with both hands, ripping a strip of flesh from his arm.

Dosseh screamed and kept screaming as he punched the thing in the face with his free hand, once, then again. The blows seemed to have no effect at all. Then with a sudden movement that was uncanny, it scuttled up his arm, jaws clamping on his throat. Dosseh fell backward from the boat, losing his footing and falling, his head slipping under the water, the thing crashing down with him.

Etse reached into the water. He grabbed hold of the thing with both hands by its shoulders, straining to pull it off Dosseh. It clung to the downed man with a fantastic strength. Then it whirled on him, launching itself clear of the water, claws scrabbling for Etse's throat. He thrust out both arms, just barely keeping the snapping jaws away. But the momentum of its charge lifted him from his feet and threw him back into the water.

The waves closed over Etse's head, those deadly claws still locked in their grip around his neck. Etse struggled but was unable to even lift his head from the sand. His lungs burned for air already. His arms were getting weaker. Any moment now they would falter and the thing would have him.

Then it was gone. Firm hands grabbed him by his woven armor shirt and hauled him up. Etse felt cool air on his face and gasped, gulping deep breaths. Breathing had never felt so good!

"Are you all right? Are you wounded?" It was Kwadwo who'd hauled him up from the water. Etse struggled to bring his gasping breaths under enough control to answer.

"I'm not hurt," Etse managed to get out. "Dosseh?"

Tetteh shook his head, and Etse looked down into the water. Dosseh's body lay there on the sandy bottom, staring up at them, eyes wide open. *That could have been me,* Etse realized. Almost had been him. If Dosseh hadn't stepped in to block him, it would be Etse's body still on the sea floor.

"Damn it," Etse said. He snapped his attention back to the thing, which was surrounded now by the rest of the patrol. They baited it in turns, working together to keep it from getting to any of them. One would get its attention, back away – and then another man would sink his sword into it from behind.

But their swords didn't seem to be doing much good. One of the thing's wrists hung limply, half severed. And it oozed blood from more than one gaping wound. Rotted intestines had spilled from its side. Yet it kept fighting. And Etse could see the men tiring.

Then one guardsman jumped back a hair too slow, and the thing had him. Its claws caught his sword arm, and its mouth followed, snapping down like a vice on the fleshy forearm. The man screamed for help, pummeling the thing over the head with his free fist while it gnawed on him. Two other men stepped forward, stabbing their swords into its back with little effect.

The scene sickened Etse. But more than that, he felt hot anger. Those were good men the thing was hurting. Killing. And he'd had enough.

His sword came free from its scabbard almost without a thought. Kwadwo said something behind him, but he couldn't hear. He was lost in the movement of the sword now, gliding in to face this horror. His blade whistled, almost catching it in the head, but instead struck one of its arms, detaching it at the elbow.

That got its attention! It turned from its prey, jaws snapping at Etse. The man it had savaged collapsed to the ground, clutching his wounded arm.

It darted in at Etse, trying to get past his sword, but he sidestepped the movement and it lost several fingers. He'd take the thing apart one bit at a time if that's what was required to finally kill it.

It rushed again, and he stepped off to the left, avoiding its good arm. It turned, following his dancing movement impossibly fast. Etse's blade sang through the air as he blocked three slashes. The monster leaned in toward him, jaws trying to bite his face, and he only just got his sword between him and that terrible maw.

Its teeth gnashed on his blade, some snapping off as it tried to bite through the steel.

He twisted the sword, pulling it clear of the creature's mouth and opening a gash across its cheek. Ichor dripped from its wounds.

Two patrolmen closed on the thing from behind, stabbing swords into it to pin it in place. The creature hissed, and tried to turn on the men, but the men grimaced and held on. Their swords held it fast.

"Now, honhommawne (*demon*), we will see how well you do without a head," Etse said. His sword split the air one more time, taking its head from its shoulders.

The thing collapsed in a heap as soon as it was headless. All semblance of life was gone in an instant. The men withdrew their swords hesitantly, and who could blame them? Etse half expected the thing to come back to life and attack them again. But it stayed there, oozing putrid blood onto the sandy beach.

"Sir, over here," another patrolman called. Etse fought to recall his name – Kudowor. He'd never felt it was so important to remember the names of these men before now.

"What is it, Kudowor?" he asked, working to cement the name in his memory. The guard was standing near where the creature's head had landed, his sword drawn.

Etse came up alongside him and gaped down at the head. It was gritty, covered with damp sand. Oozing ichor from its neck. Rotting flesh dangled in tatters where it had been damaged during the fight.

But still the thing gnashed its teeth together, trying to reach them.

"It still didn't die?" Kwadwo asked. He'd followed Etse over, and his eyes promised a conversation later that Etse did not relish. He winced inwardly – he was supposed to stay out of harm's way on these patrols, not step into it. But he worked hard to keep his outward demeanor calm and still. If he'd had to do it over again, he would have done the same anyway.

"No, it didn't." Etse poked it with his sword tip, and it hissed up at him.

"There must be a way to kill the thing," Kudowor muttered.

Kwadwo drew his sword. "This was blessed by the Ahene Akamfo (*Chief Shaman*) himself," he said. "If any weapon can end this honhommawne, it can."

He stepped forward, the thing hissing wildly at them, teeth clashing together. Then Kwadwo stabbed his blade downward, punching through the thing's skull. It went suddenly still.

Everything was quiet for a long moment, and then the men began cheering. Etse felt a wallop across his back and turned to see Kudowor grinning at him.

"Well fought, Etse," Kudowor said.

"Thank you," Etse replied. He tried to keep the pleasure out of his voice, and the heat from his cheeks at the compliment. Kudowor was, after all, a warrior veteran. He'd seen more battles than Etse had years. But behead a monster, and it seemed much was made equal that was not before.

"Is Utuka's wound bound? Good!" Kwadwo was barking orders, snapping the men back to reality. "Anatsui, Nii, wrap that thing up in a cloth. We'll drag it behind the kwapawnkah. I want the obirempon to see it."

"What the hell was that thing, Kwadwo?" Nii asked.

"Damned if I know. Perhaps the Asantehene will," Kwadwo replied.

Etse wondered what his father would think of the creature. Wondered if in all Ki Khanga, anyone had ever heard of such a thing.

"Kudowor, give me a hand, would you?" Etse murmured. The other man tilted his head sideways a moment, then nodded. Etse stepped back out into the water, Kudowor following behind.

Dosseh lay there on the bottom, still staring up sightlessly at the sky, his mouth open in a wide "O," his neck ripped open even wider where the thing had gnawed at him.

"Help me get him to shore?"

"Aane, of course," Kudowor replied. Together, they lifted the dead man from the water.

CHAPTER TWO

Etse was tired and sweaty by the time they made it back home. Kwadwo sent riders ahead to warn of their approach. So naturally a crowd had gathered to greet the warriors as they rode through the gates. Young children had been tucked away, although a few of the older ones had been allowed to stay. Most were curious onlookers, but Dosseh's family had been warned of his fate, and they were there as well. It was easy to tell who was there for curiosity and who was there in grief.

"Keep well back!" Kwadwo called. The patrol brought their kwapawnkah about the wrapped body of the monster, forming a wall to ward away onlookers. Etse walked his kwapawnkah out a few feet, carrying a precious burden tied to the saddle behind him. One woman from the crowd, her face already burnished with tears, saw his movement and broke out crying again.

Etse knew Dosseh's wife on sight but had never learned her name. They'd been wed for longer than he'd been alive, and her shattered face told him everything he needed to know about their relationship. He dismounted and slowly led his mount to the woman.

"I am sorry for your loss. Dosseh was a good man, and he fought for us all," Etse said to her. She nodded, crying all the while. A couple stepped from the crowd, the woman taking Dosseh's wife by the shoulder and leading her away. The man stepped up to Etse, grief clear on his face.

"I will take the body for burial," he said.

"I'd be glad to help–" Etse began to say but was cut off.

"No need, Etse. We will care for him." The man waved a pair of younger men over, and together the three of them carried Dosseh away, leaving Etse to wonder about the madness of a world where such creatures could exist, and where good men like Dosseh could simply end, in an instant.

Over and over in his mind, Etse saw Dosseh hold him back from the boat. If he had not, their roles might have been reversed.

He looked back at the rest of the patrol. Kwadwo had things well in hand. The kwapawnkah were being taken away by stable boys. Utuka was walking away toward the physician's house to have his wound tended. Etse was glad; he'd watched the man and seen sweat pouring from his brow on the ride home. He was surely more hurt than he'd let everyone know at the beach.

"Come with me, Etse," Kwadwo said. "We need to report to your father."

Etse managed to not roll his eyes. Barely. He couldn't avoid the sigh that escaped his lips, however. He'd rather have faced another of those things from the beach than deal with his father, right now.

Kwadwo strode down the long stone hallway, Etse unwillingly following close in his wake. He tried to keep from smiling. He needed to appear stern. It wouldn't do to smile.

Kwadwo spoke. "You know your father has explicitly said you are to come with my patrols, but stay clear of actual battle, yes?"

"Aane." Etse sounded quiet, but not petulant. Good so far.

"Yet today you disobeyed those orders and engaged that...thing."

"Aane."

"Why?" This was the question that mattered most to Kwadwo. This answer would tell him much about the man Etse was at his core.

The boy hesitated. "Because I was angry," he said at last.

Kwadwo looked over his shoulder at the boy – young man – sharply. That was not the answer he'd been hoping for. "Angry? At what?"

"These men may be my father's guards but they are my people too. That makes an attack on them an attack on me. Dosseh died, for me! I fought it because I could. And because..." Etse trailed off.

"Because you owed it to the men who serve you?" Kwadwo said quietly.

"Aane."

That was more like it. Kwadwo stopped dead in the hall. He turned, took Etse by both shoulders. He stared deep into the boy's eyes, trying to see his soul there. He'd known Etse since birth, twenty years. He'd watched the boy's father, Kwesi, pamper and shelter the boy since birth. All the while Kwadwo struggled to do the opposite, exposing the boy to everything he could, as safely as he could.

Because Kwesi was wrong. Kwadwo could feel that in his gut. Kwadwo didn't pretend to understand all the complex politics involved, but he was a lifetime soldier: he knew discord and anarchy when he saw them.

Without strong leaders, Asanteman would be doomed within a generation. It would rot from the inside, as much as fall apart from without.

Did Etse have the spark that could make men follow him? Kwadwo hadn't seen it before. But after today, he felt something he had not for a long time.

Hope.

"Boy, your father is a good man. He's done well by his people. But he is...not always right about some things."

Etse laughed sharply. "You don't need to tell me that!"

"No, perhaps not. But hear me out," Kwadwo said.

A booming sounded in the hall, as the doors on the far end flew open. "Kwadwo! What is this? What has happened? Is Etse safe?"

Portly, almost round, and getting on in years, Kwesi had nonetheless retained the light step of a duelist. He strode down the hall toward the pair, and inwardly Kwadwo cursed. Who knew when he might get another chance to speak with Etse alone?

He kept such concerns to himself, for today. "We were on our way report to you, Kwesi."

"We were attacked on the beach," Etse broke in.

"By whom?" Kwesi replied. "The Oyo? Or have the Gbawmehi Fawji become bold enough to raid this far west?"

"Neither, Kwesi," Kwadwo said. "I think perhaps it is better that we show you. I am not sure I would have believed the tale had I not been there to live through it."

Kwesi looked puzzled, but curious. "Lead on, then," he said.

Kwadwo turned, taking long strides down the hall. He loved Kwesi like a brother, but the man was lost in these times. He was a consummate politician. He should have gone to Kiswala when the last merchants left. Out here, on what was suddenly a cast off and wild frontier? Kwesi was not in his element, and that could doom them all.

He hit the big double doors at the end of the hall without breaking his stride, thrusting one back with each of his arms so they flew open. Bright sunlight was sharp contrast to the cool dim interior of the stone mansion. His men had surrounded the thing, to keep people away from it, and it was still wrapped in the heavy cloth they'd used to drag it from the beach. He gave a sharp nod to Amuzu, who bent over and carefully lifted the cloth away.

"What have you got, Kwadwo? The man acts like there's a lion wrapped up, ready to take his arm off!" Kwesi said.

"Something worse," Kwadwo murmured. "This thing attacked us on the shore."

And then the cloth was pulled back, the corpse revealed. It was as motionless as it had been on the beach. All signs of unnatural life had vanished. Now it was just a stinking corpse, flies buzzing about it. The crowd backed away, those who had caught a glimpse murmuring to others in confused voices.

Kwadwo watched Kwesi, not the crowd. His old friend was examining the body carefully, eyes taking in every detail, that ferocious mind analyzing everything the eyes saw.

But most important, Kwadwo never saw even the slightest hint of disbelief in those eyes. Not a scrap of incredulity. Instead, he saw the glimmering of fear.

Somehow, Kwesi had known such a creature existed.

CHAPTER THREE

Seeing the creature a second time didn't diminish the horror for Etse. Not even a little. If anything, this viewing seemed worse. He picked out small details now that he had missed during the fight. The thing's chin was intact enough that he could see stubble there, perhaps a two-day beard. The shoes it wore were leather, well-made but badly worn. Tangled around its neck was a thin silver chain, and he could just barely make out the sun-shaped Nsoromma Adinkra symbol dangling from it. This wasn't some hell-spawn, then…

"This thing was once a man," Etse said aloud.

His father shot him a sidelong look, eyes squinting as if to bore into him. "Aane, I think so."

To the guards around the body, Kwesi said, "Burn it."

Then he turned to Kwadwo and said, "Come with me. We need to talk."

"Etse should join us," Kwadwo said.

Kwesi shot him an incredulous look. "This is a serious matter, for serious counsel. Not a place for boys." He took a step back through the double doors to go inside, then turned as if in an afterthought to add: "Etse has studies to attend to, anyway."

Kwadwo gave Etse a long look. Etse could see the pity in his eyes. He turned away, but saw it echoed again in the eyes of all the guards. The men who'd just accepted him as one of them, if ever so briefly, turned away one after another, embarrassed. For him? By him? To Etse, it didn't matter which. Their looks turned his recent accomplishments to dust and roiled his gut.

He fumed quietly as he stalked away from the courtyard. He didn't like being left out of things, but his father cutting his legs out from under him like that was infinitely worse! Kwadwo was no better, really – setting him up for his father to humiliate him in front of everyone.

He'd fought and killed this thing! Of course, his father didn't know that yet, but he wished he thought that news would earn him a proud look rather than a wrathful one. Best to get out of the palace for now. He exited the gates, unsure where he was going. There were taverns in town, where he could drown his problems in wine, and always a few admiring women around who would spend some time with him.

All of that felt as hollow today as it always did. And for once, hollow was not going to do for him.

Instead, he set off toward where Dosseh had lived. The man had saved his life. Had given him his life. The least Etse ought to do was pay his respects properly.

That would not be hollow.

* * *

Kwadwo followed Kwesi down the hall to the conference room, then through that into Kwesi's private study. It was not a room he generally used for meetings and spoke volumes about how serious this matter was. More often, Kwadwo and Kwesi spoke in the larger room they'd just left.

"Shut the door please, Kwadwo. And slide the bolt," Kwesi said.

His tone was deadly earnest and brooked no discussion. Kwadwo did as he bid without a word, then stood quietly by the door while Kwesi busied himself with taking two goblets and a wine urn down from his cabinet. He set them on the table and filled the cups, beckoning Kwadwo to sit.

Kwadwo broke the silence first. "You knew about these things. How?"

"Rumors only, Kwadwo." Kwesi sighed deeply, staring down into his goblet. "Rumors I hoped were untrue."

Kwadwo sank into his seat, his mind racing to take in the implications. "This is not an isolated thing, then."

"No," Kwesi said. "I have heard of some curse or affliction which is spreading across Ki Khanga. At first, I had hopes that it was simply a fiction. But – you know I have spies throughout the continent."

"Of course." Not news that Kwesi kept a dabbling hand in Ki Khanga politics.

"They've brought me more than one tale, these past few weeks. Of a deadly illness. It began in Sati Baa. Men eating flesh – their own and the flesh of others…then the sickness changed, transformed…the dead rising from their graves to attack the living. Gbohii (*The Dead that Eats*)."

"Gbohii. Like the one Etse slew today on the beach," Kwadwo said.

That got Kwesi's attention fast. "Etse slew it?" he asked. "Was he injured? Bitten? Cut?"

"No. His skill with a sword is quite remarkable, you know."

Kwesi glared at Kwadwo. "You are supposed to keep the boy from danger still!" He paused a moment. "Perhaps it was inevitable that eventually he would be at risk. You said he killed it. How?"

"He cut off its head," Kwadwo said. "That didn't quite kill the thing, though. The body died, but the head kept going until I stabbed it."

"Nothing else was hurting it," he added. "The men had stabbed or slashed the thing a dozen or more times."

Kwesi nodded, closing his eyes. He seemed deep in thought, but that wasn't unusual. He'd always been more of a thinker than a man of action. Sometimes, though, Kwadwo felt that Kwesi thought too long, and acted too late. The situation unfolding here suddenly had all the hallmarks of one of those times.

"You knew about these things," Kwadwo said, trying to prod Kwesi with his words. "You're not surprised that it took beheading to stop it. You've obviously heard a great deal about something that I know nothing of. How am I to keep you and yours safe if you hold back such information?"

Kwesi opened his eyes and glared across the table at him.

"I think it's time to share information, don't you?" Kwadwo asked.

They held each other's gaze for another long moment. Then, Kwesi sighed, looking away and nodding. He took a long gulp from his cup before speaking again.

"At first I'd hoped it was just a story," Kwesi began. "A frightening one, but fiction, not fact. Then, as I heard more versions of the same tale, I knew that something terrible was happening. A curse, a plague. And worse, that it was evolving…and spreading."

He stopped for a breath and then went on. "I hoped even then that it might miss Asanteman. Might burn itself out in the deserts of Mali or on the Sati Baa River before it crossed here. So I held my tongue, to not panic people over nothing."

"What are they?"

Kwesi looked startled at the question. "I don't know. The stories spoke of the those slain by these undead things rising again to join the other creatures. The curse seems to spread that way."

Kwadwo's eyes went wide as he considered the implications.

"Those slain by it rise?" he asked. He could feel the blood drain from his face.

"Aane, that's what I said." Kwesi looked confused – and then his face filled with sudden clarity as he understood. "Who?"

"Dosseh," Kwadwo said, rising from his seat. "He was slain by the thing before the rest of us could react. We turned his body over to his family."

"You'll have to go at once. I have no idea how long it takes for them to rise," Kwesi said. "Bring whatever Gyase (*personal bodyguards*) are on duty and burn the body as soon as you've arrived."

Kwadwo went for the door. Every second might count. If one of those things got loose in the town, it would be a disaster!

He hit the outer doors still moving at a good pace, and barreled out into the daylight, almost knocking over the man lingering on the other side.

"Kudowor!" Kwadwo said with surprise. "Where's the rest of the patrol?"

"They dragged that thing outside the city," Kudowor replied. "To burn it as Asantehene Kwesi ordered."

"They won't be back in time," Kwadwo said. "Come with me, quickly. I'll fill you in on the way."

Kudowor gave Kwadwo a look that begged him to spill what was going on, but Kwadwo just kept moving. He was filled with dread, his head playing images of Dosseh's family being killed horribly by his Gbohii.

"Kwadwo, do we need kwapawnkah?" Kudowor asked.

Kwadwo thought for a moment, then replied. "They're already back in the stable. By the time we got them saddled, we could already be there. It's not far." He felt in his gut that time was very much of the essence. How long did they have?

He didn't know. There were so many things that they didn't know right now. That lack of information might be their undoing if they didn't catch up, and fast! Know your enemy was an axiom that had been drilled into Kwadwo his entire career.

"Kwadwo, what's going on?" Kudowor asked. "Why the rush?" He was puffing, trying to keep up with the pace Kwadwo had set.

"That thing we fought on the beach?" Kwadwo replied. "You become one of them by being killed by one."

"Dosseh," Kudowor breathed.

They doubled their speed.

CHAPTER FOUR

The door was closed when Etse arrived at Dosseh's house, but he could hear voices inside. He reached out to knock on the door, hesitating. Would they even let him in, or turn him away? He'd had enough of looking like a fool for one day.

But he owed Dosseh his life. He made a thin line of his lips, clenching his jaw against his fear, and rapped gently on the door.

Someone inside shuffled around for a few agonizingly long moments, and then the door creaked open a short span. An elderly man stared back at him through the narrow gap. "See here, young man," he said, "now is not a good time. There is grief enough here. Be on your way."

Etse took a deep breath before answering. "I was with Dosseh today when he fell. I tried to save him, and I... failed. I share in your grief."

"Do you, boy? I've seen you. Heard stories of how you waste the life Nyame gave you. Now you come here, for what purpose?"

"He saved me, today. I just..." Etse stopped, looking down. "He saved me, and I couldn't save him. I wanted to thank him."

Just another man who saw a useless boy when he looked at Etse. He turned to go but stopped when he felt a gentle hand on his shoulder.

"For that you may come in," the old man said. He stepped aside and opened the door the rest of the way, and Etse felt his shoulders sag with relief. He stepped into the candle lit entryway.

"My thanks," Etse said.

"He is in the back of the house," the old man replied, gesturing down a dark hallway.

But before he could guide Etse further, a scream echoed from deeper in the home. The screams continued, again and again.

"Stay behind me!" Etse said, following the sound. He drew his sword as he stalked down the dark hall. All his senses were tuned ahead. His sword reflected bits of candlelight from both the room behind him and the one before, but mostly the hallway was oppressively dim.

The person screaming was a woman. Etse thought it was likely Dosseh's wife. Three more strides carried him to the open doorway. He didn't hesitate, plunging through into the room beyond.

Sunlight streamed through the one small window in the room beyond, but it didn't reach the corners. The gloom was broken by the light of candles, several of which had been set on a long table in the center of the room, and a few which had rolled to the floor, guttering there fitfully. Movement caught Etse's eye, drawing his attention to the far corner of the room. A woman was trapped in the corner there, holding a chair between her and a burly man struggling to catch hold of her. She screamed again.

"Hey! Over here!" Etse cried. The man turned to face him. But it wasn't a man. Etse's jaw dropped, his eyes growing wide. What he was seeing was impossible, a nightmare. It was Dosseh's body, with empty eyes and a hungry mouth full of gnashing teeth. It looked at him for a moment, then came at him with quick strides. It was clothed only in a loincloth. His family must have been washing him for burial when he…rose.

"Dosseh," Etse said. "Do you know me?"

It didn't reply. It was Dosseh, and yet it wasn't. The face was his. The arms, the legs. It looked like him. But there was nothing human about the grotesque look of rage and hunger on that face.

And no man could continue walking with a wound like the one on its neck.

This thing seemed slower than the one on the beach. It was moving quickly, but not with the incredible speed of the other creature. Perhaps it was slower because it was newly revived? Etse was glad, regardless of the reason. He wouldn't have wanted to fight the faster one within such narrow confines.

"Eeeeat," the Dosseh creature moaned. "Skiiin."

Dosseh was still coming forward, and Etse held his sword carefully between himself and the Gbohii. It ignored the blade, kept moving closer.

Etse pushed his other hand out, and Dosseh slammed into his open palm, his chest hair coarse under Etse's fingers. The creature grabbed Etse by the arms, meeting resistance from the woven armor he still wore from the patrol.

Etse's mind lit back to the scene on the beach. He remembered Dosseh telling him to back away – taking the attack that might well have been his. The man had saved his life. Etse owed him everything. The thing in front of him snarled, drool dripping from its open maw, and snapped its teeth, trying vainly to bite him.

This thing wasn't Dosseh. It was something dark and evil.

He stared into the thing's eyes, looking for some semblance of humanity there. He saw none.

"Goodbye, Dosseh. I free you," Etse said. Then he raised the tip of his blade and slid it home between the thing's teeth, slicing upward into the skull.

It dropped immediately, like a puppet with the strings cut.

He withdrew his blade from the still body, blood staining the tip. In the corner of the room, Dosseh's wife had dropped the chair and slumped to the floor, sobbing. Etse heard a sound from the doorway behind him and turned, sword raised to face the new threat. But it was Kwadwo, and behind him Kudowor. The men had their own swords drawn, as well, but their mouths were open in surprise.

"We'll need to burn this one, too," Etse said, looking back down at the body. To his own ears, his voice sounded hollow, empty.

Kwadwo grasped him by the shoulder, pulled him around until they were face to face. "Were you hurt?"

"No, it never touched me. My armor kept it from me." Etse thought for a moment. "Why are you here?"

"I ought to be asking you that question!" Kwadwo replied.

"I came to pay my respects. And found...this." Etse waved his hand at the body. "Kwadwo, did it seem slower to you?"

"Aane," Kwadwo replied. "The one on the beach moved faster than any man I've ever seen." He shuddered a bit.

"This one was slow, almost like it was taking its first steps. In a way, I suppose it was." Etse wiped his blade clean and then sheathed the sword.

"What do you mean?" Kudowor asked.

"This thing wasn't Dosseh," Etse replied. "I don't know what these things are, but I don't believe there is anything left of the people who died once they rise as these monsters."

"In a way, that's a good thing," Kwadwo said. "Imagine being trapped inside that body and having to watch while some honhommawne possessed it and killed your friends, your family."

Etse stepped away from the other men. Dosseh's wife still crouched in the corner, sobbing silently in her grief. She saw him coming and shrank away.

"I'm here to help," he said, reaching out gently with one hand toward her. "Were you hurt?"

He prayed she had not been, that he'd been in time. He'd never repay the debt he owed Dosseh; it wasn't possible. But if he'd saved the man's wife, perhaps it would at least be a start.

She nodded and held out her own hand to show him. Etse inhaled sharply. Two crescent moon bite marks stood out bright on her skin, a trickle of blood running from the wound. It was a shallow cut. It would need cleaning, but she'd be fine. Not the perfect rescue, he mused ruefully, but nowhere near as bad as things could have gone. He stepped up to the table, where he found a bowl of water and long, clean strips of cloth that had been placed there to prepare Dosseh's body. He took two of those, wet one, and stepped closer to the wounded woman.

"Here, let me see," he said. She held out her hand again, and he gently washed the blood away from the wound. Then he bound it with the clean, dry length. He stood up, taking a step back.

"Keep that clean, and it should heal well."

She nodded silently, clutching her hand against her chest, tears welling in the corners of her eyes. Etse couldn't think of anything else to say to her. Nothing he said would help, anyway. The woman had seen her husband dead this afternoon, and then had seen his body rise and try to eat her this evening. There were no words to heal those wounds.

Instead, he turned back toward the door. Kwadwo and Kudowor were already gone, back down that dark hall. The body still lay where it had fallen, though. Etse wondered if he ought to do something to straighten it out, but the thought felt ghoulish.

He heard the heavy tromp of many boots. Etse's hand went to his sword almost without thinking about it. It had just been that sort of day.

But the men who poured through the doorway into the room were his father's. The leader was Gnama, one of the oldest men in Kwesi's personal guard. Nowhere near as fit as Kwadwo, he'd nonetheless managed to move his portly body with good speed. His face was reddened, his breath coming in hard rasps, but he hammered out a smart salute for Etse.

"Kwadwo told me of the goings on. Your father sent us to help, but it seems we've arrived a bit late to do more than clean up the mess." Gnama wrinkled his nose in distaste. "You can be on your way. We'll dispose of the body."

"This man was one of ours, Gnama. His body needs to be burned but give him all the honors you can accord." Etse's voice held a steel that surprised even himself – and he could see from his wide eyes that it outright shocked Gnama.

"He saved my life today," Etse went on, more gently.

"We will, Etse. You have my word," Gnama replied.

Etse nodded his assent, and then stepped from the room, taking long strides toward the door, out of this cramped space. He wanted to be back outdoors, in the fresh air, where he could breathe. He didn't stop moving until he was and then exhaled a breath he wasn't sure how long he'd held, sucking in a great lungful of air. The night had fallen, the sun's lingering radiance casting the western hills in red, and the city streets into pools of blue shadow. The cool evening breeze was a welcome relief.

Kwadwo and Kudowor were outside, as were a half dozen kwapawnkah – brought by the guardsmen, no doubt. Etse shook his head. How had his father known to send the men?

Kwadwo was exchanging quick words with a messenger boy. Then he stepped away, looking worried. He handed Etse a set of reins. "Asantehene Kwesi wants me back straight away. And I want you there with me, Etse."

Etse cocked an eyebrow. "What now?"

"Utuka is burning up with fever," Kwadwo said. "He's the man bitten by that thing on the beach."

Etse grabbed the reins Kwadwo tossed to him and stepped up into the saddle of his mount, feeling his heart freeze at Kwadwo's words.

CHAPTER FIVE

Etse was bone tired by the time he slid from his saddle in the courtyard. He barely noticed the man who took his mount's reins from his hand, but his steps were still firm and solid as he approached the main doors. Lights were everywhere – candles and lanterns alike brightening the night. It was a huge expense, all that light, but Etse gathered his father felt the situation was bad enough without being unable to see.

"This way, me wura (*my lord*)," one of the servants said. He guided Etse and his two companions not into the main building, as Etse had thought, but into the east wing. Flanking one side of the courtyard, it was attached to the main building only by a single corridor. Asantehene Kwesi had used it in the past for visiting dignitaries whom he felt a need to honor but didn't quite trust.

He was being very careful. Which meant he was very worried.

They followed the servant down one well-lit hall, then another. Finally, they ended outside a set of private suites – again, someplace generally reserved for visitors of some prestige. Not where someone would usually bring a man for an illness. Two guards stood outside the suite door – in full beaded armor, swords belted at their waists.

"Where is my father?" Etse said.

"Inside, me wura," one of the men replied.

"Step aside. We'll join him."

The two men looked uncomfortable, but did not move.

Etse looked from one of them to the other. "Well?"

The same guard replied again. "We're under orders not to let you in, sir," he said. Then he added, "No disrespect meant. It's your father's orders."

Something inside Etse snapped.

He looked back over his shoulder at Kwadwo. The older man seemed to see sense his mood and simply gave him a small nod. Kwadwo would back him. Good enough.

Etse took a step forward, and the guard stepped forward with his left leg, raising an arm toward Etse's chest to stop his advance. Instead, Etse fluidly stepped to the outside of the man's arm, grasping his wrist in a steel grip, and twisted. The guard went down, hard, crashing into the floor with a jangle of steel. But Etse had already released his wrist, spinning toward the other guard. Steel flashed in his hand, and before the other man could do more than flinch, the tip of Etse's blade rested on his throat.

The guardsman swallowed hard. He didn't move. The man on the floor behind Etse didn't try to rise, either. Kwadwo had a boot on his wrist, and stood above him, shaking his head very slowly.

"I mean neither of you any harm," Etse said. "You're good men. But understand this: you are to obey me, not just my father. And should you stand in my way again, I'll not be so gentle." He sheathed his sword.

Neither guard gave him any more trouble as he went through the door into the suites beyond.

The space beyond was another long hall, smoky from the oil lamps hung on the walls. Three doors were evenly spaced on each side of the hallway, but Etse heard voices coming from the door set into the far end of the passage, so he walked past the nearer doors. He was about to open the far door when he felt a hand on his shoulder. He turned. It was Kwadwo.

"I have your back," he said.

Etse nodded, grateful. Time to face his father. He opened the door.

Kwesi whirled as he heard the door creak behind him. He tried to shout at whichever of the damn fool guards was disturbing him now, but his voice croaked instead. Incense smoke hung thick in the air, coating his throat with its cloying sweetness. He rose from his seat, gathering his voice.

"I said we were not to be disturbed for any reason!"

"And you also said I was to come to you directly," Kwadwo replied from the doorway. Etse stood there beside him. Etse opened the door the rest of the way, waving his hand in front of him as if he could waft away the haze of smoke.

"I would rather you waited for me in the main villa," Kwesi replied. "And would rather my son was anywhere but here, Kwadwo."

"I thought it important that I come to see Utuka," Etse said. "And don't blame your men in the hallway, father. They did try to stop me." He came the rest of the way into the room, followed closely by Kwadwo. Kwesi could see another man in the hall beyond who didn't enter but stood guard outside instead. One of Kwadwo's warriors, Kwesi was sure, but he didn't know which one.

He gave Etse a careful, measuring look. Kwesi sighed. He still saw a little boy whenever he looked at Etse. But then that boy would do something to remind him that he wasn't a boy anymore and hadn't been for quite a long time.

"I wanted to keep you out of here so you would be safe," Kwesi said, hating how his voice sounded petulant even to his own ears.

"Father, none of us are safe right now. But I think we would all be safest if we pool our knowledge and resources."

Kwesi grimaced. The boy made sense; galling is it might be. "Fine, fine. Stay clear of the bed, though."

He turned back away from his son to return his attention to the tableau in front of him. The injured soldier lay on the bed, covered with blankets. Only his wounded arm and his face were visible. The man's face was tinted bright red, and slick with sweat. His eyes were closed, his breath coming in ragged gasps.

Alarming as that might be, the wound was worse. Kwesi had never seen a limb wound turn bad so quickly. It was almost like there had been poison in the bite. The skin around the wound was green. Pus and blood oozed from the wound itself, and the skin around the bite looked almost as if it was coming apart from inside.

"My god, what's happened to him?" Etse whispered, standing beside Kwesi now. *When had the boy grown taller than me?* Kwesi thought.

Kwesi ignored the question. The answer was fairly obvious: the bite was festering, and it would kill the man unless something was done. The two physicians standing on either side of the bed were making ready to perhaps save his life. If not his limb. One of them was even now fastening a leather strap tight around Utuka's upper arm, while the other carefully washed a hand saw. Kwesi spared Etse a sideways glance, to see if the boy knew what he was looking at. The ashen face told him that he did.

"Will it save his life?" Etse asked.

"We'll know by tomorrow," Kwesi replied. He tried to hold his annoyance in check. The boy should know better than to ask questions that no one could answer. The surgery might well save the guard's life. It might not. Which result occurred was less relevant than the data he would acquire from the experiment.

A bit of information was more valuable than a thousand cowries. That was nearly always true, in Kwesi's experience. But perhaps never more so than now. He felt gallingly unprepared. The scraps he'd been able to glean out of tales from Sati Baa were woefully incomplete, and some had to be flights of fancy. The trouble was, it was hard to tell which were true and which were not. He'd never have believed that the dead were rising to attack the living, had he not seen the evidence of it with his own eyes.

One of his surgeons spooned a bit of thick syrup into the man's mouth. It would keep him unconscious through this next bit. The other was already carefully laying the saw against flesh. The cut would be just above the elbow. The bite was in the lower arm, but the physicians must have felt they couldn't save the elbow. A shame.

The cutting started. There was little blood. The tourniquet had been skillfully applied and cut off the flow. Kwesi heard his son gulp loudly as the saw struck bone. The grating buzzed at him, too, but it was like a fly. He spared the briefest of glances for his son, and saw not the horrified face he expected, but grim determination.

Another surprise. Etse seemed full of them today.

The cut was complete. Kwesi examined the wound, as his surgeons prepared to seal it with hot pitch. The flesh seemed good. The rot perhaps had not traveled so far from the wound. The surgery might have had saved the man's life after all. Time would tell. The surgeons cleared up their equipment and made ready to depart.

Then he turned to his son. "Come. We have more to discuss." Without another word, he strode from the room, shouldering past Kwadwo without looking to see if they followed him.

He knew they would.

CHAPTER SIX

Hours had passed since Asantehene Kwesi and his annoying son had left, and Narko was having a hard time staying awake through his guard shift. He'd been handed many boring tasks in his years of service, but this? This one was the most obnoxious thing he'd been ordered to do in a long time. As if that wasn't bad enough, he was still stinging from the embarrassing stunt Kwesi's boy had pulled, taking him to the floor like that.

"I should be in bed, asleep," he complained.

"You should be keeping your mouth closed and be glad you've got work," grunted Trebi. The old man had been annoying him with such sage advice for their entire shift.

He sighed, eyeing the candle. They'd be relieved in only a few more hours. But it was cursed late, after the middle of the night, and he'd been up since dawn. He yawned again.

"Quit that," said Trebi.

Narko yawned again, just for the sake of doing it. He saw Trebi roll his eyes and look away.

"Listen, why do they need two of us to guard one sick man? Who do they think is going to bother him?"

Trebi grimaced. "I'm not so sure that we're protecting him, boy. I've heard rumors about how he got hurt, and..."

Something crashed in the room behind them, startling both men. They turned to face the door, straining for long moments to hear another sound, but there was only silence within.

"What was that?" Narko said.

Trebi shook his head. "I don't know. I don't want to know. Let it be, boy. My gut says bad things about this."

A series of thumps, from beyond the door. Then silence again.

"We ought to make sure he's all right," Narko said. Trebi was making him nervous, which made him angry. The superstitious old fool was jumping at shadows. Narko could see the lines of fear etched in his face. Was he unmanned by some bumps in the night? He stepped forward to the door.

"Boy."

Narko turned to look back at Trebi.

"Don't do this."

Narko's face became a mask of scorn. "Fearful old man," he said, lifting the bar from the door, "go hide in a shadow and..."

He never finished whatever it was he had planned to say.

The door crashed open, and something that had once been a man stepped out into the candlelight. It moved faster than Narko could have imagined possible.

He didn't even have a chance to scream before its teeth were tearing out his throat.

* * *

Etse's eyes flickered to the door. Had he heard something, out there? It was late, and his ears were probably playing tricks. He yawned and stretched, trying to rejuvenate his mind.

"Too tired, Etse?" his father asked.

Etse searched his father's face, but as usual couldn't tell if he saw mockery there or not. He chose his words carefully. "It has been a long day. Perhaps we'd be better continuing in the morning, after some rest? We need to be at our best to figure out how to deal with this matter."

If Kwesi was really telling all he knew – which Etse rather doubted – then they didn't have much more information than what he'd already told. The plague was in Sati Baa, Mali, and Oyo, and all Kwesi knew was that it was spreading fast. Those slain by the dead rose to become like them – Etse had already seen that happen firsthand, so they'd confirmed that bit of the story. The gangrenous corruption of Utuka's wound had surprised even Kwesi, though.

Etse mentioned the small bite Dosseh's wife had sustained shortly after they'd left Utuka. Kwesi sent guards to take her into custody, and for tonight at least she slept safely under their roof, men posted at her door to ensure she stayed there. The wound had not shown any signs of the corruption when she was brought in, for which Etse was grateful.

There was so much they needed to know! About the plague itself, and the creatures, but also about how badly this had struck their allies in Oyo. Etse could imagine the nightmare in some of the larger cities, if even a handful of the Gbohii managed to get in. All Asanteman and even all Ki Khanga itself could be in danger.

Kwadwo yawned, too. "Perhaps you're right, and we should resume this in the morning."

Kwesi looked from one of them to the other, then shrugged. "As you wish. But early."

Etse heard a yell, from somewhere outside. And a loud crash, followed by more shouts. He was on his feet in an instant, hand already on the hilt of his sword. He stepped to the door, only to find Kwadwo's arm blocking his path.

"I go first, Etse," Kwadwo said, in a tone that brooked no argument.

Etse nodded his agreement.

"Stop, both of you! We are safe in here. Let the men deal with this," Kwesi said.

Etse looked back at his father, seeing the frank fear in the man's eyes for the first time. He'd always thought of him as a big man. Bigger than life, bigger than whatever the world could throw at him. His father had always been able to think his way through anything the world threw at him. Negotiation. Diplomacy. Talking through problems.

"This is the moment for action, father. Not for talking. Our people need us," Etse replied. "Open the door, Kwadwo."

Kwadwo held his eyes only for a moment, then complied, pushing the door open hard, stepping out into the hall beyond with sword already drawn. Etse followed close behind him, ignoring his father's protests. He pulled the door shut tight and heard the bolt slide home on the other side of the door. The sound of metal scraping against wood echoed in his mind. It sounded final, like the closing of a book.

The hall lamps guttered in a faint breeze blowing down the passage. Up ahead, Etse could hear more noise, and now smelled smoke, too.

"Fire?" he asked aloud.

"The whole place could burn down, if it gets out of control," Kwadwo replied. "The yelling is coming from the courtyard." With that, he started down the hall, sword out and held at the ready. Etse drew his own sword and followed. His eyes flickered from side to side, seeing movement where there was none as the lamps cast dancing pools of darkness on the walls. The light was growing brighter as they moved toward the main doors.

The courtyard was a cacophony of light and noise. Fire engulfed the east wing of the palace. That was where Utuka was being treated, and Etse felt his stomach sink as he felt his worst fears confirmed. He'd been hoping that the emergency was something unrelated to their current crisis. Worse, the courtyard was full of people. Servants and soldiers alike were carrying buckets from the well to the fire, trying to keep it from spreading. Etse couldn't see any sign of a Gbohii, but he could feel in his bones that one was about.

"Utuka," Kwadwo said. Etse thought he was merely naming aloud the most likely source of the current trouble, but then he realized Kwadwo was pointing with his blade. Looking down that way, he saw a form, hunched over in a dark corner next to the stable. The thing reached down, pulling something from the ground to its mouth, and Etse realized with a start that it was eating.

"The corruption," Etse said. "It was just the first signs of his turning."

"If just one bite spreads the infection…" Kwadwo shook his head. "This is worse than we had feared."

"We need to stop the spread," Etse said. "Right now."

He was walking toward it before he'd realized he had started moving, anger filling his gut. Not at Utuka, but at this curse, whatever it was, that turned good men into these creatures. He could hear the crunch of gravel that said Kwadwo was stalking the thing beside him.

But before they could reach it, there was a crash of breaking wood from the burning building, and an unearthly shriek. Firefighters fanned back as something shambled forth from the burning building. It wore the armor of Kwesi's house guard, but it was on fire, and the flames had burned its face past recognition. The fires seemed to do little to slow it down, though, and it staggered toward the crowd.

"Two of them!" Etse cried. Utuka must have slain at least one of his guards. But it had risen so quickly! How fast could the curse cause the slain to rise? They could find themselves overrun. "Kwadwo, take Utuka. I'll deal with this one."

"Be careful," Kwadwo said.

Etse turned without replying. How do you respond to something like that, when you are on your way to slay something out of fireside stories and nightmares? Still, he'd stopped two of the things so far, and this one still had the slow, jerky motions

Dosseh's Gbohii had shown. It was freshly raised, and not full of strength like the one on the beach.

"Get back!" he yelled to the crowd, striding through them. They broke like water around him, making way. "Men, grab your weapons!"

That was all he had time to say before it was on him, and it was all he could do to keep his blade between himself and the horror. It still burned – he could feel the heat of the flames on his face as it closed. Worse yet, the thing still wore its armor and helm. That left almost no gap for a strike to the neck. Removing the thing's head was going to be impossible.

It slashed at Etse with a claw, and he cut the hand off. Blood oozed from the thing's wrist. It kept coming though, and he was forced to give ground again and again. The Gbohii's neck was too well guarded. How could he get in a blow that would stop the thing?

Etse was forced back once more, dodging a grab. His heel turned on a rock, sliding sideways, and he felt the ground rushing up to meet him. He hit hard, and the impact drove the air from his lungs. His sword skittered from his hand.

The thing followed him to the ground, on him in an instant. Etse pushed back with his left arm and barely kept its jaws away from his throat. The Gbohii snapped its teeth at him, trying to bring its mouth closer to his face, his neck. He could feel the heat from the beads of the thing's armor, heated by the flames, burning his arm and chest, feel the scorching on his face like a fierce sunburn.

Etse screamed, fear and pain filling his world.

His scream was cut off by water. Blessed, cooling water, splashing down over his face, over the Gbohii, quenching the fire, cooling his burns. The Gbohii lifted its head, snapping at the woman who'd been brave enough to pour the bucket of water over the combatants.

The brief respite was all Etse needed. His fingers found the hilt of his sword, and he pulled it close. When the Gbohii saw him moving, it snapped its head back to face him, maw opening wide. It lunged down at him.

He brought the tip of his blade in front of that open mouth. The thing's weight drove it down onto the sword. Etse felt the crunch of bone as the blade bit through the back of the mouth, up into the thing's brain.

It stopped moving as quickly as the others had. Pus-filled blood dripped down Etse's blade, and he turned his head to avoid being covered with the stuff. With a heave, he pushed the monster off him.

Getting to his feet was an effort. He felt a hand on his arm, helping him when he almost slipped back to the ground. He looked back up and saw the woman who'd thought to use her bucket of water.

"My thanks," he said.

She smiled and nodded, melting back away into the crowd. Etse looked around, seeking Kwadwo. He couldn't see him at first, but a scuffle on the far side of the courtyard drew his eye. There! Kwadwo was leading a trio of troops, and they'd pinned the Gbohii to the wall with spears. Etse started their way, but before he'd cleared half the distance, Kwadwo lopped the thing's head off. The body sagged against the spears, slumping to the ground as the men withdrew their weapons and recoiled in disgust.

The bodies of three more men lay on the ground nearby. It had not gone into the abyss quietly. At least one of the men was rocking on the ground, groaning in pain. Etse grimaced. What should they do with men who were wounded by these things, if the wounds were not fatal, but passed the curse? He looked down at the Gbohii's head where it lay on the ground. The head was still moving, teeth still gnashing. It was indeed Utuka.

Etse stabbed it through the eye, and it stopped moving.

"Well done, men," Kwadwo was saying, as Etse withdrew his blade.

"What was that thing, Kwadwo?" one man asked. The other two were helping the wounded soldier, binding his injury.

Kwadwo looked up and saw Etse approach. The men followed his gaze, and Etse found them all staring at him expectantly. They wanted him to answer? What could he tell these men that would not terrify them even more than they already were?

"Were any of you hurt?" Etse said aloud.

"Just Atukwei here," one of the soldiers replied. "Obo and Gimfo are dead, not hurt."

"We'll need to get him to my father's physicians as quickly as possible. The things carry some sort of poison in their bite," Etse said. "You're sure none of the rest of you were bitten?"

The men blanched but shook their heads. "No, sir. We're fine."

He hoped they were telling the truth. But the wounds would be hard to disguise in a barracks once they turned bad.

"What are they, sir?" asked Atukwei in a voice tight with pain. His arm had been savagely bitten, a wound so much like Utuka's own. The men had dressed the injury, but Etse knew the real danger now.

The man was probably already dead. He had a right to know what had killed him.

"That," Etse pointed at the dead Gbohii with his blade, "was Utuka. Some of you knew him."

He pointed back at the one he had slain. "I'm not sure who that one was. Another of our men, by his armor. Killed by Utuka after he died and turned into that thing."

The men were staring at him with open mouths. Etse knew just how they felt. It was something out of stories told to children to scare them, not something grown men would believe. Except they'd seen the things with their own eyes. They knew that this story, at least, had come to life.

"If they kill you, you become one of them," Etse finished.

The men were looking with horror at the bodies of the two guards who'd been slain by the thing. Two had aimed their spears at the corpses as if they might rise at any moment. And they might.

"Thrust into the head," Kwadwo said. "That kills them." He followed his own advice, stabbing his sword into the head of one of the men Utuka's Gbohii had slain.

"Maim our dead?" Atukwei asked.

"No," Etse replied. "Save them from becoming monsters. And if I fall to one of these things, I hope you men offer me the same service."

He thrust his own sword into the head of the other body.

"And what about those of us hurt by the things?" Atukwei asked. He clutched his wounded arm. His eyes were wide and full of fear.

"We will do what we can for you," Etse said. But what could they do? Kwesi's surgeons had failed. The curse spread even after they removed Utuka's arm. Even one bite from one of these fiends was deadly. Worse than deadly. How could they fight such a thing?

CHAPTER SEVEN

Kwadwo wondered for a while if the dawn would ever break, but eventually it did. Rays of light chased away the shadows, revealing tired, frightened, and soot-stained men and women. The battle to stop the blaze was a long one, and eventually they'd given up on saving the east wing. They'd been able to contain the damage there, which was a victory. Once they were sure the blaze was truly out, the danger past, most people had dropped where they stood.

Kwadwo stayed awake, along with a few others. Etse had stuck by his side through the night, despite the young man's obvious exhaustion. They'd piled wood and burned the bodies of the dead. Few words were spoken through the grisly task.

The change in the young man was heartening to see. But now Kwadwo wished more than anything that it had never happened. That they could return to yesterday, when Etse was a fickle boy and none of them knew such monsters existed.

Once most folks were rousing, Kwadwo called for a roll to be taken. Trebi, one of the older guards, was missing. He'd been on duty guarding Utuka. Kwadwo presumed they'd find his body after they went through the rubble of the east wing.

They were now up to three injured: Dosseh's wife Baeta, Atukwei, and another villager named Kofi who'd been bitten by the armored Gbohii before Etse slew it. A room in the main building of the palace had been set aside to treat the wounded. But the news about Utuka had spread even to the injured. Kwadwo visited the room, and it was thick with despair.

Atukwei was crying when Kwadwo left, weeping through the thick narcotic syrup the physicians had force-fed him, while they were preparing to remove his wounded arm. It had yet to begin the rot, and they hoped they might still save him.

Kwadwo found himself on the roof of the main building. The building dated to an early era of Asanteman where raids by the Kongo were common, and the roof was open, with battlements from which men could fight. Kwadwo supposed that was one reason Kwesi had chosen to base himself here, when things began to unravel.

From here, he could see miles in all directions. It was a sunny day, bright and fresh, with a clean wind blowing in from the southwest. It carried just a hint of the sea with it.

But there – coming up the road – he spied a lone horseman. At a flat gallop, from the looks of it, racing his kwapawnkah.

More trouble? He looked down into the courtyard. Most of his guards were off to their beds now. Only a skeleton force remained awake. It had been a long night. Kwadwo spotted Kudowor down by the stables, brushing his kwapawnkah.

"Kudowor! Get to the gate. Rider coming fast," he shouted down. Kudowor dropped his brush and set off across the courtyard.

Kwadwo left the roof, heading for the gate himself. He picked up a jog coming down the stairs, jingling as he went. He'd still not changed from his iron mantle armor. There hadn't been time, and he felt safer in his gear. Too many men were dead or maimed this past day for lack of good armor.

Now he was glad to still have his armor on his back. Something had to be wrong. Nobody drove their kwapawnkah like that unless the need was dire.

Still, he reached the gate long before the rider did. The palace was surrounded by a ten-foot wall with a single gate, which was still closed, even though it was day. Kudowor was standing atop the wall, watching the rider. Kwadwo took the steps two at a time to join him.

"What do you make of him?" Kwadwo said, panting a little from the run.

Kudowor was squinting into the sun. "Still coming fast. Been going like that a while. Going to kill his kwapawnkah if he's not careful."

Kwadwo heard the jangle of mail behind him. He looked back over the shoulder and saw Etse climbing the steps behind him.

"What's going on?" Etse asked.

"I should have guessed you'd show up," Kwadwo said. This time, he didn't even try to hide his smile. "Shouldn't you be asleep?"

"I heard the shouting," Etse replied.

"Rider coming up fast," Kudowor said, jerking his chin toward the road.

They waited in companionable silence another ten minutes while the rider finished his approach to the gates. He dropped back to a canter a quarter mile distant. Kwadwo could see even from there that the kwapawnkah was spent. It would need care soon, or it would likely suffer injury from exhaustion, or even die. He could feel the tension building as the man rode closer. What fresh crisis was coming at them?

"Ho, there! What's your business?" Kudowor shouted once the rider was close enough for his voice to carry over the distance.

"Urgent message for Asantehene Kwesi!" came the reply.

Kwadwo snorted, then started down the stairs. Both men followed him down and helped him raise the bar from the gates. They opened the iron bound doors and went outside. Kwadwo looked at the three of them – stained with soot, grime, even a splash of black slime decorating Etse's tunic. They were quite the sight.

In contrast, the man riding up was wearing silks, elaborately embroidered with threads in a rainbow of colors.

"Where the hell did he come from?" Kudowor muttered.

"A good question," Kwadwo said.

The rider stopped his kwapawnkah a dozen feet from the gates, a puzzled expression on his face. Kwadwo stepped forward to greet him.

"This is the palace of Asantehene Kwesi, is it not?" the man asked.

"It is," Kwadwo replied.

"What has happened here?"

"We had a fire last night, and some casualties," Kwadwo replied.

The rider's eyes narrowed. Kwadwo felt his scrutiny fall on each of them in turn, but it wasn't until he examined Etse and saw the black stains that his eyes widened again.

"No," the stranger said. "Even here? There is no refuge, then." He seemed to sag a bit in his saddle.

Kwadwo stepped forward and took the man's reins. "Who are you?" he asked.

"My message is for Asantehene Kwesi alone," the rider replied, jerking himself upright again.

Etse stepped forward then. He stood, one hand resting on his hip, the other on the hilt of his sword. Kwadwo eyed the boy's face, observing how much it had changed from the carefree look – was it really just the morning before?

"My father is busy elsewhere," Etse said. "You may give me your message."

He held the rider pinned with his gaze, and the tone was one which brooked no refusal. Kwadwo saw nothing haughty in the boy's – *the young man's,* he corrected himself – posture or voice. But there was steel.

"Me wura," the rider said. "Your pardon. I have not seen you since you were an infant."

"You know me?" Etse asked.

Kwadwo blinked. This was a surprising turn of events.

"Know your father, really. Know of you, certainly, Etse," the man said. "I'm here because your father and I go back decades, boy. I'm here to warn him."

"Warn him of what?" Kwadwo asked.

"I am Shabani," the rider said, then paused as if that should mean something. When all he saw was puzzled expressions from the three men, he sighed. "From Kiswala," he said, looking skyward.

Shabani went on. "I am here to inform your father that Okere has arrived on his shores and wishes to meet with him. At once."

Kwadwo blanched, his mind whirling. Impossible. The Wakuu (*Great Man*) would never leave Kiswala, unless…

"The Wakuu is here?" Etse said, his voice almost a whisper.

"Aane, boy. The Wakuu is here," Shabani said. "Kiswala… Kiswala has fallen."

CHAPTER EIGHT

Amon stood on the city wall, watching the parade enter. He'd never seen so many kwapawnkah all in one place. Never seen such fine clothes. Nor seen so many men in armor. He'd lived in Nicran all his life, but while grownups spoke wistfully of Mikijen and Kiswala, he'd never in all his seven years seen one. The mercenaries went away over the sea, or so he'd heard. Never to return.

Yet here they marched, like something out of a story. The Wakuu himself had come to Asanteman, people were saying. He was somewhere out in that parade of people. The whole city moved even faster than usual, everyone rushing about. Amon had a sense that things were going to change forever. He could feel it in his gut.

"Anomagyanan (*Bird Poop*)! Better run!"

But some things never changed. Amon was moving almost as soon as the hated nickname registered. Nobody who called him by that name meant him any good, and he'd learned that running remained the best way to survive in Nicran's slums. When you were scrawny but fast like him, flight was better than staying and getting beat.

He leapt from the wall onto a rooftop, sparing a peek over his shoulder. Saka and his pals followed close behind him. Time to run for sure. The last time Saka caught him, Amon almost lost his eye from the swelling, and his hip still hurt sometimes.

He jumped from the roof to a tall post and shimmied down to the ground. As soon as his bare feet touched dirt he started running again, darting between people on the street. Behind him he could hear the other boys laughing as they gave chase. He knew that this was a game for them. They'd try to stretch it out some. They were bigger, older. They could run faster. His only chance was getting someplace they didn't want to go.

There was a crack ahead in a sewer drain, just big enough for him to slip through. He'd used it to escape before. Maybe it would work again? He fled, just ahead of their catcalls, almost knocking over a cart of melons in his haste to get to the hiding place.

There it was! He hit the ground with a slide, losing skin from his elbow and knee, but slipped into the narrow gap. His feet splashed down into the shallow water under the grate.

A hand caught his wrist. He looked up in terror.

Saka was there, holding him in a grip that felt like iron. An evil smile blossomed on his face.

Amon did the only thing he could think of. He pushed his head back through the grate and bit Saka's hand, hard enough to draw blood. Saka cursed but let him go. Amon darted back down through the grate.

"Little Anomagyanan. I'm going to kill you for that," Saka said. His voice sounded so matter of fact that it made Amon shiver.

Panting with fear, Amon backed down the sewer away from the light spilling through the grate. It was a narrow space, only a few feet high by a few feet wide. A shallow stream ran through the middle, and the whole space smelled as foul as it ever did.

He could hear the boys talking above, Saka giving orders. Then there was a clanging sound, metal on metal. Amon jumped at the noise. The clanging turned into a scraping, and Amon realized that the boys had found a metal bar somewhere. They'd lift the grate.

They were going to come in after him.

Amon scurried deeper into the shadows. He'd never ventured far down here before. The bullies had never chased him deeper. They'd always given up after a while and let him slink back out to freedom.

"I'm coming for you, Anomagyanan. Gonna make you bleed."

Saka's words chilled him to the bone. Amon didn't doubt he'd make good his promise. It was time to flee.

He stumbled back into the darkness, splashing his way into deeper gloom.

***

Mercenaries in padded armor and Mikijen regalia stepped aside to let Etse pass as he went from the heat of day into something incredible. The building they stayed in was astounding. Tall, made of mudbrick blocks and towering over most of the city, Wakuu Okere had chosen this as his new edifice. The noble who'd been living here gave over his quarters; word was he'd left for a country estate. Etse supposed there hadn't been much choice in the matter. When the wealthiest man in Ki Khanga asked you for something, how could you say no?

The building was a ring of rooms, encasing a massive courtyard garden. Level stacked upon level high above the ground – it was a towering structure. As Etse stepped through the entryway into the verdant space within, the scent of fresh growth and water overwhelmed his nose. A brook burbled through the greenery, leaving him wondering how the water had been cunningly wrought to flow through the room that way. Trees, ferns, grasses, and many more elaborate plants grew everywhere.

In the center of the garden stood a young man, wearing a white silk robe with expensive gold thread embroidered in patterns across the cloth. His belt looked to be of solid gold, as well. His hands were clasped behind his back, and he stood staring at the brook as if deep in thought. Etse held his breath. This was the Wakuu. No man alive wielded more wealth than the person standing quietly before him.

"You are Etse?" Okere asked, without looking up from the water.

"Aane," Etse replied.

Okere turned. "Come closer. I would speak with the man about whom so many stories are told."

Etse was surprised to see that the man he faced wasn't that much older than him. Mid-twenties, perhaps? Etse didn't remember. He did as Okere bid and stepped out onto the carefully manicured lawn. All around him, vegetation draped from the walls of the courtyard like tapestries. Several stories above, sunlight shone down. But it only rarely cast direct light on the garden, leaving the place in a nearly perpetual twilight.

"I only did what I could to help our people," Etse said.

"You slew three of the things," Okere said. "That is more than any of my mercenaries have done. It's more than any man I have heard of has done." He paused a moment, and Etse held his tongue to see what he might say next. "Tell me. How did you slay them?"

"The head, Wakuu. You must strike it from their shoulders or do damage to the brain inside the skull. The thing dies when the brain dies."

The Wakuu nodded, rubbing his hands together. "That much I knew. But they are too fast for most to deal with well."

Etse had been giving thought to the battles to come. The way they had fought before – really, most of how he'd seen men trained – wasn't going to work well when it came to fighting this new enemy. "I have some ideas for killing them. Spear teams, working in concert with swordsmen, would let us pin them and—"

"Aane, I can see you have given this some thought. I will let you discuss the matter with General Okoth. Perhaps you can help him improve our training. We must be ready for them."

"I will assist any way I can, Wakuu."

"Good," Okere said. "Then there is something else. Rumor is spreading about why I am here. Soon, everyone will know that Kiswala has fallen – that there is nothing left there but the Gbohii and the slain."

"I think word is already spreading," Etse said. It had been devastating news. The heartbeat of Ki Khanga, gone! True, Kiswala had left Asanteman to defend itself, and the people here showed an independent spirit. But Kiswala was...Kiswala. Eternal, unyielding, unbreakable.

Except it had been broken. Aane, the news was already on everyone's lips.

"Which makes my plan all the more important. People need hope, Etse. And for hope, they need to see us victorious. They need heroes."

Etse blinked. "I don't understand, Wakuu."

"Think, man! You've slain three of these demonic things. No other man has done so much. You are the perfect person to show the people that there is still hope."

"I... don't know what to say, Wakuu." Etse hoped to help train troops, maybe get some of his ideas for re-organizing the famed Mikijen put into motion. What was Okere asking of him?

"I am planning a parade," Okere went on. "In your honor. You will ride with me. The people will see that these things can be slain. And you...you get a place of pride and purpose. What do you say?"

"I'm your man, Wakuu!" Etse replied. He could barely keep his excitement in check. What a chance! To be so esteemed by the ruler of Kiswala, to be at his side and honored? Etse could hardly wait to tell Kwadwo.

CHAPTER NINE

Amon shook with fear. The bullies chasing him had levered the grate free a few moments before. He heard them drop down into the sewer – three splashes, followed by some curses. Amon couldn't see them – he'd retreated so far down the tunnel that it was nearly pitch black around him. But he could feel in his gut that wouldn't be enough to stop Saka. He was coming. Any minute now, he'd lay a hand on Amon's neck.

But he couldn't flee further, even blindly. He'd hit a brick wall. Probably the foundation for one of the buildings, but the tunnel just stopped there. Amon felt his way along the wall, looking for any kind of opening. He could feel a whisper of wind on his fingers, which gave him hope.

There! A crack between two bricks. The stones on either side were loose, too. He pulled at one, and it came away in his hand. He dropped it next to him with a splash, then pulled the other free as well. The space that he made wasn't enough to wedge himself into, but it was a start. He tried to wiggle the other bricks, but they wouldn't budge.

Something over his shoulder caught his eye, and he looked back. There, far down the tunnel, he saw the light of a fire.

"We're commmmmming," Saka called down the passage in a sing-song voice.

Amon was frantic to get away. He picked up one of the bricks and hammered it against the wall. Once, twice, and then a third time he hit the wall with every ounce of strength in his small body.

He heard a crack, and several bricks fell free from the wall, tumbling into darkness on the other side.

Amon peeked through the hole, which was now more than wide enough for him to pass through. Inside was utter darkness. It stank. The air smelled like rotting meat. He wondered what was down there and felt a sudden sense that something watched him.

But another quick look over his shoulder showed the torchlight coming ever closer. He had to flee. He slipped his shoulders through the hole, feeling around the space on the other side with his hands. The rocks sounded like they fell at least a few feet, so there was a floor down there somewhere. But Amon had no idea how far below him it was.

He reached as far as he could, and his fingers met wood. It felt like the edge of a beam, some sort of support for the ceiling. He had to be in a basement. But where?

Carefully, he eased himself through the hole, using the beam for support. He found a narrow ledge of stone that he could stand on, and holding the beam with his hands while slipping his toes along the ledge, he made his way painstakingly along the wall.

Then he froze. Was that a sound, somewhere below him? Something moving?

Cold fingers clamped over his right ankle, and he screamed. Then he felt pain as something bit down on his foot. He yelped again, yanking his foot back. He almost slipped from the wall, hanging for a moment from the wood edging. But with an effort, he managed to get his footing again, stepping quickly away from whatever bit him.

He could hear it following. But then there was light near the hole he'd entered, and the thing moved that way, attracted to the light.

One of Saka's bullies stuck his torch into the basement, then followed with his head. Amon had a moment to see the space – stone walls, old wooden posts and beams, and tattered things moving about on the floor. It was only a moment, though, because after that one of the things on the floor burst into motion so fast Amon could barely see it, grabbed the boy with the torch, and hauled him through the hole.

The boy never even had a chance to scream. He landed with a sickening thump, and the torch went out.

"Hey! Korahm! You clumsy oaf!" That was Saka. Amon tried to make himself very small against the wall. He held completely still.

"Korahm?" Saka said. Korahm didn't answer. "Mmarato, go see where he is," he said to his other crony.

"I don't want to go in there. It's dark."

Amon could just barely see the outlines of both boys as they peered into the basement through the hole. The light from day was dim, barely reaching this place at all, but it was just enough to outline their shapes. And he knew that if he could see them, whatever lived in here could see them too...

No sooner had the thought crossed his mind than he felt the air moving below him. Something grabbed both boys from their perch and yanked them down to the basement floor. These two did have time to scream. And Saka kept screaming for a while before he stopped.

New noises came from the floor. Amon tried to put them out of his head as he worked his way swiftly back over to the hole in the wall. They were tearing sounds. Chewing sounds. He hoped that whatever the monsters in the pit were, they stayed too distracted to pay him any mind.

***

The sun shone brilliantly overhead. Heat beat down and added its own brand of misery to the day's humidity. Kwadwo found himself streaming with sweat. The men out on the practice field were even more drenched than he was, working hard under the direction of their drill masters.

"It's good to see so many men training together again," he said to the man next to him. Kwadwo chose his words carefully. This Okoth Akokoawduro was young for his command, not even in his thirtieth year. But the Wakuu had brought over a thousand mercenaries with him, and this young man was in command of them. Which made him one of the most powerful men in Asanteman.

"I can't imagine," Okoth replied. "You've done well out here, fending for yourselves with what you had."

"We've done what we could. I'd always hoped Kiswala would return someday."

"And so it has," Okoth said. He barked a bitter laugh. "Although not under the circumstances you must have hoped!"

They marched along, inspecting the men practicing on the field, all the while also examining each other. Kwadwo had asked Kwesi what he knew of Akokoawduro, as soon as he'd heard the name. Kwesi hadn't heard too much. The man was a rising star in the Mikijen – the mercenaries in the employ of Kiswala – though. He'd seemed destined for a major generalship, even before the Gbohii.

"I'm impressed," Kwadwo said as they marched past yet another rank of men beating at each other with practice swords. And he was. The men were good.

"I'm glad," Okoth replied.

"How did you adapt your training to account for the Gbohii?" Kwadwo asked.

Okoth grimaced. "We haven't. Not yet."

Kwadwo stopped in his tracks. That wasn't what he'd expected at all. "Why not?"

"I was actually hoping you might be able to help us with that. You've fought them here, yes?"

Kwadwo nodded. They'd already reported the early encounters. What baffled him was why their own meager experience would matter to a nation that was overrun with the things.

"That's good. You'll have to tell me about them."

"Surely you've fought them yourself?" Kwadwo asked, surprised.

Okoth shook his head. "Not these troops. None of our men have fought even one Gbohii and lived. We fought one brief engagement as we fled Kiswala. No one who stood their ground survived."

Kwadwo looked back over the field of mercenaries, suddenly seeing them in a new light. He'd thought they were all veterans of battles against the undead. The idea of having many men who'd survived this terrible new enemy had filled him with hope. Now, he looked out over that sea of faces and saw men who had no idea what they would face.

His heart sank.

"Okoth, you must change your training. The Gbohii are too fast, too deadly. A single bite from one of them kills – no one we've seen has survived a bite, so far. And when you die..."

"You become one. I know."

Kwadwo stepped off to the side, grabbed a pair of spears. "May I?"

Okoth waved him ahead. Kwadwo stepped over to where some of the men practiced swordplay and handed two of them the spears.

"You two – work with this one," he pointed at a man still using his sword. "The spears pin the thing. The swordsman cuts off the head."

"You're saying it takes three men to slay one of these things?" Okoth asked, incredulous.

"I fought one with myself and five other men. Two of the men died, a third was bitten and died a day later." Atukwei had grown the rot in his arm, despite all the efforts made to save him.

"Walk with me please, Kwadwo," Okoth said. His voice was tight with anger, his back stiff with it. Kwadwo followed him away from the Mikijen, curious what he'd done to arouse such ire from the younger man.

Okoth held his tongue until they were out of earshot. "I'd appreciate if you avoided frightening the men. This is bad enough for them, without adding to it. None of them have faced this enemy yet. They must not be terrified before their first battle!"

Kwadwo blinked. "You'd have me lie? Tell them the enemy dies easily?"

"Half the troops will hear that tale before dinner, Kwadwo! If they all desert out of fear, where will that leave us?"

With the brave men who actually cared about protecting their people, Kwadwo wanted to say. With the sort of men he was used to leading, and the sort of men who would actually stand their ground when the dead walked into their ranks, ravenous and terrible. But he kept those words to himself.

"How is it that you and your men have never fought them?" he asked instead.

Okoth looked at him sharply, searching his face for mockery or scorn. Kwadwo kept his face blankly professional, and Okoth seemed to finally accept his question at face value.

"The Wakuu was at his holiday villa on Shamsa Island. My troops were sailing back from Haiset and had stopped for provisions at a village on Barke Island, when Shabani came riding into town screaming about the dead rising and devouring the main island."

He paused, then went on. "The Wakuu didn't believe at first, but eventually Shabani convinced him to board our ships with us to see for ourselves. We planned to sail up the Eternal Sea, but we never got that far." Okoth stopped speaking then, lost in his memories.

Kwadwo gave him a few moments. He knew how hard those memories could be.

"One of our ships led the way," Okoth said, when he could go on again. "The tide was out when we arrived, which we thought would help. We could ride the tide inland a ways. But the water was shallow, forcing us to enter slowly. That's when we saw them."

"The Gbohii?" Kwadwo asked.

"No. People. Men, women, even children, all fleeing for their lives. Over a hundred of them, crying and screaming. The scout ship's captain tried to get closer to the shore, to bring them aboard. But he grounded his vessel on a sandbar instead."

Kwadwo kept his face cool, but inwardly he winced. Already, he thought he knew where this story was headed.

"They screamed for help from the beach. Then those things came boiling out of the wood line, rushing toward the helpless people. The Gbohii tore into them, ripping them, eating them... Some of the people trapped on the shore tried to swim to the ship stuck on the sand. It was so close, not a hard swim at all."

"But all of those people thrashing into the water must have caught the things' attention," Okoth said. "They waded out into the river too, but they didn't swim. They just walked out, and then you'd see someone swimming only to vanish a moment later."

"The dead reached the ship before it could free itself. No one survived the carnage that followed."

"So what did you do?" Kwadwo asked.

"Nothing," Okoth replied. "The Wakuu forbade us to help the trapped ship. He was terrified that the Gbohii would walk out to us, swim up to our boats and kill us, too. He ordered us to sail away."

"So you came here, hoping to, what? Make a stand? Rebuild Kiswala? What is the Wakuu's plan, Okoth?"

Okoth shook himself, as if trying to make the memories fall away like drops of water from a dog's back. "I suggested to Okere that we come here, because if any place in Ki Khanga was likely free of the monsters, it would be here. So far, that seems to be true."

The man seemed to calm himself with his own words, but for Kwadwo, they had the opposite effect. These people ran away when some of their own were in danger. Worse, they had no plan, no scheme to recover Kiswala or even defend their people. Kwadwo had felt such hope when he saw fresh troops arriving on Asanteman from Kiswala, but he was starting to think his people were better off before these Kiswalans came.

CHAPTER TEN

Kwesi swore for the third time in less than a minute. And with good reason. The letter he held was penned by an imbecile and might as well have been a death sentence – for him. He'd worked so hard, for years, and in just a few days this cretin of a Wakuu was going to ruin everything he'd sacrificed so much to accomplish.

A hard rapping on his door gave him a fresh target for his anger.

"Enter!" Kwesi shouted.

The door cracked open, Kwadwo peeking around the edge. "A bad time, Kwesi?"

"It's been a bad time since Okere arrived. Come in, though. You should hear this," Kwesi replied, waving the letter.

Kwadwo entered, shutting the door behind him, and sat down in one of the several chairs set about the room. At least the accommodations Okere gave him were appropriate to his station, Kwesi mused. Spacious, well lit, and right in the same beautiful old building as the Wakuu himself. Of course, that last might not have been intended as an honor, and might have been intended to keep Kwesi close, where Okere could more easily keep him watched. Or both. Kiswalan politics were all about achieving two ends with one action.

"What's happened?" Kwadwo asked.

"Okere seized my guardsmen. He's letting me choose a handful of my men as a small personal guard. The rest he is folding into his Mikijen and moving us to Nicran."

"Does he plan to leave Takoradi undefended?" Kwadwo asked, incredulous.

"It seems that way. He wants to concentrate all his strength in one place."

"A single unified force would be the best able to defend against invasion," Kwadwo said.

"It would also represent a single point of failure," Kwesi said. "And it neatly traps me here."

"Because you can't very well leave the one defended place in Asanteman? We can train more troops, Kwesi."

"I'm not sure we have time." Kwesi stared out his window. He had always been able to sense the flow of events around him, to have a feel for the direction things were going, and how to take advantage of that movement. A valuable skill for a politician. But right now, Kwesi felt like a man adrift in a raging river, the current rushing him along and threatening to dash him against the rocks. There had been no more Gbohii found since the Wakuu arrived – but there were rumors. Troubling ones.

"What have you heard?" Kwadwo asked.

Kwesi chuckled softly. "You know me too damnably well."

Kwadwo waited quietly. Kwesi picked up the goblet of wine he'd poured himself before reading the missive from the Wakuu. In these dangerous times, he couldn't afford to lose any edge his mind might provide. He took a sip, collecting his thoughts.

"Nothing solid. Just stories. But the thing is, these tales are coming from places they ought not. The people in Asanteman know too much about these things. They seem to know what they look like, how they smell, how they feed..."

"Spreading from our men and the Wakuu's troops?" Kwadwo suggested.

"Perhaps. But I want you to look into it for me. I worry. Nicran is a huge city, and virtually none of it is patrolled in any organized manner. If there is an outbreak somewhere in the city, quietly brewing..." His thoughts trailed off. He didn't need to tell Kwadwo – they'd already discussed what a nightmare an outbreak of Gbohii would be in a city this big.

"I'll go and see what I can find out," Kwadwo said. "But for once, Kwesi? I hope you are wrong."

"So do I," Kwesi murmured as Kwadwo turned to go.

***

Etse was exhilarated. It wasn't every day you dined with the Wakuu, and no matter how unimpressed his father chose to act, Etse felt like his whole body was alive with energy. That Okere liked and appreciated him was obvious from the seating arrangement. His general sat to his right, and Etse to his left. The table was beautifully appointed, the meal created by the best chefs the Wakuu's men could find. Etse tried to recall when he'd last eaten so lavish a meal and couldn't bring another to mind.

He glanced at his father, seated next to him, and met a scowl. Etse turned away again, trying hard not to let his father's mood infect his own. Why couldn't the man be happy to see his son elevated and honored by so important a patron?

Kwadwo was seated next to Okoth, across from Kwesi. Shabani was the sixth person at the table, seated across from Okere. He sipped from a second cup of wine already.

Etse caught his father quirking an eyebrow at Kwadwo, who replied with a subtle shake of his head. He wondered what that was about, but doubted he'd be told. Being taken into his father's confidence seemed to be something he'd have to fight for every time he wanted it.

And he wasn't sure it mattered that much anymore. What seemed so important just a few days ago paled now.

There were few diners at the table, and all were men of influence. That meant there was sure to be discussion of their next moves, their plans and possibilities – although so far everyone had been mostly silent, with little idle chatter while they ate their meals. Etse finished his plate and sipped from his wine, wondering. The Wakuu surely planned to go back to recover Kiswala. Probably with an army of Asante at his back. Etse pictured that army with himself at the vanguard as it marched to recover the seat of Kiswala.

The Wakuu slid his own plate away from him. A servant wordlessly removed the dish, and another brought him a bowl to wash his fingers. He flicked them dry and cleared his throat.

"I trust you all enjoyed the meal," Okere said. "But we have things to discuss."

Everyone was already finished except Shabani, and he reluctantly pushed his plate away from him to give his full attention to the Wakuu.

"We do," Kwesi said. "I would like to discuss your plan to move the troops from Takoradi to Nicran."

Okere eyed Kwesi. "It is not a plan. It's done. The troops are already here."

Etse saw his father's cheeks pink the smallest bit. It was a sure sign that he was furious, but subtle enough that he doubted anyone at the table caught it except himself and Kwadwo.

"I am not sure it is the wisest course to put all our troops in one place," Kwesi said.

"Why would it not be?" Okoth broke in. "Once we fold those men into my Mikijen, we'll have even more forces here. The more troops, the better defended the city will be."

"As well defended as Kiswala was?" Kwesi asked. His tone was flat, but Etse could hear the undercurrent of disdain in his voice.

Okoth sank back in his seat, looking troubled. Of course, even with the additional troops, they'd have nowhere near as many as

Kiswala had housed. And Kiswala had fallen. That was his father's point.

"But we have the advantage of having fought the Gbohii before," Etse found himself saying. "We can train the men to fight them better. A smaller force might do here if they are better trained and equipped."

"Aane," Okere broke in. "I believe it was fear – terror even – of this strange and unnatural foe which broke our Mikijen in Kiswala. It is that fear we must battle before we can beat the Gbohii."

"And how do you intend to fight that fear, Okere?" Kwesi's voice was biting.

"By naming a champion," Okere replied, smiling broadly at Kwesi. "By giving the people a hero to believe in. Someone they can look up to. Someone who already faced the things and beat them not once, but three times."

Etse watched both men carefully. Okere's face had victory written all over it. Kwesi was glaring back, the pink spots of his anger gone, replaced by pallor. Etse had rarely seen his father go this cold. Kwesi's icy anger was his most dangerous mood.

Then his racing mind caught up with what the Wakuu was saying. Beaten the Gbohii three times? But he had...

"We will parade through Nicran tomorrow, and I will name Etse as my champion, if he will accept."

Time seemed to freeze for Etse. His eyes took in each face as they swept across the table. Shabani's bored look. Kwadwo, with a deep sadness in his eyes. Okoth, whose own eyes narrowed as he looked Etse over.

Then there was Kwesi – who wouldn't even meet his eyes right now. Etse didn't know how to feel about his father. He'd struggled to win some shred of attention from the man for so long he despaired of it ever happening. Even now, when he'd slain creatures from legend, won the attention of the Wakuu himself, his own father wouldn't even look him in the eye.

Damn him to the Cleave.

Etse turned his eyes again to Wakuu Okere, who beamed at him with a smile wide enough to break the room.

"It would be my honor, Wakuu," Etse replied.

CHAPTER ELEVEN

Kudowor felt a tug on his sleeve and turned tiredly to see who was accosting him now. This city was exhausting. Every minute someone demanded something of you. And he'd been up all night last night on the wall, watching for enemies the Wakuu feared might assault them at any moment.

The new commander was a dolt and ran his unit like a despot. Kudowor's new warriors were mostly men from the Mikijen. There was only one other from Kwesi's troops.

He'd been stunned to hear Kwesi's guards had been disbanded, and that they'd been remanded into General Okoth's Mikijen. Kudowor had half a heart to simply take off for the hills. He had plenty of friends to the east, and while he'd miss the pay, he knew he'd have a warm welcome. Okere and his Mikijen would never venture out that far.

He wasn't sure what kept him here. Nostalgia? He missed Kwadwo. Even missed seeing Etse, something he never thought he'd feel, and wouldn't admit to anyone but himself.

Kudowor tried to shake off his moodiness as he turned. He was overtired. He'd feel better after some sleep.

He looked, but didn't see anyone standing beside him. Still, the tug came on his sleeve again, and he brought his tired gaze down. The boy tugging his tunic with one grimy hand was young, shoeless, and dirty enough to look like he carried his own dust cloud with him wherever he went. Probably looking for a cowry for a meal. Kudowor's heart went out to the young boy.

"I don't have any money with me, boy, but I kept a bit of bread from dinner, if you want it," he said. He reached into his pocket and made good the promise, pulling out the crust of a loaf he'd saved to eat with breakfast. He held it out.

The boy snatched it from his fingers, sitting down right there in the street and wolfing down big bites.

"Here now," Kudowor said. "Slow down! It's not going anywhere." Kudowor knew the boy wouldn't listen. He remembered what it was like to be that hungry, and to not know when you might eat again. He eyed the boy, wondering if he could do anything else to help him.

Kudowor's inspection stopped cold when it reached the boy's ankle, visible now that he was sitting. He had a wound there, two festering crescent moon marks. Kudowor inhaled, sharply. He'd seen those marks before, seen that purulence.

His next thought was a pang for the boy. He was so damned young.

And he was dead. Or would be, soon enough.

Kudowor walled off the grief he felt. He couldn't let the boy get away. He reached down, his grip snagging the child's wrist.

"Let go!" the boy yelped, trying to scuttle away from his captor but failing.

Kudowor held fast. "Relax boy. I'm not going to hurt you. How did you get that wound?"

The boy tugged harder, still trying to break free. He whimpered a little in distress.

"Boy, calm down. I'm Kudowor. What's your name?" His heart went out to the child. This damned world was too cruel.

He still looked frightened but stopped pulling away for the moment. "Amon," he said.

"That's your name?"

The boy nodded.

“Amon, I want to try to get some help for your wound. It is infected; it will get worse unless it is treated.” Inwardly, Kudowor cursed himself for his lie. He’d seen several people bitten by the Gbohii now. Not one person bitten survived. And all turned into monsters like the ones that bit them after they succumbed to death. This boy was doomed to join them. From the flush in his cheeks, he already had the fever. Delirium would follow, then seizures, then stillness and death. Followed by undeath.

Kudowor would spare the boy that if he could. He silently cursed a world so cruel that murdering a child was mercy. Even more, a world that made it his duty not to bestow that small mercy. But even more important was finding out where the boy had been infected.

“They was in the sewers, sir,” Amon said. “The monsters.”

It sounded like a child’s tale. Monsters in the sewers? But then, everything that had happened since that ruined boat arrived had been like something from an old tale. Why not this, too?

“Monsters? Do you know how many?”

The boy shook his head.

“Can you show me, Amon?” he asked. “It’s important that I make sure no one else is bitten. Then we’ll get you help for your foot.”

The boy nodded, his eyes wide and trusting. Kudowor cursed himself again for his lie.

***

The dawning sun had crested the horizon only an hour before, but the palace started buzzing with activity far earlier. Etse yawned as he plucked up an apple from a breakfast table laden with foods of all sorts. He didn’t feel like his stomach could handle much more. Too much rich food and wine last night, and his stomach roiled with nerves over the day ahead, as well.

Okoth joined him in the dining room, striding through the doors like he owned the world. Etse eyed the man carefully. He hadn't missed the baleful glares the general shot him last night. Right now, Okere was favoring Etse, but Okoth was still the Wakuu's one remaining general, commanding what might be the last Mikijen in Ki Khanga.

And he didn't like Etse much. Or didn't like all the attention he was getting, anyway.

"Good morning, General Okoth," Etse said, trying to break some of the tension.

"Good morning, Etse. Or should I call you by title, too? Champion?"

Etse shook his head. "Just Etse, please. We have too much work to do together to be worrying about titles."

Okoth cocked his head at an angle, searching Etse's face carefully. Then he closed his eyes, shaking his head sharply. He opened them again, staring directly at Etse again. "You're right, of course. Far too much. Call me Okoth, then. No titles between us."

He reached out his hand. Etse took it into his own.

"Ah, it does my heart good to see my left hand shaking my right!" Okere said. He strode into the room, long legs quickly carrying him to where the two men stood.

"Wakuu," Okoth said, bowing.

"Come, men. We must be off. Both of you will ride with me, in a war chariot. Men from the Mikijen will be arrayed around us to remind the people that Kiswala is still strong."

"I've handpicked men for the job," Okoth said. "They're already standing by outside."

"Excellent!" Okere said. "Shabani has arranged criers to set out ahead of the parade, to inform the people of the good news. They'll announce our coming and tell the people of Etse's heroism – and his new title."

Etse tried to keep the flush from his face. Part of him had trouble believing all this was happening. He couldn't hold back his grin, though, and Okere noticed.

"I can tell that you're excited. But you'll work for the title often enough. It won't be an empty posting," Okere said.

"I'm not worried about fighting for a good cause," Etse replied.

"Excellent! I knew I could count on you," the Wakuu said. "Now, we should be off. Okoth, see to the men and then join us. Kwesi and his captain of the guard should be following us in a second chariot. Make sure they have everything they need."

Okoth bowed and went outside without another word.

"What will you have me doing, Wakuu?" Etse asked. He was curious. Champion was a noble title, and he was honored, but he was too much his father's son to miss the political nature of such an appointment.

"Mostly, you'll help ensure I stay alive," Okere replied. "Etse, I'll be honest with you. Much of your value to me is as a symbol. I will tell the people you are a hero. They will believe me, because when people are afraid, they want a hero to save them."

Etse felt his gut clench at the notion. He'd fought these things, but he remembered Dosseh – and all the other people he hadn't saved. He was no hero. The idea of people looking to him as one terrified him.

"Wakuu, I am no hero. I've failed people."

"Aane, and you will again. Something you'll need to learn, Etse, is that people fail. The ones who eventually succeed are the ones who get up and try again." Okere seemed lost in some memory and paused for a long moment before going on. "I learned that lesson at great cost, from someone who meant more to me than I ever knew until it was too late."

"You'll fail people, Etse. All you can hope to do is to save more than you fail. Still think you want the job?"

Etse looked down at his hands. He'd fought monsters out of nightmares with those hands. He knew he'd do it again, with or without a title. In his mind, he saw Dosseh's face, staring up at him from the sandy bottom of the river. His death had given Etse a chance to become something more than he had been. Wasn't that what this was, now? A chance to be more than he was?

"I'm still your man," Etse said firmly, if with less enthusiasm.

Okere searched his face and seemed satisfied. "It's not a boy's job, Etse. If it was, I could put anyone into the role. Oh, I'll admit I enjoyed tweaking Kwesi's nose a little. Your father has a bit of a rod up his ass."

Etse stifled a chuckle. "That's one way to describe him."

"But don't for a second think I would name you my champion for that reason alone."

"I understand, Okere." He hoped it was really true, and at the same time could barely fight back the fear he felt at the notion. As a champion, he would be held up for everyone to see. His failures would become obvious to all. They would all see him for what he was, surely – a boy with a sword. He was no hero. How long would the Wakuu's illusion hold? And what would be left of him once it failed?

Still, he had to try.

"Good. Let's go let the city meet their new hero."

CHAPTER TWELVE

Kudowor winced, scraping his shoulder as he squeezed through the open grate. His boots landed in the muck at the bottom of the sewer tunnel with a splash. He'd probably have been able to squeeze down here much more easily without his iron mantle shirt and sword, but the boy had been bitten by a Gbohii. The idea of meeting one – or curse it, more than one – of the things down here unarmed chilled his guts.

"Boy, what the hell were you doing down here, anyway?" Kudowor asked. Amon had led the way in, jumping down into the muck before Kudowor could stop him.

"Running away from Saka," Amon said.

"This Saka, he another boy?"

Amon nodded.

Kudowor eyed the damage to the grate, where a small hole had been pried at to make it larger. "Older than you, I suppose? Bigger? And he followed you in?"

Amon nodded again.

A sudden thought struck Kudowor. "Amon, where is Saka now?"

Amon's eyes grew very big. "The monsters got them."

Them? Inwardly, Kudowor cursed. The Gbohii made more of themselves when they killed. How many of the things were there down here? For a moment he considered turning around. He could go back to Kwadwo, return with a squad of guards. Or a company.

But if he tried to turn about now, the boy would flee. He could see it in Amon's eyes even now, that he wanted to bolt. He was only holding steady because Kudowor was. Without the boy he might not find the nest in time to stop it. He had to find out where the things were hiding and how bad the situation was, then get back to Kwadwo and report the situation.

"We need to be quiet, Amon. Can you lead me to where the monsters are, silent as a mouse?"

The boy nodded, then set off down the passage. And he was pretty quiet. His footsteps barely made any sound at all. If anything, Kudowor was the one making more noise. He had to hunch over to fit in the passage at all, and his boots sloshed through foul smelling fluid with every step.

Finally, they reached a crumbling wall of stones. It looked like the edge of an old foundation. Kudowor tried to figure out where they were, but it could have been any of a number of old buildings in this part of the city.

"Through there," Amon said, pointing at a hole in the wall.

Kudowor could see nothing but darkness beyond. He had no light except the dim illumination reaching this far from the grate hole back down the passage. Carefully, he leaned against the wall, staring into the darkness, straining to see or hear anything beyond.

Nothing stirred in there, as near as he could tell.

"Amon," he whispered, "are you sure this is..."

Before he could finish his words, the rock shifted under his hands, falling away in front of him. Kudowor yelped, losing his balance as the stones dropped into the dark space beyond. He couldn't stop his own fall and tumbled down headfirst.

He hit the bottom hard, jamming his right hip and shoulder. He cursed, but softly as he could. Fear clenched his gut. He couldn't see anything here – the room was in total darkness.

But he could hear movement. The whisper of rustling cloth. The slosh of something moving through liquid. All around him, it seemed, he could hear things beginning to stir.

The hair on his neck and arms prickled. His hand went to his sword, slowly drawing the blade from its sheath. His shoulder screamed in pain from the simple movement.

There was more movement around him now. He tried to back up toward the hole he'd fallen through, but couldn't find the spot in all the rubble, and had a horrible feeling the noise he made was drawing the things to him. He stopped moving, went completely still, barely drawing a breath.

Long moments passed, and the movements began to settle again.

The room was as silent as a tomb again. Kudowor dared not even lean back against the wall, for fear he'd set the things into motion again.

Then, from above and to his right, Kudowor heard Amon's voice whisper down. "Are you there? Are you OK?"

The movements began again, in earnest this time. The things had heard prey. They were awake. They were hungry. They were coming for Amon.

And Kudowor was right in their path.

***

Kwesi fumed in silence, his face a carefully constructed mask. He was in public, after all, riding in a chariot behind the Wakuu himself. And his own son was being lauded a hero today. The crowd would take his stoic pose as pride.

His son knew better. He could see that in Etse's face, every time he turned back from his place in the Wakuu's chariot. The boy was growing uncannily good at reading his moods. Kwesi wasn't sure if that pleased him or upset him.

This...the insanity of everything Okere was doing set him on edge. To bring the last fighting force Kiswala had into a large city like Nicran was bad enough. It was almost certain that the Gbohii plague would arrive here soon, if it had not already. It would be far safer for the Mikijen to be based away from major population centers. Kwesi had been drawing up plans, putting his mind to work on ideas. Asanteman was not the safe haven Okere seemed to think it was. They knew that one Gbohii had arrived on the shores, and if Etse hadn't managed to slay it, there would likely have been many more.

There was no safety here. Kwesi's gut clenched as he scanned the crowd. He wasn't sure what he was looking for... Sick, feverish faces? He couldn't tell if any were there in the masses crowding around the parade.

They were here to see a man be made champion. A hero. Kwesi knew better. There were no heroes, only scared men trying to stay alive.

He kept his focus on the crowd as the parade stopped and Okere began to speak again, telling all assembled of Etse's deeds. It was no wonder the boy had a swelled head – the Wakuu made it sound like Etse alone could carve his way through the undead enemy. Like he was a magic weapon the Wakuu would wield to rebuild a lost Kiswala.

Kwesi understood the power of hope. But his gut told him this wasn't the place, or the time. He glanced at the sun. It was late morning, and no word from Kwadwo yet. Kwesi let a flicker of that worry crease his brow before restoring the stoic mask to its place.

CHAPTER THIRTEEN

Kwadwo wasn't sorry to be missing the parade. He'd never enjoyed them, and being ordered to not attend this one was pleasure, not pain. He only wished it had been for some other reason.

Kwesi was right. The city was rife with rumors of the undead. And there was too much of it to be accounted for as just tales being spread by the troops. Some stories were clearly made up. Kwadwo didn't think the Wakuu was raising a group of Gbohii for circus games, for example. Nor did it seem likely the Gbohii were a Gbawmehi Fawji weapon.

But the story that there was a temple here in the old quarter, where the sick could come and be cured, if they had a bite that festered badly? That troubled him. It had the ring of truth to it.

He'd asked around, carefully. He could play the doddering old man, if he needed. He could play the desperate father of a sick child, too. He'd used both ruses, and finally he'd tracked down the location of this miracle temple.

The fact that few people knew where it was seemed like a good thing to him. It implied that there were not many people with such bites in the city. But the fact that everyone with their ear to the ground knew the place existed at all was worrying, because it meant that there were at least some Gbohii near enough to be a threat.

If there were any at all, there were probably going to be quite a lot more, and soon, unless they were slain.

Kwadwo stood in the doorway of a building next to the temple, and watched a man in a white lappa slip in through the side door. The man was carrying a large bag. Kwadwo wondered what was in that sack... Bits of the mystery cure? What if these shamans had actually found a cure for the pestilence in the Gbohii' bite? But if that was the case, why not tell the Wakuu? Why not spread the word?

He had to find out what was going on in there.

Kwadwo left his perch, casually sauntering across the courtyard. Once he reached the far side, he stepped quickly up to the same door the man in the lappa had used and pushed gently.

Locked.

There was a hook latch, inside the door. Not a complex lock. Kwadwo drew his knife, sliding it through the gap between door and mudbrick wall. He had to gouge the wood a bit, but a few moments later the door was open.

The room inside was small, poorly lit, and smelled of blood – both old and fresh. An open doorway was set into the middle of the wall across the room from him, leading deeper into the temple. A single table filled the center of the room. The sack sat open on the table, chunks of flesh and bone spilling from the top. Blood pooled on the table and ran onto the floor, where it joined older stains to color the floor a deep crimson.

Kwadwo sheathed his knife and drew his sword instead. He wondered briefly if the Ahene Akamfo who'd blessed the weapon was even still alive, or if he'd died in Kiswala when it fell. Whether the man was still among the living or not, Kwadwo believed in the blessing. And his gut said he'd need every bit of Daarila's grace in this profaned place.

Kwadwo closed the door behind him quietly. He took another step into the room, his feet sticking a bit to the tacky blood spread over the floor. There was no cure here. There was only death.

The man in the white lappa stepped back into the room from wherever he'd been. He didn't notice Kwadwo immediately, seeming preoccupied. He carried a large butcher's knife and stepped up to the table. He pulled a large chunk from the bag, lay it on the table, and raised the cleaver to chop the flesh up.

Kwadwo cleared his throat.

The man whirled, seeing Kwadwo for the first time. He gave a yelp of alarm, saw the sword in Kwadwo's hand, and dropped his cleaver, squealing like a pig and dropping to his knees.

"Please sir! Don't hurt me! Please!"

The man shuffled on his knees, dragging them through the grime and decaying matter on the floor. Kwadwo didn't even try to conceal his disgust.

"What the hell is going on here?" he asked.

"I'm taking care of them! Honest, I am," the strange man said.

"Taking care of whom?"

"The Head Priest. And the others. I'm taking good care of them, see?" he said, gesturing at the bag set on the table.

"Show me," Kwadwo said.

The man squealed again, prostrating himself on the floor. Kwadwo's mouth wrinkled, watching the man press his face into the slippery mess of the floor.

"Show me!"

"No!" the robed man shouted back. "No! You'll take them away, and I'll miss out. I want to have the life after death too! The pastor, he said the life after death was special and was only for Daarila's special chosen."

He got up on his hands and knees. Kwadwo eyed him warily. The man's face was flushed. His eyes were glassy and sweat stood out on his brow. All the signs of fever. Kwadwo had missed it before, but the signs were unmistakable once he looked closely.

"You've been bitten, haven't you?" he asked.

The man cackled, rolling back a sleeve to show a festering wound. "Aane! And soon I will have the life after death, too! Just like the others! Just like all the rest! And you can't stop me!"

With that last yell, the robed man snapped his cleaver up from the floor where he'd dropped it and rose quickly to his feet. He slashed the air in front of him, taking swipes at Kwadwo.

Kwadwo sidestepped quickly, but the man kept coming, still swinging the cleaver. Kwadwo leaned away, letting the gleaming blade pass only inches from his face. He batted the cleaver aside with the flat of his sword.

"Stop this," Kwadwo said. "Let me try to help you."

The man cackled wildly as his only response, lunging again with his blade. Kwadwo wasn't wearing armor. This madman could hurt him, and his pity was fast running dry.

He snaked his blade up and around the man's wrist, slicing flesh, trying to force him to drop the blade. The man ignored the fresh wound and almost drove his cleaver into Kwadwo's arm.

A crash from deeper inside the temple drew Kwadwo's attention for a moment. His opponent took the chance and hacked his cleaver straight at Kwadwo's head. Kwadwo saw the movement, took a step back to avoid the blow – and was stopped by the table.

The cleaver drove into his right shoulder with a dull thud. The waves of pain that followed a moment later made him grit his teeth against the taste of iron and bile in his mouth.

"No one can take the life after death from me!" the maniac shouted again, pulling the cleaver free. The withdrawal of the blade hurt almost as much as the blow itself. Kwadwo clenched his teeth past the pain, saw the man raise his weapon for another blow.

Kwadwo never gave him the chance. He drove his own blade forward and up, through the man's throat and into his skull.

His body sagged against the blade, then he dropped to the floor twitching, but quite dead. It wouldn't be rising again with a wound like that, either. Kwadwo withdrew his sword. He could feel his own blood pouring from the wound on his shoulder. It was time to get out of here. He sheathed his sword and tore a strip of cloth from his shirt, pressing it against the wound.

The sound of shouting drew his attention back to the interior of the temple. The first noise had been like masonry coming apart. Now shouting. Was someone else trapped here?

Kwadwo took his shirt off and tied it around his shoulder to hold the makeshift bandage in place. He'd had worse. A date with the surgeon and some time to heal, and the wound would be one more scar on a body that bore many scars. In the back of his mind was the niggling worry that he might not have time to heal this wound though. That death was coming for all of them far sooner than healing.

Drawing his sword again, he stepped through the doorway into the main area of the temple. He heard a second shout, this one coming from the back of the temple, behind a stout wooden door. The door was barred from this side. Which meant the door was intended to keep something in.

His heart was pounding. The maniac in the lappa had been bitten. He'd said enough, too, that Kwadwo had a good idea what was on the other side of that door. He gripped his sword tightly, his other arm in agony. Opening that door right now, in his condition, would be foolhardy. He hadn't lived this long...

The shout came from the other side of the door again. This time, Kwadwo was close enough to recognize the voice.

"Kudowor?" he said, astonished. Impossible! But he'd known the man for long enough to recognize the sound of his voice anywhere.

Kwadwo was already moving, his decision reversed. Still holding his sword with his wounded arm, he lifted the heavy bar with his good hand. With a yank on a thick iron ring set into the middle of the door, he pulled it open.

Past the doorway was a set of wooden stairs, descending into darkness. Kwadwo grimaced down into that blackness, his courage faltering. He'd never believed monsters lived in the dark places, even as a child. But now?

Now he knew the monsters were real. And it terrified him.

He steeled himself and shouted into the dark. "Kudowor?"

"Kwadwo?" came the incredulous reply from below.

"This way man! Up the stairs!" Kwadwo called.

He heard the sound of hasty footsteps below. Then he saw a boy ascending the stairs, with Kudowor close behind him.

"Run!" Kudowor shouted, his face pale.

More shapes were moving in the darkness beyond him. Moving fast and coming their way.

Kwadwo grabbed the man by the shoulder, hauling him up the last two steps, and then turned to slam the door shut again.

Too late. A grotesque arm reached through the doorway as he tried to close it. The bones in the arm shattered as the door hit them, but they stopped it from closing all the way. Kwadwo threw his shoulder into the door, trying to force it closed so that he could set the wooden beam into place again. Kudowor joined him, adding his own weight.

He could feel the impact of dead fists on the other side, dead bodies piling up, heaving upward with their uncanny strength. Inch by inch, steadily, the door was opening despite their best efforts.

"How in the Cleave did you get down there?" Kwadwo asked.

"Long story," Kudowor replied, panting. "Tell you later."

"You bitten?"

"No. Still had my armor on. Was too close though." Kudowor shuddered.

"We're going to have to run for it," Kwadwo said. Three more hands were reaching around the door now, clawed fingers scrabbling for their flesh.

"I'm ready," Kudowor said. "Where's Amon?"

"Who?"

"The boy," Kudowor replied.

Kwadwo looked around, but there was no one else here. The front door to the temple hung open, though.

"He's run for it. And so should we. On three?"

Kudowor nodded, breathing hard.

Kwadwo counted. "One."

The door opened further, their boots slipped on the mudbrick floor. A Gbohii managed to stick its head out through the widening gap, jaws snapping.

"Damn it to the Cleave – three!"

The two men released the door together, turning to sprint through the temple as what seemed like all the monsters of their childhood nightmares boiled out of the dark space behind them.

CHAPTER FOURTEEN

The parade was beginning to blur together for Etse. They'd ride a ways into the city, then stop while the Wakuu spoke to the assembled crowd. Then they would ride on a bit further. Some of the listeners would drift away, while others picked up and followed along, so that the crowd swelled as the morning went on.

The chariots had just stopped again, and Okere was beginning his speech.

"Most of you have heard by now: Kiswala has fallen," Okere began. Wails came from a few in the crowd. Most people had heard the rumors, but some had perhaps not believed them before now. Hearing the truth from the Wakuu himself was hard.

"We face a great challenge. An evil none of us had ever dreamt of invades our lands, slays our people – and then they rise up against us to join that demonic force."

Etse scanned the crowd. The wailing had stopped, and they were all listening to Okere intently.

"But all is not lost," Okere said. "Kiswala has returned to Asanteman. I have come here, with my finest Mikijen, and here we shall make a stand. Together we will defend these lands. And in time, we shall take back what they have stolen from us!"

The crowd cheered. Etse almost shook his head in wonder. Okere knew how to manage a crowd. His oratory was perfect.

"And here, among you all, I have discovered a hero who will help me achieve those goals. One of you – an Asante – who has slain not one of the honhommawne, but three!" Okere reached down and took Etse's hand, raising it high.

"You know him as Etse, son of Kwesi. But today, he becomes my champion. And he is your champion as well! Etse, kneel."

Etse bowed and knelt before his Wakuu. This was a new twist on the speech. It seemed Okere felt the crowd had reached enough mass to take the next step. The Wakuu laid hands on his head.

"I would name you champion of Kiswala and Asanteman and defender of their people," Okere said. "It is a grave responsibility. Do you accept this mantle, Etse?"

Etse felt the weight of those words crash down upon his shoulders. If he consented to this, his life would be gone. He would never be able to live up to the expectations these people had of him. He would die, trying. Etse knew that. His failure was certain as the sunset.

His eyes closed, and he could see Dosseh's face staring at him from the blackness. The eyes did not accuse. They simply watched him.

What was his life, at this point, but something borrowed? A gift from a dead man? Could he do less for these people than Dosseh had for him? Etse knew his next words would change his life forever. He swallowed hard and spoke.

"I do," Etse said, his clear tenor carrying well over the sudden silence as people strained to hear every word.

"Then rise, champion, so your people can see you."

Etse stood, and the crowd erupted, hundreds of people calling his name. He stood, dazed, and looked out over the people whose lives he'd just sworn to protect, wondering how he could possibly ever succeed at the task.

The roars became a chant: "Etse! Etse!" they called, again and again.

***

Kwadwo raced through the streets, Kudowor one step ahead of him. His lungs were beginning to burn with the effort. There was no way to bar the front door of the temple, and the Gbohii had chased them down the steps, running after them with that strange, loping gait they had. Kwadwo glanced back, then swiftly tore his eyes back to the path ahead of him. *There have to be at least twenty of the things!* He thought.

"There's a guard post a few blocks away," Kudowor said. "If we can make it there, we'll find help."

Kwadwo nodded, too out of breath to speak, and redoubled his efforts. The things were gaining on them. At least the streets were mostly clear. People had gone to see the Wakuu speak, gone to watch the parade. Somewhere ahead of them, he could hear the roar of a crowd.

He felt a cold chill in his spine. "Kudowor," Kwadwo gasped out. "The parade..."

They rounded the corner and were blocked by a mass of people, all standing and shouting, roaring out a name. Kwadwo couldn't stop in time and smashed headlong into the rear of the crowd. Two people went down and yelled angrily in protest.

"Run!" Kwadwo shouted. "Flee!" He drew his sword, grimly. The crowd was packed too tightly here. He met Kudowor's eyes, and the man nodded, drawing his own blade. They'd both been soldiers too long to flee when there were people in danger.

"Run, you fools!" Kwadwo shouted. The nearest of the crowd stared at him like he was mad.

Then the first of the Gbohii rounded the corner, a slavering fiend with bits of decaying flesh hanging loosely from its bones. It slowed its advance when it saw the people ahead, jaws clacking together with a hollow sound. There was a moment of shocked silence.

Another one rounded the corner, and another. Like a startled herd of duiker, the crowd panicked, taking flight in every direction at once. First, they surged away from the undead, and Kwadwo tried to cover their retreat, slashing at the first of the Gbohii as it came toward him. Kudowor joined him, and their swords wove together to stall the advance. Bits of the things began to drop to the street, carved off by their blades.

But panic spread through the crowd faster than it could disperse, and soon people were trying to flee in all directions.

Including straight into the waiting jaws of the Gbohii.

The people nearest to the undead tried to stop the mad rush, but they couldn't stem the flow, and were shoved aside or worse, shoved back toward the monsters, screaming all the way. Kwadwo was hit from behind by one man struggling to stay upright. He saw the man's face, contorted in a scream, but he was helpless, pressed by the flowing crowd away from the fight into the mudbrick wall of a building. Kwadwo felt his head crack hard against the brick. Dizzy, he tried to keep his feet, and managed – only just. He couldn't see Kudowor anywhere. His hand went to touch his forehead, and came away red.

With no swords to slow them, the Gbohii tore into the crowd. Kwadwo watched, helpless. Blood spattered the wall around him; screams tore through the air. Men, women, and children alike – the dead had no care who they slew.

Keeping himself carefully pressed against the wall, Kwadwo slipped away from the horror happening behind him. He was too hurt to help save these people. And his duty lay elsewhere.

***

Etse's head snapped up at the first scream.

It was hard to make out where it had come from at first. Hard to hear at all, over the hundreds chanting his name. But he'd heard screams of terror too often lately to mistake that sound for anything else. Swiftly, he spotted a commotion near the back of the assembled mass. People were pushing, shoving – a panic.

And there, at the very back, he saw a Gbohii. Someone turned from the crowd to face the thing, and Etse recognized him instantly.

"That's Kwadwo!" Etse said, pointing.

Okere looked, and blanched when he saw the Gbohii. "Not here," he whispered. He sank back into his seat, pale and silent.

Okoth swore. "Men, clear a path back to the palace. We need to get the Wakuu to safety." The Mikijen troops surrounding the chariot moved sharply, fear making them swift. They used their shields to plow aside any people in their way. In moments the chariot was moving again, turning around.

"Okoth, we have to help those people," Etse said. Kwadwo was still there, fighting, but Etse could see more than one Gbohii now – how many were there? Kwadwo was outmatched, giving ground.

"We have to protect Okere," Okoth replied.

"If we don't stop those Gbohii now, none of us will survive this. We need to kill them before this spreads!"

Okoth stopped, looking Etse in the eye. "You've sworn to serve the Wakuu. Protecting him now is that service."

Etse glared back at the man. He glanced down at Okere, who was still sitting, speechless in his terror. Etse straightened his back and stared back at Okoth.

"I swore to defend those people, too," he said.

Then he leapt over the side of the chariot.

Etse hit the ground with his knees bent, stepping up quickly into a long, loping stride. Behind him, he heard Okoth swear again, but the chariot didn't turn. The general was sticking to his duty and getting Okere clear. Etse was fine with that. He had his own duty to attend to.

The plaza was beginning to clear. Enough people had fled that Etse could pick his way through what was left without too much trouble. There were bodies lying on the ground, though – knocked over and trampled by others in their haste to escape. He drew his sword, and the people left gave him a wide berth, opening a path for him.

He saw the first Gbohii before it saw him. It was occupied, teeth tearing into a woman's shoulder. Etse's blade whistled through the air and cleaved the thing's head from its shoulders. The body toppled to the ground over the still screaming woman. Etse's gut churned from knowing it was too late to save her – she was already dead, it just hadn't quite caught up to her yet. Grimly, he kept striding forward into the carnage.

The next two of the monsters he came across worrying at the dead body of a man. He removed the head from one. The other tried to rise and face him, but he stabbed it in the eye. His sword punched out the other side of the skull and stuck fast. Etse tried to jerk the blade free but couldn't pry it loose from where it stuck in the bone.

A claw grabbed his shoulder, jerking him around. Jaws snapped at his face and he cried out, sticking his forearm between those deadly teeth and his face. The Gbohii bit down, teeth snapping off on his beaded armor.

A sword flashed, and the thing's head rolled from its shoulders. The body dropped in a heap at Etse's feet.

"Etse, don't you know better than to turn your back on an opponent?" Kudowor asked. He was battered, his armor a mess, his sword coated with blood. And with his left arm he was helping to support Kwadwo, who looked even worse than he did.

Etse grinned weakly in reply. "It's good to see you two."

"Good to see you as well," Kudowor said. "Now, let's get out of here before we become something's dinner, shall we?"

"What are you doing out here, Etse?" Kwadwo demanded.

"Came to rescue you!" Etse replied, jerking his sword free at last. The crowd had scattered now, and most of the Gbohii were busy...eating. Etse felt his stomach roil at the sight.

But several of the dead were taking notice of them. And as Etse watched, some of the newly dead were beginning to twitch. He looked around.

There were a lot of newly dead laid out on the ground here. And they were all going to be Gbohii soon.

"We need to go!" Etse said. There was no way the three of them could fight so many of the things.

He heard hoof beats behind him and whirled. A chariot pulled up alongside the trio, Kwesi holding the reins.

"Get aboard!" Kwesi yelled.

Etse grabbed Kwadwo's other side and helped Kudowor get him onto the chariot. Kwesi didn't wait any longer but jolted the kwapawnkah into a run. Kudowor hopped on and reached out a hand to Etse. He jumped aboard as the chariot picked up speed.

Behind them, a couple of the Gbohii gave a brief chase, but they couldn't outpace the kwapawnkah and quickly lost interest.

"Father, thanks," Etse said.

Kwesi merely nodded in reply.

"We need to get the Mikijen in here, clean this up," Kwadwo said. "Or we'll lose Nicran for sure."

Fires were starting somewhere in the city. Etse could smell the smoke, and fire would rage uncontrolled in the panic gripping the city. Between fire, and the undead, he had a bad feeling.

"Nicran is already lost," Kwesi said. "We need to save what we can."

Screams broke through the air, cries for help from people they had left behind. Every one broke Etse's heart. He sank to the floor of the chariot, a tear leaking from one eye as he stared backwards at the terrible evidence of his fresh promise, already broken.

CHAPTER FIFTEEN

Etse stood atop the battlements of the Wakuu's palace, staring out at the city around him as the sun played its first light over the rooftops. Cloying smoke filled the air, rising from a hundred burning buildings. Dawn didn't make the ruin of Nicran more pretty. His bleary eyes took in the ruins. It was quiet – an uncanny silence for a place where just yesterday so many people had lived, punctuated now and again by the sounds of terror or torment. But even those were less frequent than they had been.

He hadn't slept well last night. He didn't think anyone in the palace had. Etse knew he'd hear the screams of those trapped outside in his dreams for a long time to come. Every cry of torment had been another stone added to the guilt he felt, until the pile was tall enough, he thought it might smother him.

The palace towered over other buildings in the city, so Etse could see a long, long way. In the distance, he could spy bands of people fleeing along the road to the west. Back toward Takoradi. Toward home.

But not everyone had left, he knew that. By now most of those slain by the Gbohii yesterday would have risen and would be out there adding their own grisly tally to the total dead. Kwadwo said there were perhaps two dozen undead hidden in the temple cellar. This morning, there must be hundreds of the things. By tomorrow, there could be thousands. Nicran was a large city, the biggest in Asanteman.

He shuddered. He'd slain a few of the things. But how could they prevail against so many? This, he knew, was how the cities on the six islands of the Kiswalan archipelago had fallen, how Kiswala had died.

Maybe there was no hope left. Asanteman might have been the last place left in Ki Khanga free from the things, and now they were here, too. They'd scatter from this place as soon as they ran out of prey. Thousands of them would take to the countryside, killing until there was no one alive to slay.

He heard a noise behind him and half turned, his hand going to the hilt of his sword. But it was Kudowor, not a Gbohii. He turned back to watching the city.

"Up early," Kudowor said.

"Didn't sleep," Etse replied.

"Neither did I."

A long silence, as the two men stood side by side. More plumes of smoke billowed from the east side of Nicran. The fires there were spreading fast.

"Did you ever find him?" Etse asked.

"Who?"

"The boy you mentioned, the one who led you to the temple."

"No," Kudowor sighed. "But he was bitten. If he's not...one of them yet, he will be soon enough."

Etse could hear the sadness in the man's voice. "Was he someone you knew?"

"No. He was just a boy."

Etse nodded. He remembered the Gbohii he'd slain yesterday, chewing on the shoulder of a woman in the square. She'd kept screaming even after the thing was dead, and he'd left her there. He just kept on walking. She was bitten, so she was already dead. It just hadn't caught up with her yet. His mind railed against the idea, but he knew that was the grim reality of this new world they found themselves in.

"How did you survive in the cellar?" Etse asked. Kudowor had fallen into a pit of the things but somehow came out alive.

"If Kwadwo hadn't opened the door, I wouldn't have. When I fell, they came to life, but Amon – the boy – called out, and they went after him instead. I found a wooden beam on the floor and pushed it into them. Knocked them back, and it bought us a little time. There wasn't much light, but I could see a bit coming from the cellar door, so I ran that way."

"And then Kwadwo arrived?"

"Aane. If he hadn't..." Kudowor's voice trailed off. Etse saw the man's gaze following a band of the monsters down in the street, ambling along aimlessly, seeking prey.

"If he hadn't, I'd likely be out there right now. One of them."

Etse tried to still another shudder but wasn't especially successful. That was the worst of this. Not the monsters. He could face monsters. Had faced them. But the constant, nagging fear that one bite would finish you was terrible. And the knowledge that the comrade standing next to you could be bitten and turn into one of those horrors tomorrow was perhaps even worse.

Kudowor seemed to sense his melancholy. He put an arm over Etse's shoulders. "Come. You've been alone up here long enough, and Okere is calling a council meeting."

Etse raised an eyebrow at that. "I wonder what he plans to do?"

"You'll find out before I will," Kudowor said. "The Wakuu wants his new champion in attendance."

Etse was the last to arrive to the large dining hall the Wakuu had set aside for his council. Everyone else had already taken seats at a long table. He saw his father there, with Kwadwo beside him. Okere sat at the head of the table, of course, with Okoth by his side. The other seat next to the Wakuu was empty.

Etse was surprised to see three other men there as well, people whose faces he vaguely recognized. He couldn't place their names, but they sat like soldiers, with the same sort of dangerous grace at rest that he always saw from Kwadwo.

"Etse, good! I'm glad they found you," Okere said, smiling a little too broadly. "I apologize for calling a meeting on such short notice, but..."

"Wakuu, I'm at your service when you need me," Etse replied.

"Good, good. Please, join us." Okere motioned to the empty chair next to him.

Etse took the seat offered. He looked around the table. The mood in the room was tense, thick enough to cut with a blade, but that was to be expected given the circumstances. Which were about as dire as Etse could imagine them becoming.

Almost as soon as Etse was seated, Kwesi launched his outburst. "It's clear what we need to do at this point. The trick of it will be in the execution."

Okere cocked his head sideways a bit. "I am not at all sure we have the same thing in mind, Kwesi. Do elaborate?"

"Nicran is lost," Kwesi said, speaking slowly. Etse fought to maintain a cool exterior. Kwesi had used that same voice many times over the years. It was the voice he used when he thought someone was being especially stupid. His father wasn't as good at masking his sarcasm as he thought he was. A quick glance at the clouds growing on Okere's face showed the effect Kwesi's words were having. Etse wanted to warn his father to take more care, to convince and guide, not harass the Wakuu. Where was the cunning politician Kwesi had always been when he was needed most?

"We need to escape the city, bringing the bulk of the troops clear of the immediate threat," Kwesi said. "And then we need to find a place we can fortify. Big enough to support us all, small enough to be defensible."

"Like Takoradi, you think?" Okere replied.

Kwesi shook his head. "Sadly, no. Even Takoradi is simply too large to patrol well. And as we've seen, if even one Gbohii gets past our troops into the civilians, the results can be devastating."

"So you'd have us...what? Drop all of the trappings of civilization and run off into the mountains?" Okere didn't even try to hide the scorn dripping from his voice. "You'd have us simply surrender?"

Kwesi shrugged, looking around the table. "You all saw the same thing I did, yesterday. A couple dozen of the things overran us, slaughtered hundreds of men, women, and children, and forced us to flee like rabbits." He gestured around the room. "This place won't keep us safe for long, and we don't have supplies to keep hundreds of soldiers stationed here."

Okoth moved as if to speak, but the Wakuu shushed him with a wave of his hand. "I know your mind, Okoth. I would hear from your captains." He gestured to the three Mikijen Etse didn't recognize.

The man seated next to Etse looked a little worried and cleared his throat hurriedly. He glanced at the other two captains, sitting next to him, but neither seemed inclined to open their mouths first, either.

He cleared his throat again, then spoke. "My name is Abigaba, and my apologies Wakuu, but he's not wrong. My men are bunked on a mudbrick floor, on blankets. They've eaten today, but we've about run through the provisions stored here. An army runs on its stomach, and morale is terrible being trapped in here with those things outside."

Okere nodded sharply. "Thank you, captain, for your candor." He gestured to the next man.

This man seemed more relaxed on the surface, but Etse could see the muscles in his jaw tense before he spoke. The man was like a drawn bowstring.

"I'm Musongola." His words were quick, clipped, like he was rushing through every syllable with intensity and intent. "Abigaba isn't wrong, Wakuu. As things stand right now, we have food for another day, two at most. And the longer we hide in here, the more of those things will be out there."

The Wakuu held his tongue, gesturing to the third man. Etse examined this captain closely. He seemed interested but strangely detached. There was something in his manner that made Etse feel ill at ease, but he couldn't put his finger on what it was.

"I'm Rwamirama, one of the good general's captains, as are my...brothers...here." The third captain waggled his fingers at the other two men. Then he pulled out a knife, and with everyone watching, he played the knife over his fingers, spinning it around them like a toy. Etse inhaled sharply. Drawing weapons in the presence of the Wakuu?

With a snap of his wrist, Rwamirama flipped the knife into the air and let if fall point down, embedding itself an inch into the table in front of him.

"It seems to me, we're balanced on a knife edge here," Rwamirama said. "On the one side, we face starvation and disaster if we stay. On the other, we face the dead if we try to leave, and we face disaster from starvation once we are out of the city, too."

"What would you have us do, Rwamirama?" Okere asked.

"Find another path."

Etse blinked. Suddenly, he was certain Okere and these captains had spoken before the meeting. The Wakuu had set this up, planned for them to say these things. The question was why? His father's plan sounded sane, if risky and complex. What did Okere have in mind, if not flight?

He didn't have to wait long to find out. Okere waved them all to silence.

"Which is what we shall do," the Wakuu said. "I do not believe for an instant that Nicran is dead to us. And if we have any hope of reclaiming Ki Khanga from these monsters, it must not be dead. We need a point to rally from. Nicran will be that place."

"Against thousands of those things?" Kwesi said. "How will we win the place back from such a foe?"

"Your own son has shown us again and again that they can be slain, Kwesi," Okere said. "But it isn't enough to slay a few. We must wipe them from the city, and we must be systematic about it. Okoth, explain my plan."

Okoth unrolled a large sheet of paper. Etse peered at the diagram there – a map of Nicran, with scrawled notes swarming all over.

"Here we are," Okoth said, stabbing a finger down at the map. "The rest of the city is largely overrun, but we will restore it to our control. Most critically, we will restore safe access to key points, like the granaries here and here." He touched points on the map less than a mile away.

"That's a long way to travel through ruined, half burnt out city with packs of Gbohii hiding in the shadows," Kwadwo drawled.

"Which is why our first step will be to ensure there are no shadows to hide in," Okoth replied.

Kwesi was still studying the map. "You plan to burn the city down?" he asked, his brows knotting together.

"Not all of it," Okere replied.

"We'll go block by block," Okoth confirmed. "We'll clear what we can and burn enough buildings down to clear a path to key resources."

Kwesi heaved a sigh and sat back hard in his chair. Etse felt sorry for his father. He'd clearly been outmaneuvered here. The Wakuu had planned this out, set him up to make a suggestion with no intention of doing what Kwesi wanted.

"What do you think, Etse?" Okere asked.

Etse hesitated for a moment. His father's plan was safer. He knew Kwesi well enough to know the man had carefully thought through the angles, and probably already had one or two places in mind to flee into. But the Wakuu's plan was audacious.

"It seems a risky venture," Etse said. "But if it works...we would have much to gain by holding the city and killing as many of the things as we can."

Etse looked over at his father, feeling his apology on his face. "And if it goes badly, we can retreat from here as a back-up plan, right?"

Kwesi stared him down, the fury in his eyes casting aside his unspoken apology. *Fool*, those eyes said.

Etse turned his face away from his father, toward Okere.

"Aane, we could retreat if we fail here," Okere said. "But to retreat without even trying to fight? It smacks of cowardice, to me."

Etse winced inwardly. It did sound like a coward's move. But Kwesi was no coward, and he opened his mouth to say as much.

While he was still trying to reconcile the feelings in his head and heart, Kwesi stood from the table. Etse looked up, but his father was no longer looking at him. He glared daggers at the Wakuu now, his face red.

"If that is to be the plan, and my own words are called cowardice, then I trust you have no more need of me in this council." Without another word, he turned and strode from the room, his angry footsteps a steady drumbeat on the mudbrick floor.

Silence filled the room for long moments.

"Well," Okere said. "I have decided we will stay and try to win this battle. Now I leave it to you gentlemen to decide how best to manage that task." He rose, and without another word followed Kwesi out the door.

As soon as he was gone, Okoth shook his head. "Politicians will be the death of us," he muttered.

"No doubt," Rwamirama said, a sly smile playing at the corner of his mouth.

"We need to work out plans for this operation," Okoth began. "You three each have an asraafo dawmno (*battalion*). You'll have your men work in cycles. One asraafo dawmno will rest while the other two are active. Of the two active asraafo dawmno, one will engage the Gbohii in the city, burning a path to those granaries. That's our first objective – achieving reliable access to food. The other will guard the palace, ensuring the gates are clear of monsters when the active fighting force returns..."

CHAPTER SIXTEEN

"That man will be the death of us," Kwesi fumed, stalking back and forth.

Kwadwo watched him for another moment before settling himself down carefully in a chair. He winced as his right arm brushed the wood. A surgeon had sewn up the wound, but it was still painful. Kwesi paced back and forth a few more times. After the meeting was over, Kwadwo had gone straight to Kwesi to pass on details of Okoth's planning. He knew he'd find the man in this room, which he'd made into his office. The furnishings were spartan, but Kwesi had a desk and a few chairs in place.

Since Kwadwo had arrived and passed along his information, Kwesi had taken to this pacing back and forth like a caged leopard. There was no rage in the man's body language, though. Kwesi was cool, each footstep deliberate, and each turn precise. Kwadwo knew that even now he was plotting something.

"Perhaps," Kwadwo said, when Kwesi stopped speaking. "But you won't do us any good wearing a groove into the floor. What do you have in mind?"

Kwesi stopped pacing. "What makes you think I have anything in mind?"

"I've known you a long time. You always do."

Kwesi threw his head back and laughed. "I suppose so," he said. He took a seat in a chair opposite Kwadwo.

"So?"

Kwesi took a deep breath. "I wasn't expecting Okere to agree with me."

Kwadwo nodded. Kwesi had given up too quickly. Which meant he'd already known what to expect from the meeting, or at least to expect Okere would disagree with retreat.

"But I wasn't expecting him to call me a coward to my face, either," Kwesi said.

"That was more for Etse's benefit than yours, you know," Kwadwo said.

"So he could sink his claws deeper into my foolish son, yes."

Kwadwo knew he was treading on dangerous ground here but plowed ahead anyway. "I think you do him a disservice to call him foolish, Kwesi. He is your son. Very much so."

He wanted to add that if Kwesi had spent a little more time trusting his son, guiding him to manhood instead of treating him like a child, then perhaps Okere's claws might have found a much more slippery target. But Kwesi was a smart enough man to figure that out on his own. It would not heal their rift to point it out for him.

Kwesi grunted in reply. He tapped his fingers on the desk for a few long moments, staring out the window. All Kwadwo could see out there was a plume of the ever-present smoke rising through the morning air. At the rate the city was burning, Okoth might not have much to do.

"There were over two-hundred fifty-eight thousand people living in the city, before Okere arrived. But when he came here, people flocked to the place. Rumors had spread. Some came to curry favor. Others came for safety. Still more came to make money from the thousands who flooded the place. My best guess is that there were over two-hundred sixty-two thousand souls here, yesterday. Perhaps as many as two-hundred sixty-five thousand."

Kwadwo whistled. He had no idea there were so many people in Nicran.

Kwesi went on speaking while Kwadwo absorbed the news. "We know some people fled the city. Thousands of them. Thousands more are still out there in hiding. But the death toll was much, much higher than Okere is thinking, and it is still rising."

"He thinks he is up against hundreds of the things, maybe a thousand," Kwadwo said. "But from what you are saying, there could be tens of thousands of the things out there."

"Or will be, soon enough."

"My god. How can we fight that?"

"Not all at once," Kwesi said. "That's how."

***

Etse marched in the center of Abigaba's asraafo dawmno, trying not to feel like he was a token addition to the force. The cloying smoke was ever-present here, so much worse at the street level than it had been from the roof of the palace. And the soldiers were adding to the mess. They'd acquired barrels of oil from somewhere and were splashing it over a row of houses. Nearby, a half dozen men stood with torches, ready to go in and set the buildings ablaze.

The rest of the men were fanned out on either side of the street, watching for Gbohii. Several dozen men formed shield walls on each side, with spearmen at the ready in a second row. Every single man had a job. Even Abigaba was giving orders and directing his men into position. Everyone but Etse, that is. Abigaba had made it clear that he tolerated Etse's presence only because the Wakuu commanded it. He'd told Etse bluntly to stand there, look pretty, and be out of the way.

And Etse had to admit, it had all the appearances of a well-planned operation. The men moved with a cohesion and skill born from long practice and drill. But there was a weakness to the plan.

"Those buildings are going to smoke once they're set alight," Etse said aloud.

"Hmm?" Abigaba was standing next to him, watching his men at work.

Etse sighed, exasperated. The man had all but ignored him the entire time they'd been outside the palace walls. Okoth had sent him along to help the mercenaries if they ran into trouble. None of these men had ever actually faced a Gbohii in combat. Etse had. The idea that he was the most experienced man out here scared him more than anything else, today.

"I said, the buildings will smoke a lot," Etse repeated.

"What of it?" Abigaba asked.

The torch bearers were running in now, each carrying a torch to one of the doused homes. Other men had already scoured them for necessary supplies, especially food. The whole of the palace would be on short rations until they gained access to the granaries, and that might be days from now.

The houses lit quickly, and as Etse expected, they gave off huge plumes of smoke. The wind blew hot air and soot back into the street, and the warriors quickly pulled away. In seconds, the street was so full of smoke that everyone was coughing.

And Etse couldn't see the troops who were on guard through the haze. He peered as best he could through stinging eyes, trying to catch glimpses of the warriors, but they were too far, the smoke too thick.

He heard the yells when they started, though. And he heard the screams. Etse drew his sword – the cries came from the west side of the street, about fifty feet to his left. He took off at a jog, careful not to trip over the bits of debris littering the road and watching the smoke for trouble.

It didn't take him long to find the latter.

A small band of Gbohii were tearing into the shield wall. Shields, Etse saw quickly, simply didn't work on the undead the way they did on the living. Living men feared a wall of shields, hesitated when they saw the bristling spears behind that wall. The Gbohii didn't pause, though. They stepped forward and grabbed hold of the shields, tearing at them with inhuman strength. Some of the more battle-wise men simply let go. But Etse saw one man holding fast to his shield, dragged out of the line and into the midst of the monsters. He vanished from sight, but his screams were terrible.

One of the spearmen tried to close that gap in the line, but a Gbohii stepped into the hole, impaling itself on his spear – and then kept stepping forward. It pulled itself down the shaft, while men with swords hacked bits of it off. When it reached the spearman, it had no arms left, but its teeth locked into his shoulder before Etse could arrive to help.

"Go for the head!" Etse shouted, swinging his sword hard at the thing. His blade smashed into its skull, breaking it open. The Gbohii dropped to the ground, and the spearman collapsed under its sudden weight. Etse had no time to assist the man further, and he knew that the bite would be lethal no matter what he did.

"Form a line!" he shouted. "Spears, pin them. Swords, cut off their heads!"

The men fell into ranks alongside him, with Etse forming the center of their line. He took a step forward, and miraculously, the men stepped forward with him. He'd worried that they were too broken by the attack to continue the fight, but these were Mikijen, and they advanced with him. Etse's sword sang again, and he took the head from a second Gbohii. There were no more immediate threats, so he looked left and right down the line. The men were following his orders – spears on both sides stuck into the undead, slowing their advance, giving the swordsmen time to cut them down.

In a few minutes of heart-pounding work, it was over. Six Gbohii bodies lay on the ground.

"Gather our dead and wounded," Etse said. "We're pulling back to the palace."

He stood guard, watching for more movement in the smoke, but no more Gbohii came at them. He counted four dead, and three more wounded men carried from the field. Which effectively meant seven dead, he reminded himself. Six enemies slain, and seven of their own lost. And this was a small cluster of the Gbohii. If it had been a larger band, the entire force might have been destroyed.

More men from the asraafo dawmno arrived to help drag the wounded to safety. Etse covered the rear, walking backwards away from the smoke. They were out there. Watching. He could feel it.

There had to be a better way.

"What the hell were you thinking?" yelled Abigaba, coming toward him through the smoke.

"I was saving your men," Etse replied.

"Why are they pulling back?"

Etse gritted his teeth at the man's stupidity. He'd surely seen the wounded, and the dead. "You've lost seven men, captain. Another attack like that will wipe out the entire flank."

Abigaba grunted. For a moment, Etse thought he would countermand his orders out of sheer spite. Instead, he cupped his hands to his mouth. "Pull back to the palace!" he shouted. "Orderly formation, rear guard watch for attack!"

Etse sighed with relief. He started to follow the mercenaries in their retreat, but Abigaba grabbed him by the arm, turning him back around.

"You, boy. You make me look bad again, I'll feed you to those things out there. Don't think I won't."

Etse gritted his teeth, fighting the urge to draw his sword. He yanked his arm free from Abigaba's grasp. The man was incompetent, and worse, he was stupid. He'd get them all killed.

"You might try," Etse said, his voice cold. Without another word, he turned his back on the captain and followed the men back to the palace.

CHAPTER SEVENTEEN

Kudowor was on his rest shift, snoozing lightly. The mudbrick floor made for a rough bed, even with a blanket spread out underneath him. But it was dry, and there was some sense of security in the thick walls of the palace. He felt like he'd just begun to doze off when a hand gently touched his shoulder.

He woke instantly, hand sweeping down to touch the hilt of his sword on reflex. He'd taken to sleeping with the thing, of late. It seemed wise to be armed. Always.

Kudowor opened his eyes, trying to adjust to the dim light in the room. Other men were laid out across the floor in neat rows, packed in just a little more tightly than was comfortable. There were a lot of soldiers bedded down in the palace right now. His glance swept around to the hand on his shoulder, then up the arm to Kwadwo's face. His friend had his other hand up to his face, one finger across his lips in a signal for silence. Once he saw Kudowor understood, he released his grip and stood quietly, beckoning Kudowor to follow.

The two stepped silently from the room. Kwadwo didn't stop in the hall outside, but kept going down the hall, down one flight of stairs, and then another. They were in the basement of the palace now. The rooms here were piled high with things. Much of it was furniture cleared from the upper floors to make room for soldiers to sleep and live. The rest was items deemed critical – spare weapons, foodstuffs, and other crucial supplies.

"We can talk, here," Kwadwo said, sitting down on a large bag of grain.

"Where's the guard?" Kudowor asked. There should have been one posted over the supplies.

"He's using the latrine. I've taken his post for a short while so he could go. One of our men, from Takoradi."

Kudowor nodded, understanding. Kwadwo had set this up so that they'd have complete privacy. That was a lot of effort. "What's going on, Kwadwo?"

"You saw what a disaster the clearing operation was, right?" Kwadwo asked.

"I understand it went okay for the first shift," Kudowor said.

"Because Etse saved their asses."

"Well, he wasn't there for the second group. I was. It was a disaster. The men here have never fought these things before. We lost a lot of men. Too many," Kudowor said.

"And the numbers of Gbohii swarming out there are growing. By tomorrow, when Okoth sends his men out, I have no idea what they'll be facing."

Kudowor paced a bit, kicking one of the sacks with his boot while he thought. "You didn't drag me out of my bed to tell me we're all going to die, Kwadwo. What's the plan?"

"We're getting out of here, that's what. Kwesi. Me. And he's asked me to grab a few men loyal to him."

Kudowor whistled. "This is without the Wakuu's approval, I assume?"

Kwadwo didn't reply, he just glanced sideways at Kudowor.

"Right. Stupid question. So, when do we go? And how do we get past the Wakuu, all his men, and then," Kudowor gestured at the space outside the walls, "get past all of those things out there?"

The other man chuckled.

Kudowor's heart sank in his stomach. He hated that sound.

"Oh, god, I'm going to dislike this plan, aren't I?" he asked.

"Aane, you probably are," Kwadwo said, still laughing.

***

Kwadwo climbed the long staircase slowly. His feet felt like lead; his head stuffed with cotton. It had been a long night, and he needed to rest. One more person to talk to, though. And he was fairly sure where he'd find the man he was looking for. So here he was, as the first light of dawn cracked over the horizon, stepping up to the rooftop.

And there he was, standing out by the edge of the battlements, looking out over the city. Etse hadn't been in his bed when Kwadwo had sought him out. He had a feeling he might find him here again.

"Did you sleep at all?" he called out softly. The two guards posted to the rooftop were a good distance away, and he pitched his voice low enough to not carry.

Etse looked back at him over his shoulder. The boy's carefree face was gone. It was replaced by the gaze of a man who's seen horror and despair, who'd lived through it but wasn't sure how. Kwadwo kept his face straight but winced inwardly. He'd hoped to see Etse wake to his responsibilities, but the last weeks had been a harsher way for that to happen than anything he could have imagined.

"Some," Etse said.

Kwadwo came up alongside him. Down in the street below, he saw the work of the day before. The row of houses the first asraafo dawmno had burned had been torn down by the second asraafo dawmno, and the third had managed to get the next row alight before being forced to retreat with heavy casualties. Now, scores of the dead roamed through the cleared-out area. Pushing ahead today was going to mean a pitched battle, and there were still several blocks to burn through if they wanted to clear a path to the granaries.

"Okoth is sending out all three asraafo dawmno today," Etse said. "We discussed it. It's the only way to clear the area and push ahead. One asraafo dawmno will guard each flank while the third tears apart the next row of buildings."

"I heard you had a row with Abigaba, yesterday," Kwadwo said carefully.

"The man is a fool. I'll be with Musongola's asraafo dawmno today."

Kwadwo cleared his throat. Etse cocked his head at the noise, and to Kwadwo's relief, cracked a smile.

"Say what you have in mind, Kwadwo," Etse said.

"You know me too well," Kwadwo grumbled. "Etse, you know this operation cannot succeed, right?"

Etse nodded. "I've done the math too, Kwadwo. On short rations, we have two days of food left, and even if all goes well, four days to clear the way to more."

"And the men can't fight those things well on short rations."

"I know. But Kwadwo... You know we rescued fifty people yesterday? Saved them from those things. Some we found hidden inside the buildings when we searched them before burning them out. Others simply stumbled across us. That's fifty lives saved."

"And thirty-two soldiers dead, or soon to die from their wounds," Kwadwo said. "Warriors whose expertise we cannot easily replace and cannot afford to lose."

"Those men will not leave here unless the Wakuu orders it. They'll follow his commands. I'm not the one my father needs to convince, Kwadwo."

Personally, Kwadwo doubted that. Already grumbling had started among the men. Kiswalan mercenaries were a disciplined bunch, but what was happening in Nicran was so horrific that morale was falling fast. Men sent out to face monsters out of myth day after day, with more of them dead each day, would not keep doing so to the last man. But he kept the thought to himself.

Instead, he said, "Kwesi cannot convince him. He's tried. Okere is set on this mad course."

"So what does my father want, Kwadwo? I assume he's sent you to me?"

"I came because your father asked me to gather a few men that he can trust. And you are a man I know that I would trust with my life, Etse," Kwadwo replied, surprising himself a bit with his words. He tested them in his head and was more surprised to see that they were true. He would never have trusted the callow youth he'd once known with anything of importance. But this man?

Etse turned and stared Kwadwo eye to eye. "Thank you. That means...a lot, Kwadwo."

"Then you'll join us?"

"I can't. I swore to defend these people," he cast his hand out in a sweeping gesture over the city below. "I have to at least try."

"You'll die here, if you stay," Kwadwo said, his voice flat.

"Maybe," Etse replied. He grinned, a bit of the boyishness suddenly returned. "But I find that I am not that easy to kill, so maybe not."

"Eda's own luck to you, then," Kwadwo said. He was about to leave, but an inspiration struck, and he turned back.

"Etse," he said, unbuckling the sword from his waist.

"Aane?"

"I want you to take my sword. If you're to survive, you will need Eda's grace. Maybe a sword blessed by an Ahene Akamfo will help."

"Kwadwo..." Etse reached out for the scabbard but paused. "I can't. I know how much your sword means to you."

"You mean more," Kwadwo said. Unable to resist the impulse, he reached out and embraced Etse. The young man went still for a moment and then wrapped his own arms around Kwadwo.

Etse stepped back first. Both men's eyes were damp. "I will keep it safe for you," he said, taking the sword.

"You'd better," Kwadwo said, with the hint of a joking growl to his tone. In a more serious voice he added, "And come join us. As soon as you can. Things will be bad here, soon."

Etse nodded. "I know. Where will you be?"

"I don't know. But we'll leave some sort of word at Takoradi."

Kwadwo turned away, leaving Etse to his thoughts on the roof. Etse would weave his own fate, now. He'd done all he could.

CHAPTER EIGHTEEN

Day was in full bloom over Nicran when Etse made his way down to join the soldiers massing by the great front doors of the palace. They were double doors, sturdy mahogany, and barred from the inside. The entry hall was large, but the force being sent out today numbered some three hundred soldiers and mercenaries, almost all remaining fit for duty from the asraafo dawmno they'd gathered. Half of Okoth's force was still missing. They'd been at the encampment, in the north part of the city, when the Gbohii had attacked and everything had gone to agyanan (*feces*). Perhaps they were still holding out there, but there had been no word from them.

"Etse, good to see you. I hear you are with my men and I today?"

He turned to see Captain Musongola striding toward him, already decked out in full tortoise armor. He'd added a few refinements to his armor, Etse noted. In addition to the leather covered in pieces of turtle shell all Mikijen wore, Musongola was wearing sleeves of overlapping steel plates.

"Steel, Musongola?" Etse asked. He'd never seen steel sleeves worn outside of an arena fight before.

"I found a set on a display here in the palace, and it seemed like it might be useful, given the nature of the enemy."

"It might, at that," Etse admitted. The Gbohii would have a hard time biting through that armor. He glanced down at the short sleeves on his beaded armor and found himself wishing they were longer. Thick leather bracers protected his wrists, but steel would have felt good there.

Musongola drew close. "I'm glad to have you with us. I spoke with some of Abigaba's men about your actions yesterday. The man is a fool. You probably saved his entire asraafo dawmno."

Etse smiled at the compliment. This man, at least, was no fool. He felt his odds of surviving the day improving by the moment. "Thank you, Musongola. I hope that there won't be too much action today, but..." His voice trailed off.

"But I think we both know better than that," Musongola said, his face grim.

"Aane."

"Excuse me, please. My asraafo dawmno has the vanguard, and I should speak to my men."

"Of course," Etse said.

He watched as Musongola set off through his troops, clasping one by the hand, slapping another on the helm. He pulled tight loose straps on one man's armor, admonishing the soldier to better mind his own gear in the future, then spoke briefly to some spearmen, reminding them that their spears had more weight now that the blacksmith had soldered crossbars near the tip – so the Gbohii could not force themselves up the shaft. Etse's idea, that, and he was glad to see so many of the altered spears out here today. The smith must have been up all night working on the project.

No grand speeches or proclamations from Musongola. Bit by bit he worked his way through his men, talking to one man by himself, then to a small cluster of his troops, until he'd spoken to most of them. And wherever he went, the mood was brighter, the men standing a bit taller. It was clear they all looked up to Musongola, and Etse could see why. He had a gift for leading others.

Finally, it was time. Musongola had worked his way up to the front rank, closest to the great doors. Etse stepped forward to join him, and the men parted before him. He touched the sword Kwadwo had gifted to him, belted at his side. He didn't believe an Ahene Akamfo's blessing would somehow slay these monsters at a touch. But any ounce of grace he might be lent today would be welcome. He'd just been on the rooftop. He knew what was waiting outside those doors.

Musongola gave a sharp command to two men, and together they lifted the wooden beam holding the doors closed. Without another word, Musongola stepped out through the doors as they opened. Etse was close on his heels. Rank after rank of men followed them out into daylight.

The nearest Gbohii were only a spear-length away and came at them as soon as they saw the doors opening. Etse drew his blade. Musongola had his in his hand already, and the two struck the oncoming undead as one, cutting them down. The men continued to spill out of the doors, flowing into the open yard beyond. They set a shield wall, spears behind the shields. Gbohii hit that wall and were impaled by the spears. Then the shield men sliced into the Gbohii necks with the short swords they carried. Another Gbohii rushed the center of the line, and Musongola's blade stabbed it in the throat before Etse could even react. He'd never seen a man move like that with a blade! He was quick, but this Mikijen was even faster.

The troops began to advance, pushing deeper into the cleared territory. More Gbohii rushed them but were quickly dispatched. By the time the entire asraafo dawmno was outside in good order, there were no more of the undead to be seen.

"Is anyone injured?" Musongola called.

Down the line, Etse saw men checking with their comrades, but every man shook his head. He saw at least a dozen of the monsters broken on the ground, and not a man from the asraafo dawmno hurt.

For the first time since the disaster of the parade, Etse allowed himself to feel a ray of hope.

Abigaba gritted his teeth. The shame of it, his entire asraafo dawmno reduced to manual labor. No burning today, Okoth had ordered. Too much smoke, too much confusion. They were to somehow tear down these buildings with force alone. The other two asraafo dawmno were on guard duty, protecting his men. Pah! Protection? More like shaming them all. Stealing all the glory.

He'd heard the triumphant shouts of Musongola's men after their little show at the doors. Now they stood off to his left, guarding the flank. Rwamirama and his men had the other side. Except for a few of Abigaba's men who were keeping watch for Gbohii ahead, his men all had their weapons sheathed, and were tearing apart houses with hand tools and improvised battering rams.

And this place? How was he supposed to tear this down? He wasn't sure what the building had been before, but it was well crafted from mudbrick, three stories tall, and huge. He peered at the sign hanging from the door. A school, perhaps?

"You!" he growled at a runner. "Go tell the general we'll need to go around this one. No way to tear it down. Hurry!"

The man dashed off. Okoth was back near the doors, with a small cluster of guards there, covering their retreat should they come under attack. Except there hadn't been any attacks, barring a few of the dead things that had stumbled across them, and been dispatched rapidly. Kwesi and his tens of thousands of dead couldn't possibly be right. If there were tens of thousands of the things, where were they all?

The runner returned a few minutes later. "General Okoth says we can skip demolishing this one. He says if it's sturdy we might be able to put it to use."

Abigaba squinted at the building. It might work as a barracks, at that. The ground floor windows had all been broken, but those could be replaced, barricaded.

"But the General says we need to clear the building, first. He says he doesn't want to leave any Gbohii behind our ranks, sir," the runner continued.

Abigaba grunted. "Fine. We'll clear his damned building."

A few minutes later, he'd gathered up a dozen men to search the building. He stood outside the front doors with the rest of his men, waiting, while they stepped into the gloom within. Abigaba had ensured all his men had their weapons close to hand, just in case the men inside met more than one Gbohii.

Then the screaming started from inside the mudbrick schoolhouse. Instead of dying down, the volume increased, as more men cried out in agony. His men standing outside began to look wildly at one another.

"Captain!" one shouted. "We have to help them!"

Abigaba shivered. What in the Cleave was in there that would take down all twelve of his men like that?

He had an answer a moment later.

A small figure appeared in the doorway, looking like a lost child. It staggered down a couple of the stairs and then looked up at the warriors arrayed in ranks in front of the building. It was a child, but its eyes were empty, as soulless as any of the other Gbohii. The thing made a high-pitched noise in its throat and started toward Abigaba.

"Eda's womb," he heard one of the men swear, standing next to him. "It's a child."

"No, it's a monster," Abigaba said. He stepped forward to slash at the thing, but it darted sideways. His blade only nicked its arm. It dashed in, teeth going for his leg. Abigaba tried to back away but tripped over a chunk of rock, falling flat on his back. His breath went out of him in a huff, and then the thing was on him.

But before it could bite, two of his men impaled it with spears, and three more stepped forward to cut its head off. Blood sprayed from the wound, splashing down all over Abigaba.

"Damned thing!" he shouted, scrabbling back to his feet while trying to wipe the blood from his face. At least it was dead, though. He pulled a strip of cloth from a pouch, wiping at his face.

Abigaba heard more scrabbling noises from the doorway.

"Daarila, take pity!"

He wasn't sure whether he'd said that, or one of his men.

He didn't have long to wonder about it though, as hundreds of dead children swarmed from the school and engaged his men.

CHAPTER NINETEEN

Etse panted hard. Blood dripped from his sword. But he was whole, and unbitten. That was more than some of Musongola's men could say. It had been a hard morning of fighting. The Gbohii weren't organized, so they never came at the line in a mass. But they did come, a steady stream of them. And if anything, the attacks had seemed to grow more numerous as the day went on. The men were making a lot of noise – three hundred armored warriors would do that. Etse wondered if the noise was drawing more of the dead out.

"Still alive?" Musongola asked, clapping him on the back with a grin.

"So far," Etse replied.

"We've lost ten men. I've had a report that Rwamirama has lost twelve."

"But we've slain a lot more of the enemy," Etse said.

Musongola wiped the sweat from his brow with a free hand. "And yet they keep coming. How many people lived in Nicran, Etse? How many of them are Gbohii now?

Etse didn't know. He knew only that the city had been teeming with life days before. It might well be just as full of the undead now.

"And that damned fool Abigaba is taking his sweet time, too," Musongola grumbled.

Etse looked over in the direction of Abigaba's asraafo dawmno. There did seem to be an awful lot of his men standing around. They'd cleared a row of buildings, but now they just stood there. What was going on?

Every row of buildings cleared meant more streets to guard, which meant the flank asraafo dawmno were more spread out. That meant less men at any one point to stop Gbohii who attacked. Eventually, they were going to simply be spread too thin.

He looked back at Abigaba's position and saw furious activity there. "What the Cleave?"

Musongola followed his gaze and swore. "He's in trouble. They must have found a nest of the things. Bakka, take your squad and go reinforce them, on the double!"

The Mikijen he'd ordered took off at a jog, bringing nine other men with him. Abigaba's troops were being cut down like wheat. How many of the things were there? He heard one of the men from the beleaguered asraafo dawmno blow a horn, three loud blasts. The sound to retreat.

"No!" Etse said. "They can't..."

"We need to begin pulling back to the palace," Musongola said.

Etse stared back down the street they guarded. He thought he'd heard a noise from the no-man's land out there in the uncleared streets. Then he heard it again – the tromp of many feet.

"Damn," Etse said, his voice hollow.

"What is it...?" Musongola asked.

"What we've all been afraid of."

A Gbohii came into view from a side street a few hundred paces ahead of them. It shrieked and began loping toward them. The men set themselves to deal with the thing.

But Etse realized its shriek was being echoed. By many unearthly voices.

They rounded the corner as a mass, boiling into view. Etse had no idea how many of them there were. However many it was, he knew it was too many.

"We need to go, now!" he shouted. Musongola's men hesitated, their line faltering as a few men took a step or two back.

"Pull back in good order!" Musongola shouted. The men formed their ranks again, shield wall at the ready, spears bristling. Against any imaginable human army, it would have been enough to allow the asraafo dawmno to escape. But this was no human army.

The Gbohii hit the men like a tidal wave, some of them literally hitting the shields and going over, pushed along by the force of the undead behind them slamming them forward. They fell on the troops from above, tearing into them like lions.

The ranks fell apart in an instant, half the men turning to flee, and the ones who stood their ground found themselves surrounded by ravening dead. The carefully ordered line of troops collapsed into chaos. The dead swarmed everywhere. Screams echoed. Men shouted curses as they died in place or ran away. This battle was over – there was nothing further they could do here.

"My men!" Musongola shouted.

"Run!" Etse grabbed his arm, trying to drag Musongola clear. The man hacked down one Gbohii that had gotten close and turned to follow Etse. Together the two sprinted back toward the palace doors.

Etse spared a glance toward Abigaba's asraafo dawmno, but he could no longer see any men there. The Gbohii had completely overrun them, and were now running toward the palace, their strange gait carrying them swiftly.

"They're going to cut us off," Etse said between gasping breaths. Where was Rwamirama? He looked back toward the palace and saw his answer. Rwamirama had already pulled his men back, and they were filing in through the doors.

"If they close those doors before we get there, we're all dead men," Musongola said.

"Or worse," Etse replied. They both redoubled their run. Behind them, they heard the screams of men who were slower, cut down as they tried to flee.

The dead things that had slain Abigaba's men were coming closer now. Horribly, Etse saw that they were children. Hundreds of dead children, making ready to feast on their flesh. The fastest of the dead children were already between them and the palace.

"We'll have to cut our way through them!" Etse shouted.

His sword sank deeply into one of the undead, cleaving a leg from it. Not a finishing blow, but it kept the thing from chasing them further. Beside him, Musongola helped carve a path, and the handful of surviving troops cut into the undead with desperate strength. One man went down, three child-things tearing at his arms and throat. Then another fell, one of the things attached to his ankle, only to be swarmed by still more of them as soon as he fell.

"Damn them! My men!" Musongola roared.

They were at the base of the palace steps now, and there Musongola turned to face the foe.

Etse had sprinted halfway up the stairs, so close to safety that he could taste it. He saw men in the doorway, beckoning him in. But Musongola was down there, facing that horde alone. Instantly Etse saw what he was trying to do – one squad of his men had held a tight formation, and fought their way almost to the palace, but the main force of Gbohii was going to cut them off.

Unless someone stopped them. Etse had never seen such courage. This was the man who should have been named hero and champion. This was the person he should have been and knew in his heart he would never be. And he was about to die.

Musongola screamed a challenge, and the mass of undead turned to face him, coming on at a rush. His blade was a brilliant blur, flashing in the sunlight, and a pile of the dead quickly formed at his feet. But Etse knew he could not hold. He was a dead man. The best among them, and he was about to fall. Etse felt his heart shatter with despair.

All he had to do was take those last few steps, and he would be safe.

But he knew he would never be able to live with himself if he did.

"With me now!" he shouted to the men guarding the palace door. Without waiting to see if they followed, he charged back down the stairs. As he started down, he saw one of the undead grab Musongola by the arm, pulling him off balance. One of the child-dead latched itself to his leg, gnawing. Etse cried out in horror, sprinting to close the distance. But before he could arrive, Musongola went down under the weight of the dead.

Grimly, he took the man's place. He wove a deadly web with his sword, taking the head from one Gbohii, then another. He danced back a step to avoid the rush of one – but a spear struck its side, pinning it. He swung his sword backhand and struck the side of its head, shattering its skull. All around him were other warriors now, shouting, roaring their fury.

The men who'd been cut off gained the steps, but instead of running for safety they joined the others trying to protect Etse.

There! A glint of steel, under the unmoving body of a Gbohii.

"Keep them off me!" Etse shouted, sheathing his sword.

He heaved the thing over, and saw Musongola, laying on the ground. His face was bloody, but Etse was grimly determined not to leave the man to die here. He heaved the unmoving form over his shoulders and turned to make for the waiting doors.

A few moments later, and he was through, into the welcome dimness of the protective stone walls. He managed a few more steps before stumbling and falling to one knee. Two men ran forward to help him set Musongola down. Etse looked back to the door, but the last men were coming through now, and the heavy doors were being shut against the undead tide. With a booming noise, the beam was set in place.

They were safe.

Musongola coughed.

"God, he's alive!" one of the men said. "I thought you were carrying a corpse!"

Etse looked Musongola over carefully. If he'd been bitten, he would be dead soon anyway, no matter that he still breathed now. But miraculously, the man's armor seemed to have protected him. The blood on his face was from a blow to the head, probably from when he'd fallen. Etse could find no bite marks. His head spun. If he'd hesitated even a moment longer, Musongola would have been lost. But this time, he had not failed.

"You have to be the luckiest man alive, Musongola," Etse breathed.

Musongola coughed again, and his eyes opened a bit. "That I seem to be," he said.

"And the craziest," Etse said, smiling.

"I think my luck is mostly having you by my side, Etse."

Etse clasped his arm, and Musongola used the grip to help pull himself back to his feet.

"Hail, Musongola!" one of his men called.

"No," Musongola said, staring into Etse's eyes. He straightened his back and said in a voice which carried well over the crowd, "not I. Hail Etse, who saved my life."

There was a pause, as the men's admiring looks shifted from Musongola to Etse.

"Hail, Etse!" the men shouted together. As one, they surged forward, clasping Etse's arm, buffeting his back, each giving their thanks in their own way.

The shouting had only begun to die down when Okoth came down the stairs from the floors above.

"The Wakuu wants to see both of you right away," he said.

CHAPTER TWENTY

Kwesi stood by the window, ignoring the seats arranged around the conference table. He noted each man as they came in. Kwadwo was already there, speaking softly with Rwamirama. Okere sat in silence at the head again, sipping a goblet of wine. He noted when Okoth came back, leading Etse and Musongola, but still he held his position in the window.

He'd always been a curious man, driven to investigate things. He'd always been good at seeing patterns, too. Even for him, it was proving difficult to see any sort of order in the chaos swirling around the palace.

The one thing he'd been able to pick out is that more Gbohii were arriving, but none were leaving. He'd watched, carefully. Once they stumbled into the cleared area near the palace, they stayed near it. They entered in ones, and in twos, and sometimes in bands numbering dozens or scores. But while Kwesi had been watching them, not a single one had drifted away from the place. Only toward it.

He'd noted one other curious thing as well. It didn't seem likely that the Gbohii could drown – they were already dead, after all. But most of them avoided the river. The few he'd seen stumbling in were quickly swept away. The palace had city on only three sides – and the Densu River on the fourth.

They were not entirely encircled.

Kwesi caught Kwadwo's eye with a look. He responded with a tiny nod of his head. Good. The plan was underway. No matter how this meeting went, he'd have a chance to get away. He'd need to, because if this went badly, everyone who stayed behind would be doomed.

"Gentlemen," Okere said, "we face a great problem. We need solutions."

Everyone seated went silent.

To Kwesi's surprise, Etse spoke up first. "Wakuu, the position is untenable. Nicran had a couple hundred thousand of inhabitants, and it looks like most of those are now dead – and trying to kill us."

Okere narrowed his eyes.

"We must find a way to withdraw," Etse continued, ignoring the Wakuu's displeasure. "We can't fight through them, so we must find a way around them or a way to draw them off long enough to escape."

"Did I name the wrong man as my champion, Etse? So quick to tuck your tail between your legs," Okere said, scorn dripping from his voice. "Just a boy after all. So disappointing."

Etse flinched but then steeled himself to glare back at the man. Kwesi watched his son through narrow eyes, examining the exchange. How had he missed seeing such change in his boy? Where had this spine come from?

Okere met Etse's glare, their stares matching across the table briefly. Then the Wakuu looked away, shaking his fist. Okere stood and slammed his hand into the table.

"I am Kiswala!" he shouted. "Understand me now. Kiswala will retreat no further. We shall defeat the enemy here!"

Kwesi turned completely from the window, his curiosity finding a new target. He watched the faces of the other men at the table. Okere was easy – the man was broken, his terror bringing him to the edge of madness. And his insanity would kill them all if allowed to go further. Boring. Rwamirama looked bemused. That one bore watching. Kwadwo had a poker face on, revealing little. But then, he knew the game Kwesi had in mind.

On Okoth's face Kwesi saw fear warring with loyalty. He wondered which would win. Musongola – he watched that handsome face dissolve in anger, turning red. He'd been furious at Okere for scorning Etse, and Kwesi wondered what his son had done to win the man over so completely.

But Etse – his face was by far the most interesting. He'd half feared that the boy would act as a whipped puppy, bowing instantly to the power in the Wakuu's position. Or that he'd react in heat and anger, lashing out with words of his own.

Kwesi saw that anger appear on his son's face, only to be banished in an instant. He saw Etse scanning the Wakuu's face intently. His lips were tight, but his face was calm. Kwesi stood silently, watching to see how this played out.

Etse stood.

"Wakuu, your titles are your own to give or take. Do with mine as you will."

"I will –" Okere started to say, but Etse's strong tenor voice continued over him.

"But understand this. Every one of us is also Kiswala. Every Asante is Kiswala. And Kiswala survives so long as the ideals of civilization do. If we all die here – and if we stay, we will all die here – then that much of Kiswala dies with us.

"Let us choose the time and place of the battles ahead. But to do that, we must escape the trap this place has become."

Kwesi found himself nodding, despite himself. Damn! Kwadwo was right. His son had truly grown up. He felt something odd welling in his chest... Pride.

Okere slowly sat back down. His hands were shaking.

"Okoth, arrest this upstart," he said.

Okoth took a long look at Etse. Then he returned his gaze to the Wakuu. He did not move.

"Will none of you stand with me?" he whispered. "Am I betrayed from all sides?"

Kwesi heard shouting from below and turned to look back out his window. The pattern of the Gbohii had changed. They were milling about less aimlessly now. They seemed directed. Focused. What the Cleave was going on?

A pounding at the conference room door startled all of them.

"Enter!" Okoth shouted, his voice shaking with tension.

The door opened, and a panting Mikijen stepped in. "They're breaking through!"

"Calm down, man. What's going on?" Okoth ordered.

"The dead, sir. They're tearing apart the wooden doors with their bare hands. They'll break through any minute!"

Etse exchanged the briefest of looks with Musongola before both men rose from their chairs and started to the door. Musongola reached the doorway first and vanished down the stairs. The noise from below was growing more intense.

Okere was staring at his hands. He wasn't going to be much use to anyone for the next little bit.

"Okoth," Etse said, "gather all the men you can. We're going to need to hold the doorway, and it isn't going to be an easy fight."

Okoth nodded, beckoned Rwamirama, and the two men set out.

"Father," Etse said, "I think it's time you got your plan into motion and got everyone out of here."

"What makes you think I have a plan?" Kwesi said, raising an eyebrow.

Etse rolled his eyes. "You always have a plan."

Kwadwo laughed at that, and when Kwesi scowled at him, he laughed again, saying "You do, you know."

"Get the Wakuu out, if you can," Etse said. "Save who you can. We'll hold them as long as possible."

Then he turned and followed Musongola down the stairs. His feet flew over the mudbrick steps, and he took the corners with what was probably too much speed, but he had a feeling every second would count.

The courtyard was a scene of confusion. Some citizens who'd taken refuge in the palace were running about madly, like ants trying to escape a boot. Etse saw one woman kneeling in the middle of the grassy garden, two children clutched to her. She was sobbing in terror.

The area around the front door was one calm spot in the midst of the chaos. Etse could hear Musongola calling out orders before he even left the stairwell. The men gathered by the door had to know they were in trouble, but they stood in ranks and files anyway. Shields were set. Spears held at the ready. They would hold, at least as long as they knew someone would be there to lead them.

Etse stepped up into the entryway and stopped cold. He could see daylight through the doors. Those doors had been four inches thick, made of strong mahogany. But the Gbohii had torn at the wood, gouging holes with their hands. As he watched, one hole grew suddenly wider as a big chunk was torn away, and a rotting arm reached in through the opening. One of the men in the first file stepped forward, hewing at the appendage with his short sword. He struck twice but couldn't quite cut the arm off before it was withdrawn.

"Steady, men. Be ready for them when they come," Musongola said.

Etse stepped up beside him to whisper in his ear. "We need to buy some time here."

Musongola gave him a look that begged the question: time for what? But he nodded understanding. Etse hoped that he was right and Kwesi did have a plan in mind. Because once that door broke completely – and it would – nothing was going to hold the Gbohii out for long. There were too many of them.

Another chunk tore away, and Etse saw hands grasp the door from either side and pull hard. The Gbohii's strength was terrific, and the mahogany tore free from the iron bands that held the door together. That opened a huge gap, not quite large enough for a man to slip through.

A short form flickered past the opening, and almost too late Etse remembered the child undead. "Watch for the short ones!" he shouted.

Because the opening was too small for a man – but big enough for a child. A moment later, the first of the dead children slid through the gap, followed by another, and another, and another. They ripped into the front ranks of horrified men, and the battle was joined in earnest.

Behind the dead children, the larger Gbohii tore the rest of the door to splinters.

CHAPTER TWENTY-ONE

"Join the army," Kudowor muttered to himself. "See exciting places. Meet fun people. They didn't say anything about those people being dead, though."

They hadn't said anything about crawling through the muck of the palace privy drain, either. That had been one of the foulest things he'd ever had to do. When Kwadwo showed him the grate, he'd almost lost his breakfast. It was a man-sized gate that led into a tunnel. The tunnel which every privy in the palace dropped into. The muck and human waste ran from there out into the Densu River, but every so often it needed to be cleaned out if things got stopped up. Thus the locked gate.

Then Kwadwo pulled out keys for the lock. Kudowor had already figured out that his day was about to get very, very bad.

He wondered if he'd ever be able to get the stench from his body, after swimming through that. Even once he'd gotten out into daylight, swimming against the strong current in the river, he could still smell the stink left by hundreds of people using too few privies for too many days.

He drifted back down the river, holding tight to the side of a large rowboat he'd acquired a short way up the river. Kudowor kept as still as possible. As smelly as he felt, he preferred being alive to being dead, and there were a lot Gbohii gathered around the palace now. They didn't seem to swim well, but he had heard the stories Okoth's mercenaries told about how they'd walked across the bottom of a river to board a ship. He didn't want to be noticed right now.

He could hear yelling from the palace. Something was going on up there. The Gbohii were all wandering away from the river, up toward the main doors. Had Okere tried to send his men to break out through the dead? Kudowor shook his head. That would be mad. There had to be thousands of the things out there now.

Slowly, he brought the boat up to the sewer opening. He sighed. He was going to have to go back through that mess to get in. He grabbed the rope tied to the prow of the boat.

"This truly stinks," he whispered. Then he swam from the river into the filthy muck inside the sewer. Floating things bumped into him as he swam, and he tried his best to ignore them. His feet touched the stone bottom but slipped in the slimy stuff. He was chest deep, and desperately didn't want his head to go under, so he flailed for the nearest wall. His hand caught on the stonework, almost slipping but finding purchase on a sharp rock just before his head went into the muck.

Panting, he pulled himself back upright. His hand was burning where the rock had gouged his skin, and he was bleeding. But it wasn't that bad a wound.

"Provided I can get it cleaned out, anyway," he said to himself. It would be irony indeed to die from a wound that went bad from swimming in sewage, there at the end of the world.

He slid his way deeper into the tunnel, using the walls to keep himself upright. At long last, he reached the grate and tied the rope off on the bars. Still breathing through his mouth, he reached for the door.

Locked.

"Kwadwo?" he called out softly.

No answer.

He heard a splash from behind him, back toward the river. Something had fallen into the water back there, and his hand went to the sword he'd carried strapped to his back during his swim.

More splashing. Something was in the water, pawing around at the entrance.

Then he saw it – a Gbohii, splashing through the muck. Kudowor pressed himself back against the wall, trying to be as invisible as possible.

It took a few halting steps and turned. For a moment, he thought it might go away. It splashed to the wall and started sniff-ing.

He cursed silently. That was the spot he'd cut his hand.

It turned toward him again, still sniffing away like a hound. Following the scent of his blood – right to where he was trapped like a rat in a cage.

The fighting downstairs was growing more intense. Kwadwo could hear it from the clash of weapons, and from the screams of dying men. He wanted in his gut to join them there. He'd been a soldier all his adult life, and part of him was horribly offended at not being there, with the men, when they were doubtless in the middle of the fight of their lives.

But his place wasn't there, this time.

***

"Kwadwo, go make sure the way out is clear," Kwesi said.

Okoth was as useless as the Wakuu. He knelt next to Okere, trying to coax him into sense, but the Wakuu was still staring at his hands with wide, unseeing eyes. Rwamirama had vanished down the stairwell, probably to go join his men.

And Kwesi? Kwesi was like he always was. Cool. Calm. De-tached, even. Kwadwo envied the man that, sometimes. Other times, like this, he wondered if his old friend was even human, to stay so cold at the hottest of moments.

Kwadwo nodded to him and started off. Kwesi would join him; Kwesi was a survivor and would do what was needful. He stood up and started to the door. Before he'd even reached the doorway, he heard a loud crack and turned.

Kwesi had slapped the Wakuu across the face.

If he'd been trying to get Okere's attention, it worked. The Wakuu of Kiswala was staring up at Kwesi now, his face red and angry.

"You dare strike me?" he said. His voice trembled somewhere between rage and terror. Rage that someone would treat him so, and terror at a world so changed that someone could.

"Damn you and your pride!" Kwesi roared, all detachment gone in an instant. "Your men are down there dying! For you! My son is down there – dying for you!"

His hand descended a second time, striking Okere on the other cheek, leaving matching red welts on both sides of his face.

"On your feet! Daarila knows why those men are all willing to die for a pile of shit like you. But they are. Make it worth something."

He grabbed Okere by the collar and hauled him upright. Kwesi was a big man, and if he was quiet much of the time that only served to keep many from realizing how strong he was.

Seeing Kwesi had the situation well in hand, Kwadwo started down the stairs. He passed by the ground floor, able to catch a quick glimpse of the fighting. So far, the men seemed to have kept the undead in the entryway. It was hard to tell how well or poorly things were going. He could hear the screaming of wounded men, and some troops had been pulled back from the front lines, clutching an injured limb or bleeding on the floor.

They were holding. But for how long? Kwadwo hurried on, feeling the pressure of time passing with each moment. He went down another flight of stairs into the basement level.

With luck, Kudowor would already be back. He'd had to lock the gate, just in case one of the Gbohii found its way in somehow, but he hoped Kudowor would be sitting there in the muck cursing at him when he arrived. If not... They'd have to make do without the boat and try another way to get down the river and out of Nicran.

Because if Kudowor hadn't returned yet, it was too late to help him.

Chapter Twenty-Two

Etse shifted left, Gbohii claws only barely missing him. He slashed down at the hand, but the thing withdrew before he could cut it. A spear pierced its side, thrust by one of the men in the second rank, and the man to Etse's right cut off its head.

He was slowing down. They'd been fighting without pause, the rush of the things never slowing. If anything, the pace of the melee was increasing, as the dead tore the hole in the door wider. It was a wave now of snapping, snarling monsters, bits of decaying flesh dripping from them. The floor was slick with blood.

Then all at once the things pressed. They came at a rush, driving into the men. Spears punched into dead bodies, holding some of them back, but as they went down, they brought most of the spears to the ground with them. The Gbohii behind them drove on, climbing over their still-snarling fallen to grapple with the front ranks. Etse found himself face to face with one of the things. It grabbed his shoulders, open maw coming in lightning fast. He thrust upward with his sword, taking it under the jawbone. The thing became dead weight, hanging there from Etse's shoulders. And the dead behind it kept pressing, driving into it and over it. Etse found himself falling backward to the floor. His head struck hard, sparking stars all over his vision.

All around him he could hear the sounds of men dying.

Another Gbohii face appeared behind the one he'd slain, but his arms were pinned. He stared, helpless, as the thing scrabbled up to his face and opened its mouth wide. Etse's vision narrowed – suddenly all he could see was that mouth, the teeth that would kill him, as they closed toward his throat.

A sword seemed to blossom from the thing's head. Red ooze splashed all over him. Then a strong hand had hold of his armor at the shoulder and was dragging him clear. Etse managed to hang on to Kwadwo's sword as he was hauled free. His rescuer didn't stop until he was well clear of the melee, back down the stone steps which led from the entryway to the central courtyard.

"Are you hurt?" Musongola asked.

Of course it was Musongola. Etse tried to smile but groaned instead. His head was hammering.

"Did it bite you?" Musongola asked again, now looking him over for wounds.

"No," Etse said. "Was a near thing, though."

"And you said I was the one with all the luck," Musongola said.

"Looks like we're both lucky to have the other around," Etse replied. He tried to sit up, but the pounding in his head was too great. He eased his head back to the floor, groaning again.

"Rest a bit," Musongola said. "I've committed the third asraafo dawmno, pulled mine back. We lost the entry room, but we're holding them inside it. For now."

Etse slowly brought himself up to a sitting position. His head hurt, but the stars in his vision had faded out.

"We can't hold them," Etse said.

"No. Does Kwesi really have a plan to get us out of here?"

"I hope so."

***

Kudowor sank into the muck, dropping everything below his nose from view, and slunk back against the tunnel wall. He'd rarely been so terrified. Even down in the temple basement, he'd been more worried about saving the damn fool of a boy than he was about the Gbohii biting him. Here? He was trapped against a steel cage, with the only way out blocked by a dead thing, slowly shuffling through the muck toward him.

His sword was unsheathed, in his hand. But he'd seen how fast these things could move, how strong they were. And there was precious little room here for him to move around and use his sword well. Any moment now, it would see him, dash in, grab him with those horrible hands, and bite down.

He shivered, and mostly not from the cold of the watery muck he was immersed in. The damned thing was coming closer.

"Kudowor?"

It took him a second to realize where the voice was coming from. It was Kwadwo! He must be right outside the grating.

But he wasn't the only one who heard Kwadwo. The Gbohii looked up sharply and started toward him. He'd been seen! Kudowor lunged up from the water, his sword slicing in an arc toward the thing.

"Kwadwo! Get me out of here!" he shouted. He heard Kwadwo curse, heard metal scraping on metal, then the clang of dropped keys.

The thing was on him. He had time for only another quick swing that fell uselessly against the Gbohii's shoulder before it plowed into him. He shifted his sword, grabbing the blade with his left hand and tried to keep it between himself and the dead thing coming at him. It drove his shoulder hard against the tunnel wall, knocking the wind from his chest. He felt the steel bite into his leather glove as the creature put weight against the blade, but the sword kept those snapping jaws away from his face.

His foot slipped on the slimy floor, and he went under. The thing dropped beneath the muck on top of him. He couldn't see anything, could only feel it thrashing above him. Without sight, he couldn't keep it away with his sword, so he dropped the useless weapon. Instead, he reached out, hands finding the thing's shoulders, then its neck. With all his strength he clung to it, fighting to keep the lethal bite away.

But without air, his arms were getting weaker. The Gbohii was too strong. Kudowor felt hands close around his skull, pulling his face up toward the teeth he knew were waiting. He opened his mouth to scream – he couldn't help himself – and his throat filled with foul fluids from the muck in which he was buried. He was drowning, dying, and all he could feel was gratitude that he wouldn't have to feel the teeth tearing into his flesh. If he could just keep it away another moment, he'd be gone.

And then something was hauling him out of the muck, slamming his body down on cold stone, pounding his back. He vomited a mess of fluid that looked as horrible as he felt, coughing and sputtering water and worse from his lungs.

"Can't you stay out of trouble for even a little while?" Kwadwo asked.

"But then you'd get bored," Kudowor said weakly, trying to crack a smile that he suspected was more a grimace. "We do need to stop meeting like this, though."

"Was there just the one?" Kwadwo asked.

Kudowor nodded, still coughing too much to reply.

"And you have the boat?"

"Wouldn't have come back without it," Kudowor said, pulling himself up to a sitting position.

"I know. Can you hold the door if more of them come?"

"Lost my sword. In there," Kudowor said, gesturing at the muck and shuddering. Somewhere down there was the Gbohii's body. He had no interest in going after his lost weapon.

"Here. Take mine," Kwadwo said, offering the blade. Kudowor took the weapon and pulled himself back to his feet with an effort.

"I'll hold the door here. You get...who are we bringing, anyway?"

"Everyone," Kwadwo said. He started back toward the stairs. "The palace is falling. We're bringing everyone we can."

CHAPTER TWENTY-THREE

Etse heard his father coming down the stairs before he came into sight. And it was a sight – he had Okere firmly in hand. Or hands. One of Kwesi's hands gripped the Wakuu's shoulder, the other held his arm. Etse winced. He knew from experience how tight that grip could be when his father was angry. And he could see the storm in Kwesi's eyes.

He levered himself to a standing position. The world had stopped spinning, but he was still dizzy. His head throbbed. He tried to shake it to clear it but that only increased the dizziness and pain.

"Etse, are you hurt?" Kwesi asked.

"Hit in the head," Etse replied. "No bite."

He saw the relief flash briefly in his father's eyes, replaced almost instantly by cold calculation as he scanned the battle still being waged in the entryway to the palace.

"We haven't much time," Kwesi said.

Etse had seen the same thing. The number of wounded men was climbing, and there was no longer a reserve of uninjured men to rotate troops out when they grew tired. Many of the men who'd been bitten were still out there fighting. They knew they were already dead and simply kept going because they had nothing else to lose. Other bitten mercenaries were scattered across the garden, sobbing softly as they cradled bleeding arms or legs. Etse wondered how he'd handle that doom if it came to him. Would he be able to die well?

There had to be worse ways to die, but he couldn't call any to mind.

"What's the plan, father?" Etse asked.

"There's a way out through the basement. Sewer opening, into the Densu River."

"And the monsters?" Etse asked.

"They seem to avoid the water," Kwesi said. "It's our best chance."

Etse looked around. Small clusters of women and children were huddled here and there in the garden, and he knew more had to be upstairs somewhere. Hundreds of people had taken refuge in the palace.

"How can we get all these people out? They'll never make a swim to safety," Etse said.

Kwesi shrugged. "We can show them the way. Kudowor was sent to get a boat, but if he managed, it'll be small. Enough to help a few of us."

Etse felt his face flush. He stalked up to his father, until they stood almost nose to nose. "You'll just leave these people here? Abandon them?"

"I can't see a way to save them," Kwesi said. "Can you?"

His voice rang with challenge. Etse looked about, trying to think of a way. He needed something for people to hang on to. Something that would float.

"I can," he said. Without another word, he turned toward the basement and almost bumped into Kwadwo coming back up the stairs at a jog.

"Kudowor got the boat, Kwesi. He's guarding the sewer grate downstairs," Kwadwo said, huffing.

"Good," Kwesi replied. "Trouble?" he asked, eying the red stain on Kwadwo's armor.

"Nothing we couldn't handle." Kwadwo eyed the battle. "It's time to get out of here. We need to let people know."

Etse's mind was still racing. "Kwadwo, how many of those big oil barrels did we have? The ones we used to douse the buildings so they would burn?"

Kwadwo blinked. "I'm not sure. Several dozen, at least. Why?"

"We tied ropes to them because they were too big for one man to haul. Where are they?"

"The cellars."

Etse turned to Kwesi and saw recognition dawning in his father's eyes.

"That's how we'll get the people out," Etse said.

"Roll the barrels out through the sewer, and have people hang on to the ropes. It could work," Kwesi said, pulling at his beard. "Okoth, have some men get all those people into the cellars," he added, gesturing to the crowd huddled in the garden.

"What about the ones upstairs?" Etse asked.

Kwesi whirled on him, his face growing red again. "They're dead, boy. Your idea will save some. Would you give up protecting all of them to try to save a few more?"

Etse turned, watching the men dying to buy them all time. He knew their reprieve was running out despite the troops' best efforts. Soon they'd break. With luck, some of them might survive to escape out the cellar, but most of the Mikijen committed to the battle would die. And anyone not already out when that line broke would probably die with them. He turned away from his father.

"Kwadwo, hold the stairway for as long as you can. We need to get some of the mercenaries out. When the line breaks, show them where to go, but don't get trapped," Etse said.

"I will," Kwadwo replied. "But where will you be?"

"Upstairs, saving who I can."

There wasn't any time for more words. Etse sprinted up the stairs, headed to the third floor, where most of the civilians had been housed. Once he reached the floor, he started banging on every door.

"Up!" he shouted as loud as he could. "Out! The palace is falling! Escape through the cellar!"

People started coming out of their rooms, peeking out into the hall. They were terrified, but his shouting roused some of them to start running, and then others followed. Soon there was a steady stream of men, women, and children running down the stairs. Etse finished the circuit of the floor, and joined the throng headed down.

Kwadwo still waited at the top of the cellar stairs. He'd grabbed a few of the soldiers, who stood in line with him, showing people the way down.

"Good work, Etse. They're rolling barrels out below. You've saved a lot of lives today," Kwadwo said.

"Not yet. We still need to get clear," Etse said. But he was feeling good. This was going to work. They were going to get away and get most of these people out with them. For the first time in hours, he didn't feel like he was going to die today, and the sense of relief was overwhelming.

Then he heard a child crying.

She'd been left behind by some parent when people fled the third floor. Or maybe she was an orphan, with no one to look out for her. Now she was alone on the upper floor, standing by the rail and looking over the edge down to the garden, sobbing her eyes out.

Etse looked at the battle line. It was cracking. The Gbohii would break through any moment now.

He looked again at the child, alone up on the balcony.

Kwadwo must have seen the decision in his eyes. "Etse, there's no time..."

But he was already gone.

Etse was moving before he thought about it, but the long climb up six flights of stairs to the third floor gave him an eternity to consider what he was doing. The battle line was falling apart. He glimpsed it as he ran past, saw the men retreating from the undead horde, the Gbohii hacking down mercenaries only to begin gnawing on them once they fell. It was too late to save the little girl. He knew that.

And he kept going up the stairs anyway, sprinting like all the hordes of the Cleave were chasing him. Which felt more than halfway true. Somehow it seemed like if he failed that one girl then everything he'd done would be for nothing.

He could still hear her, wailing like a lost soul. He focused on her cry, trying to ignore the screams of the men dying below. But the sound when the line broke was unmistakable. The screams changed pitch. Men shouting to fall back. Kwadwo yelling for men to rally and hold the line at the cellar stairs. And above it all, the sound of the dead, their unearthly shriek as they fell on the prey too slow to escape them.

Etse had made the third floor. He kept going, breathing in ragged gasps, his head pounding with each footfall. There she was, just a little way ahead. She couldn't have been more than five or six years old. He scooped her up into his arms and whirled back toward the stairs. She kept crying but clung to him like a burr.

He reached the first steps, but before he started back down, he heard them. The dead had already made the stairs. They'd heard the child crying too, perhaps, or maybe there were so many of them pouring into the palace that they were flowing to fill every nook, every room, spreading out like water. It didn't matter. They were on the second floor now, and even if they delayed a bit to hunt there, he'd never be able to fight past them to safety.

Etse peered over the edge. A ring of men still held the stairs. Kwadwo was there and saw him.

"Etse!" he called, his voice breaking with emotion. "Damn it!"

He could see the Gbohii climbing the steps to the third floor now. In another few moments, they'd be on him.

"Sorry," Etse shouted down. He kept his words light, but his heart hammered in his chest. "I had to try."

"Stay put! We'll force our way through, get you out!"

Etse shook his head. "There's too many and you know it. Get the hell out of here, Kwadwo."

Then he had no more time for words. The first Gbohii made it up the stairs and came loping along the balcony toward him.

CHAPTER TWENTY-FOUR

The first Gbohii came on fast. Etse held the girl tightly in one arm, his sword in the other. Behind the dead thing he saw another, and another, more and more of them pouring up the flight of stairs. He was cut off from escape – Kwadwo and the last mercenaries had already fled down into the cellar, where hopefully they'd escape the death trap this place had become by floating down the Densu River.

The thing came at him, light on its feet and swift. Etse did the only thing that made sense.

He ran.

They chased him as he fled around the balcony, sprinting with everything he had. He burst through the huge double doors to the room they'd used as a conference chamber and slammed them shut behind him. There was no bar here, though. He rammed a chair against the door handle to barricade them out, but they'd be through in a few moments. He continued his flight, nearly tripping on soft velvet carpet, the opulence that was so completely out of place and useless now. The young girl whimpered into his shoulder as he twisted his hips, fighting to keep his balance.

There was a side door, another exit from the room. He opened the door, dashed through, and slammed it closed as the Gbohii smashed through the first door and came into the banquet room. He was in a narrow hall, with stairs at the far end that spiraled up into one of the rooftop towers. On the far end of the hall was a door which led back out to the interior balcony. He knew that way would be full of Gbohii by now. Only one way to go: up.

He took the stairs two at a time, panting, breaths ragged, pushing himself up, and up. The stairs opened on the fourth floor, and again on the fifth, but he kept going all the way to the roof. Behind him he heard the dead scrabbling their way up the steps. He'd bought himself a few minutes, but that was all.

The top of the stairs opened into a small tower, with slits to look through and a stout door. This door had a bar – on the inside. That wasn't going to help. He sheathed his sword, and lifted the bar away, then shoved the door open with his shoulder, stumbling out to the roof.

The rooftop was flat, and the bright sunlight dazzled his eyes for a moment. Daylight seemed a stark contrast to the dim palace interior, and for a moment he was trapped in the strangeness of the things chasing him through broad daylight. Shouldn't evil horrors evaporate or hide from the day? It seemed wrong that creatures of darkness could exist under the sun.

He knew they would follow him soon. He slammed the door closed with a booted foot, and looked across the roof for anything which might help him or the girl he carried survive. The roof was flat, broken only by the towers and battlements at the edges.

He looked down at her, tucked into his shoulder, legs wrapped tight around his waist, arms locked around his arm and neck. His left arm burned from the strain of running with her. When it came to fighting, he'd never be able to face even one Gbohii while holding her. They were too fast. He'd have to put her down, and then she'd die. He couldn't allow that to happen.

"Hold tight," he said. "I'll find us a way out of this."

She whimpered quietly in response.

He had to find a way to keep running. How? He couldn't see a way. They'd simply run out of places to flee. He hoped that Kwadwo and the others had escaped, at least. Etse staggered to the far side of the roof, hoping to catch a glimpse of them in the river below.

The sunlight playing off the water hid them from his view for a moment, but there they were – Kwadwo and his father, with Okoth and Okere and a few other men in a small rowboat. And all around them floated empty barrels, with men, women, and children clutching to the sides. Dozens of barrels drifted with the current, and every single one had at least four people bobbing in the water next to it. They'd done it, then. Some people had escaped the disaster.

He smiled. His idea, those barrels. He'd managed to save a lot of lives today.

It was something.

There was a crash behind him. The Gbohii had made the roof and boiled out of the tower door. Some of them saw Etse and sprinted straight toward him. He had seconds left.

He looked down again. The river was sixty feet below him. He'd never fallen so far, and the thought of jumping made his legs shake with more than just exhaustion. But the thought of being eaten alive by those things was far worse. Death from the fall would be cleaner and faster. He carefully examined the drop. Bricks jutted out at each level, overhangs to create shade for the windows. He'd need to leap out far enough to reach the water.

He stepped up onto the battlements wreathing the roof and prepared to jump.

A clawed hand grasped his shoulder.

Etse yelled, twisting his body to tear away from the thing. He pivoted and started to fall, staring into the dead eyes of the Gbohii, holding fast to his armor. He kept spinning as he fell, the world dizzy in front of his eyes and slammed his head against the brick wall. He heard a crack, and the thing released him. He was dropping, wind whistling in his ears. He tried to tuck his body around the girl, to protect her.

Then he slammed hard into something. Pain flashed through his legs, his back, his head, and he stopped feeling anything at all.

***

Kwadwo sat at the rear of the longboat, holding the rudder, steering their little craft out away from the shore into the deeper water. The further they got from the palace, the better he'd feel. He looked over the men in the boat. Okoth, especially, kept glancing at the shore, where hundreds of the Gbohii milled about. Kwadwo could see the haunted look in the man's eyes, and he recalled the tale about how the dead had simply walked out into the water and then swarmed a grounded boat from his fleet.

That could happen here. The river was only deep in the middle, where a channel let larger ships come up as far as Mali and Kenja from the Sati-Baa River.

"Row gently, men," Kwadwo said softly. "Let's avoid any admiring looks from the beasties there if we can."

His attempt at humor was rewarded with a few chuckles, and the men with oars in their hands kept at their work, slowly moving the rowboat through the water. Behind and all around them, small clusters of barrels bobbed on the current, each with a little batch of people clinging to ropes the mercenaries had tied on days before. Still other people were swimming for it, no barrels to hold to. Kwadwo wondered how many of them would actually get clear of the city before they either succumbed to exhaustion and sank beneath the water or tried to reach shore too soon and fell prey to the Gbohii waiting there.

Yelling caught his attention. He swept his eyes back to the palace. People were pushing and shoving out of the hole where the sewer emptied. The hole they'd just escaped through. There were no more barrels, but in desperation those left behind were still trying to swim for it. They were jumping into the water, frantically trying to swim away from the death trap of the palace behind them. They'd started screaming. Kwadwo knew what that panic meant. The Gbohii had reached the cellars.

Which meant that Azumah and the other men he'd left behind were dead. They'd been bitten, all six of them, but not so badly they couldn't fight. They'd volunteered to a man to hold the stairs for as long as they could so that others could get away.

The panic must mean they'd fallen, and...

More screaming. This time from inside the tunnel itself. And then they poured out of the hole in the palace wall, boiling into the river like pus from a lanced wound. The dead hit the water and kept coming, seeing their prey trying to swim away. They didn't swim out. They simply kept walking, until their heads vanished beneath the waves.

"Come on, keep going," Kwadwo said quietly, urging the desperate swimmers on. Some of them were already spent, exhausted. He could see them struggling to stay afloat.

"Look! Up there!" Okoth said, pointing up at the palace.

Kwadwo looked. There was a man atop the roof, clutching someone. He knew in an instant it had to be Etse. Kwadwo saw him come to the edge, look down, and hesitate. How had he even made it to the rooftop, still carrying the girl?

"Jump for it!" he shouted as loudly as he could. He had little hope that Etse would hear him from this distance, but he called out anyway.

He watched as Etse looked back over his shoulder, then seemed to steel his resolve. He stepped up onto the battlement and was about to leap off when something grabbed him. Kwadwo watched, horrified, as one of the things snagged him. Etse fell, smashed against the palace wall, still held in place by the thing's arm. Then it released him, and he dropped. But instead of falling clear into the water, he smacked into one of the mudbrick outcroppings on the side of the palace.

"Get up, Etse. Get back up," Kwadwo heard himself whispering.

But Etse didn't move again.

"Kwadwo."

He blinked, his eyes still watching Etse's body where it had come to rest.

"Kwadwo!" Okoth repeated.

He brought his attention back to the boat, which was now out into the current and starting to move downstream. All looked well. "What?"

"Over there. Look at the swimmers."

A good number of people had made it into the water. Scores of them now swam for the barrels. Some of them had even made it, and now the rearmost barrels had a lot more people clinging to them. Arguments were starting as the extra weight slowed the barrels down.

Then Kwadwo saw what Okoth was talking about. The rearmost swimmer, an old woman who'd been struggling, vanished. One moment she was there, straining with each stroke. The next she was pulled beneath the water. She never even had time to scream.

"They're under the water," Kwadwo said.

"We have to warn them," Kudowor replied, staring back over the water. The place where the woman had been pulled under was only a few dozen feet from the rearmost barrels.

Kwadwo stood up in the rear of the rowboat and cupped his hands to his mouth. "They're under the water!" he shouted. "You need to swim for it!"

The people out in the water looked around frantically. Another swimmer was swept under, and this one managed a strangled yell before he was gone from sight. The river was still too shallow. The Gbohii must be walking out under the water and pulling people down as they came upon them.

"Get into the deeper water!" Kwadwo yelled.

Then a child vanished, yanked into the depths. This time Kwadwo could see the pool of red rise to the surface, and so could the other swimmers. They frantically swam in all directions, scattering like a school of fish. Some of the ones who kept their heads heard his shout and made for the deeper water. But he saw one barrel that had seven or eight people clinging to it, each trying to pull their makeshift life raft in a different direction. The people around that barrel started to disappear, one after another. By the time the others realized what was happening, it was too late. Moments later, the Gbohii had dragged them all to the bottom.

Splashes came from the shoreline. The yelling and screams had attracted attention, and hundreds of Gbohii were pouring into the water, taking long strides out into the river until they, too, vanished from sight.

"Kwadwo, do we have a rope?" Kwesi asked. Kwadwo flinched at the sound of his voice. Kwesi hadn't said a word since Kwadwo had fled into the cellar without his son. Now his words were ragged, laden with grief, but as sharp as ever.

"Aane."

"Rowers, backstroke. Get us upstream, but keep to the deep channel," Kwesi commanded. "Kwadwo, once we're in range, toss the rope to a barrel. Have them tie on, then pass the end to the next barrel."

"The weight will slow us down," Okoth warned.

"Once we're in the channel, it won't matter how fast we're going. But we need to save as many of these people as we can," Kwesi said. "My son died for them. It's the least we can do."

***

In the end, they managed to save twenty-one barrels, all bobbing along behind the rowboat like links in a chain. One hundred and thirty souls clung to them like barnacles, shivering as the afternoon turned into evening. With the ten men on the rowboat, they'd managed to escape with only a tiny fraction of the people who'd gone into the palace. The rest were lost.

Kwadwo steered the boat, a job made much more complex by the long tail. He had to watch for shallows now, too. Many of the dead had been pushed downstream by the river's current, and the first time they'd come past a spot where the river shoaled, they'd lost one man to Gbohii pulling him under and dragging him away.

The rowers kept the boat downstream of the barrels, and Kwadwo kept the whole chain away from spots which looked like they might harbor a waiting Gbohii. The strain of keeping constant watch was wearing out his eyes and his back. He stretched and winced as tight muscles complained.

"We'll need to find a place to stop soon," Kwadwo murmured to Kwesi. "I won't be able to see the shallows in the dark."

Kwesi nodded and scanned the shoreline. "I've been thinking about where we could stop. There's a small temple which ought to be just a few miles down the river from here. If it hasn't fallen, it might serve as shelter for the night."

"And then?"

"And then we go home," Kwesi said. "If we move swiftly, we can get to Takoradi before the Gbohii spread that far."

Kwadwo shook his head. They were traveling east down the Densu River with the current. Takoradi was west. And they had far too many people to travel so far with any speed. "You mean to leave all these people, don't you?"

"Not entirely. I mean to go ahead of them with you and a few men. We can leave the others with some soldiers as support, to guide them after us," Kwesi replied. "But the sooner we get to Takoradi, the better off we'll all be."

"We can't hold Takoradi any more than we could Nicran."

"No, we can't," Kwesi agreed. "But we can get supplies from there and then go someplace better."

Kwadwo shook his head sadly. Leave it to Kwesi to already be planning three steps ahead. Also to ruthlessly give up on the entire town full of civilians he had governed for years. He hoped they would be able to at least rescue the people of Takoradi, even if the town itself could not be held. But he wasn't certain that was on Kwesi's agenda.

"Where?" Kwadwo asked. Where in the Ki Khanga could be safe from the dead? Where could they go that the dead would not simply follow them, smash their way in, and slay them all? It seemed hopeless. Kiswala was gone. The Mikijen were destroyed. The Gbohii were moving out from Nicran even now, to hunt in the countryside and spread the plague. There were nearly a half-million people living in Asanteman. How many of them would be Gbohii in a week? In a month? In a year?

Kwesi didn't reply.

CHAPTER TWENTY-FIVE

They reached the temple an hour later. The sun was getting close to the horizon by then, the shadows longer. Kudowor watched the water carefully as they eased in toward shore. The shallows were death. They'd seen that over and over all day long, but here they were rowing into them anyway. At any moment he expected to see a dead face lunge out of the water, grab him, and pull him under.

He could still remember the feeling of the Gbohii's weight, pushing him beneath the sewage in the cellar tunnel. He could remember in vivid detail the horror of knowing the thing was about to bite him. He remembered trying to scream, his lungs filling with water when he opened his mouth. He knew what it was like to almost die, and the thought terrified him.

But he kept to his duty. He pulled the oar in time with the men around him. Too many people were counting on him for him to let his cowardice get in the way.

They made the shore without incident. Sand and gravel scraped over the bottom of the boat, telling him that dry land was near. With all the danger that implied.

"Rowers, stand guard," Kwadwo said, keeping his voice pitched low. "I'll reel the rest of our people in from the water."

Kudowor and the other five soldiers stepped out of the boat, landing in the shallow water, and drew their swords. If anything came, they'd be as ready as they could.

"I will go see about arrangements for the night," Kwesi said. "Time for Okere to make himself useful." The Wakuu hadn't said a word since Kwesi had dragged him through the slime and muck in the sewer tunnel and tossed him unceremoniously into the bottom of the boat.

Now Kwesi grabbed his shoulder and hauled him to his feet, pulling him out of the boat toward shore. The Wakuu didn't struggle or complain, but Kudowor caught the look Okere gave Kwesi – black hatred. There was no mercy in that gaze, just the promise of pain. Kudowor shivered. He hoped Kwesi knew what he was doing.

Okoth accompanied the two as they went up from the riverbank to the mudbrick wall surrounding the temple. The walls were fifteen feet tall. Designed to repel casual raids from the Gbawmehi Fawji who'd begun pillaging the area on occasion in recent years, they ought to also keep the Gbohii out, at least for a while. At least for the night, Kudowor prayed. Someplace to rest was all he needed. What they all needed.

One barrel at a time, Kwadwo pulled the people in. Drenched, shivering, they came ashore in little clusters huddling together for warmth. They rubbed their hands together; they rubbed their shoulders. Some staggered about, looking dazed. Others fell to the ground sobbing as soon as they reached the shore. He saw families finding each other and crying for the ones they'd left behind. None of them made much noise, though. They all knew better.

By the time Kwadwo was pulling the last barrel from the water, Kwesi had returned.

"It's safe," he said.

"They'll let us stay?" Kwadwo asked.

"Aane. It's amazing what impact 'open in the name of the Wakuu' has on a bunch of frightened old men hiding behind a door," Kwesi replied.

Kudowor breathed a sigh of relief, overhearing their words. They'd be safe – for tonight, at least. They'd have refuge. He didn't know what tomorrow would bring, but...

"Kudowor, a word please?" Kwesi called.

He sighed. It was never, ever good to be singled out of the crowd. He knew that, but it kept happening to him anyway. He walked over to Kwesi and Kwadwo.

"Walk with us," Kwesi said, heading away from the river and the people huddled there. Once they were out of easy earshot, he stopped and turned back. Kudowor stood silently, waiting.

"I'm taking Kwadwo, Okoth, the Wakuu, and a couple of soldiers with me at first light," Kwesi said. "We're making for Takoradi."

Kudowor blinked.

"These people can't travel fast enough. I need to reach Takoradi before the Gbohii arrive," Kwesi went on. "Even riding as fast as we can, I don't know if we'll make it in time. But we have to try."

"Why are you telling me this?" Kudowor asked. "I'm glad to come along with you, if you're asking for volunteers."

Kwadwo looked uncomfortable. He looked down at the ground, avoiding Kudowor's face. That was bad. When Kwadwo had sent him swimming through sewage and dodging Gbohii in the river to get a boat, he'd smiled and chuckled about Kudowor's discomfort. Whatever was going down, Kwadwo thought it was a lot worse than that.

"There are over a hundred people here. Men, women, and children that we've saved," Kwesi said. "I need a man to bring them home to Takoradi."

Kudowor's heart sank. He'd avoided leadership his entire military duty. He liked having Kwadwo in charge. He liked being told what to do next. Whenever he went off on his own, he ended up in some sort of trouble – like in the cellar of a temple, surrounded by dead things that wanted to eat him! He looked back to where the shivering refugees stood or sat on the beach.

He knew Kwesi. The man would do what was needful, whether or not it killed every one of those people. He was going to go. And if they were left here alone, they would all die.

"Are you a man I can count on, Kudowor?" Kwesi said softly. "Will you bring these people through safely?"

Kudowor opened his mouth to refuse, to say no. It was insane. It would take days to cross all that distance, longer if they had to forage, and they'd be easy prey for Gbohii the whole way. He glanced over his shoulder where the shivering refugees were being guided through the temple gates.

"I can only try," Kudowor found himself saying instead.

***

Kwadwo was awake before dawn. Kwesi wanted to be gone before anyone else was up and about. He'd said it would make less of a scene, and it would be better for everyone if they simply left. Kwadwo wasn't sure it would be better for everyone... He had a feeling it would make poor Kudowor's job harder. But Kudowor was a survivor, and people liked him. He thought the man would do well. As well as anyone could, anyway.

Besides, Kwesi was right. If they didn't get to another major city before the Gbohii, the chances of anyone surviving this disaster at all diminished. The Mikijen Okoth had commanded would have been an amazing tool to fight off the Gbohii threat, if it had been wielded well. Instead, it had been tossed into the place most likely to fall and lost. What a waste.

The center had fallen apart. All they could do now was try to pick up the pieces. That meant carrying word faster than the danger would spread, and they'd already lost too much time.

He made the kwapawnkah ready. The priests had four in their stables, and Okoth had sent men to nearby farms looking for more. People were already fleeing and no one was willing to sell their kwapawnkah, but the men had found several abandoned in a farmhouse. Whether the owners were dead or fled, Kwadwo didn't know.

They had enough kwapawnkah for their entire party to each have a mount. But they had no remounts, which meant they'd be traveling slower than he'd like. No help for it. They'd do what they could with what they had.

He cinched the last saddle as Kwesi came out of the temple. Okoth, Okere, and two soldiers followed close behind him. One of the soldiers was Mensah, a Takoradi guardsman Kwadwo had known for years. The other was one of Okoth's men. Kwadwo didn't know his name yet. Kwesi left the others by the door and came over to join him.

"Packed and ready?" Kwesi asked.

"Aane. Are you sure you want to bring these others? We could travel much faster with just you, Mensah, and I." They'd have remounts, then.

"Am I sure?" Kwesi glanced over his shoulder and grimaced. "No. But I think they could prove useful to us. And they're certain to be trouble if left here."

Kwadwo inwardly agreed. Kudowor would never be allowed to command if the Wakuu was left behind. He'd take charge with Okoth to enforce his wishes, and Eda knew where that would lead. Most likely to the deaths of all these people. He'd seen more than enough of the Wakuu's incompetence these past days.

That didn't mean he'd be a good traveling companion. Quite the opposite. Kwadwo lowered his voice. "Kwesi, I do not trust those men."

"Trust them? Never. But I'll keep them where I can see them," Kwesi said. "Let's be off. Daybreak will come soon, and I want to be far away from here. We have a long way to go before dark."

Kwesi took a set of reins from Kwadwo's hands and mounted up. He noted the jangle of gold rings on leather as Kwesi slung his leg over the beast—ringed armor, and saw he'd picked up a sword somewhere along the way. It was belted at his waist.

"Been a long time since I saw you wearing one of those," Kwadwo said.

"I think I will need it, before all this is done."

The others saw Kwesi mount and hurried over to do the same. Okere went to Kwadwo and sniffed when he saw the mount.

"Dog food, these animals," Okere said.

"They'll be the difference between life and death, for us," Kwesi called down from his mount. "Unless you'd prefer to walk?"

Okere sniffed again, pretending to ignore Kwesi. But he took the reins and mounted with the assistance of his Mikijen. Kwadwo shook his head. Okere had seemed so confident, so full of himself. Now he acted more like a petulant boy. What a difference a few days had been. Without his Mikijen, what was left of the man? His title was empty, and his throne was in the middle of a city full of dead things.

Okoth was already on his kwapawnkah, so Kwadwo mounted up. Kwesi started out, and again they all followed his lead. The first light of dawn was cresting the hills when they left the relative safety of the temple walls behind and set out into whatever waited beyond. Once they were a bit away, riding at a light pace so that the kwapawnkah could sustain it, Kwadwo looked back over his shoulder. One man stood atop the wall, staring down at them. He knew that would be Kudowor. He hadn't come to see them off, but he'd known when they were leaving.

Kwadwo wondered if he'd ever see his friend again.

CHAPTER TWENTY-SIX

Kwesi's party stayed to the north side of the Densu River as they went west. The nearest easy ford was at the bridge in Nicran, and none of them wanted to go anywhere near the place. So they swung wide around the city, keeping to the open fields as much as possible. Here and there they saw fires burning. Once Kwadwo caught a glimpse of a whole village alight. They avoided such places. The dead were careless about lamps and candles, and wooden buildings aflame were a clear sign that a place had been visited by the Gbohii. The creatures were spreading fast into the countryside.

Going slow as they were, watchful at all times for the dead, it was several hours before they crossed the great road leading north out of Nicran. Here the signs of the Gbohii's carnage were more obvious. Bodies lay hacked and torn apart on the road. A wagon stood, laden with a family's belongings, with both kwapawnkah slain and half eaten, still in their harnesses. Kwadwo shuddered and was glad when they'd left the road behind again.

It was only a short while after passing that scene that Okere began to complain.

"This is madness. We can't reach Takoradi by nightfall, at this pace," he said. He groused repeatedly about the futility of their mission.

The worst of it was the man was right. They'd be better than halfway, but they'd have to ride well into darkness in order to reach Takoradi. And in the dark, they'd be easy prey for any Gbohii they ran across.

"I say we should make for Asamankese," Okere went on. It was a city just a short distance north from Nicran. "We can gather the garrison there and then figure out what our next move should be."

"Asamankese doesn't exist anymore," Kwesi said.

"How can you possibly know that?" Okere said. "They have walls, guards. They could be perfectly fine."

"No one is perfectly fine anymore!" Kwesi roared. Then, more softly, he said "You saw how many of those things were in Nicran. Hundreds will have reached Asamankese by now. It's not a long walk, and the dead don't tire."

"But..."

"The city is gone, Wakuu," Kwesi cut in. "But if you must see for yourself, it's on the way. We can skirt the city and get close enough for a look."

The Wakuu subsided at that and fell back a bit behind. Kwadwo overheard him talking to Okoth. He was making plans for his triumphant entrance into the city, and what they would do from there to fortify their position. Okoth wasn't saying much in reply, and Kwadwo felt for the man. Okoth was loyal – to a fault. He'd given his service to a man he had learned wasn't worth it, but his honor wouldn't let him withdraw. What a terrible trap. Kwadwo kneed his kwapawnkah ahead a bit so he didn't have to listen to Okere blather on.

Another hour's ride brought them close enough that they'd be able to see Asamankese soon, from a high enough hilltop.

"Something's going on, up ahead," Kwesi murmured to him.

Kwadwo could hear it, too. The tromp of many feet, just over the next rise. They'd been carefully winding their way through the hills, to stay as invisible as possible. But this bore investigating.

"I'll check it out," Kwadwo said. He kneed his kwapawnkah into a trot, climbing the slope of the hill. He felt tense as a bowstring as his kwapawnkah stumbled a little over the rough terrain. If the kwapawnkah went down, either it or he could be injured. Either might be lethal to him. But he was loathe to leave his kwapawnkah behind in case they had to make a run for it. He opted to ride all the way to the top, proceeding with as much caution as possible.

The other side was a sea of the dead. Kwadwo's mind couldn't take in their numbers – thousands, certainly. Maybe tens of thousands. The nearest saw him and began loping toward him. Kwadwo turned his kwapawnkah about and fled down the hill faster than was safe.

"Time to run," he said, and kicked his kwapawnkah into a gallop. The others followed him, and they raced around the side of the hill. Behind them, Gbohii poured over the broken ground, giving chase. The kwapawnkah could smell the dead, and their riders' fear, and put everything into their run. Kwadwo looked back over his shoulder. Fast the Gbohii might be, compared to a man, but they couldn't keep up with the kwapawnkah. They soon lost the pack and everyone coaxed the kwapawnkah back down from their gallop.

"Now we must get to Asamankese," Okere said, breathing hard. "We have to warn them."

"No, we don't," Kwadwo replied.

"Of course we do! That horde would wreak havoc on the city, unless they're prepared," Okere said, his eyes a little wild.

Kwadwo shook his head. His eyes met Kwesi's, seeking help.

"It's too late for Asamankese," Kwesi said. "That's where the horde was coming from, isn't it?"

Kwadwo nodded, his face grim. If Asamankese had fallen so completely, what hope was there that Takoradi would still exist by the time they arrived? What hope was there for any of them?

***

Kudowor sat on the wall for a long while after Kwadwo and the others left. He sat and thought about where he'd come from, and how he'd ended up here. He had been a simple storyteller, once. He'd enjoyed traveling from town to town, singing and telling tales in one place after another. He was good at the job, too. He'd never lacked for a place to sleep, never gone wanting for food.

The Asante especially valued their nwontofo, but even among the Kiswalans he always felt welcome. One Kiswalan wura had been so pleased with his service that he'd offered him gold as a reward. Instead, he'd asked for a small sailboat, and with that boat he'd explored Asanteman's shores, visiting as many towns and cities as he could.

And then he'd come home, back to the village where he'd been born, where his family lived. Except they weren't there anymore, and neither was the village. It had been burned to the ground, the people slaughtered or taken.

It was probably raiders from Kongo. But it could have been anyone. The ruin they'd left behind was as total as what the Gbohii had done to Nicran. Everything Kudowor had been until that moment died in the ashes of his home.

Furious and full of rage, he offered to join Asanteman's army and ended up under Kwadwo as a guardsman. Kudowor supposed he had been longing for a quick death at the end of someone's sword. Yet Kwadwo must have seen something in him worth salvaging, although Kudowor had no idea how. He remembered how black his mood had been, in those days. He sought solace in killing the invaders. And he'd fought them. But he'd found no respite in bloodshed.

He'd finally found it, instead, in the eyes of the people they'd managed to save. With Kwadwo, he helped stop whole villages from sharing the same fate as his old home.

Kwadwo knew that about him, damn it. Which was why Kwadwo knew he'd do his best to save these people.

But how?

There were hundreds of thousands of the damned dead things in and around Nicran by now. He could do the math. They'd spread out in all directions, infecting new towns and spreading the curse still further. Even on horseback, he knew Kwadwo and Kwesi would have a hard time finding a safe path through the center of Asanteman to Takoradi. On foot, with people unused to hard travel? Impossible.

Kudowor was lost enough in his thoughts that he didn't hear anyone approaching until a gentle hand came to rest on his shoulder. He jumped, turning and standing in a single motion, his right hand already flowing to the hilt of his sword. But it wasn't a Gbohii, just an old man in a simple white lappa, holding both hands up in front of him palms out in a placating gesture. One of the priests who'd given them refuge here.

"I am sorry. I didn't mean to surprise you," the man said. He was an old man, white beard not quite covering a long scar on his ebony face. He had a wiry frame used to hard work. But he didn't seem like he intended to be a threat.

"No, I'm sorry," Kudowor replied, his hand relaxing from his sword. "I'm a little jumpy."

"Understandable."

"Did you need me for something?" Kudowor asked.

The man cocked his head sideways, his eyes looking Kudowor over carefully, taking in every detail. Kudowor blushed under the scrutiny. He wondered what those old eyes saw in him.

"You are the man Asantehene Kwesi left in charge of the people here, yes?" the priest asked.

"Aane," Kudowor said, after a moment of hesitation. Wishing it were not so wouldn't relieve him of the burden. "I am."

"Then I don't need you, but your people do. They've seen that the Wakuu and Kwesi have left. They're frightened and upset."

"They ought to be afraid. I am." The admission left a bitter taste in Kudowor's mouth.

"That makes you wise. Now, you need to also be smart. What will you do with these people?"

"Kwesi wants me to bring them to Takoradi, to join him there," Kudowor said. "If we don't get there soon, he'll have already left for wherever he plans to go next. But we can't go closer to Nicran – it would be madness."

The old man nodded. "Go on," he prompted, like Kudowor was a slow pupil. The thought drew a crooked smile from Kudowor. Perhaps he was being a slow pupil here. He'd play the game, though.

"But if we circle widely around, then it will take too long. The Gbohii will spread from Nicran in an ever-wider circle. I don't think we can move fast enough to reach Takoradi before they do. They'll catch us somewhere on the road, no matter how wide we try to go around."

"I am sure you'll find some answer to the problem. In the meantime, I think you should see to them."

Kudowor shrugged, tired. But he followed the old man down the stairs from the wall. In the courtyard, the three soldiers Okoth had left stood side by side in front of a mass of citizens. These people had gone from frightened to angry, and things were going to get ugly if everyone didn't cool down.

And somehow, making that happen was going to be up to him.

He drew a deep breath and called out. "Aane, the Wakuu and Kwesi have gone ahead." He'd set his voice to carry over the noise of the crowd.

If there was one thing he knew he could do well, it was be heard. He'd had plenty of practice in both of his careers. Everyone hushed a moment and turned toward him. Well, he had their attention now, anyway. Now to do something with it.

"They've gone ahead to warn Takoradi of the danger, to prepare people there," Kudowor said.

"And what of us? Why were we left behind?" one man shouted back, his face red. Kudowor watched that one's eyes – they were too wide. He was terrified, and close to lashing out.

"We're to join them," Kudowor said. "But if they didn't ride ahead, Takoradi wouldn't be there by the time we all arrived."

"Who says it will be now?" the man countered. "Maybe they'll grab what they can and run off. Not like they need us."

Kudowor shook his head. "They'll be there. Have a little faith, man."

"Why?"

Only a few feet separated them now. Kudowor bridged the small gap, gently laying a hand on the man's shoulder. He looked into those wide eyes, full of fear, and spoke softly but in a voice that still carried, "Because that's what we have left. That, and each other." He held his gaze another moment. The man looked down.

Kudowor stepped back from the man, who lingered a moment and then went elsewhere. The crowd slowly dispersed, talking quietly among themselves. Kudowor managed to hide his shaking hands by clasping them in the small of his back until he had them under control. He walked over to the three soldiers he'd been left with.

"Thanks, sir," one of them said. "That could have been bad."

"What is the plan, then?" another asked.

He needed to get these men firmly under his command, and quickly. He'd won some respect from them just now. But they were Okoth's mercenaries, not Kwadwo's soldiers. They didn't know him at all. Time to change that.

"First, my name is Kudowor Toto. Kwesi and the Wakuu have left me in command," he said, snapping off each word. "We are effectively at war. I expect instant obedience to orders from each of you."

"Aane, sir!" all three said together. They were Kiswalan mercenaries, which meant they'd been forged into fighting men under a system where discipline was everything. Kudowor intended to use that.

"Now, what are your names?" he asked.

The three men quickly spat out their names and recent histories. Magezi was the one who'd answered first. Baryomunsi was the questioner. And Oyite was the third, and most quiet of the three. He seemed like a thoughtful sort, with a quick wit. All three had served with Okoth since they'd joined the Mikijen, although Baryomunsi had served five years, and the other two had joined together only two years ago. One veteran and two relative novices. It could have been worse. He'd need more people able to fight, though. Four men weren't going to be enough to defend so many. Four men would be touch and go against even a single Gbohii.

"We need to secure more weapons, and with luck some armor," Kudowor said.

"Arm these people?" Baryomunsi asked. "Is that wise?"

"It's necessary," Kudowor said sharply. "They have a right to help defend themselves. And we could use some more fighters on our side. Now, I think the best bet to find more weapons is the fort near Fosu."

"But that's east," Baryomunsi protested. Kudowor was already beginning to tire of his questions. "It's in the wrong direction."

"No, it's not." Kudowor had the beginning of an idea. There might be a way through to Takoradi after all... Or rather, around to Takoradi, not through. "If we take the river down to Fosu, we'll find river-ships. It's not the port Nicran is...was," he corrected himself. "But we should find something there."

"You're assuming the dead are not walking there too, sir," Oyite said quietly.

"We seem to be ahead of the main wave of them for now. Let's try to stay that way. We'll need to begin organizing people to move out. The river is safer than overland, and we'll make better time."

"You mean to use the barrels again, then?" Oyite saw his idea immediately. Kudowor was taking as much a liking to the young man as he was growing annoyed with Baryomunsi.

"Aane. Get people ready to move out. The Gbohii will be spreading out from Nicran, and I don't know long we have."

Then someone screamed, a long shriek of horror and terror, and Kudowor knew they were already out of time.

CHAPTER TWENTY-SEVEN

The first thing Etse felt was heat. He felt hot all over, like he'd been basking in front of a fire. The next thing was pain. His entire left side felt like it was one raw nerve, and his head hammered like he'd cracked his skull wide open. He blinked once and hastily closed his eyes again. Damn, it was bright!

Someone was sobbing nearby. Was that what had woken him? Who was crying? His head felt full of cotton, and he struggled to recall where he was. He felt hard brick under his fingers, and someone was tugging at his boot, trying to get his attention.

"A minute," he said, the words slurring a little.

The tugging continued, and if anything grew even rougher. Someone was pulling at his boot, trying to pry it from his foot. He withdrew his leg in frustration. He just needed more sleep. But as he swung his leg away from whoever it was, it slid out into...nothing. He dug his fingers into the brick beneath him on reflex and pulled his leg back closer to his body. Wearily, he opened his eyes again, slowly, shielding then from the bright daylight.

He was on a narrow mudbrick ledge. Why was he on a ledge? There was a little girl there, a few feet away, sobbing. And a little window next to him. Someone was standing in the window. That was the person yanking on his boot. He squinted, and saw that it was that ass, Abigaba.

"What the hell do you want?" he asked groggily.

Then he recalled that Abigaba was dead.

All the rest of his memories came back in a rush. He tried to sit up, felt dizzy, and threw up over the edge. There was nothing but bile in his stomach. The noise and smell seemed to make the dead-Abigaba even more crazy, though. It raked claws through the narrow window, scraping rotted flesh from its bones in a desperate attempt to reach him.

"You were an ass when you were alive, and you're a failure as a dead monster, too," Etse told it.

He heard noises above him and looked up. Gbohii were gathered along the rooftop battlements, looking down hungrily at him. He'd only fallen about fifteen feet. Lucky – more than that, and he'd probably have died in the fall. As it was, his whole left side throbbed.

And now that they'd noticed him, Etse didn't think it would take long for the Gbohii on the roof to try their luck at a free lunch. Abigaba's Gbohii might not be able to reach him, but all the ones above had to do was leap down. He looked up again, nervous, and saw some of them testing the bricks, starting to clamber over. Etse leaned forward, hauling up on his beaded armor shirt, shimmying out of the thing. It slithered over the edge of the stone catwalk and splashed into the water far below. He already regretted not having it. But he'd never be able to swim far enough while wearing it.

"Time to go, little one," he said to the girl. He marveled that she was still alive. That either of them had survived so long was nothing short of a miracle.

"Sefadzi," she said.

"What?"

"It's my name," she replied, pouting.

"Fine. Time to go, Sefadzi!"

The first Gbohii fell from above, and missed the ledge, plummeting down the side of the palace, smacking against the ledge below with a wet slap before splashing down into the river. A second dropped, and this one hit his ledge, slipped, and fell away to join the other. Etse looked up again and saw what looked like another dozen Gbohii scurrying over the edge.

He stood, testing the strength of his injured left leg. It would do. He took a step toward the girl and scooped her up into his arms. Another step carried them both over the edge, and he pushed off and away with every ounce of strength in his body. Behind him he could hear the crash of bodies hitting the mud-brick, the growl and hiss of the Gbohii as their prize escaped them yet again.

Etse was flying again, floating through space. He'd jumped into water before, but never from so high! He clutched the girl close to him and tried to straighten his legs so that he went into the water feet first. Wind rushed past his face, whistled in his ears, and the drop seemed to go on and on.

He hit the water so fast that he was under the surface before he realized his feet were wet. He kicked up hard for the surface, for the light he could see above, pulling the small girl along with him.

And then they were in daylight again. The girl was coughing, but she was alive and clung to him like a burr. The Gbohii on the ledge jumped into the water after them, hitting the surface with huge plumes of spray and vanishing from sight. A few more saw them from the shore and came out into the water after them, walking deeper and deeper until they were gone from view. The skin at the nape of Etse's neck prickled, and he had sudden visions of the dead things walking along the bottom of the river until they were beneath him, reaching up to drag him down into the depths.

"I think we should help the current along a little," he said. He kicked his legs, pushing them out into the deeper middle of the river. The current there was stronger, and the water ought to be deep enough to keep them safe from the things.

"What about the bridge?" the girl asked.

"What do you mean?" Etse replied.

"The bridge!" she said again, drawing the word out like she was speaking to someone unaccountably slow. Etse found himself filled with a mix of amusement and annoyance, until he looked down the river ahead of them.

"Daarila," he said.

Nicran had been built on the first easily fordable spot in the Densu River that the Asante found when the abosua (*familial clans*) first unified into one people. But a ford was soon not enough to manage the traffic of the growing town, so a bridge was built. Over time, as the city grew, the bridge was rebuilt, until it was a huge thing of magnificent stonework.

The current was pushing them straight toward that bridge now, and it was crawling with Gbohii, all looking down at them hungrily. The damned things didn't seem able to swim, but if enough of them dropped down at once, it wouldn't take much luck for one of them to hit him. And one of the dead things clinging to him is all it would take to drag him down into the depths, where all the others would be waiting...

He shook off the thought. He still had a little time before they were under the bridge. Time to come up with some sort of plan. He gauged his speed against the riverbank. Maybe half a minute.

Fifteen seconds passed, and he still had no ideas.

"We need to dive," the girl said. Then she pushed away from him and followed her own advice, diving deep under the water and swimming straight toward the bridge.

She was right. If they dove deep enough and swam fast enough maybe the things wouldn't see them. Or at least maybe they'd have a harder time leaping down atop them. Etse dove, pushing deep beneath the surface. Above him, he could hear the impact of the things tearing into the water, see the bubbles floating back upwards that marked the passage of the dead on their way to the bottom. One Gbohii fell directly in front of him, claws clutching toward him as it fell. Etse backstroked hard. One claw brushed his arm as the thing fell past him. He gave a powerful kick to start moving forward again. Just in time – one fell into the water where he'd just been a moment before. And then there were no more impacts. He kept swimming until his lungs couldn't hold out any longer and his body ached for air. Only then did Etse kick back toward daylight again, hoping he was through the gauntlet.

He broke the surface and gasped for air, filling his lungs, the breath a sweet taste that he'd wondered for long moments if he would ever have again. He looked around – he'd cleared the bridge. Ahead lay the open river.

The girl surfaced a little closer to the bridge than he did, and she paddled her way through the water toward him. Once she'd gotten within arm's reach, she grabbed hold of him again and resumed being his personal barnacle.

"So, who's saving who here, little one?"

"I told you, my name is Sefadzi," she said. "And we're taking turns saving each other," she added in a practical tone.

"I can live with that," he replied, wondering a little at the precocious child he was suddenly traveling with.

"Good," she said.

Together, they floated down the river through the ruins.

CHAPTER TWENTY-EIGHT

The forest ahead looked like a wall. Kwadwo didn't love the forest. He preferred the open spaces of the hills and grasslands. But he'd rarely seen one which felt so dark. Of course, he'd never worried that a forest might be filled with creatures interested in eating him before, either. Most animals would flee from a man, not hunt him.

"We'll have to go through. This wood stretches for miles in each direction. We'd lose hours going around," Kwadwo said.

"You're sure we can't just work our way back up to the road?" Kwesi asked.

It was a fair question. A good road cut right through the heart of the forest, and it lay not far to the north. But Kwadwo had tried to bring their party toward the road three times since running into the huge band of Gbohii. And every time he turned them north a bit, they ran into more of the dead than they could hope to handle. Right now, speed and avoiding the enemy was their best bet.

"Not without running into more of our friends." he said.

Kwesi nodded, then dismounted. "We'll need to walk the kwapawnkah," he said. "Too risky to ride through such dense growth."

"Those trees could hide a host of the things," Okere said, his voice hushed, for once.

"So keep your eyes open," Kwadwo told him.

Kwadwo dismounted and drew his sword. Holding the reins in one hand, his blade in the other, he led them under the trees. Instantly the sun vanished from view, and they were in a twilight world. These were old trees, never felled. They'd lived a long, long time. That was good, in a way. The lack of sun stifled growth on the ground. Ferns grew on the forest floor, as high as his waist, but not much grew higher than that except the trees themselves. And those towered overhead, leaving a gap that should reveal any Gbohii ahead.

Unless the Gbohii thought to crouch down. If the things were smart enough to try an ambush, they were in trouble. Kwadwo was gambling that they were not.

He'd been thinking a lot about the things over the past two days. He'd seen them fight singly, and now in huge bands as well. They didn't seem especially intelligent. Fast and strong, yes. But not that smart. They worked together more because they all tended to follow one another around like a flock of birds, rather than as groups of soldiers fought. They didn't use teamwork or concerted action – instead, the Gbohii seemed to rely entirely on instinct.

It was possible that might be something which could be used against them. But first they had to survive, and that meant getting out ahead of the dead things spreading across the land and safely to Takoradi.

They proceeded through the wood in a single file, Kwadwo leading the way. He kept his senses open to any noises in the woods. All felt normal for the first hour of their travel, and he grew confident enough that he began to curve their path back toward the north, hoping to link up with the road.

It was the birdsong that made him realize something was wrong. The lack of it, rather. He had been hearing birds chirping in the trees ever since they'd entered, but suddenly – nothing. No birdsong, no animal sounds at all. Kwadwo froze in place, and the rest of the party stopped behind him. He stood there, straining with his senses.

Nothing. No forest sounds. No squirrels running from tree to tree. No birds. No noise but the whisper of wind through the branches.

Which meant something was out there.

He waved a hand, beckoning Okoth forward. The man slipped silently toward him, setting each foot down with care. Kwadwo gave him an approving smile.

"What?" Okoth said, barely a whisper.

"Listen."

Okoth looked out into the woods intently. Then he looked back to Kwadwo, his eyes widening with understanding. "Fall back," he mouthed to the other men, and then started to follow his own direction, taking one careful step backwards at a time. Kwadwo followed him back, keeping his eyes on the silent woods ahead of them. They'd have to backtrack, go around this area, and they'd lose hours. The road was so damned close, he could almost feel it. But if there were Gbohii here, they were better off going around.

Crash!

Kwadwo jerked, turning around to see what had made the noise. Okere had fallen and was staggering back to his feet. At least he was being quiet about it, but...

Something was stirring in the woods ahead. He heard it first, and scanned the trees, looking for the source of the sound. It took him only a moment to see them, loping through the trees, drawn by the noise.

"They've heard us," he said, fighting to keep his voice calm. "Kwesi, do we run or fight?" He prayed for the former, risky as flight would be. One, two, three – there were at least half a dozen of the things.

Kwesi could do the math as well. "Run!" he said, swinging his leg up into his saddle. "Make for the road!" Then he bent low over his kwapawnkah and kicked her sides, sending the mount into headlong flight through the forest.

It was risky, foolhardy even. The roots here were large, and any of them could tumble a kwapawnkah at a full gallop. But it was better than the odds they had staying. Kwadwo lunged into his own saddle. The Gbohii would be on them in seconds. He watched one of the men struggling to mount up. Okoth had the Wakuu's belt in one hand, hauling him up into his own saddle. They'd get clear, and Kwadwo realized he'd waited almost too long. He squeezed hard with his knees, but his kwapawnkah needed no urging to sprint away from the dead things coming at her.

Behind him, Kwadwo heard screams. At least one of the men hadn't been quick enough to get into the saddle. He didn't have any attention to spare, though. Branches slapped at his face, threatening to dislodge him from his seat. It was the roughest of rides, him half blind and the kwapawnkah more than half panicked.

The sudden burst of broad daylight was the sweetest relief he could imagine. The forest came to a sudden end a few feet from the road, a gravel bed preventing most growth from coming too close to the paved bricks. When his mount's hooves clacked on the bricks of the road, Kwadwo whooped, laughing with the joy of being alive. He brought the kwapawnkah back down to a canter, then to a walk. The mount trembled; it had been a rough ride for both of them.

Kwesi was a few feet ahead, already starting on down the road. Kwadwo shook his head. If the man had been the only survivor, he'd have kept on with his course regardless. He had to admire that single-minded pursuit of a goal. But it made Kwesi damned hard to be a friend to.

More crashing in the wood-line. Kwadwo made ready to push his kwapawnkah back into a run – on the road, they could get away from the dead much more easily. But it was Okoth, with Okere riding on the same steed behind him. And Okoth was bleeding – his pants leg was wet with bright red blood.

"What the hell happened?" Kwadwo asked.

"His kwapawnkah went down, broke a leg," Okoth said. "I scooped him back onto my mount, but they reached us before I could get away clean."

Kwadwo was impressed. Running through those woods, it was all he could do to stay on his kwapawnkah. Okoth had noticed the Wakuu's danger, stopped his own mount, grabbed the man, hauled him onto his mount, and then gotten away. But at what cost?

"The wound – did they...?" Kwadwo couldn't say the word 'bite.' They all knew that the bite of one of these things was worse than death.

"No, one of them caught me with its claw, before I got clear. Nasty gash. I'll tend to it once we're away safely."

Kwesi brought his mount up alongside Okoth and looked him in the eye. His eyes flickered to the man's leg, taking in the blood. "You're sure you're well to ride for a bit?"

"As long as I don't need to walk for a while, sure," Okoth laughed. It was a hollow sound.

Kwesi nodded. "Then let's go."

"The other men?" Kwadwo asked, already knowing the answer. He'd heard at least one of them screaming.

"If they were able to join us, they already would have," Okoth said. "Nothing is alive back there."

The mood was somber as the four men set off again. They'd found the road, but it was still a long way to Takoradi.

CHAPTER TWENTY-NINE

Kudowor grimaced, looking down from the wall. There was at least a dozen of the things. The gates were still closed, or they might have wandered straight into the court and slain everyone inside. Now the monsters were all outside the big doors, worrying at the wood. It was a stout door, but he'd seen them tear through one several times as thick at the palace. It was only a matter of time.

They needed to get to the river to escape. Which meant they needed to break through these things. But he was going to need more than himself and three guards to manage that. He stepped off the wall, looking for the old priest who'd spoken to him earlier. He wasn't out in the courtyard. Plenty of other people were – his refugees. Many were sobbing. Others pressed back as far as they could from the doors. One man was on his knees, praying.

Praying. Where else would a priest be, right now? Kudowor headed for the shrine.

It was a small mudbrick building, set in the middle of the walled area. No fortress, this. Just a simple door on a simple building, with a bell set above it. He opened the door, trying to disturb things as little as possible.

The old man was within, as were another four men in similar lappas. All of them were at the altar, praying. About a dozen of the people they'd brought out of Nicran had found their way into the shrine as well, joining the priests in their prayers.

Kudowor quietly went up to the old man and gently laid a hand on his shoulder. This time, it was the priest's turn to be startled, and he turned his head sharply, his hand grasping Kudowor's in a grip like steel. Kudowor felt his eyebrows raise. The man had the reflexes and strength of a fighter, not a priest. And if he wasn't mistaken, those were the calluses of a swordsman on that hand.

He saved his questions for later. "I need your help," he said.

The priest nodded, stood, and followed him quietly from the building.

"I can't help you fight them," he said.

"I think you can," Kudowor said. The more he watched the man move, the more certain he was that he hadn't always been a priest. That hand had held a sword for years before it clutched at a priest's rattle.

"I cannot!" the priest repeated. "Please don't ask that of me."

"Then help me find another way!" Kudowor said. "Do you have weapons here? Anything?"

The priest rubbed his chin in thought. "No weapons, no. But we have things which might help. How long before they are through the door?"

"I have no idea," Kudowor said. "Minutes? Not long."

"Come with me quickly, then."

He led Kudowor around the side of the shrine, to an old wooden building. The place stank of animals, and Kudowor could hear sheep chattering within. The priest opened the door to the place.

"Careful not to let the flock out," he said. "We brought them in when we first got word about the trouble. To keep them safe," he said, laughing bitterly. "Like we could." Then he stepped inside, and Kudowor followed.

Two dozen sheep wandered about inside. Several went up to the old man, looking like they were dogs begging for treats.

"Not today," the priest told them. Then to Kudowor, he said "These might help you."

He pulled a pitchfork down from the wall and handed it over. Kudowor looked at the implement. It was just a farming tool, but the tines were iron, not wood. Expensive, but they'd been made to last – and the metal might make them passable as weapons in a pinch. There were three of them.

"We'll take whatever we can get," Kudowor said. He scooped up all three into one arm and made for the door. There couldn't be much time left. Before he left the barn, he turned back to the old man. "You can use a sword. I felt it in your grip. We could use your help."

The old man's shoulders sagged. He shook his head sadly, staring at the floor.

Kudowor had no time for the mystery. He went back into the light, carrying the makeshift weapons. It would have to be enough. Somehow.

The situation in the courtyard wasn't any better than it had been when he'd left. Daylight shone through the door in one spot where a Gbohii had clawed a hole, and now it reached hands through the wood, greedily pulling splinters loose. His three guards stood in a ring around the failing door, swords drawn. Two men he didn't know, civilian refugees, had found stout sticks someplace, and stood alongside the soldiers. But they all looked like they'd already accepted defeat and stood there only because they had nowhere else to go.

"Kudowor! Thank god," Baryomunsi said.

The other two men straightened their backs as well. Kudowor was glad to see it.

"I need three brave men!" he shouted.

Five stepped up.

"You three – take these." He handed over the pitchforks. "You two, start escorting everyone who can't fight back to the shrine. If you can find more cudgels somewhere, join us. We'll fight with whatever we have."

The three men joined his small force, circled around the door. Kudowor drew his own sword.

"They'll be through in another minute. Use the pitchforks to keep them at bay, so the swords can kill them. Take the heads off, or they won't die," he reminded his men.

A board fell loose from the door, a dead arm reaching inside, questing for flesh. Kudowor swung his blade out, severing the arm. The Gbohii made a hissing sound, and withdrew the stump, ichor pouring from the wound. He knew it wouldn't kill the thing, but it made him feel better to be doing something.

The door twisted, turned, tearing apart. Bits flew back at them, sharp shards of wood. And then the real threat was upon them. The dead swarmed through the narrow doorway, forcing his men back. If the things broke through their line, Kudowor knew everyone within the walls were doomed.

Kudowor thrust his sword straight in front of him, stabbing the Gbohii through the throat and up into its skull. It gagged, and then died, nearly yanking the weapon from his hands before he could pull it back. There was no time to crow about the victory, though. Two more clambered over the fallen thing, reaching their arms out to grab hold of him. A man with a pitchfork stabbed, slowing one of the things, but Kudowor had to step back to avoid the other while he withdrew his sword. It followed him, grabbing his shoulders. A sword whistled. Kudowor ducked, and the blade took the thing's head from its shoulders. Magezi smiled a toothy grin, spinning the blade around again to fend off another of the things.

"Thanks!" Kudowor gasped.

Baryomunsi was hard pressed, on his other side. He'd stabbed, but the sword wedged into the thing's collarbone, and as he tried to wrest it loose, the Gbohii grasped his arm with its claws. Kudowor stabbed at it but missed. The things were too fast! He couldn't do anything but watch as it pulled itself down to his arm and bit hard. Baryomunsi screamed. The thing tore a chunk of flesh from his arm, and blood splashed everywhere.

"Hold the line, Baryomunsi!" Kudowor shouted.

But it was too late. Baryomunsi was falling back, the dead following close on his heels. Kudowor heard Magezi curse. With one man gone from the line, the Gbohii could flank them, and the whole thing fell apart. Magezi and Kudowor ended up side by side against a wall. The men with pitchforks were torn apart, screaming as most of the dead stopped in place to eat them alive.

Baryomunsi hadn't made it far either. The one which had bitten him snatched his leg, tripping him. He went down, trying to scuttle away on all fours, but it simply snagged his leg again, dragging him back, and began to tear chunks of flesh from his calf. Two more pulled Oyite screaming to the ground.

Two of the things chased after Kudowor and Magezi, and they found themselves backed into a corner of the wall desperately fending them off with their blades. Kudowor felt crushed. He'd failed just as utterly as he'd feared he would. In another moment, those things would finish with the men they'd slain and move on to the rest.

He heard a yell. No, more than a yell – it was a battle cry, full of anger, fear, and rage. The Gbohii pinning him in place turned at the sound, and he had a moment of breath to look.

A woman – one of the refugees – had picked up Baryomunsi's sword and cut the head from the thing eating him. Too late for Baryomunsi; he'd already stopped screaming. But she'd attracted the attention of all the remaining Gbohii, and nine of them were loping toward her.

"Now!" he said to Magezi. The man nodded, and the two of them struck as one, slicing the heads from the undead who'd pinned them into the corner.

That still left seven of the things closing on the woman. She held her ground, sword unwavering in front of her, but her face blanched with fear. Kudowor ran to help her, Magezi right behind him.

They'd almost reached the rearmost Gbohii when a blur of silver dashed through the smashed gate. It was a man, dressed head to toe in Kiswalan tortoise shell armor, a sword in his hand. He tore into the rearmost Gbohii, his blade slicing clean arcs to sever an arm, then flip back to cut through the neck. He moved fluidly from the fallen opponent into the next, cutting it down as well.

"Etse?" Kudowor whispered. Could it be? He'd rarely seen such swordsmanship.

The woman used the distraction of a new opponent to good effect, slaying another of the things. Magezi smashed into one with his shoulder, knocking it to the ground. Kudowor drew his dagger with his left hand and stabbed the fallen thing in the temple before it could recover.

Moments later, it was over. The Gbohii were slain.

Kudowor walked over to the man in armor. "Gods, man. We thought we were lost. Thank you."

"Glad to be of help," the man said. He turned at last so Kudowor could see his face inside his helmet.

"Musongola! We thought you'd died in the palace!" Kudowor said.

"It was a near thing. I was in battle to hold the gates but got split off when they broke through. I couldn't meet up with you all, so I hid. Slipped out through a second story window, found a kwapawnkah, and followed the river east."

"Just slipped out? Past thousands of those things?" Kudowor asked, aghast.

"It was no picnic. I'm glad I found you all."

"So are we," Kudowor said.

"Is Etse here? And who is the beautiful swordswoman who fought alongside us?" Musongola asked.

"Etse...didn't make it out of the palace," Kudowor said. Musongola's face fell. "And as for the lady, I'm afraid I don't know."

He turned to the woman in question. She was young – mid-twenties perhaps. She had brown hair which rolled in curls at the nape of her neck, striking hazel eyes and sepia-brown skin. Kudowor noted that the clothes she was wearing, while grime and blood coated now, had once been very fine indeed. Some sort of noblewoman then, drawn to Nicran by the presence of the Wakuu.

"I am Diata," she said. "And my thanks as well. You saved my life, probably all our lives."

"It was my pleasure," Musongola said, smiling.

Kudowor watched the two of them. Neither could take their eyes off the other. He rolled his own eyes, just a little, but couldn't help smiling. The entire world was coming apart at the seams, but nothing – not even the dead rising from their graves – seemed able to stop people from falling for one another.

CHAPTER THIRTY

Etse found a chunk of charred timber as the pair drifted their way out of town. It floated and gave them something to cling to. The dead were still everywhere on the banks. Getting out of the water was impossible, and even the water was perilous. In one spot where the bottom changed from dark mud to yellow sand, Etse looked down and saw three of the Gbohii walking along the bottom. They reached up as he floated by, claws raking futilely through the water. He reached for his sword reflexively, but it was long gone – he'd lost it somewhere back at the palace.

They were far too deep to reach him. He found himself tucking his legs up anyway.

Sefadzi drifted down the river alongside him, each clinging to one side of the log. She'd been silent for a while now. Maybe lost in her own thoughts. Etse looked at her, and she stared back at him briefly, then looked away.

They were carried on by the current, drifting out of the city walls. They went past rows of homes near the city, then into farmland dotted with houses at regular intervals. Etse studied the sky. It was past noon. He wondered how far behind the main party they were.

"A long way," Sefadzi said. Etse hadn't realized he'd spoken aloud. "You were asleep all night."

"All night?" Etse was aghast. They'd been well and truly left behind, then. A few hours gap they might have closed, but not a whole day. His father might have led those people anywhere by now. And she'd sat beside him, on that mudbrick outcrop, the whole while. "That must have been a rough night for you."

"It was. I kept them off us."

She was a little scary. Sefadzi's quick intelligence was a wonderful gift, given the situation. But Etse wasn't used to speaking with young children who acted like adults. Everything about her tone and manner suggested she was much older than she looked. It was uncanny at first, but he found himself slowly becoming accustomed to her as the day wore on.

There was no more conversation for a while, and Etse spent the time scanning the shoreline. The houses had grown fewer, and he'd seen no signs of any Gbohii for a little while. At last, he saw what he was looking for – a little cottage, right on the water, with a dock sticking out from the shore into the Densu River. And tied to the dock was a small boat.

"Let's push our log over there," he said, pointing to the dock.

"Are you sure it's safe?" she asked, her voice dubious.

"I think we'll be safer in a boat than with our legs dangling in the river," Etse said, shivering at the memory of the dead reaching up to them from below. He wondered how many more of them they'd passed, in murkier water where they couldn't even see the things. He tried to put the thought out of his head.

"And there might be supplies there," he went on. As they got closer, he saw signs of a hasty flight. The front door was wide open. A few bits of clothing were outside on the ground, fluttering a little in the breeze. But there were no splashes of blood. Maybe they'd gotten lucky, and they were ahead of the Gbohii wandering their way out into the countryside.

His eyes scanned for movement as they got closer to the shore. Unarmed, there was no way he could fight one of the things. Their only chance would be to get back into deeper water.

With a hollow bump, their timber raft came up alongside the dock. The water was still too deep here to stand, and he wasn't sure what might be down in the dark depths. He grabbed the side of the dock swiftly and yanked himself clear of the water. Then he reached down and hauled the girl up as well.

Still no movement from the shore. They could untie the boat and be off on their way in minutes. Or he could check the building and see if there was anything inside they could use. Hunger was beginning to gnaw at his belly.

"Is there food here?" Sefadzi asked softly.

That decided for him. As hungry as he was, he could perhaps wait a little longer. But the girl had been without food for over a day. And fresh water would be welcome, too – the Densu River downriver from Nicran was not exactly clean.

"Wait here," he said. "I'll go see."

He stood up and carefully walked down the dock toward the cottage. The wind blew through the bushes around the house, ruffling things. No other sounds, no other motion. The cottage was stone, with a thatched roof. There was a well out front – he could get water. That should be his first step, to find something inside that they could fill with water for the trip ahead. Sooner or later, they'd need to leave the river.

"Hello? Anyone here?" he called out.

No answer. He wasn't really expecting one. The place looked abandoned. Someone had packed up and left in a hurry.

The cottage door was ajar. The interior was dark. A few gaps in the shuttered windows let some light in. Etse stepped carefully inside. A pile of firewood was stacked by the hearth, and he grabbed one stout-looking branch. He smacked it against his palm, which made a satisfying thwack. It wasn't a sword, but at least it was something.

The main room of the place was kitchen and living area. A door in the back led to what might be a bedroom – the door was closed. And a ladder led up to a loft. He carefully climbed the ladder for a peek and saw several straw-stuffed pallets laying on the floor. Whatever other bedding had been there was gone, but a few toys were scattered on the floor, testament to the children who'd once lived there. Nothing useful remained.

He slid back down the ladder. His stomach was grumbling louder than ever, so he went to the kitchen area, hoping for some luck. The shelves were mostly bare, but there was a bag of oats they might be able to do something with, and some cheese. Best, there was a large skin full of wine. He could empty it out and fill it from the well, and they'd have something to carry water in. A few plates sat dirty on a table. Washed up, they'd do for mixing some oats and water into a porridge. It wasn't great food, but they wouldn't starve.

A noise from behind Etse startled him. He whirled.

The bedroom door creaked again.

Horrified, he realized that in his worry about food, he'd neglected to search the entire house.

The latch on the door lifted. Etse eased his way toward the door out of the cottage. His fingers tensed around the stick he'd found.

The door slammed open, and a snarling Gbohii stood in the doorway. It had been a woman. She still wore her wrap-skirt and a long tunic. She obviously hadn't turned too long ago. Her face was pale in death, her eyes empty, but her skin hadn't yet begun to decay. Her right arm was a festering open wound.

She'd been bitten, died, and her family had fled. Etse wondered for a moment if she'd been left here alone, feverish and cursing them, or if she'd passed before they went.

Then the thing leapt at him, and he had no more time to wonder about anything except staying alive. It crossed the room in three bounds, its loping stride carrying it faster than a human could have moved. Etse dove out through the doorway. He whirled as the thing came at him and slammed the cottage door shut.

It impacted the door just as he shoved it closed, crashing against it with a bone-crunching noise. There was no latch. It wouldn't hold her more than a moment.

"Untie the boat!" he yelled to Sefadzi, who still sat on the dock. He ran toward the shore to join her. Behind him the door crashed open, and he knew the thing would be on him before he could make the deep water.

Desperate, he turned back to face the monster. It was coming fast, head low. He swung his makeshift club as he turned, putting all his momentum into the swing.

The club connected with the thing's head, and he sidestepped. It shrieked, the sound audible even over the crack the stick made when it connected. Between the force of his blow and a few quick steps, the thing missed Etse by a couple of feet. He backed up.

Behind him, he heard a splash and looked back over his shoulder. Sefadzi had jumped from the dock into the water and was wading toward him.

"Get out of here!" he shouted to her. He was going to die at the hands of this thing. Quick as he was, it was faster. Without his sword, he wasn't going to last long. He only hoped to hold it long enough for Sefadzi to get away.

Then it was trying to tear into him again. He swung the club, batting aside its arm as it reached for his throat. The other hand whipped in, and he only avoided it by taking two more skittering steps back. His feet were in the water now; it had backed him into the river. It lunged; he swung and gave more ground. It wasn't giving him another shot at its head.

And he knew that if it could lock one of those hands on him for even a moment, it would pull him in close for the kill.

He was up to his knees in the river now. He swung the club, hard, and took the Gbohii at the left elbow, smashing the bone there. With a crack, the stick broke, splitting down the middle. It was useless. He stepped back again. The force of his blow had bought him a moment while it found its balance, but then it would be on him.

"Etse!" Sefadzi called. She sounded right next to him!

He looked over his shoulder. She was there, just behind him. She was soaking wet, water pouring down from her hair in rivers of silver drops. She looked like some creature from the sea, risen up out of the depths. Her eyes were a deep brown that was almost black, and the intensity of her stare startled him.

She had a sword in her hands. She held it out to him, both her hands clutching the scabbard, hilt facing him.

His fingers found the hilt without trying.

The blade flowed from the scabbard into his hand, and he whirled back to face the Gbohii. Icy hands closed around his throat. He'd turned away a moment too long. He saw teeth in front of his face, the thing's maw opened wide to bite.

Etse thrust upward.

The sword bit home, stabbing through the monster's neck, into the skull, into the brain. The teeth clacked closed, inches from him. It sagged against him, dead. Etse fell to his knees in the cool water, breathing hard, amazed to be alive.

CHAPTER THIRTY-ONE

Kwadwo woke to Kwesi shaking him gently. Dawn was just beginning to brighten the sky. The air smelled of fresh grass, but Kwadwo thought he could catch a whiff of the sea now and again. They'd be to Takoradi soon.

It had been a tough call, whether to continue to ride through the night or find someplace to stop. Okoth's wound was paining him, and his kwapawnkah was exhausted from having Okere ride double. Kwesi finally made the call, saying that at night they'd never see the Gbohii coming. Kwadwo scouted ahead and soon found a place to stop – a small, abandoned shrine a ways off the main road. They brought all the kwapawnkah inside and barred the doors, then took turns keeping watch through the night.

Kwesi had been last watch. Kwadwo saw that he'd woken none of the others yet, and he beckoned now for Kwadwo to follow him. Something was up. Kwadwo stood slowly, careful not to rouse anyone else. Okoth slept fitfully off to one side of him, tossing and turning a little. But no one woke.

Kwesi went outside, and Kwadwo followed.

"When we get to Takoradi, what then?" Kwadwo asked.

"Hmm? Oh. We prepare to move out. We can't hold Takoradi. It was never designed to defend against an enemy like this. But there are things I need there."

"So where, then?"

"I was thinking Kamit, perhaps," Kwesi said. It was a place Kwadwo knew from a few trips there in the past. A technological marvel, with its monumental pyramids and advanced systems of engineering, architecture, medicine and mathematics, and location of the oldest – and many believe greatest – university in Ki-Khanga: Ipet-Isut.

"That might serve," Kwadwo said.

"But that's not what I wanted to speak with you about," Kwesi said. "Have you noticed Okoth?"

"Noticed what about him?" Kwadwo asked.

Kwesi sighed deeply. "Well, noticed that he is awake and behind us listening, for one thing. I should have woken you earlier."

Okoth pushed the door open and stepped out into the morning air to join them. He limped, favoring the injured leg heavily. His face was flushed, his cheeks pink. Almost, Kwadwo would have credited that with embarrassment at being caught eavesdropping. But his brow was wet with beads of sweat. Coupled with the flush...

"Fever," Kwadwo said. "God, Okoth – were you bitten?"

Okoth pulled up the leg of his trousers. He'd covered the wound with strips of cloth, but blood and pus had oozed through the dressing. He let go of the pants leg.

"It was a bite, out there in the woods. Not a claw," Okoth said.

"And you chose not to tell anyone," Kwesi said.

"If you'd turned last night, you'd have killed us all!" Kwadwo said.

"Damn it, I know the course of the curse!" Okoth cried. "I'm a dead man, all right? But I'm not dead yet. I can still help you get the Wakuu to safety." He sat down heavily on a stone bench outside the shrine.

Kwesi stared down at him through half lidded eyes.

"Please," Okoth said.

"You should have told us," Kwesi said. "But he was no danger to us, Kwadwo. I stayed awake through his watch as well as my own, last night."

"You...how did you know?" Okoth said.

"Please." Kwesi's voice was dripping with sarcasm. "You can no more hide that sort of wound – or the growing fever – than you could grow wings."

"Will you tell Okere?" Okoth asked. Kwadwo could hear the fear in the man's voice.

"I will kill you myself, when the time comes," Kwesi promised. "I won't let you turn. But I will keep this between us for now, if you wish. You might want to tell him yourself, though. You've given your life for the man. He owes you something for that."

Okoth shook his head. "He owes me nothing. It's duty."

Kwadwo looked at the dying man. They'd argued. They'd each worked for men who'd been at odds with each other, not long past. But now? He wished he could do something, anything, to help. Okoth was a brave man, and a good one. Kwadwo realized with a start that he was already grieving a man not even dead yet.

"Come on, I'll help you rebind the wound," Kwadwo said.

"I'll get the kwapawnkah ready. The sooner we are gone, the better," Kwesi said.

***

The road ran straight and true from there to Takoradi, and they saw very few of the undead as they rode on. The handful they spotted were easy to outrun on horseback. By noon, Takoradi was in sight.

"Damn," Kwesi said as soon as he saw the city.

"What's wrong?" Kwadwo asked.

"I'm not sure. But something is. My banner is gone."

Kwadwo scanned the city, looking to the palace atop the hill, where Kwesi lived. His hippopotamus banner should have hung there, above the palace. But there was nothing at all fluttering in the breeze.

"What do we do?" Okoth asked, his voice pained but steady.

"We press on," Kwesi said. "Carefully."

The closer they got to the town, the more signs of something out of place they saw. There were people on the road, but fewer than there ought to have been on a normal day. And those they saw hurried away as soon as they saw kwapawnkah coming. They dashed off into the fields, away from the roads.

"What the hell is going on?" Kwesi muttered.

"Not the homecoming you expected?" Okere smirked.

Kwesi glared daggers at the man and rode on ahead.

Then they came to the gates, and what they saw there stopped them in their tracks.

The gates were closed. Guards walked the walls and stood in the towers. All that was as it ought to be, if the city was warned of possible danger. The decorations just outside the gates were new, though. Rows of spikes had been set into the ground on both sides of the road, each with a head stuck atop it. They were Gbohii heads, and all of them had been placed so as not to pierce the skull. The result was that to walk up to the gates, you had to pass a gauntlet of six half-decayed, snarling, growling, hissing heads on each side of you.

"Who has done this!" Kwesi roared. "I'll have someone's head."

"Kwesi, we should go. Something is very wrong," Kwadwo said. In his head he went over who would have been in charge in their absence, but no one he could think of would set up such a grisly spectacle. Someone else was in command of the city now. Someone new.

"Like hell. This is my city! How dare they!" Kwesi said.

"Kwesi, listen to Kwadwo. We can't risk it," Okoth said.

"Maybe you're right," Kwesi muttered. "We can go around outside, ask what's going on." He made to turn his kwapawnkah.

But as he did, the gates opened wide, and a patrol of mounted men poured out.

"Too late," Kwesi said. "Okere, Okoth, keep your identities to yourselves until we know who is in charge here."

The horsemen crossed the ground swiftly, forming a circle around the party. They all wore leather armor covered in iron rings, with swords belted at their waists, and spears in their hands. Kwadwo recognized not a one of them.

"Asantehene Kwesi," one of the guardsmen said. "We've been instructed to escort you to the palace. Please, sir – welcome home, and come with us."

Kwesi shot Kwadwo a quick, questioning look, and Kwadwo shook his head slightly. He had no idea who any of these men were. He'd never seen any of them before, which meant they were not from Takoradi. It also probably meant that despite the welcome, they were not going to be allowed to leave.

Kwesi turned back to the man. "Well then. Please do escort us."

They rode through the streets, which were empty. No one wandered about. The market was closed. Citizens peeked at the parade of kwapawnkah through shuttered windows. Kwadwo wondered how so much change could be wrought in so few days. This was a vibrant city! Even if the people had heard of the Gbohii, even if they were terrified of them, there still should have been some folk up and about.

The guards dismounted, and Kwesi followed suit. Kwadwo stepped down from his own kwapawnkah and then helped Okere and Okoth down as well.

"This way, please," said the soldier who'd spoken before. None of the other men had said a word, which was unnerving.

Usually soldiers were given to some idle chatter, but not these men.

Okoth was limping, but gritted his teeth and shook off Kwadwo's offer for help. Kwadwo shrugged and kept close to Kwesi instead. They entered the main doors of the palace. At first Kwadwo thought they were making for Kwesi's private study, but instead they made for the main hall. Kwesi rarely used the room, preferring to keep important meetings small. The space was large – big enough for a large dinner party, or for an audience hall. It was clearly being used for the latter purpose now.

Kwadwo thought the heads outside were the worst horror he would see today. He was wrong.

Iron bolts had been driven into the walls on either side of the room, and heavy chains attached to those. Held fast by those chains was a pair of Gbohii. Snarling, slashing the air with their claws, snapping their jaws, they flanked a huge chair which had been set, throne-like, at the far end of the hall. A young woman sat in the chair, long dark locs flowing over her shoulders in stark contrast with the white silk gown she wore.

The guardsmen drew themselves up into positions along the walls, forming a passage for Kwesi's company to walk down, but Kwesi stopped short as soon as he saw the woman.

"Why, father! Welcome home!" she said. "No kiss of greeting?" She faked a pout.

"You are not my daughter, Lugu," Kwesi grated out. "I've asked you not to call me that."

"Ah, but you married my mother," she replied. "That makes you at least a stepfather, yes? But I prefer father."

She stood, the dress floating about her legs, clinging to them as she stepped forward. The undead snarled at her movement, spittle dripping from their lips.

"Do you like how I've redecorated?" she purred, gesturing to the monsters chained to the walls.

"I think I preferred the place without dead things making a racket," Kwesi replied drily.

Kwadwo's mind was racing. He knew of Lugu, of course. Kwesi had married her mother when she was just a young girl. He'd heard the child had never forgiven her mother and hated Kwesi. He'd never met her before now, though.

Somewhere, that hatred had turned into madness. It was insane to keep these dead things so close. But more than that, he could see it in her eyes, in her step, in her posture. Something was broken inside her. Something twisted in her heart. He wanted to flee from the room. With an effort, he stood his ground, staying next to Kwesi.

"A shame, father," she said. She reached out to one of the Gbohii as if to stroke its face, drawing back her fingers languidly when it snapped at them. "Because you'll be staying here with me for a long, long time."

CHAPTER THIRTY-TWO

It was daylight outside. Kwadwo could see that much through the cell bars, but little more. The palace house only had three cells, and they hadn't been used in all Kwesi's time residing there. A constable in the city had managed the larger jail near the center of town. Kwesi preferred to keep his hands out of local justice, leaving it instead to the people of the town. But if these cells had been ill-used during his time here, his daughter certainly seemed to be trying to make up for it.

This cell had a sole window, sitting about a foot over his head, and barred. Kwadwo knew from memory of the place that the window was at ground level. When it rained, the water would drizzle into the cell from the palace wall. It left the cell slimy and dank.

"If I'd known I was going to end up locked in a cell down here, I would have left a key behind. Or a knife. Or something!" Kwadwo said aloud, frustrated.

Okoth chuckled from the one bunk in the room. The laugh was a hollow sound. His fever had come on in force since Lugu had cast them down here. Kwadwo didn't think the guards had noticed yet. But at some point Okoth was going to die, and then it was going to get very nasty in here very fast.

Locked, unarmed, in a room with one of the Gbohii? Kwadwo couldn't think of a worse way to die, and he had a good imagination.

Okoth saw him shudder and shook his head. "Won't come to that. Just end it now. Damn it, man. I'm already dead. Just end it and bash my head in before I turn into one of those things."

"We discussed this already. We wait for Kwesi to get back, right?" Kwadwo said. He was scared, sure. But he was damned if he'd just kill the man outright. Even if he knew Okoth was a dead man already. The bite would kill him, sure as anything. Which was better? To end the suffering now, or to let him linger. Kwadwo didn't know.

Okoth exhaled, a long, rasping breath. For a moment Kwadwo thought the man had died and he tensed, ready to crush his skull before he rose again. But then his chest lifted with a new breath. Kwadwo took a sip of air himself, not realizing he'd been holding his own breath for a moment.

"Just pray he doesn't take too long," Okoth whispered.

Lugu had tossed all four of them down here. But just an hour later, her guards came back and grabbed Okere and Kwesi, leaving Okoth and Kwadwo behind without so much as a glance.

That was six hours ago. What the hell was going on up there?

That Lugu and Kwesi had unresolved issues was beyond obvious to him. Most children don't lock up their fathers. It was equally clear that Lugu was dangerous, perhaps even mad. No sane person would keep living dead monsters in their throne room. But Lugu did. She even acted like the things were her pets.

Kwadwo wondered who the men had been, before they turned. Had they somehow captured the Gbohii? That seemed unlikely. The things were fast and deadly. Hard enough to kill them, let alone trying to snare them! No, it seemed more likely she'd had those men chained in place while they were still alive, already bitten and dying of the fever.

A clanging from out in the hall jerked his attention back to the present. That was the door at the end of the hall. Someone had opened it, which meant someone was coming their way. Kwadwo went to the door and peered out through the small, barred hole, but all he could see was lantern light.

"Step back from the door!" The command was a man's voice, from outside. "Back, or we'll make you wish you had."

Kwadwo stepped back. These guards hadn't been too gentle bringing them down here in the first place. He knew they wouldn't hesitate to beat him bloody if he gave them a reason. For now, at least, he needed to appear docile. The right moment would come, but not if he were beaten too badly to move.

The door opened, and Kwesi came through. He was moving slowly, pale and drawn. He must have been moving a bit too slow for the guards outside – one of them planted a booted foot into his behind and pushed. Kwesi tried to keep his balance but fell forward onto his hands and knees.

"You bastards, show some respect!" Kwadwo shouted as the door closed again. He went to Kwesi's side to help him up. The men outside didn't bother saying anything back – just walked away laughing to one another.

"I'm all right, damn it," Kwesi said. He stood, brushing the dirt from his knees.

"What happened? Where's Okere?" Kwadwo asked.

Kwesi exhaled. "Lots to talk about. Less time to do it in, I think. How's Okoth?" He walked over to the bed.

Okoth smiled gamely up from the bunk. "Still here," he croaked.

"But not, I think, for long," Kwesi said, his voice quiet and grim.

Okoth shook his head. His face was a mask – pale patches in some spots, bright flaming red in others. He'd stopped sweating a while ago. His skin was bone dry now and burning hot to the touch. Kwadwo hadn't looked at the wound recently, but the stink had grown so much that it was overpowering even through the wrapping. The man's leg was probably covered with rot. All three men had seen a few people die of the curse – they all knew Okoth didn't have much longer.

"I fear I may have to break my promise to you, Okoth," Kwesi said, sitting down on the bunk beside him. "That pains me, because I never break my word. But Kwadwo and my survival probably depends on my not fulfilling that promise."

Okoth looked as confused as Kwadwo felt. "What promise?" Okoth whispered.

"I swore to kill you before you turned, Okoth." Kwesi shifted, looking up at the wall, out the window. "I'm not going to be able to do that."

***

Okoth was dead. It was a matter of time, now. The nerve-wracking question was: how much time? Kwadwo had seen someone turn within seconds. He'd also seen the process take hours. The goal, of course, was to stab into the dead man's brain before the body could turn and rise as a Gbohii. That stopped the process cold.

He'd never before had to stand in the same room with a cursed corpse, waiting for it to turn. Kwadwo was terrified. Every hair stood out on his arms. He watched the body, barely even blinking. At any moment, Okoth's body would rise as something unnatural, a hungry demon out to slay anyone nearby and make more of its own kind through its bite. And he was locked in with the thing without even a knife to defend himself.

"You're shaking, Kwadwo. Get a hold of yourself," Kwesi said.

"How can you be so damned calm?" Kwadwo asked.

"Because either this will work, or it won't."

Kwadwo grunted. "You haven't gone hand to hand with these things before. I have."

The corpse twitched and Kwesi flinched. A bead of sweat broke out on his forehead.

"Fair," Kwesi said.

That Okoth had agreed to this crazy plan at all spoke more to the man's character than anything else Kwadwo had seen. They'd moved Okoth from the bed, set him gently on the floor wrapped in the blankets. Then they'd taken the wooden cot and set it up on end, against the wall. After that, it had been a long wait while Okoth slowly died.

As they waited Kwesi let Kwadwo know what had transpired while he was out of the cell. Someone had recognized Okere and told Lugu who he was, so instead of just bringing Kwesi upstairs to play with she'd brought them both. Okere had immediately been all bluster and played the regal emperor. Lugu went along with him and let him talk. Then she'd left with Okere to 'give him a tour,' while Kwesi remained in her throne room under guard. It was a long wait.

When they returned many hours later, both were flushed and a little rumpled. Rather than taking his place beside Kwesi as a prisoner, Okere went to stand next to Lugu at her seat.

"That was a long time to tour such a small building," Kwesi said, sarcasm dripping from his voice.

"But father, you would want me to be an adequate host to our illustrious guest, would you not?" Lugu said.

"I'm sure you were more than adequate," Kwesi said.

"I always am," Lugu purred. Okere blushed.

"Lugu, your taste in men has never been that good. But Okere, I'm frankly startled. Haven't you noticed, man, that there is only one seat at the head of this hall?" Kwesi asked.

Lugu glared daggers at him. "Chairs can be moved," she said. "Sadly, no seat for you, father. I think I will plan something more permanent for you than a chair."

Lugu nodded to someone at the main doors behind Kwesi, and a workman came into the room. He bowed quickly to Lugu.

"Over there," she pointed at a spot on the wall. The man went to the place quickly and began drilling out holes in the mudbrick. Kwesi saw what he was about – he was setting a ring into the stone wall of the room. In fact, the ring looked identical to the ones that the two Gbohii in the room were chained to.

That was when Kwesi started to sweat a little.

"Aane, father dear. I will keep you close to me...for always. Right there, on the end of a chain."

Then Lugu's guards hauled Kwesi back to his cell.

CHAPTER THIRTY-THREE

Kwesi had laid out his plan to Okoth and Kwadwo as soon as he returned to the cell. It was simple enough, and almost certain to get two of them killed. Only two of them, because the plan relied on the third man – Okoth – already being dead.

Kwesi wanted to wait until Okoth died of the curse and rose as a Gbohii, then somehow survive that first few minutes while making an enormous racket. The noise would bring the guards, who would open the door and be faced with a hungry monster. In the chaos, Kwadwo and Kwesi would escape. Okoth had agreed, provided Kwesi swore to kill his Gbohii.

"I don't want that thing loose, killing innocent people," he'd said.

Kwesi swore.

Kwadwo thought the entire plan was a terrible one, and he'd made no effort to hide his opinion. Once Okoth had stopped breathing, he and Kwesi slid behind the bed frame. The thin wood shell between them and the soon-rising corpse didn't make Kwadwo feel any better.

"You know, I watched those things tear through a six inch thick mahogany door, back at the palace in Nicran," he said.

Kwesi grunted softly.

"This bed frame will last all of a few seconds," Kwadwo said.

"Maybe," Kwesi replied. "You have a better idea?"

Kwadwo didn't, at least not at this late date. Okoth's body was twitching again. A hand rose. Air escaped dead lungs in a low moan. He watched the process with a mixture of horror and curiosity. He hoped Okoth's soul had already fled that shell and gone on to its reward. But what if it hadn't? What if the soul was trapped there, in the rotting body, doomed to watch as the monster inhabiting it committed vile acts?

He resolved to ensure Okoth's wishes were carried out, at any cost. He owed the man that much, and more.

That was assuming he survived the next few minutes, of course.

The thing stood up from the floor. It seemed unsteady on its feet, like a calf trying to take its first steps. The body hadn't decayed at all – the thing was very clearly still Okoth's body. But those eyes! There was nothing human left in the dead eyes. They were empty, black pits. The thing cast about for a moment, looking around the small room. It sniffed the air. Then it locked its gaze on them.

"Now!" Kwesi shouted.

They surged forward, pushing the frame hard across the mud-brick floor. It hit the Gbohii, almost bowling it over. The thing howled at them, shrieking like a damned thing – which for all Kwadwo knew, it was. The bed smacked into the Gbohii and their rush carried it back two more steps to pin it against the wall. The thing struggled, but they'd caught it off balance. It had little leverage to use its strength against them. Still, it pushed hard, trying to heave them away from it. If it escaped from behind the bed, it would be on them in moments.

Now it was on to the next stage of the plan: make noise and hope the guards come. "Help!" Kwadwo shouted.

"Fire!" Kwesi shouted. "Fire!" Kwadwo looked around wildly for a moment – fire was a huge threat anywhere, and he had an instant of instinctive fear as soon as Kwesi said the word. Even stone buildings would burn if a blaze grew strong enough. Which made it the perfect thing to say, he realized. Nothing would draw the guards here faster than the threat of the entire place burning down.

He joined his voice to Kwesi's: "Fire! Fire!"

The Gbohii was pushing harder against the wall now. Even with both of them leaning into the bed with everything they had, it was shoving them back a little. Kwadwo worked his feet against the brick floor, trying to find the best spots to place his boots. One of the thing's hands got free, waving about in the air dangerously close to his head. Then the claw tore into the mattress, ripping chunks of cloth and straw away. Another few moments, and the mattress would fall apart. Then all that would stand between them and the thing would be a few thin bars of wood. Kwadwo kept shouting for everything he was worth.

From out in the hall, he heard the jangle of armored footsteps. Men were coming their way!

"What is all this noise about?" someone hollered from the hallway. "You two – back away from the door!" A key was inserted into a lock.

The Gbohii tore another huge chunk out of the mattress, revealing its snarling head. The face was a mask of rage, drool dripping from the open maw. It lunged in, teeth snapping, but the wooden frame held it back.

The door was about to creak open.

"Pull now!" Kwesi shouted to him. Both men grabbed hold of the wooden frame and pulled, instead of pushing. The Gbohii was already pushing against them with such force that as soon as they stopped resisting, the frame shot away from the wall. They kept going, continuing their retreat until the frame boxed them in, with a mudbrick wall against their backs.

Okoth's Gbohii had let go about halfway across the room. It stood there a moment, saw them, and took one loping stride toward them.

Then the door swung open and two armored men stepped through into the room. They saw the Gbohii about the same time it saw them. Kwadwo could tell from the instant look of horror that flashed across their faces that they'd faced the things before. He almost felt pity for them. Almost.

The one closer to the door tried to draw his sword – neither man had drawn a weapon yet. The one closer to the Gbohii backed away from the thing fast, and stumbled into the other guard, fouling his draw. Both of them tumbled to the floor with a *thud*, cursing and shouting.

It was on them in an instant, and the curses turned to screams. It bit down on a thrashing leg. Blood splashed from the wound across the floor. The bitten man screamed, agony mixed with dread and grief. That wasn't just the scream of a wounded man. Kwadwo had heard the same sound too often over the last few days. The guard knew he was already dead even though he was still breathing.

The Gbohii released its grip on the leg and scuttled, lightning quick, up the body of the other guard. He screamed and beat at it with his fists, but the blows had no effect at all. It held the guard's head almost lovingly with both hands for a moment. Then it darted in, quick as a striking viper, and tore out the guard's throat with its teeth. His screams turned into gurgling, and in another moment he was still, while it continued to gnaw at him.

Kwadwo couldn't do anything to save the men. And he found that he wished he could. Kwesi's plan was working, but it was a foul one. Using the curse as a weapon like this, even against enemies, seemed…wrong. Evil. He glanced at Kwesi's face but saw no remorse there. Only a grim stare. Kwesi had always been a hard man, and these dark days had only made him more so.

The guard whose leg was bitten pulled himself free from under his dying friend. While the Gbohii was distracted, he made it to the doorway, stood up, and staggered off down the hall, shouting for help.

He'd left the door open, though. His screaming attracted the dead thing's attention, and it left the cooling body for new prey, loping off down the hall after him. As soon as it was out of the room, Kwadwo pushed aside the fragile shelter they'd hidden behind and grabbed the dead man's sword. It felt incredibly good to have steel in his hand again.

"Let's get out of here," Kwesi said.

"We need to deal with Okoth first," Kwadwo said.

Kwesi raised his eyebrow. "The man is dead."

"And you gave him your word."

For a moment, Kwadwo thought Kwesi would explode in anger. His face grew red, and he could see the angry retort forming on the man's lips. But instead, Kwesi frowned, and nodded.

"Aane, I did. Let's do this swiftly, then," he said. He looked down at the dead body on the floor of the cell. "We need to get out of this place."

CHAPTER THIRTY-FOUR

Kudowor supervised a makeshift door being put in place over the gaping hole where the old door had been. It wouldn't hold long, but if it took even a few minutes for a Gbohii to hack its way through the pile of wood and the wagon they shoved into place to hold the boards up, then it might save lives. He smiled, satisfied.

"The Wakuu left you in charge?" Musongola asked, brushing dirt from his hands. He hadn't asked any questions before this, merely jumped in to help. Kudowor had always liked the man, but never so much as now.

"Kwesi did," Kudowor said. "The emperor is with Asantehene Kwesi, riding to Takoradi as fast as they can."

Musongola nodded. "What were their orders, then?"

"To get these people to Takoradi," Kudowor said, shrugging helplessly.

"Damn," Musongola said, looking around at the haggard men and women struggling to clean up the mess left behind in the aftermath of the desperate fight.

"Just so," Kudowor said.

"Well, you're the man the emperor put in charge," Musongola said. "You have my sword at your disposal."

He reached out his hand, and Kudowor took it into his own. The two men stared across at each other. Kudowor smiled first, then Musongola joined him. Kudowor was torn between gratitude for the man's support and annoyance that he wasn't going to just take charge and lift this burden from his shoulders. He wasn't used to command, damn it! Musongola was. Why should he be giving orders to this man?

"My thanks," Kudowor said, keeping his other thoughts to himself. It seemed this burden was his to bear whether he wanted it or not. His heart lifted a little, despite his misgivings. What he'd hoped to do had seemed impossible before, but maybe there was a chance with Musongola alongside him.

"Now, do you have a plan in mind to accomplish this mighty feat?" Musongola asked.

"I might. I was thinking the river, down to the old fort, where the Densu River reaches the Sati-Baa."

"And then what? By ship around the coast?"

"That was the idea."

Musongola rubbed his jaw. "It might work. It's a long trip, but it would be just as long overland, and the dead don't seem to swim well. But how to get them down the river? The barrels got you this far, but..."

Kudowor grinned. "Come with me," he said.

He led Musongola around the wall, off to one side of the temple grounds, to a shed. The cluck of chickens was clearly audible through the walls. Kudowor waved his hands with a flourish.

"Chicken soup?" Musongola asked.

"No," Kudowor said. "Wood for a deck. Lash the planks to the barrels, and we have rafts. Get several rafts..."

"And you have enough space for all these people to float down the river safely," Musongola finished. "I like it. Will the priests come?"

"I am hoping they will come with us." Kudowor wasn't sure they would want to. The old priest he'd spoken to had been...odd. A strange man. And he seemed to be in charge here, or at least well respected by the others. If he went along with the plan, it would probably fly. Without his approval, it was hard to say.

"I know who we should ask," Kudowor said. "Come on."

It took him a few minutes to find the old man. He wasn't in the shrine, which is where Kudowor had assumed he might be. Several of the other priests were still there, praying and keeping scores of the refugees calm.

Kudowor went back outside, Musongola following close behind him. He scanned the grounds with his eyes, looking for the strange old man. Somehow, he had a feeling that was the one he needed to convince of his plan. If he agreed, the other priests would fall in line.

And then Kudowor saw him. He stood on the wall, facing west. He looked for all the world like a sentry at his post, and if it hadn't been for the priest's lappa billowing in the wind Kudowor might have taken him for a soldier.

He went up the stairs to join the old priest as quietly as he could.

"Most priests were not always priests, you know," the man said, his gaze locked somewhere in the distance beyond the wall.

Kudowor kept his silence, hoping he would go on talking. He was more than curious. The priest had clearly been someone else before he put on his robes. Who?

"Some of us came here from other lives. Some of us maybe came here to try to forget those lives." He turned to face Kudowor then, anger creeping into his voice. "And then you bring your swords and your war and your needs here!"

"I'm sorry." Kudowor couldn't think of anything else to say.

"Sorry doesn't cure the world," the man grumbled.

"No. But neither will hiding from the world cure...all of this," Kudowor said, gesturing with both hands. "The world is crumbling. I don't think this place will be a refuge much longer."

"I don't need it to last much longer," the priest said. "I've lived long enough."

Kudowor leaned into the wall next to the old man. He could see it clearly now that he knew what to look for. The corded muscles in the shoulder and arm. The small scar on the cheekbone. The way the old priest stood, straight and ready, balanced. He was surprised that he'd missed it before, but then – one didn't think of priests as warriors. This one clearly had been, though. A swordsman, Kudowor guessed. And someone important, judging by how the other priests treated him.

"Who are you?" Kudowor asked.

"I am no one of importance."

"Every living person is important, now," Kudowor said.

The priest sighed. "What is it you would ask of me? Out with it."

"I want to tear down two of the priests' sheds and use the lumber to build rafts. Get us all to the river, and from there to the ocean and then to Takoradi."

The priest harumphed, but he nodded as he did. "It's not a bad plan," he said. "I'll speak with the priests and get you their permission. They will want to go with you."

"I think that would be wise," Kudowor said. He turned as if to go and then put a hand on the old priest's shoulder.

"And I want you to come with us," he added.

The old man shook his head. "This is not my world, son. Nor my time."

"Just think on it?" Kudowor pleaded.

"I already have."

Kudowor walked away. He had much to do, and you could not save a man who didn't want to live. You could only offer him a chance to save himself.

Kudowor didn't see the old man again before they left. Everyone else pitched in and made short work of demolishing two of the outer buildings, turning the lumber into boards for rafts. The resulting mess wouldn't last two minutes in the open sea – but it would get them safely down the Densu River. Once they'd gotten near the mouth of the river, they had only to acquire a ship and ideally some more weapons and armor. With luck, they'd arrive at Takoradi only a couple of days after Kwesi!

He stepped aboard the last raft and nodded sharply to a man holding its mooring line fast. The man relaxed the rope, letting the boat drift out into the current. A couple of men with long poles kept the raft drifting evenly down the river. They didn't want to lose any of the rafts to rocks, mud banks, or other perils.

Musongola was somewhere up ahead in the rowboat. He was already out of sight. With Magezi, the woman Diata, and two volunteers, they were scouting the river ahead of the ungainly rafts. If there was danger ahead, the rowboat would be able to come back upstream to warn them. That was the plan, anyway. But it left him as the only trained swordsman watching over five rafts, each carrying about twenty souls. It was a heavy load to carry.

He looked back at the temple. There was a man standing atop the wall, looking like the loneliest person in the world. Kudowor knew that had to be the old priest. Who had he been? Why stay, when even the other priests had left? Kudowor burned to know the man's story. But he seemed almost desperate to not come along. Kudowor hadn't pushed. The man had to have heavy burdens of his own.

Which he'd most likely bear to his grave soon enough. Kudowor doubted one old man would survive long out there alone.

He brought his attention back to his people, to bringing them safely out of this disaster. They had a long way to go, and everyone counted on him to see them through it. Kwadwo had believed in him. He was determined not to let any of them down.

CHAPTER THIRTY-FIVE

Etse knelt at the edge of the river and did his best to wash the blood from his clothes in the shallow water. The cloth was stained beyond belief – the Gbohii had bled out all over him, and the vile stuff stank. He'd done the best he could, but he'd have to find new clothing at some point. What he was wearing had once been fine enough, but it was stained, tattered, and torn now.

He belted the sword around him, the comforting weight settling on his hip. How helpless he had been without it! The club he tried to defend himself with was next to useless against the dead. Having a sword was the difference between life and death now.

Sefadzi was hiding in the boat, still tied to the dock but ready to cast off if any more Gbohii attacked. If he had to, Etse could swim out to the rowboat and climb aboard once they were away from the shoreline. Somewhere east down the Densu River was his father and the other survivors from the palace. Etse hoped that with the boat, they might link back up with the others.

He really didn't want to go back into the house. The Gbohii he'd slain had been a woman, before she'd died. Etse had seen the little toys in the loft. Children had lived here; the woman had perhaps been their mother. Would they grieve to know she was gone to her rest? Were they even still alive? He had no way to know, but the building felt more like a tomb than a home.

They needed supplies. This was no time to be squeamish. He steeled himself and went back in. He grabbed the small bits of food he'd found and filled the large jug with water from the well.

All this he piled into the boat in silence, Sefadzi watching him with those big eyes of hers.

When he had everything that made sense to bring, he cast off. A few strong strokes of the oars carried them out into the middle of the river where they'd largely be safe from the undead. Gbohii didn't seem able to swim.

Only when they were safely out into deep water did Sefadzi speak.

"You're mad at me," she said.

Etse found that he was. "You had my sword. All that time we were floating down the river, you had it. I almost died for not having a weapon in my hand."

She cast her eyes down. "I'm sorry."

He shook his head, trying to fight down words that would only frighten the child. "We survived. It's past. But why, Sefadzi? Why didn't you tell me you had it?"

"It made me feel safe," she mumbled. "I thought you were dead when we fell on the ledge. So I took the sword and used it to poke any of the dead who came too close to us. It made me feel safe."

Etse nodded. Hadn't he felt the same sense of security just a short while ago, belting the weapon back on his waist? It was impossible to fault the child for being desperate to protect herself. She'd lost people. Everyone alive had, at this point, but she was a child. It was only natural she would cling to whatever would provide her with a sense of security. It was a mad world where that sense of safety was provided by a deadly weapon that she was too small to use anyway. But that was the world they lived in now.

"I understand," he said. "We'll see about getting you your own weapon."

"Really?" she asked, brightening.

"I don't see how any person who wants to live can go without one, at this point."

They drifted on for some hours, Etse working the oars periodically in hopes that they might gain on his father's larger band. There would be safety in numbers, security in having more people around them. Kwesi seemed to have pressed on for a long way, and Etse's head began pounding again after rowing only a short way. He had to take breaks in between, to allow the pain to diminish. His skull had taken a couple of hard knocks, and he still didn't feel right. He knew injuries like that could be dangerous, so rest seemed like a wise course.

Etse took to scanning the banks during those times, watching for any sign that his father had passed. It was during one of those rest periods when he spotted the first living people he'd seen since leaving Nicran.

He was lying back against the stern of the little boat, shaking out his arms and allowing the boat to drift with the current. Sefadzi sat in the bow, looking into the water ahead for sandbars, rocks, or waiting dead. Etse scanned the shoreline while he rested, but in a more or less casual way. It had been miles since they'd seen any of the dead, and he was starting to hope they'd gotten out ahead of them. So he almost missed the movement off to the north side of the bank.

He saw the Gbohii first. Two of them, standing at the base of a tree, growling up at something above. He scanned the branches and saw at least three people hidden in the boughs. The Gbohii began tearing at the trunk of the tree. Chips of wood flew away. The tree was only about a foot thick. It wouldn't last more than a minute or two. The people trapped in the tree knew they were doomed. Etse could hear their sobs even from the river.

"Can we help them?" asked Sefadzi. Etse hadn't realized that she'd seen them, too.

"Maybe." It would be a terrible risk. He'd fought the things mostly one at a time, or as a mass with other men near him to help. Two against one wasn't odds he liked. In another minute, his rowboat would drift past, the Gbohii would tear down the tree, and those people would be torn apart by the things. The safe, sane choice would be to stay the course, to continue on to his father.

He looked down into Sefadzi's eyes. Saving her hadn't been safe or sane, either. Etse picked up the oars and made for the shore.

"Stay in the boat," he told Sefadzi. "If they come your way push off and get to deep water. If anything happens to me, stay on the river until you find my father and the others."

Sefadzi nodded, her eyes still and serious.

The boat scraped bottom and Etse jumped over the side into the shallows. There was no time for anything fancy. Another few moments, and the things would tear down the tree. It already wobbled with the force of their blows. He sprinted straight for them, hoping to take one down before he was noticed.

The nearer one turned just before he was in range to swing. His sword was already raised, the stroke about to fall, but the thing got an arm between the blade and its neck. Etse's sword half severed its right forearm, but it slashed at his belly with its left. He barely dodged, the fingernails scraping along his clothes. He sorely missed the armor he'd had to leave behind in Nicran.

The other Gbohii was suddenly there, alongside him. Etse yelped and planted his boot in its sternum. It kept coming, bowling him over onto his back. Roots and rocks stabbed into him from behind, but he held his leg firm. He pushed hard with his leg, and the thing flew through the air over his head.

No time to breathe. The one he'd wounded was on him before he could get back to his feet. It closed its good hand around his ankle, hauling him toward it. His head hit a rock as it dragged him, bringing stars to his vision. He blinked to clear his eyes. It was leaning forward now, about to tear a chunk from his calf!

Etse screamed rage and defiance. His sword sang in an arc that passed through the thing's neck, cleaving its head from its body.

Where was the other one?

He got back to his feet, dangerously unsteady. And there it was, in front of him. But it was facing the wrong way. Instead of chasing him, it was after Sefadzi. Etse started to move toward it, then stopped. She was standing there before it, not backing away, just whirling something about. He squinted, and saw that it was a rock, tied to a string. She whirled it about, weaving patterns with the rock in the air. The Gbohii stood as if spellbound, watching the movement, occasionally reaching out as if to bat at the rock.

It looked like a cat, enjoying a toy. Etse had never seen something so strange before.

But he could feel blood trickling down the back of his neck. He'd been hurt, again, in that fall. He could see black starting to creep in around the edges of his vision, and knew he needed to end this quickly. Three steps brought him behind the thing, and one well practiced swing cut its head free.

Etse fell to his knees, dizzy.

"Etse? Were you bitten? Etse?" He could see Sefadzi's worried face in front of him. He tried to shake his head, but the motion made him nauseated, and he sank closer to the ground. He could hear a roaring in his ears, and the blackness filled his vision completely.

CHAPTER THIRTY-SIX

Kwesi and Kwadwo didn't have to go far to find Okoth's Gbohii. It had caught the fleeing guard at the bottom of the stairs leading up from the cell block. By the time they arrived the guard was dead and the Gbohii was chewing strips of flesh from the body. Kwadwo held a finger to his lips for silence, creeping forward as soft-footed as he could manage. In a straight up fight, he might be able to beat one of the things, especially if he had armor to protect him. But unarmored, already tired from the struggle in the cell, and with an unfamiliar sword? He'd rather not take chances.

Distracted, the thing was vulnerable. Kwadwo closed the distance. One step. Two. Three. It lifted its head from the body, sniffing the air. He was out of time! With a cry, he lunged across the last of the distance, sword licking out at the thing's neck. The blade bit deep but didn't sever the head entirely. It whirled, snarling, Okoth's head lolling off to one side horribly. Just a few more inches, and he'd have killed the thing!

Kwadwo cursed, dodging back away from those grasping claws. He swung his sword again, the blade crunching against wrist bone. It kept coming. Kwadwo backed away, trying to bring his sword up for a killing blow, but the thing was already too damned fast.

He ran out of room with a jolt. Kwadwo's back hit the wall with enough force to knock the wind out of his lungs, and then it was on him. The hands reached for his throat, closing like a vice. The mouth snapped in at his face. He punched the thing in the nose, hard, and that slowed it enough that the jaws closed inches away. Kwadwo grabbed the thing by the chin and forehead and tried to tear the head from the Gbohii's shoulders. But the grip it had on his throat was tightening. He could hear blood roaring in his ears. Kwadwo pulled hard once more, twisting with all the strength he could muster, but he simply didn't have the strength.

Then the head flew free from the body with a splash of blood. The Gbohii collapsed against him, blood pouring over his tunic. He coughed hard, trying to avoid getting the stuff into his mouth. The lifeless body slumped to the ground.

Kwesi was standing there, a sword in his hand, blood on the sword. Kwadwo realized Kwesi had slain the thing, had cut the head off with his sword while Kwadwo grappled with it.

"Thanks," Kwadwo said, breathing long, deep gasps of air. He picked his own weapon back up from where it had fallen on the floor.

"Don't mention it. Not like that guard needed this sword anymore," Kwesi said, stabbing the Gbohii's head to finish it off. "There. Our duty to Okoth is complete. Now it's time to take care of ourselves, eh?"

"We're both armed. Should we try to make a run for it? I know a spot on the back wall we can get out fast," Kwadwo said.

"There are things in my study I'd like to acquire first, if we can."

"The woman wants to turn you into one of those things and keep you as a pet. What could possibly be worth going back for?" Kwadwo couldn't imagine anything worth the risk.

Kwesi didn't answer him, at least not directly. "We'll be quick, and then be off," he said. Then he started off up the stairs.

Kwadwo followed, grumbling about madmen.

The halls were mostly empty. Lugu must have scared the servants away. Or maybe she fed them to her pets. She didn't seem to have very many troops, though. Kwadwo tried to guess the total number from what he'd seen. She might have a few dozen men, but he doubted that she had many more. A small force, then. Enough to cow the Takoradi militia, once Okere had stripped all the professional soldiers and taken them with him to Nicran. But not really enough to hold even the palace against a concerted attack. And if the Gbohii showed up in any serious numbers, they'd be completely overrun.

Lugu struck Kwadwo as mad, but brilliant. She had to have a plan. What was she thinking?

Outside Kwesi's office they ran into the first guard they had seen since winning their freedom. Just about literally ran into him – Kwadwo rounded the corner, and there he was, right outside the door. Kwadwo already had his blade out.

The guard didn't.

A moment later it was over, and fairly quietly. Kwadwo laid the dead man on the floor and beckoned Kwesi over. Kwesi opened the door to his inner sanctum and went through. Kwadwo followed, dragging the body. Kwadwo slumped the corpse over in the corner, eyeing it nervously. This one hadn't been bitten by a Gbohii – it shouldn't rise. But he'd seen too many dead men doing things they oughtn't be able to do, lately. It made him nervous to be around the dead.

He looked up. Kwesi was busy with something on the hearth. Fiddling with a statue of a kwapawnkah.

"Now what was so blasted important?" Kwadwo asked.

Kwesi didn't reply right away. Instead, he lifted the kwapawnkah free from the mantle and twisted the statue's base. It opened up, and a small key popped out. He turned they key over in his hand. Then he ran his fingers over the marble hearth, tracing the stone just under the mantle. He seemed to be looking for something and then paused. As Kwadwo watched, Kwesi slipped the key into a tiny crack in the stone and turned it.

The entire block had been cunningly crafted into a lockbox! Kwadwo was astonished. He'd never seen such fine work.

"I never knew you had this built here," Kwadwo said.

"I didn't. The man who built this palace did, a hundred years ago. I stumbled across the secret myself," Kwesi said.

The stone opened to reveal a small space inside, barely large enough for a book or small chest. Kwadwo peeked over Kwesi's shoulder and saw a small bag of fine black leather inside.

"This is why Lugu is here, Kwadwo. Somehow, she knew about my secret. Damn her."

"What secret?" Kwadwo reached out for the bag, and Kwesi didn't stop him. "What do you have in there that's worth risking your life? A few jewels?" Kwadwo lifted the bag, and it had something inside. Metal, from the weight. Coins? How much would gold be worth if the dead ruled the world?

Kwesi looked at Kwadwo, a wry smile on his face. "We've known each other a long time. Have you ever known me to get my thoughts addled by money? By cowries, jewels, or gold?" He still smiled, but Kwesi's eyes held reproach.

"No. Never." Kwadwo looked down at the bag. "So what...?"

"It was Etse's legacy, before he...before. And it might just save us all, now. But only if we can get it out of this place, away from his mad sister." Kwesi hastily shut the hiding place and secreted the key back in the statue. "Now, we can fly from here!"

But before they could leave, the door opened with a crash, all but flying from its hinges. Kwadwo turned to face the threat, his sword already in his hand. He saw Kwesi draw his own blade out of the corner of his eye and noticed that small bag he said was so important slip through the man's fingers to fall near Kwadwo's feet.

Kwadwo carefully placed his boot over the top of the bag, hiding it from sight.

Armed men poured into the room, swords drawn and at the ready. Four, eight, a dozen of them. And behind them came Lugu herself. She had a wicked smile from ear to ear. Kwadwo had the feeling they'd been in much better company when they were locked in a room with Okoth's Gbohii.

"Why father, it's wonderful to see you again so soon," she purred.

CHAPTER THIRTY-SEVEN

Diata ran her hands over the unfamiliar sword belt, her fingers playing with the leather, touching the heavy brass buckle, running at last to the hilt of the sword itself. It was so unlike the ones she'd used before. She'd been trained on short blades, like the spearman's short sword but thinner, lighter – faster. This sword was a cleaver in comparison. It was long, too long for tight formation fighting. Long enough to be used even from horseback, but still short enough to be easily carried in one hand by a strong man.

She was strong enough, but too short so she'd had to swing it with both hands in order to use it well during the fight. It wasn't a fighting style she was used to. Yet. She figured she would have plenty of practice in the days ahead.

"You'll wear that out, if you keep playing with the leather so," Magezi said, chuckling.

Diata blushed.

"I'm just glad to have it," she said. They only had five swords between everyone. Kudowor carried his, back behind with the rafts. Magezi and Musongola each wore one. Oyite had died in the battle at the temple, and his sword had gone to Isufu – who claimed to have some proficiency with the weapon, although privately Diata doubted that. He didn't look to have even the familiarity she had.

And the fifth had gone to her. She'd been a little surprised that the men had so readily agreed to let a woman keep one of their handful of weapons. But most people didn't carry swords. Most people had little understanding of the weapons beyond 'pointy end goes into the enemy.' So even the scant training her father had arranged for her made her far above someone with no training at all.

And besides that...

"You dealt with two of the things, my lady," Musongola said. His eyes smiled at her, even though his face remained serious. "One was...occupied."

She shuddered a little. It had been eating the man who'd once owned the sword and armor she now wore.

"But the other you slew in the middle of combat. Not many men can say they've beaten one of those things," he said. His eyebrows lifted. "I confess to curiosity about how you came by such skill with the weapon, but I am not about to second guess the good luck of having you here with us."

"My father taught me," she said. She dropped her eyes to her lap. She had no idea if the plague had reached Aburofasu yet or not. But it would. Her father would try to defend the place, but how could he prevail, when even Nicran's soldiers and the emperor's mercenaries had failed?

Musongola seemed to sense her distress, and didn't ask any more questions for a while. Diata let her thoughts return to the crew of their little vessel. Magezi seemed solid, confident. He was a big man, with a dome of black hair on his head and a beard to match. He was quiet but laughed when it was called for.

Isufu seemed more farmhand than soldier. He had short hair, and a deep tan to his sepia skin that spoke of long hours out in the sun. She wondered what he had done before the disaster in Nicran. She hoped he was good enough with that sword he carried.

The only man without a sword was an interesting one. He called himself Tay-Natey. He was slim, but his arms were corded muscle, and he'd clearly been used to battle. For weapons, he carried only a long dagger and a long bow, both of which he'd managed to keep safe while floating down the river all day. Diata wasn't sure how he'd managed to keep the bow above water, but she was glad he had. He'd put an arrow through the eye of one of the Gbohii in the battle at the temple. The man was an amazing shot. His accent sounded like he was from near her father's lands, in the northeast of Asanteman. But she had never met him before. An enigma.

And then Musongola... He still wore his tortoise shell armor, even out here in the deep water. If the boat tipped, he'd have a hard time struggling his way to shore, but the man seemed utterly without fear. He'd walked into the middle of the melee at the temple with no care to the consequences. There had been seven of the things, and he'd waded into them. Near as she could tell, he'd slain at least three of them himself, too. She'd never seen such swordsmanship, not even from the master who'd taught her. And her father hired the best.

Musongola looked up at her, and she realized she'd been staring too long at him. He smiled, and her pulse raced. Damn the man! She wasn't some peasant he could charm with a smile. She pulled her gaze away, casting it ahead, down the river.

***

Such an interesting woman! Musongola couldn't help but admire her. Not at all like the pretty faces that had thronged Okere's court. She wasn't just wearing that sword. He'd seen her use it, and he meant every word of the praise he gave her. He'd watched men with years of training fall in an instant to a single Gbohii. But she'd held her ground with seven of the things rushing at her! She wasn't lacking in courage.

He shook his head gently to clear it. He'd never travelled this river before, but he knew that they ought to be getting close to their destination.

"Isufu, you know this area at all?" he asked.

"Some," the man replied. "Not well." He spoke between breaths, his arms working hard at the oars. They'd been swapping in and out – right now, Isufu and Magezi were rowing. It would be his and Tay-Natey's turn next. In unspoken agreement, the men had not asked the lady to row. She was posted to lookout instead. She'd looked ready to protest more than once when they swapped seats. He'd seen it in her eyes. But she'd abated, and he was glad of it. It wasn't that she was weak – but she didn't have the arm strength to keep up with any of the men here, and they needed strong arms at those oars.

"We should be getting close, yes?" Musongola asked.

"Any time now, I think."

"Diata, keep a close eye out," Musongola said. "We don't know if we've beat the dead here or not. And we don't know what sort of reception we'll have, either way."

"I think we're almost there," she said. "The banks are growing further apart. We've almost made it to the Eternal Sea."

She was right. There was a lot more chop here than there had been, too. The little rowboat was fine for such water, although it might be a rough ride if the weather got any worse. But the rafts might have a tough time ahead.

"We'll stay close to the shore and watch for a settlement. Someplace we can stop, rest, and wait for the others. I think we want to be all together before we try crossing."

"Gebisa more risk on land than out here," Magezi said.

"At night? We could risk it in this boat, but the rafts could sink if a good gust came up. And the people will need food, besides," Musongola said.

"I'll watch for something promising," Diata said.

Already little fishing villages dotted the shores. But the boats were all gone. No fishing vessels were out in the river. It was late afternoon, but there ought to have been plenty of daylight left for work. Where were the people? Musongola examined the houses on the shore. Not a one had smoke rising from them. The weather was hot – no one was lighting fires for heat. But no one here was cooking dinner yet? He narrowed his eyes, watching for even the smallest sign the dead had been here already. But there were no torched buildings. No wandering Gbohii.

Then they rounded a corner in the river and found something at last. An entire village burned to the ground, and recently. Not a building was left standing. Every structure had burned to its foundations.

"What happened there?" Diata asked aloud. "Did the dead do that?"

"No," Magezi said, saying Musongola's thoughts aloud. "Too thorough. Too complete. Only men destroy everything like that."

"We'll pull in there. I want to see who did this," Musongola said. No one raised a protest. There were a hundred basically unarmed people coming down the river behind them. The sort of people who would burn an entire village to the ground might well murder every one of their refugees without a second thought. They needed to find out if the danger had passed by, or if whoever had done this was still nearby.

CHAPTER THIRTY-EIGHT

Etse came awake with a start. He tried to sit up quickly – he was lying on his back. But the instant he rose even the smallest bit, his head felt like it was splitting wide open. He had no choice but to lay back down with a weak groan.

He heard someone say, "You're awake, good. I'll bring the little girl." But he couldn't see the speaker without moving his head, and his neck didn't seem to want to cooperate with that operation. His hands would still move, so he carefully reached out, trying to feel more about where he lay.

He was on a straw pallet, with a rough wool blanket laid over him. His head was wrapped with some sort of cloth. On his left side, he felt raw stone. Unworked, unshaped, like the wall of a cave. His boots were gone, and he didn't feel his sword or scabbard near him. That jolted him to the core. It was frightening to be without a weapon again. That meant being helpless.

"Etse? Agboko said you were awake," Sefadzi's voice floated to him from somewhere nearby.

"I am," he replied, his voice a faint croak. "My neck is stiff. How long was I asleep?"

"Just a day," she said.

Another day lost! Kwesi would be well on his way to wherever he was going next. He'd never catch up, now. And they thought he was dead. There'd be no markers left, no way to easily find out where they'd gone. Etse was betting they'd head to Takoradi, though. It was home. His father had resources and people there. But Takoradi was a long way away, and there was no guarantee they'd risk the journey. They might have gone anywhere.

"Etse, are you OK?" Sefadzi asked, in a small voice.

"Aane," he said. "Just worried. Where are we?"

"Caves near the river," she said. "Through a forest and up a hill. Those people you helped were out gathering food. They have a lot of people here."

Etse slowly turned his head to face her. His neck still hurt, but it was getting better. "I'm glad you're safe."

"They almost didn't bring you," she said, her eyes fierce. "When you fell down, they wanted to leave you—"

Footsteps sounded behind her, and she stopped talking abruptly. Her eyes flashed a warning. Etse eyed the man entering the little chamber carefully. He'd learned to trust the girl's intuition.

He was middle aged, in good shape. He was balding a little, but he had a salt and pepper beard and mustache to make up for the loss. He was wearing armor. Mikijen tortoise shell, from the looks of it, with a Mikijen sword at his hip.

"One of General Okoth's men, I presume?" Etse asked.

"Aane. And you are Etse? Kwesi Panin's son?"

"Aane," Etse replied.

The man sat down on his haunches next to Etse's bed. "It's good to see another fighting man," he said. He smiled, though it didn't quite reach his eyes. Etse was willing to believe that might be from the stress of the past days. True happiness was thin on the ground for everyone.

"My name is Agboko Gbahbilah. I was a file leader in the Mikijen, yes. I was with the troops cut off in the camp when disaster befell Nicran."

Etse managed to sit up a little bit. He looked at the man with new curiosity. "We'd wondered what happened at the camp. We were trapped in the palace but hoped to make contact."

"Things went badly there," Agboko said, his face grim. "We had no walls. Just tents. They tore into the place. It was horrible."

"How did you escape?" Etse asked.

Agboko stood. "I didn't."

He paced across the room, gathering his thoughts. "I'd gotten drunk the night before and lost my temper. Hit another man. So I was on punishment detail."

Etse slowly hauled himself to an upright position. His head still hurt, his neck was outright painful. But he found that if he moved slowly, he could get around a little.

"I was north of the camp, digging a new set of latrines, when the Gbohii hit the place. Two hundred meters away, and I could hear the screams."

"So you ran," Etse said. He worked to keep his voice even, to hide the disgust he felt about a man who fled and left his fellows to die. He hadn't been there. He didn't have the right to judge. And yet Etse couldn't help but feel those things anyway. When it came to flight or fighting to help others, he'd struggled to always do the right thing. This man had turned tail at the first real danger.

"Aane, I ran! Stay and die, or run and maybe live? Damned right I ran. So did Ekpaka. He wasn't so lucky though. Died to one of the things the next day."

"But you've kept a group of people alive," Etse said, putting a smile on his face. "That's something good that's come out of it. Think, man – if you'd died alongside your fellow soldiers, how many of these people would still be here?"

Agboko's shoulders sagged. He looked down at his feet. "Thank you, Etse. I've told myself that, too. But it doesn't stop me from seeing their faces when I sleep." He looked back up at Etse, his face bleak.

The man was nearly broken. That he'd held these people together was a miracle. That he'd kept himself sane was even more of one. Etse had never seen men like this before, but he'd heard

Kwadwo talk about it. Survivor's guilt, the curse of still breathing when the battle is over and the dead are counted up.

"But now you're here," Agboko said. "You can help me keep these people safe."

"Aane, I can," Etse said. He winced, his headache starting to come back.

"You're still wounded," Agboko said. "Rest, for now. I'll give you a tour later, when you feel better." He turned and left the room.

Etse watched him go and looked from there to Sefadzi's face. The girl had been uncharacteristically quiet the entire time Agboko was in the room. Now she was staring out the exit Agboko had taken, her eyes wide, round, and alarmed.

She turned to Etse, and her eyes looked relaxed and normal again. Had he imagined it?

"Rest is good," she said. "Can I sleep here too?"

"Of course," Etse replied. She smiled and curled up next to him like a kitten. She was asleep almost instantly. Etse, bemused, took a little longer to drift off. His last thought as he went to sleep was that he'd forgotten to ask about his sword.

***

The cave system was large. And it had to be, for all the people it housed right now. Etse hadn't been able to get out of bed until the next day. But he woke early with his headache mostly gone. He still felt weak, but a breakfast of warm pap helped quite a lot with that.

Agboko was eager to show off his little domain. The room where Etse had slept was one of dozens. Scores of people were scattered through the little warren of caves. Here and there a few small holes in the ceiling provided light, but overall the roof of the place seemed sound enough. There were only two openings large enough for a man – or a Gbohii – to pass through. One, they'd blocked with a rock. The other was guarded night and day.

Etse looked out that opening now. The warm sun felt good on his face. The entrance was near the top of a little hillock in the forest. Over the tops of the trees, he could see the Densu River running, perhaps a mile away. A narrow trail winded its way down from the hill, through the forest.

"You've seen the whole of it, Etse. What do you think of our fortress?" Agboko said, smiling.

Etse returned the smile. "You did an excellent job finding such a place."

"And now, with you here, we can hold it if any of the cursed things happen upon us. And we can train some of the others to fight, too."

Etse walked out a few steps. As defensive positions went, the place wasn't bad. But his mind was already going over problems. He must have frowned, because when he looked back up at Agboko, the man was frowning as well.

"What's wrong?" Agboko asked.

"Honestly?" Etse replied. "Cold, wet season for one. You have nowhere to store enough wood, food, or water."

Agboko winced. "We've been working hard to gather supplies."

Etse held out his hands in a gesture of peace. "I am sure you have. But you just showed me your stockpiles. You're burning through it almost as fast as you're gathering it in, aren't you?"

Agboko sighed. "I know. We just need to work harder."

"And if you do gather enough to live through the cold, wet season, what happens next warm, wet season?"

Agboko looked baffled. "What do you mean?"

"Next warm, wet season," Etse said. "Man, think! We need to plan for a future here, not just live out the next day."

Agboko sat down on a large rock. His breath heaved out, and he rested his chin on his hands, elbows on his knees.

"Agboko, what you've done here is amazing," Etse said. And he meant it, too. Saving so many people was a great feat. Keeping them alive, finding them someplace relatively safe? Etse was impressed.

"Come with me to Takoradi," Etse continued. "Bring these people. We'll get them through, join my father there, and find a new home together."

Agboko stood up swiftly. "Leave here? To wander out there, and be eaten?" He laughed. "I think not. My people and I will stay right here. You may go if you want. But don't be a fool, Etse. Stay here. You can help me keep order. Keep them safe."

Etse stared at the man. He'd already explained why staying was foolish. Why was Agboko so dead set on these caves? Etse winced. His headache was starting to return, a slow pulsing ache in his temple.

"At least stay until you are healed," Agboko said. "And consider my offer. You could be my right hand. Together we could build upward and outward from here."

Etse nodded, tired. "I need to rest, clearly. I'll think about your offer, Agboko." He needed time to figure out what was going on here, and what to do next. But the longer he was here, the more Etse was certain he wanted to be gone.

CHAPTER THIRTY-NINE

Kwesi hoped he'd seen the last of Lugu when he'd married her off to a Haisetti *gooftaa* (lord) in Haiset, in northeast Ki Khanga. Obviously, she had other ideas. She'd always been a willful child. She'd grown into a nightmare of a young woman, and her temperament hadn't improved any with her years in exile.

"Drop your swords," Lugu said.

"You heard her," Kwesi said to the men accompanying Lugu. "She said to drop your weapons."

"Cute," Lugu said. "But we really don't need you both alive, you know. Kill that one." She nodded at Kwadwo. Three of the guards stepped forward to cut him down. Kwadwo raised his blade, his face grim.

"Stop," Kwesi said, stepping in front of the guards. He slowly set his sword down on the floor. "We'll disarm."

Kwadwo raised an eyebrow at him. Kwesi nodded firmly to him. There was no way they could escape, not right now, not fighting through all these men. What mattered most was that one of them got away with the contents of that bag. Which meant biding their time. Kwadwo bent over slowly and set his own sword on the floor. While he knelt to place the weapon carefully on the floor, Kwesi saw him slide something into his boot.

The bag. Smart man. Kwesi was sure no one else had seen the movement.

"So, Lugu. What now?" Kwesi asked.

"Now you show me what you came in here to acquire," she replied.

Kwesi wondered how the hell she'd heard about the legacy stores. He'd set things aside in there around two decades ago – right after Etse was born, when it had first become clear that Kiswala would eventually have to withdraw its troops. Lugu couldn't possibly have seen something then, could she? She was all of six years old at the time. She was a precocious child, but that seemed a little much even for her.

Maybe she was bluffing?

"Just hoping to find a little of my reserve money, to help us when we got out," Kwesi said. "You're welcome to whatever is left in here."

The guards seemed interested. Lugu didn't. She stalked forward, eyes hot, coming almost nose to nose with him.

"Father. You and I both know that what you were looking for here was much, much nicer than that." She ran a long fingernail down his cheek. He twitched a little. Couldn't help himself. She smiled when she saw that she'd bothered him with the gesture and brought her hand back up to repeat it.

Kwesi caught her wrist in his hand. "Child, if you insist on calling me father, then do act the part of the daughter. Obey me."

She laughed, the sound high and wild. She ripped her hand free from his grasp. He didn't try hard to hold on.

"Obey you? But as you're so fond of saying, you're not my father. Not really, anyway."

"No. I married your mother. I did try to be a father to you, Lugu. You were never good about letting anyone in."

"Lies," she hissed in his face. "My father died in battle with your men. And then you took my mother away from me."

Kwesi sighed heavily. It wasn't that simple, he wanted to say. Her father had rebelled against the rightful rule of law. He had no choice but to put down the rebellion. Her mother Nai might have died as well, as a conspirator. But she'd been a friend of Kwesi's since childhood. He'd managed to get her spared the executioner's block by marrying her.

None of that mattered to this girl. She'd been living in hate, bathed in it, clothed herself daily in it, for so long that nothing existed but meting out the punishment she felt he deserved. Kwesi looked around at these men, these sell-swords who served her. None of them seemed ready to hesitate. If she ordered him dead, they'd kill him in an instant.

"Lugu, I loved your mother. We had a good marriage. I tried to be a father to you. I'm sorry I failed," Kwesi said.

For a moment, Kwesi wasn't sure if she'd scream at him or break down crying. The woman seemed dangerously unstable. She'd always been a bit mad – but this was far outside her norm. What in the Cleave had happened to her in Haiset?

Mercurial as ever, she had neither reaction he'd expected. Her face calmed, grew almost serene. "If you won't give it to me willingly," she said, "perhaps I can find some other way to get you to tell me what I need to know."

She turned her back on Kwesi, then, and walked out the door.

"Bring them to the throne room," she said as she left.

The guards seized Kwadwo and Kwesi by the arms, while others held swords at their backs, and marched them from the room.

The throne room was the old main hall of the estate – a big dining room, now made into an audience chamber. Lugu was already seated on the throne down at the far end of the hall by the time the guards brought them in. And her pets still stood on either side of her throne – two Gbohii, a chain running from the wall to a collar around each of their necks.

"Bring Kwesi to me," Lugu called out.

The guards hauled him forward until he was standing in front of her. Then one of them kicked the back of his knees. He fell forward, his knees slamming painfully into the stone floor. Kwesi let out a grunt. He weighed too damned much and was too damned old. This was going to be very unpleasant.

Before he recovered from the fall, the guards grabbed his left ankle and fastened a manacle there. Kwesi looked down at the thing. It was simple iron, with a lock fastening the cuff. From the cuff dangled a chain – thin, but perhaps two dozen feet long.

"What is this, Lugu?" he asked, holding up a bit of the chain.

"Your inspiration to give me what I want," she replied. Then she nodded to one of the guards. The guard picked up the far end of the chain. Kwesi could see the man was sweating. Two other guards came forward with large spears with crossbars. They went to one of Lugu's pet Gbohii and stabbed it with their spears.

The thing shrieked, then hissed, trying vainly to reach the men who'd stabbed it. It tried to pull itself up their spears, but the crossbars stopped it cold. Grunting with the effort, the men pushed the thing back against the wall.

The man holding the chain dashed forward then, to the steel ring set into the wall. He ran the chain through the ring. Then, still holding the end, he ran back out until he was standing next to Kwesi, panting.

The spearmen backed away, then, carefully stepping back together until the monster was free, lashing out at the air from the end of its chain.

"You've done this before, I see," Kwesi said, standing back up. He tried to keep his voice light, but he was sweating. The chain which ran from the manacle on his ankle now ran through the steel ring on the wall – the same ring the Gbohii was chained to.

The guard holding the end of his chain grinned at him and gave the chain an experimental tug. Kwesi fell flat on his tail, his leg dragged out from beneath him. The man pulled again, and Kwesi was dragged forward a few more inches.

"Oh yes, we've done this with a few people. It makes for wonderful examples. Show the common folks a few people eaten alive, one bite at a time, and the rest fall nicely into line," Lugu said. She nodded to the guard, who hauled the chain again, dragging Kwesi closer to the thing.

"Now, where is the key, father?"

Kwesi kept silent.

The man holding his chain pulled again. Kwesi dug his fingers into the stone, trying to hold his place, but there simply wasn't enough to hold on to. He had the Gbohii's attention now. It stood at the end of its chain, dripping blood from the spear wounds, slavering and gnashing its teeth. It flailed its arms, then fell to hands and knees, trying to pull itself free. Trying to get to Kwesi. Its hands were only a few feet from his ankle now.

"Tell me where, father. Then I can let you go."

Kwesi glared daggers at her. "You'd just kill me as soon as I told you, anyway. Get on with it."

The chain dragged him another foot. The Gbohii's fingers were just touching his boot, questing, trying to grab hold and not quite being able to... Kwesi pulled hard, trying in vain to yank his leg back away from the thing.

"No, I don't need to kill you. I can lock you away. Send you elsewhere. Exile you, like you did to me," Lugu said. She'd gotten up from her throne, drifted next to him. Whispering in his ear, she said, "I don't have to kill you to destroy you, father. But I will if you make me."

Kwesi sighed. He looked deeply into Lugu's eyes, seeking some scrap of...anything there that might give him the smallest hope. But he saw nothing in her but madness. Her thirst for revenge had overwhelmed her, eaten her alive from within.

"If I thought there was even the slightest chance you might use the legacy to preserve our people, I would offer it to you," Kwesi said, knowing as he said the words that he would die for them. "But you and I both know you would never do that. It's not in your nature."

Lugu stood quickly. She took two steps, to where the guard had the chain, and took a length of it in her hands.

"Not in my nature?" she said, sarcasm dripping from her voice. "I'll show you my nature, father!"

She yanked on the chain.

Kwesi slid another foot closer.

The Gbohii locked claws about his leg, pulling him closer to it. Two more guards grabbed him by the arms to prevent it dragging him all the way into its embrace. But it already had his ankle, and his leg. It sank its teeth into his calf, tearing a chunk of the flesh away.

The pain was excruciating. Kwesi screamed.

The Gbohii kept chewing.

Kwesi lost track of the pain, somewhere. The guards didn't let it drag him any closer, so it kept gnawing on what it had in its hands. He knew he was losing blood badly, could feel the rushing of his heartbeats in his ears.

"Pull him back," Lugu said. "Bind his wound."

Kwesi lay on the cold stone, the world spinning. He was fairly sure he had stopped screaming. Why was he still hearing screams? And then he saw he wasn't the only one hearing them. Lugu and the guards all looked up toward the closed doors at the far end of the hall.

"Find out who that is and kill him," Lugu said irritably. She stood over Kwesi, glaring down at him. "Now you'll tell me what I need, if only to get the service of a clean death. Or you can rot on one of these chains as my newest pet. Your choice."

Kwesi saw her men open the big double doors, to find the source of the screams. As soon as the door opened, the Gbohii stormed into the room. Two of them, side by side. One of them ripped out the throat of the man who'd opened the door. The other jumped onto the chest of another sell-sword, biting and gouging.

Ah, yes. The two guards who'd been killed by Okoth's Gbohii during their escape from the cell.

"About time," Kwesi muttered.

The guards were all running to face the dead, now. Nobody was paying any attention to Kwesi. Not that they needed to. He tried to sit up and failed. He wasn't going anywhere. Too much blood lost, and not much point. His fate was set.

Then Kwadwo was there, kneeling next to him. "Oh, God," he said, staring at the wound on Kwesi's leg. The horror and pity in his eyes were almost worse than the pain from the damned wound.

"Kwadwo, enough. Too late for me," Kwesi rasped out. "You have the key?"

"Aane."

"Keep it safe. It was for Etse, but... Lugu must not get it."

"I will."

"It opens a vault at Kamit. Stockpiles." Kwesi sucked breath through his teeth. God, his leg hurt so much. "Set aside for time of need. Armor, weapons, food. Enough for an army."

Kwadwo's eyes grew wide. "Damn."

"Just so," Kwesi said. "That key is the only way to open the vault. I have paid a sizeable yearly tribute to Ipet-Isut University to keep the stockpile. That key might be the most valuable item in Asanteman right now."

"We'll keep it safe," Kwadwo said. "Let's get you out of here now."

Kwesi closed his eyes, shaking his head slowly. "Nothing else you can do for me. Go. Press the red brick on the wall behind her damned throne to open a secret door."

"I'll keep it away from her," Kwadwo said. "Kwesi – take this." He pressed something into Kwesi's hand.

A small knife.

Kwesi stared down at the tiny blade. It meant freedom – without it, he'd become one of those slavering monsters. But it might as well be a thousand miles away. "I am too weak to do what needs to be done." He barely had the strength to hold it. "Can you, my friend?"

Kwadwo took the knife back, his face wretched with pain. Kwesi reached out his right hand. Kwadwo clasped his forearm – a gesture of friendship, and of farewell. Kwesi looked into Kwadwo's tear-streaked eyes and felt his own eyes well up. Kwadwo was a good man. He'd been a good friend. Kwesi wanted to say all that and so much more, but he felt his strength failing him, so he closed his eyes instead. He felt Kwadwo place the sharp tip of the blade against his temple. There was one brief moment of stabbing pain, and then he was free.

CHAPTER FORTY

Diata jumped into the water as soon as they reached the shallows. The water came to her knees, and she was suddenly very glad she'd traded out her skirt for pants back at the temple. She grabbed hold of the rope tied to the prow and hauled.

She wasn't sure if she ought to feel resentful of the men taking on the rowing, or grateful. It was a mixed blessing. She could feel in her gut that being the weak link in any group would be a bad thing in the days ahead. But her hands would have been torn to shreds by those oars. She wasn't used to that sort of work, and she would need her hands to hold a sword if it came to fighting again. When it came to fighting again, she corrected herself. For there was no doubt in her mind that it would.

She salved her conscience by hauling the boat closer to shore. Magezi jumped down a moment after her and splashed alongside her to help. Together they brought the rowboat up onto a small bit of sand on the river's bank. Judging by the gouges in the sand this was where the fishermen from the burned village had pulled their own boats into the river. But there was no sign of them now. Just the gutted ruin of houses, smoke still drifting from some of them, and the stink of charred wood and burnt meat.

Musongola stepped off the bow of the boat and into the sand. "Weapons ready, all of you," he said. "Watch yourselves."

Diata drew her sword, trying to keep it in the one handed grip she was used to. It remained just a shade too heavy. She'd have to go to a two handed grip again if things got nasty. The sand shifted under her feet, and she found herself fighting for balance more than once before she made her way to the packed dirt beyond. She wasn't the only one slowed by the sand, which made her feel a little better.

The smells were getting stronger. Both the wood and…the burnt meat smell. She found herself truly hoping that the smell was coming from dead animals, or Gbohii someone had burned. But her roiling gut was telling her something different.

Magezi reached the first house before the rest of them. He prodded the rubble with his foot, then backed away. "Still hot," he said. He kept his voice low, so the words didn't carry far. "Wasn't long ago."

They continued to search the place, although Diata wasn't really sure what it was they were looking for. Whatever had happened here might not have been long ago, but the people who'd done it seemed to be gone. Once, Tay-Natey knelt by a set of kwapawnkah tracks. He looked to be counting, then held up all five fingers of his right hand to Musongola, flashing them three times. Fifteen? Fifteen what? Kwapawnkah?

"Night is coming," she said, at last. "We ought to be seeking food and shelter for the folk still on the river before they arrive."

"You're right," Musongola said. "We've learned all we can from this place." She saw him grimace, his face a mask of anger for a moment.

Her own face must have revealed her confusion, because he stepped closer to her and took her aside a little. "We have learned a great deal from this stop, my lady. We know that men burned this town. We know they killed everyone here – burned alive over in that gutted temple there. Or close enough to everyone, as best we can tell. We know there were about fifteen of them. And they used the gear of Mikijen."

"How?"

He raised an eyebrow. Then he quirked a small, grim smile. "Sadly, Magezi, Tay-Natey, and I have seen this sort of thing before."

"I see," she said, her mind working on this new information, churning through it. "So, who? The garrison?"

"Possible. But why would they burn the village? There's no sign of Gbohii. I don't understand it."

"And that worries you," she said. It wasn't a question.

"Aane, that worries me."

They walked back over to the smoldering remains of the town, far too close to the skeletal remains of a temple that Diata now knew housed the unburied dead. How many people lay there? They hadn't been her people – not the folk her father ruled, and who counted on her family for protection. But they were people, nonetheless. Horror warred with fury, and fury was winning.

"Tay-Natey and Isufu have gone back to the shore to watch for the rafts," Magezi said.

"Good," Musongola replied. "We'll join them. We need to look for some place with shelter. We'll take the boat back out and out move on. This is not a good place to stay."

The walk back to the boat was a silent one. They could see the other two seated in the boat, the boat already pulled back from the shore and drifting in the shallows. Diata felt the solid dirt shift into crunching sand under her feet again. She swore a little under her breath.

The men on the boat saw them coming when they were still about twenty feet away. To Diata, they looked incredibly tense, even at this distance. Wired taut, like that bowstring Tay-Natey always carried. But he wasn't carrying it now.

She realized something was wrong a moment before Tay-Natey shouted "Trap!" from the bow of the boat.

Musongola swore, pulling his sword back free from the sheath and taking long strides onto the beach. Diata heard arrows whistle through the air. Saw one hit Isufu in the belly. He fell back into the rowboat. Another struck Tay-Natey in the head, knocking him off the boat and into the water.

Diata heard a sound behind her and tried to turn. Her foot caught in the sand and she fell face-first into the stuff. The fall saved her life. Another arrow whistled through the air where her head had been. She pulled her sword free and staggered to one knee.

All around the beach, men in ringed-leather armor were pouring out onto the sand. One swung his sword downward at her like a cleaver. She raised her own and parried, but the force of the blow almost drove her back to the ground.

She heard Musongola and Magezi fighting, somewhere behind her. Swords clanged against one another. Men were screaming. The soldier in front of her grimaced then snarled as he raised his weapon for another blow. She raised her sword with both hands and chopped hard at his leg, down below where his armor covered. The blade bit deep and he fell over, howling and clutching at his leg.

Bright red covered her blade. She got to her feet, turned to face back toward the others. Magezi had reached the boat. He was hauling Tay-Natey from the water, tossing him into the boat before climbing in himself. Musongola was trying to fight his way through to her. But there were at least five men between them! Diata gritted her teeth and rushed toward them. She'd take them from one side, while Musongola fought them from the other. She raised her sword, slashing down at the neck of the man in front of her. She didn't cleave his head from his shoulders, but bright red splashed upwards in a spray from the wound, and he went down.

Musongola had killed one, too. Just another few fighters to cut down and she'd be back with him, and they could run to the boat.

Then something struck her in the head from behind. She felt an instant of blinding pain, and then nothing.

CHAPTER FORTY-ONE

Two more days went by before Etse felt strong enough to go outside. The warm sun felt good on his face; the fresh air, scented strongly of the deep woods, was welcome after days in the musty cave system. He had to remind himself that he wasn't on vacation out here. Agboko had asked him to go watch over some of the men and women when they went out to gather firewood.

"May I have my sword back?" Etse asked, careful to keep his voice polite. Something about Agboko's manner was still setting off Sefadzi. And strange as the child was, Etse trusted her sense about things.

"Of course," Agboko replied with a smile that seemed a little too broad to be genuine. But he handed over the sword. It was the same one – the one Kwadwo had given him, back in Nicran. Having the length of steel back in his hand did much to restore Etse's confidence.

And now he was out here, walking alongside people as they filled their arms with sticks and fallen branches. He kept his ears and eyes open, alert for the smallest sound which might indicate nearby Gbohii. They were far from major settlements in these woods, but that was no guarantee of safety.

"Why not just fell a few nearby trees?" Etse asked one older man.

"That would be much faster, me wura," he replied. "But we've no axes, and no saws." He wandered away, then, to pick up more deadfall.

Without tools, they'd never be able to secure enough wood to stay alive over the cold, wet season – let alone gather enough food and find means to store it all. Etse pursed his lips. Agboko should have been leading forays into the nearby towns, dangerous as it might be, to seek out tools. Even a quick visit to an abandoned farm or two might give them everything they needed. But the man seemed terrified to leave his hilltop.

A rustling in the bushes down the hill a ways caught Etse's attention. His head snapped around just a moment before a terrified scream broke the relative silence. Etse had his sword in his hand quick as thinking of it and bounded down the hill in short leaps.

He broke through a wall of greenery and nearly tripped over the Gbohii. It was on all fours, straddling a woman while it chewed on her belly. Its face and hands were crimson; her hands and belly were the same.

The thing looked up at him from its prey, but before it could do more than react to his presence, his sword detached its head from its body. The head rolled to the ground a few feet away, gnashing teeth at the air. Etse crushed it under his boot.

More people were gathering around, trying to console the woman, comfort her, quiet her. Nothing was working – her screams were loud enough to wake the dead.

Or call them.

"Get her back up the hill, and quiet her quickly!" Etse said. "Gag her if you have to!" He kept his sword out.

"Have some pity!" a woman called out angrily. "Can't you see she is dying?"

"My sister, the rest of us will die as well, if her screams call more of those things down on us. Quiet her!" Etse snapped.

The protesting woman got very pale. The man who had spoken with Etse earlier about the lack of tools came forward with a stick and put it in the hurt woman's mouth.

"Bite down," he said. She did, and the screams abated.

"Get her back up there," Etse said. "We need to move, now!"

It was a short walk back to the caves, and everyone went as quickly as they could. Four people carried the injured woman, and most of the others simply ran back uphill as swiftly as their legs could carry them.

So Agboko was already waiting there by the entrance before Etse arrived.

"Damn it!" he shouted. "You were supposed to protect them!"

"I'm sorry. I tried, but – in the woods, and so many people. She was out of my sight."

Agboko scratched his head, clearly worried. "They've never come up so far. Why are they coming after us now?"

Etse sighed, sinking down onto a large stone. He kept one eye watching the slope just in case more of the Gbohii tracked them. But it seemed like none had. "I don't know that they are coming after you. I think they are just spreading out, wandering aimlessly in search of prey."

"But how can we stay safe?"

"Here?" Etse shook his head. "Agboko, I don't think this place is safe. It was fine for a brief respite. But we have to get these people someplace more permanent."

The soldier stood, staring out over the woods. Etse watched his shoulders shake a little and then relax. "No," Agboko said. "I don't see or hear any more of them out there. And if any had been there, they would have come calling, after all of those screams."

"I think you're likely right. For today. But what about tomorrow and the day after?"

Agboko whirled, then, his eyes narrowing as he examined Etse closely. "Why are you so all fired up to leave here? Tired of not being in charge, Etse? Bored without troops to order around?"

Etse blinked. Had he ever been like that? He'd maybe ordered around servants and the like, but whenever he'd been on patrol, Kwadwo had kept a hawk's eye on him. Order around the soldiers? He thought back to the days in Nicran. How long ago they seemed, now. He had ordered men around, then. He'd given orders, but taken them, too. He'd tried to make things work. Instead, they'd gone horribly wrong, but he felt like he'd done his best there.

"Agboko, you're in charge. I've never questioned that," Etse said cautiously. "But these are your people. Surely you want to see them safe?"

"They are safe!" Agboko all but shouted this. Some of his people were back a ways in the corridor, whispering to one another. "I make them safe!"

Etse sucked in a breath. This was what Sefadzi had sensed in the man. Agboko's hands shook. His face was red, his eyes just a little wild. Etse could tell the man was near ready to draw steel against him. He was mad, in a way that wasn't evident at the start but showed when he was pushed.

"I think," Etse said, keeping his voice very soft, "that it's time for me to take my leave of your hospitality."

"You may go whenever you'd like," Agboko spat. "But leave your sword. I won't have good steel lost because a fool boy ran off into the woods."

"I don't think so," Etse said. He kept his voice just as soft as it had been but allowed the beginning of an edge to leak into his tone. Leave without his sword? The man was utterly mad. He might as well slit his wrists here and now.

Agboko drew his own blade. A lurid grin split his face, a mockery of a smile. He laid the tip of his sword at Etse's chest.

"Just leave the sword, boy," Agboko said.

Etse drew his own sword in a short arc, knocking aside Agboko's weapon.

"Don't do this, Agboko," he said. He had no wish to kill the man. But he would not allow himself to be disarmed, either.

"You're fast, boy," he replied. "But I've had a blade in my hand longer than you've been alive. Just leave the sword. It's not worth your life."

Etse felt his own fury rise to match that of the man facing him. His heart sang with the fierce fire he always felt in combat. But in the back of his head, he could hear another voice. That voice belonged to Kwadwo, who was telling him – it's just a sword, boy, not worth a man's life.

Not even this worthless wretch?

Not even him, the Kwadwo-in-his-mind agreed.

Briefly, Etse warred with himself. It would feel so much better to cut this bastard down to size. He could do it without hurting him – much, anyway. And it would feel very good. Plus, being without a sword out there would put him at a lot more risk. But hurting this man might doom all these other people. Even if Etse slew Agboko, would the people who followed the man want to trust him? After he'd slain their savior? He didn't think so. They'd try to stay here, and so he'd have killed them all.

That he couldn't do. He sighed and set Kwadwo's sword down carefully on the cave floor, careful not to muss the blade.

"You may have the sword," Etse said. "Sefadzi and I will be leaving now."

He turned to go. It was still early enough in the day outside that he could get them someplace safe by evening. He'd whiled away too many days in this place, anyway. Who knew where his father, Kwadwo, and the others were by now? They might already be at Takoradi. Etse doubted they would stay there long, though. Takoradi would suffer the same fate as Nicran. It was too big, too impossible to hold.

"Etse, look out!"

He was moving before Sefadzi finished her shout. Etse pivoted hard on one foot, saw the blur of motion bearing down on him. A sword flashed, sweeping in an arc toward his head. He raised his forearm and took the blow on a bracer, metal splints fending away the blade. The impact jarred his wrist to the bone, but nothing felt broken.

It was Agboko, wild-eyed, sword in hand. The man swung again, and the blow would have taken Etse's head off if he hadn't ducked under it. He turned the duck into a rolling dive, turning over one shoulder to land near where he'd dropped his sword. He snatched the blade from the floor and finished the roll on his feet, parrying another attack.

"Agboko, stop!" Etse said. "This is madness!"

Agboko kept coming wordlessly, one blow raining down after another. Etse was fending him off, but fast as he was, he couldn't keep this up forever. Sooner or later, one of the blows would get past his guard if he remained on the defensive.

His attacker was leaving huge holes in his own defense, though. Etse blocked an attack with his blade and snapped a punch into Agboko's nose with his empty hand. The blow sent Agboko staggering back, and he cracked his head against the cave wall. Etse didn't relent. Time to end this. He circled his blade around Agboko's own sword, and with a deft flip Etse forced the weapon from his hand.

The sword clattered against stone. Agboko sank to his knees, sobbing for breath.

Etse closed the distance between them in a single stride. He grabbed Agboko by the front of his collar, yanked his head up so that he could see the man's eyes.

"You madman. You could have killed me, just now," Etse said. "I ought to kill you."

He held his sword high, and for a long moment he was sorely tempted. Agboko was trouble and left to live he'd likely bring heartache for someone else. But his eyes were like empty pools. Etse realized the man had seen too many dark things, and unable to take them in or turn them aside, he'd simply broken.

Etse shoved him to the ground and sheathed his sword. Sefadzi ran to his side and hugged his leg.

"Thanks for the timely warning, my sister," he said, smiling down at her and ruffling her hair. She beamed back at him.

"Don't try to follow us," Etse warned. "Not any of you. You've made your bed. Good luck with it." Then he guided Sefadzi from the caves and the madman who ruled them. They were on their way back into the daylight.

CHAPTER FORTY-TWO

The barge rocked gently under his feet as Kudowor paced back and forth. He cursed roundly. "Taken! Taken where?"

"I don't know," Musongola replied.

Kudowor looked Musongola over and decided not to take him to task over it. He was clearly already beating himself up enough. He'd never seen the man so miserable. Musongola wasn't someone used to failure, and it obviously didn't sit well with him. He looked...worn. Haggard even. What was with the man? Kudowor could ill afford to have him fall apart now.

The barges caught up with Musongola's scout team only a short while after their disastrous encounter. Lacking a safe spot to land, they found a sandbar near the middle of the channel and dropped anchor. Then they reeled all the rafts in close to one another. Nobody was feeling very good about the arrangement. There were too many people in too small a space to be comfortable, and they weren't really safe, either. The dead could come walking up from the depths onto the sandbar any time. Kudowor's men kept a constant lookout. One of the things getting loose among them could be fatal to everyone.

"It was a scouting mission, Musongola. We both knew it would be dangerous. That's why I sent you with your hand-picked team. How are the rest of them?"

Musongola shook his head as if to clear it. Something new to focus on seemed to help him get himself together. "Magezi wasn't hurt, and he hauled Tay-Natey back into the boat before he could drown. The arrow hit Tay-Natey's helmet, knocked him out – but he'll be fine. Isufu..."

"Died earlier this evening of his wound. I know," Kudowor said, picking up where Musongola trailed off. "Which leaves us back to the question of Diata. Are you sure she wasn't killed?"

"Fairly sure. I doubt they'd have bothered hauling her corpse away, and she wasn't there when we snuck back in to look."

Kudowor sat down, staring up at the stars. They were keeping no fires on the boat. With dangers both living and dead likely haunting the shoreline, Kudowor had no intention of announcing their presence.

But the result was a staggering display of light across the sky. Simply beautiful, like someone had taken a handful of diamonds and tossed them out on display, each one sparkling with a fierce inner light. Moments like this opened a conflict in his heart; because seeing such beauty made him glad to be alive, but at the same time despairing of ever feeling like his life had value against such grandeur.

"Kudowor, I don't know where precisely those men have taken her, because I don't know the land here well. But I do know something about them," Musongola said.

"Aane?"

"I recognized the faces of a couple of them."

Kudowor stared at Musongola, trying to see his expression in the dark. "You knew them? How is that possible?"

"They were Rwamirama's men."

"Shit," Kudowor said. "You're sure?"

He'd only had a couple of run-ins with Rwamirama, but the man had been a piece of work. Cold as a snake, which was Kudowor's take on him. That said – he'd never been accounted for in the last day of the siege. He hadn't gotten out down the river with Kwesi and Okere. But he'd struck Kudowor as being a survivor. It wouldn't really be a stretch to imagine him having somehow escaped with some of his men.

"Very sure," Musongola replied. "And they were Mikijen-equipped, too."

"There's a garrison on one of the islands down the river a bit. It's where we were hoping to go for supplies, weapons, armor. I'm going to bet Rwamirama knew about it, too," Kudowor said.

Which was going to cause a major problem for them. They'd been counting on resupply from that fort. But worse, the spot was perfectly positioned to watch all river traffic. That's why it had been placed on the island in the first place. There was no way they could drift past on their little rafts without being spotted, except at night – and daring the tides at the mouth of the Densu River at night in makeshift rafts would be suicide.

"If Rwamirama is there, he'll be interested in meeting with us," Musongola said. "And if we can bluff, so much the better."

"Tomorrow, then. But we'll need to be careful. If he catches wind that we're bluffing..."

"I've known the man a long time," Musongola replied. "You're not wrong. He cannot find out."

"Then we'll be sure he does not."

***

Musongola stood in the prow of the little boat, looking outward toward the island ahead. It was more of a large rock than a proper island, or maybe a jumble of rocks tossed into a pile. The fort rising from those stones looked almost like it had been made from them, like some odd growth of the stone itself. Of course, it wasn't. Human hands had shaped those stones. Nothing from nature would cause towers to spin up from the bare rock like that.

It wasn't abandoned, either. Musongola could see the lookouts posted to the tower top. He watched one of them scurry down into the bowels of the fort. To report their advance, no doubt. He kept an eye on the other one just in case he had a bow and more guts than sense.

"I hope this works," Magezi said under his breath. He'd been grumbling ever since Musongola picked him for the foray out to the island. But he'd been an obvious choice, and he knew it. They were short on fighting men, but Rwamirama absolutely could not have that piece of information. So they needed something like a show of force.

Kudowor wanted to come, for the same reason: more fighting men on the boat would look good. But Musongola had pointed out that they wanted Rwamirama to think that Okere was in direct charge of their group. If Musongola started deferring to Kudowor's orders, it would tip their hand.

Besides, leaving all their civilians with no armed men seemed a bad idea. If things went terribly wrong in this meeting, at least they'd still have someone there to keep them alive.

The ghost of a smile traced across Musongola's lips. That last suggestion hadn't made Kudowor like the idea any better. But he'd agreed, and so it had been Magezi and Tay-Natey who made the trip back out with him.

"It will work," Musongola said. "Rwamirama will know me. He'll be curious."

He was fairly sure that he was right. Rwamirama would bring them in. No harm doing so. He clearly had enough men to overwhelm a little boat with three people in it. But how they were going to get Diata away from him after they were there, he wasn't sure.

Magezi and Tay-Natey kept rowing, and they closed the gap to the isle at a steady pace. Closer up, the place looked even more bare, less habitable. Nothing grew from those gray rocks. Which made it an absolutely terrible place to pick as a base in these times, at least from Musongola's point of view. You might survive for a while by raiding the countryside for your supplies, but what then? What did you do when those supplies ran out? They needed more lasting solutions, and a bare island without even grass wasn't the answer.

He wished he had a better one. But this place – it looked more like a tomb to him, than a home.

"Looks like there's a welcoming committee waiting for us," Tay-Natey drawled.

Men were pouring out of the front gates, forming ranks. Spearmen – and archers. Musongola grinned.

"A show of force," he said.

"Oh, like us?" Magezi asked.

"Aane," Musongola replied.

"I'd like our show of force to have as many men as theirs, next time," Magezi said.

Musongola laughed.

Keeping his mind busy helped, but despite everything going on around him, he kept worrying about Diata. Was she still alive? Had these men hurt her? Rwamirama had a reputation for running a tight ship in terms of discipline, but soldiers were not always good at treating prisoners well. Her face kept coming back to haunt him, all last night. Even in the snatches of sleep he managed, she still floated there in his mind. He watched her brought down over and over while he slept, each time his imagination painting the image more violently than the last, until he finally gave up on sleep altogether.

Damn it all, he knew he fancied the woman a bit – she was tough, and strong, and had guts. But he'd never been so worried about anyone. He struggled to bring his mind back to bear on the mess they were in. Musongola needed a clear head today. He couldn't afford to let Rwamirama see his concern for Diata, or Rwamirama would know that he had a weapon in his hands.

They were within bow range and not yet peppered with arrows. He took that as a good sign. Cupping his hands to his mouth, he called out, "Hail the fort! We come in the name of Emperor Okere!"

He saw some of the men on the shore shift a little uncomfortably at his words. Good. He was reaching them. These people had been Kiswalan mercenaries for many long years. The ideas of discipline and obedience to the Empire were paramount, even in dark times like these.

He scanned the shore, but didn't see Rwamirama. He did see some of the men hastily conferring, and one ran back inside the fort.

"Rwamirama will be coming out shortly," Musongola said.

But he was wrong. Rwamirama was still nowhere to be seen as they came in against the dock. There were three other vessels here – two long rowboats tied to the same dock their boat approached, and one even larger sailing ship, moored a little off the shore. The latter was only perhaps forty feet long, not a huge vessel. But it might suffice for Kudowor's refugees – if only they could find a way to acquire it!

No other boats were visible anywhere nearby. And Musongola had been watching. He'd seen burnt hulks near the shore, here and there. Rwamirama had been having his men burn every boat within range.

Which made sense, really. The fort was isolated. It looked like rock dropped off sharply on the sides, so there would be few approaches for Gbohii to walk ashore. The only way to reach the island was by boat, swimming, or by a pontoon bridge that the fort could always burn or cut loose.

Musongola found himself having to rethink his earlier position on the fort. The supply situation was still poor. But if they could acquire supplies somehow, then the fort would be fairly safe from Gbohii attacks, and easy to hold against anything but a large, concerted force.

The boat bumped against the wooden dock, breaking into his thoughts. None of the men on the shore moved to help them. They stood, two ranks of soldiers, waiting.

"A poor greeting, for the emperor's servants," Musongola remarked. He sprang from the boat up onto the dock. Magezi tossed him a line, and he tied it off.

"Tay-Natey, keep the boat safe, would you?" Musongola asked. Tay-Natey patted the bow next to him and smiled. Musongola had recovered the long bow from one of the men he'd slain on the beach yesterday. The soldiers had ambushed Tay-Natey and Isufu and used them as bait for the rest of the party. But Musongola had seen one of them holding Tay-Natey's bow. He'd cut the man down, and recognizing the weapon, snatched it up. Tay-Natey thought he'd lost it and had been beside himself when Musongola presented the bow back to him.

"Magezi, you're with me," Musongola said.

"Of course, I get to go do the dangerous stuff," Magezi grumbled. But he hauled himself out of the boat and joined Musongola on the dock.

They made it as far as the shore before the men on the beach reacted. As one, the front rank – six men with spears – dropped into a guard position, their shields locking into a wall, the points of their weapons bristling out. Behind them the four bowmen each drew and nocked an arrow.

"Really?" Musongola said. "I'm shocked."

"You will disarm and surrender yourselves to us or be killed where you stand!" one of the archers shouted back.

Musongola took two steps forward, bringing his chest within striking distance of the spears – but making him an impossible shot for the archers.

"You think it wise, threatening the emperor's messenger?" he asked. "Is Captain Rwamirama here? Tell him Captain Musongola is here to see him with word from the Emperor. If you're quick, I might ignore your impudence!" This last, he said with a roar, loud enough that the spearmen in front of him flinched.

Mercenaries were not complex. They'd been trained to take commands from people who ranked over them, even if they didn't know the commander well. That's how mercenaries and armies worked. It also meant that they were used to taking orders from men like Musongola, who knew how to deliver them.

He watched indecision flicker over the faces of these men. He kept his eyes on theirs, and they looked away whenever he met their gaze. He knew when he had them.

"Fine," he growled. "I'll find my own way in."

He shoved aside one of those spear-tips with each of his hands, and the spearmen parted in front of him. That left the bowmen, and they seemed to suddenly think better of having their weapons trained on an angry officer. Arrows hastily found their way from bows back into quivers, and the men who'd stood in his path a few moments before turned into an honor guard for him and Magezi, escorting them into the fort as guests instead of as prisoners.

It was a subtle distinction, and one which could reverse itself at a moment's notice if he screwed up in dealing with Rwamirama. But he wanted to keep his sword at his side, for that meeting.

They went into the fort, the archers leading the way, the spearmen following. The doors boomed shut behind them.

CHAPTER FORTY-THREE

Kwadwo felt a sneeze building. He fought hard to contain the sneeze. He could not sneeze. That simple noise would doom him and this entire family. Death would be the least of their worries – most likely, they'd be either fed to Lugu's pet Gbohii, or turned into new pets for her growing menagerie.

The word was her men had slain the loose dead during the battle at the palace. She'd lost a few of her soldiers in the process, but the people in town were more terrified of her than ever.

They'd realized Kwadwo had escaped and were out looking for him in force. Patrols stomped by daily, turning houses inside out, and she had riders searching the lands around Takoradi. All looking for him. Kwadwo wondered if Lugu knew – or even suspected – that he had the bag she'd been looking for. She seemed to know all about the 'legacy' Kwesi had spoken of. He wondered how she had come by such a carefully kept secret. Until Kwesi told him about it in the throne room, Kwadwo had no idea that anything like the legacy existed.

There wasn't much in the bag. A key, and a map of Kamit. Kwesi had spoken of going there after Takoradi. But what was the key for? What did it unlock? Kwesi had spoken of stores set against hard times. That would be valuable indeed if there was anyone left alive to use them. Who could he gather to claim that prize?

It was a problem for later. For now, he had to survive. And he had to keep the contents of the little bag away from Lugu. Somehow.

He'd had time to reflect on things. Lugu knew about the key. She must have suspected Kwesi had gone to his study to get it. She'd have torn the room apart by now, thinking she'd gotten there before him. Assuming she eventually found the compartment – empty – and no hidden keys, there was only one place that it could have gone.

Which explained why she was putting so much effort into finding him.

So far, the only thing saving Kwadwo had been that the people of Takoradi hated Lugu even more than they feared her. That and he'd lived there for years. They knew him. He was one of them. So they were willing to risk a lot for him, like the family hiding him under their floor right now.

He wasn't going to ask Ako why there was a hidden space under his floor. Ever. Kwadwo had no doubt that the hidey-hole had been used to smuggle all sorts of things in past customs in the past. Ako was that sort of man – big, rough around the edges, and just a little on the shady side of the law. But he was a good man. His son had ridden with Kwadwo and Kwesi to Nicran, among the guards. Kwadwo couldn't even tell the man for sure if his son was dead or not. Everything had been so confused in the end, he just didn't know.

Ako had nodded at the news. He hadn't smiled, hadn't cried. Never asked another word about the boy. But he'd taken Kwadwo in anyway, given him food and water, and hidden him well once the patrols started.

If only he could keep from sneezing a little longer! Dust drifted down through the floorboards above, tickling his nose. Those were the booted feet of Lugu's soldiers in the house above, knocking down the dust.

If Kwadwo sneezed, they'd find him. He'd die – horribly – along with Ako and the rest of the man's family for aiding him.

He pinched his nose hard with his fingers, fighting to not make even the smallest noise. The boots tromped across the floor upstairs for another few moments, voices saying things Kwadwo couldn't hear. Then the boots left. Ako didn't come down for him, though, and Kwadwo continued to wait in the gloom.

Has something else gone wrong? Kwadwo waited until the tickle in his nose went past unbearable and kept on holding back the sound.

After what felt like hours, the floorboards lifted away, and Ako's face appeared in the gap.

"It's safe now," the man said.

Kwadwo sneezed, and sneezed again, and again.

"Shit, man, you been holding that back all this time?" Ako asked.

"Aane," Kwadwo said, sneezing again. He chuckled. "Barely!"

"Good that you did. They hung around the street a while. Checked out some other houses. Think maybe someone is squawking."

"Maybe," Kwadwo said. He didn't think so, though. If anyone had turned him in – and there was a reward posted, Ako had told him so – then the guards would have torn the house apart, not just questioned his host and searched. Still, perhaps it was time he moved elsewhere. He didn't want to put Ako's family into harm's way any more than he already had.

"I think it's time for me to leave the city," Kwadwo said.

"Sounds good," Ako replied. "When do we go?"

"We?"

"You think we're safer here than we would be out there with you?"

Kwadwo sighed. Ako was right. His family would be in danger for as long as Lugu was in power here. Eventually, maybe she would get bored and move on. But would that happen before the

Gbohii were at the gates in enough numbers to swamp the place? Cities like this were incredibly vulnerable, as they'd seen in Nicran. For all he knew, Lugu might well sit on her throne here until the Gbohii were at her gates and then invite them in for tea.

She seemed mad enough.

The front door slammed open with a loud bang. Kwadwo was on his feet in an instant, hand reaching for his sword before he even saw who it was. He relaxed a little when he saw it was Ako's daughter, but not entirely. The little girl's eyes were too wide, too frightened. Something was up. She ran to her father, jumped into his arms.

"What is it, Korkoi? What's wrong?" Ako asked.

"Men from the northeast, Tseh'atta (*Dad*)," she said. "Hundreds of them!"

"Where?" Kwadwo asked. He was on his feet, the urge to go see for himself almost overpowering. Men from the northeast? From where? "Are they at the gates?" he asked.

What would Lugu do, with a force at her gates? Her little band of warriors couldn't possibly hold off a larger force for any length of time. Things might be about to change for the better after all.

"Not at the gates," the breathless girl said. "Through them. They've let them in. Hundreds and hundreds of men with spears and strange paint on their arms."

"What?" Ako said.

"The dark lady was there herself, letting them in. I swear it!" the little girl said.

"It's all right. I believe you," Ako said. He patted her on the head and she dashed back outside, filled with the exuberance of the very young.

Haisetti. It had to be. Kwesi said something about marrying her off to some Haisetti lord in the northeast. Kept the peace that way. Somehow, Lugu had arranged for a Haisetti army to come southwest. Hundreds, the child has said. How many men did she command? Were these all of them, or were there more?

"I have to get out of here," Kwadwo said. "Tonight. If you're coming, you can come then, but I need to leave."

"It's this army you're fearing?" Ako asked.

"It's what she'll do with them," Kwadwo replied. "She'll comb the countryside, and the city. She hasn't been able to do a proper search with so few men. But with a larger force?" He shrugged.

Ako looked around at his cottage. He stroked a heavy wood beam, supporting the wall and ceiling.

"It's been a nice place," he said. "But we'll be ready. We're going with you."

The front door slammed open again. This time, Kwadwo was almost relaxed. The sound was the familiar slam of a hyperactive little girl. But as he turned, he saw her eyes were wide with fear again.

"They're coming!" she said.

"Who?" Kwadwo asked.

"The men with spears! They're coming this way!"

CHAPTER FORTY-FOUR

Etse and Sefadzi walked in silence for a long while. They traced their way down the wooded hill, passing the place where the attack had happened just hours before. The leaves and ferns were stained red there, and they skirted around the place. Etse had no interest in lingering, so they went west through the trees a good distance before stopping to rest.

"Thank you for taking me from the bad place," Sefadzi said. She was clearly tired but was smiling anyway. The girl had seemed more at ease almost immediately as soon as they'd left. She had known. Long before Etse himself had figured out that Agboko was a little mad, she had seen it. That level of perception in one so young was remarkable, precocious, and more than a little unnerving.

They had no food. They had no water. He could have perhaps used a little more forethought in his departure, he thought a little ruefully. But it had seemed best at the time to get out of there as quickly as possible, and he couldn't regret the decision.

He stood up. They'd rested long enough and had a long way to go if they were going to find some sort of safety before nightfall. He dreaded the idea of traveling at night. At least during the day, he had a chance at seeing the Gbohii before they stumbled over them!

As he was thinking that, a rustling in the leaves from down the hill a bit caught his attention. He froze in place. Next to him, Sefadzi did the same.

Something was coming up the hill.

Silently, Etse pointed to the tree next to them. He picked Sefadzi up and lifted her to the lowest branch. She grabbed on without a word, hauling herself up into the tree. From that first branch, she climbed higher, vanishing into the leaves.

Etse jumped and caught hold of the branch with both hands. With an effort, he brought his legs up and wrapped his feet around the wood, then hauled himself up. He quickly climbed a little higher into a large V in the trunk, hoping the mass of wood might hide him from whatever was coming their way. Caution was better than carelessness, these days.

They were just in time. The first Gbohii loped into view about fifty feet away, sniffing through the woods. It vanished from sight, heading up the hill. Behind it came six more – seven of the things, the most Etse had seen at once time since Nicran! He kept as still as he could, hoping Sefadzi would do the same. Even the smallest movement might betray them, and he'd seen the things move. Jumping into a tree like this would be simple for them.

None of the Gbohii looked up, or let their gaze linger long enough on the right tree. All of them bounded on up the hill. Etse stayed put. Sefadzi was a few branches higher than him, and she held herself completely still as well.

One of the things started howling a few minutes away. It was still close enough that Etse was glad they'd remained hidden. The other Gbohii in the pack took up the cry. Were they talking to each other? Etse had no way of knowing. It seemed strange behavior for things they had assumed were mindless monsters. One in the lead – a scout? – with others following. And the howls. He'd never seen them acting so coordinated, and it frightened him. One of the things alone was bad enough! If they were able to communicate and organize…

Then his blood chilled. The howling – it had come from right about where the woman's blood still stained the grass. They'd left a blood trail when they hauled her back up the hill. They must have. There was no way she'd bled so much where she was injured without leaving a track that anyone could follow. Did the dead see her blood? Could they smell it, like hounds?

Etse had a feeling that the people in those caves were about to get a very unfriendly visit.

"Sefadzi," he whispered. "They're going to attack the cave."

"We're going back?" she asked. "To help them?"

"I am," he replied. "I want you to stay here."

"I can help."

From any other child, that would have been an odd thing to say. But Etse recalled the way she had distracted the Gbohii by the stream. She'd been the one to see the danger by the bridge in Nicran too, and she'd known just the right time to hand him his sword at the cottage. Without her, he might be dead thrice over already.

"I know. But I'd rather know you were safe. Okay?" he said.

She looked down from the tree, and he realized she was looking back up the hill, where the caves were. "Okay."

"Stay in the tree. I'll find you."

He jumped down, landing lightly in the leaves and brush. They'd walked over an hour to get where they were, but they'd travelled at a child's pace. He didn't dare run full tilt – in these thick woods he could stumble into the pack of Gbohii before he knew they were there. But he could make much better time on the way back than he'd made coming down. Etse started off, long loping steps carrying him swiftly but silently through the trees.

The Gbohii were already well ahead of him, and they moved fast. He wondered if anyone would still be alive by the time he arrived. Damn it! He could have tried to lead those people out. But would they have risked following him? Agboko wanted to stay and had some good arguments for staying put. Etse knew he was wrong – and if the dead walkers on their way to the cave didn't prove his point, nothing would. But scared people tend to hole up someplace, which is sometimes the right instinct, and other times will get them killed.

All he could hope is that he might save some of them from the fate their decision had brought on them.

It was bad. Etse could tell that even before he could see the caves. He could hear frightened screams, and the moans of the dying. He could smell blood on the air, and the stink the Gbohii left behind – the smell of rotting meat.

He was too late to stop the dead things – they'd reached the caves ahead of him, as he feared they would. His sword was already in his hand, and he increased his pace. No need to worry about running into the Gbohii in the forest, now. He knew where they were.

Etse continued moving forward through the darkness. Somewhere ahead, there was light, and sound, and people who needed help. He almost cried out when his foot landed in something that squished underneath his boot. Someone had died there. One of the people who he had lived with in his short time here had died...messily.

He kept moving as quickly as he could through the trees, between the trees, around trees, which twisted and gnarled in his path, seemed to block him from where he was trying to go. And then, suddenly, he was through. He had reached the cave. He immediately wished he hadn't.

Two of the Gbohii were crouched before the cave entrance, gnawing on the remains of one of their victims. Etse's fury surged. He snarled, and to his ears his voice sounded far too much like that of the monsters. He crossed the clearing in two bounds. His sword sang through the air, and one of the Gbohii lost its head. The other tried to rise and reach for him. But he stopped it with his sword, blocking the blow. Fingers flew from its hand. He circled his sword around, cleaving the air in a graceful arc. The second Gbohii died just like the first.

The way into the cave was open. A woman's screams reached his ear from somewhere inside. Etse stepped into the cave warily, looking carefully for foes. He didn't know what he was going to find in there, but it wasn't going to be good. Almost immediately he heard a shriek from somewhere to his left. A woman came running down the passage, her arm tattered and bleeding. One of the Gbohii loped down the passage behind her, catching up fast.

Etse stepped between her and her pursuer. It lunged at her, snagged her clothing. With one quick sword blow, Etse severed the thing's arm. Blood flowed from the dreadful wound but the Gbohii didn't even slow down. It only turned its attention to Etse instead.

That was what he was hoping for. Etse danced with the thing. His sword licked out, trying to strike its head from his shoulders. In its turn, the Gbohii tried to grab Etse, and stuck in the close confines of the cave it almost succeeded. It was so close, Etse could smell its rotting flesh. The monster lunged, grabbing him by the shoulders. Claws pressed Etse against the cave wall.

But Etse managed to place his sword in front of the Gbohii neck. The force of its own lunge pressed its neck against the sharp blade, cleaving its head most of the way from its shoulders. Etse pushed hard, and the head rolled free. He stood there a moment, panting, gasping for air.

The woman he'd saved was nowhere to be seen. If that wound on her arm had been a bite – which seemed likely – then she was dead anyway. But he'd accounted for only three of the Gbohii. Etse knew there were at least seven. And sadly, enough people had died here that there would soon be more.

Etse had no way of knowing if anyone was still alive and unhurt. How could he find anyone who might still be saved in time? He could waste precious minutes searching the caves, minutes which might mean the difference between life or death for someone still alive. Etse took a deep breath and decided to take a chance.

"Is anyone alive out there?" Etse shouted to the darkness. He hoped desperately to hear a response. But he feared the worst.

"Aane!"

"Help us!"

Etse turned toward the shouts. Someone was still alive! They were coming from somewhere off to his right. That was back toward the storage rooms, the places Agboko had set aside for cold, wet season stores. They hadn't seen much use, but Etse thought it possible that those rooms might have made a good defensive position. People who had made it there safely might still be alive.

"I'm coming!" Etse shouted back. He set off down the dark passage.

Before he'd gone more than a few feet, one of the things leapt from the darkness onto his back! He'd been moving too fast, too urgently, and not paying enough attention. Now that mistake was going to cost him. He cried out in horror, and tried to break free, but failed. The Gbohii's jaws snapped closed right beside his ear, and fear surged through him. The smallest bite would be the end – even worse than the end.

He used his fear as fuel. With a shout, he pushed back, slamming the Gbohii between his shoulders and the cave wall. He heard bones crack and snap inside the Gbohii body. It snarled, trying vainly to hold on to him. But Etse whirled away. He thrust his sword at the thing, aiming for the neck, but missing. His blade lodged in its shoulder instead.

The thing hissed at Etse. Then it did a peculiar thing. It reached out with both hands and grabbed the hilt of Etse's sword. Then it pulled with all its strength. Etse gasped. The Gbohii was actually pulling itself down the sword toward him!

In another moment, it would release the sword and those fingers would lock around his neck instead. He was out of time. Etse did the only thing he could think of. He let go of his sword. Then he grabbed the monster's head with both hands, turning to use its momentum against it. It flailed forward and smashed into the cave wall.

But it wasn't dead. Not yet. Not quite. Etse held its head in his hands and smashed it against the cave wall. Once. Twice. A third time he hammered the skull against the hard rock. There was a sickening crack, as bone splintered under the impact. But the thing stopped moving at last.

Etse was gasping for breath now. But he couldn't stop. There were still three more of the things somewhere in these caves.

With an effort, he yanked his sword free from the Gbohii's shoulder.

He was exhausted. He could feel tremors starting in his arms. Etse wasn't sure he had it in him to fight another of the things. It would be so easy to slip away right now. He'd tried, right? Did he owe these people his life? Wouldn't it be better to leave now, to live and fight another day?

He shook blood from his blade. It would probably be the smart thing to do. It's what his father would have done. But what sort of life would it be, living with the horrible memory of having let these people down? Not because he had tried and failed – but out of cowardice?

"I will save every person that it is in my power to save," he said aloud.

Simple. Crystal clear in his mind. His purpose. His reason. He knew, somewhere deep inside, that he'd signed his own death with that statement. If he held true to it, eventually he would try to save someone that he couldn't. Eventually, he would fail. And he would die. But in the meantime, the life he lived would have meaning.

He started back down the hall. His drawn sword reflected bits of light from the few torches and fires in the cave – a beacon in the dark.

CHAPTER FORTY-FIVE

Kwadwo spent the rest of the day nestled away in the hidey-hole underneath the floor. The Haisetti soldiers flooded the city, and there were hundreds of them indeed. It was impossible for him to move about, or even to plan next moves and connect with people who might be able to help him. All he could do was sit and wait.

But when night fell, things were different. The Haisetti withdrew to the palace house, away from the city-dwellers, who viewed them as hostile invaders. Everyone in the city could feel an explosion brewing, but it looked like it might not be coming tonight. The Haisetti still posted guards to the walls and the gates. He knew they were watching for him trying to get out as much as they were alert for Gbohii trying to get in.

Despite that, Kwadwo thought he might still have one way out of a city that wasn't so well guarded. It was going to take him through the sewers, and he was frankly getting tired of sewers. Takoradi, like Nicran, had its own sewer system. And those sewers had their own exit point out of the city: a pipe that ran under the walls and became a stream trickling downhill toward the sea.

It was the perfect escape route.

The down side: it was too obviously perfect. The pipe was blocked by steel bars, and Kwadwo knew just how well those bars had been welded in place. He'd supervised the work himself as part of his work to improve the city's fortifications. Worse, Ako reported that Lugu had chained a Gbohii to the bars on the inside of the sewer. Getting out that way was going to be a nightmare. But he was running out of other options. With so many additional troops, Lugu would be able to search the city even more carefully. Eventually, she'd find him. Or she'd make an offer that someone couldn't refuse, and he'd be turned in to her.

Now that night had fallen and he could move more freely again Kwadwo was nestled up beside a dark building, waiting to sprint to another hiding spot once the way was clear. Peering out, he could see no one. He dashed across the street. When he reached a pool of shadow on the other side, he froze. He waited several heartbeats, listening for any alarm raised by his movement. Nothing. Carefully, he stepped back out of the shadow and beckoned. Several dark-clothed forms shifted from beside the building where he'd been hiding and scurried across the street to join him. He held a finger to his lips as they arrived. No one nodded. They all understood the need to be utterly silent.

Kwadwo had thought over possible alternative escape plans. Perhaps he could disguise himself somehow, or hide himself in a wagon, and have a shot at exiting the city through the gates. But that would only work if he were alone, and now Ako and his entire family wanted to come along. They were the dark forms accompanying him through the shadowed streets.

Word had spread to others, Ako said. People had heard about his daring escape from the palace, and rumors were rampant about his escape plans. Many now knew that Kwesi was slain by his own daughter. They knew what Lugu was. They hated her for it. And with these new soldiers flooding to the city, it was clear that the place was coming apart at the seams. There was no safety here.

He wondered who would be waiting at the meeting point. Ako said he planned to tell a few friends, so Kwadwo expected a couple of additional families. But if anyone had gotten wind of the escape attempt and turned them in, they could be walking straight into a trap.

His hand went to the pouch slung around his neck, safe under his clothing. Kwesi's key was still safe inside. The key would unlock hidden supplies which might just spell the difference between life and death for the little band of families fleeing with Kwadwo. With Etse dead, and Kwesi bitten, the dying man entrusted the key to Kwadwo. He would find a way to get there and recover Kwesi's legacy. But he had to get out of Takoradi, first.

Another quick run down an alley, and he was almost there. Up ahead was a warehouse. It would be full of boxes, crates, and barrels of goods. That made it the perfect place to hide the refugee families they planned to meet. It would also be the ideal place to hide a troop of Haisetti mercenaries. This was the most dangerous moment of the whole endeavor.

Kwadwo held up a hand, palm out toward Ako to tell him to stay put. He looked ready to argue, but Kwadwo shook his head, and Ako subsided. No one could doubt the man's courage, but damn it all, he had a family to think of. He could come once Kwadwo was sure the coast was clear.

Nothing moved in the night. The warehouse seemed completely silent and totally dark. Kwadwo strained to hear anything at all from the place – the smallest creak, a clank of that might alert him to the presence of troops. But even after listening a long moment, the only sound he heard was a cat, yowling at something a few streets over.

He dashed across the street to the door. His heart hammered in his chest. If he were caught, he had no doubt that Lugu would feed him to her pets, just as she had her own father.

The lock was off the door. The chain which should have barred it hang limply in place, and the door itself was ajar by an inch. That was expected. The other families would have snuck in the same way he was coming now. He slid the door open another foot and slipped inside.

The warehouse was black. Only the faintest shards of moonlight entered through gaps in the wood, casting more shadows than light. He could almost make out the hulking mounds of supplies heaped in long rows. God, Lugu could have hidden her entire army in here and he'd never know it until they all came after him! He'd been a fool to agree to this meeting. Kwadwo turned to flee, his hand on the door.

He stopped himself. If the place was safe, then this was the last good shot he would have to get out of Takoradi. By tomorrow, Lugu's patrols would be everywhere. Tonight was his best chance. Maybe his only chance. He had to try.

Kwadwo stepped away from the doorway so that he couldn't be framed in the relative light outside. He took a deep breath to calm himself. Then he called out, in a quiet voice but pitched to carry through the silent room.

"I'm Kwadwo. Come out if you are here."

There was a rustling, and then the sound of footsteps. It was only the steps of one man, not a troop of soldiers, but Kwadwo tensed anyway. He'd rather be prepared than caught off guard.

"Me wura? Over here," a voice called from over in the stacks.

Kwadwo peered into the dark, but couldn't make out where the person stood, at first. Then he saw a hand waving.

"The others are all in the cellar, me wura. Waiting."

"Take me to them," Kwadwo replied. He'd let Ako wait another few minutes, to be certain there was no trap. He followed the shadowy figure deeper into the alleyways between the piles. He lost track of where he was almost immediately. The place was a maze. Whoever the person was leading the way, he knew the warehouse. He traced a winding path through the place like someone intimately familiar with all of its twisting ways.

They rounded yet another corner, and Kwadwo saw the first glimmer of light since he'd come into the place. It was warm light, from candles, or perhaps a lantern. A moment later he could see the source – the light leaked up from somewhere below, the square of light outlining a trapdoor in the floor.

"Down there, me wura," the man who was leading him said.

In the dim light, Kwadwo got his first good look at him. Asante, for sure. Not a Haisetti. And young, not really a man yet at all. But could he be trusted? That was the question of the hour. He stared into the teen's eyes, searching them. He saw confidence there, and nerves, yes, but not enough to account for betrayal. In Kwadwo's experience, fear of being discovered in the moment before putting a knife into someone's back was something that always showed.

It wasn't there in this youngster's eyes.

"Very well," Kwadwo said. "Let's not keep them waiting."

The young man lifted the trap door. Light spilled up from flickering sources somewhere below. A ladder was set up to the edge of the door, and the boy stepped down lightly onto the first rung, descending to the cellar below. Kwadwo peeked over the edge. No soldiers down there, no. But what he saw took his breath away.

Kwadwo stared, aghast. The basement of the warehouse wasn't as large as the warehouse itself, but it was still quite big. And from what he could see in the dim light of a few scattered candles, it was filled with people.

Men, women, children. Whole families. They sat in little groups on the floor, or leaned up against the wall, or huddled in corners. There must have been over a hundred people down there.

"Are you all completely mad?" he asked.

That got their attention. Every gaze in the place locked on Kwadwo's unsmiling face.

"You, boy," he said to his young guide. "Go back out there, get Ako and his family down here. Now."

The young man practically leaped back up the ladder in his haste to get away from Kwadwo's ire.

"As for the rest of you," he said in a voice pitched to carry through the room. "Who is in charge of this mess?"

Nobody answered. They were all still staring at him.

"Come on now," he said more gently. "Who's running this show?"

Another long moment of silence. Kwadwo wasn't sure anyone was going to speak at all, but then a man stood up from where he'd been sitting with a small cluster of children. Kwadwo thought he recognized him. One of his pet projects, before everything went to hell, was training a bunch of the men in Takoradi. The guards were good at what they did, but Kwadwo wanted more men who knew how to use a spear available if the city ever came under serious attack, and Kwesi agreed.

"You are, sir," the man said. He looked confused and worried. "Aren't you?"

CHAPTER FORTY-SIX

Rwamirama met them in the great hall, just across from the small courtyard from the fort's main gate. Someone had run ahead to let him know that he had company on their way in. Rwamirama was standing in the middle of the hall when the spearmen opened the big doors to allow Musongola entry.

The two locked eyes for the barest moment, measuring each other. They'd often competed with each other, each in their own way. Okoth's third captain was a buffoon – but Musongola had always respected Rwamirama's quiet competence. The man was like a cat. He always landed on his feet.

And it seemed like he had done so again.

"The dead rise, and the entire Cleave is loose on the land. Yet you stand here surrounded by a company of Kiswala's best Mikijen, drinking good wine," Musongola said, smiling to take any sting out of his words. "You are without a doubt the finest survivor I have ever known."

Rwamirama ducked his head to acknowledge the compliment. "And I see your luck has yet to abandon you, my friend; you, too, are a survivor."

Musongola closed the gap between them. Rwamirama reached out his hand, and Musongola accepted the arm clasp. The two stared into each other's eyes another moment, searching.

Rwamirama looked away first. "You must be tired, Musongola! You've come far from Nicran."

"Aane, we have," Musongola said. "This is Magezi," he continued, gesturing. "He's been helping me keep order in the fighting men who remain with us."

Rwamirama beckoned him over to a table, where plates with bits of food were set, and goblets with wine. "Come, eat, and drink something. Your man is welcome to help himself, too."

"No, thank you, Captain," Magezi said. He held his post by the door.

"Suit yourself," Rwamirama said, still smiling. But the smile seemed a bit more brittle.

Musongola went with him. To be polite, he stacked a bit of the cheese onto some bread and took one of the cups of wine. The food was decent. Fresh. Bread could be baked from stored grain, and wine would keep for years. But how had Rwamirama found a source for fresh cheese? And there were some fruits on the table as well – grapes, and sliced apples.

"You have done well," Musongola remarked.

"Aane. But tell me – you said you were here on behalf of the emperor. How the hell did Okere escape that madness in Nicran?" Rwamirama shook his head, then sipped his wine before continuing. "We barely made it out ourselves."

Now was the time to be cautious. Because they didn't precisely have Okere with them, did they? If Rwamirama knew that right away, then he'd be much less inclined to take them seriously. But if he outright lied to the man, and Rwamirama called his bluff, asked to see the emperor…

The worst of it was that Musongola knew this was more Rwamirama's game than his. Give him a straight up fight any day. This sort of word dance was something Rwamirama had always excelled at.

"He did survive, yes?" Rwamirama asked, when Musongola delayed a moment too long in replying.

"What? Aane. Mostly thanks to Kwesi," Musongola said. "There was a postern tunnel out into the river, where the privies emptied. We got out through an access tunnel used to clean the...mess."

Rwamirama's eyes bulged at that, and then he doubled over laughing. He spilled some of his wine on the floor, slapping his leg with his free hand.

"No!" he said, between gasps, trying to contain his laughter. "So Okere the useless had to escape – through the shit hole?"

Musongola nodded. He couldn't help the small smile that crept onto his face. All in all, it was sort of funny, if you had served Okere as long as they had.

Rwamirama broke out laughing again. It took him a good minute before he was able to stop and wipe the tears streaming from his eyes.

"Oh, Daarila," he gasped out. "Funniest thing I have heard in a week."

Then the laughing demeanor vanished as quickly as it had appeared. The transition was so sudden that it shocked Musongola. For a moment, he thought he was seeing a rare personal side to Rwamirama. But no, even the man's laughter turned off like a spout.

"So why are you still serving such a shitty emperor, Musongola?" Rwamirama asked.

"My oath?" he replied, trying to feel his way through what suddenly felt like a dangerous trap again.

"Your oath was to the emperor and the empire. The empire is dead. And is there still an emperor, without an empire? Can there be?"

Musongola pursed his lips. "I don't like Okere any more than you do. But we need some sort of center to cling to."

Rwamirama sat on the table behind him. He shrugged with his hands, gesturing at the room. "Look around you. I have built a center here. I could always use good men to help me."

It was a good set of questions. Okere had always been an ass, and his stupidity had largely resulted in the disaster at Nicran. Rwamirama's answer wasn't all wrong. It was simple survival for all of them at this point, and following Okere was not a good way to ensure you kept breathing, these days.

Of course, it wasn't really Okere he was serving. Okere was off with Kwesi god-knew-where, and if they didn't get past Rwamirama and acquire a ship, they might never see either Kwesi or the emperor again. Hell, even if they did get through, there was no guarantee Kwesi's party had made it.

But he couldn't tell Rwamirama too much of this. Let the man know how weak they really were, and he'd swoop like a hawk, scooping up what he wanted and destroying the rest. Musongola could see it there, in his eyes. Rwamirama had decided to make the most of this dark time and carve out his own little empire.

"What did you have in mind?" Musongola asked aloud.

"I've declared myself the Juu," Rwamirama said. That was an old title; it had been used for the man who was supreme commander of the Mikijen. But it hadn't been used for a long time, not since the Mikijen's twenty-third year.

"Any Mikijen and soldiers who join with me will get to retain their rank, and have privileges commensurate with that rank," he went on. He gestured to Musongola. "You, for instance, would keep your captain rank. You'll command men again. Real fighters. Think about it, Musongola."

"I am thinking about it," he replied. "I'll have to go talk with my men, but I have to say – I don't relish the idea of taking orders from Okere."

"Good," Rwamirama said. Then he sneered, and added, "Because it seems like you've been commanding women into battle these days. I'd hate to see that become your new normal."

Musongola froze. He was talking about Diata. Some of Rwamirama's men must have recognized him there on the beach. So Rwamirama had known all along that he was here at least in part to see to Diata's release. He wanted to wipe that sneer off the man's face. Musongola's fingers twitched, ever so slightly, toward the hilt of his sword. Rwamirama caught the gesture, and his sneer turned into a smile.

"So, she means something to you, then?" Rwamirama asked. "Never fear. She's alive, and safe here. When you join us, I'll be happy to give her back to you."

Musongola took care to keep his face calm, his features even. Inside, he was boiling. "You could give her back to me now, as a gesture of good faith."

"I could. But then she'd have to leave the fort, and wouldn't it be better for her to remain safe here, waiting for your return?" Rwamirama asked. He raised his glass. "A toast, then – to our renewed friendship."

"To friendship," Musongola said. He was careful not to mention whose friendship he was toasting. It seemed ill to toast friendship with a man he knew he'd likely have to kill before all this was over. He didn't feel too bad about it, though. They both knew each other well. He had no doubt that Rwamirama was harboring little hope he'd join the man. If Rwamirama knew he'd been on the shore, then he knew that he'd seen the burned villages, the slaughtered townspeople. Rwamirama would order such things. But Rwamirama knew that Musongola would never stand for them.

The battle lines had been drawn here today, that was all.

"I should be off. I have much to accomplish," Musongola said.

"I am sure you do," Rwamirama replied. "I trust I will see you back here soon."

"Oh, yes," Musongola said. Then he turned and took his leave from the hall, Magezi falling in beside him. They walked in silence back to the boat, and Tay-Natey didn't say anything when he saw their grim expressions. He knew things had gone badly.

Musongola felt an itchy spot between his shoulder blades until they were well outside of bow range. But no arrows spun at them over the water. Rwamirama was playing a waiting game, and that did seem a safe bet for him. After all, he held all the cards right now.

Somehow, Musongola needed to find a way to turn that around.

CHAPTER FORTY-SEVEN

Etse slowed as he approached the storage rooms. Up ahead, he could hear the snarling of Gbohii and the frightened cries of humans. He steeled himself and rounded the corner. The room he entered was a round chamber, one of the larger rooms in the cave complex. A number of small, dead-end passageways led from this room. That made the space perfect for storage. Agboko's plan had been for each of those side tunnels to be filled with a different sort of supply. Now, that plan was in tatters.

Inside the room were all three of the remaining Gbohii. They were tearing at something the defenders had laid across the passage as a barrier. Etse couldn't quite see what it was, but he knew from experience that the Gbohii were sure to break through. In Nicran, he'd seen them tear through the stout palace doors to get at prey inside. He knew it wouldn't take them long to carve up this makeshift barricade.

He ducked back into the passage before the monsters saw him. Three at once? He had never fought alone against so many. When he fought the horde of Gbohii in Nicran with the Mikijen and the Palace Guard, there was a company of men fighting alongside him. Every man would look out for the others next to him. Here, he was alone. It was three of them, against just him.

Someone was screaming, from the other side of the barrier. Etse heard wood splintering. He didn't have time to think about this. He'd made a promise. More than one, really. There was the one he made just moments before, and the one he had made at the

Emperor's behest, before everything went to hell. He steeled himself. He'd find a way to save the people trapped inside this place.

Or he would die trying.

Etse rounded the corner again, this time moving at high speed. His best chance was to take the monsters by surprise. He almost managed it – they were so engaged with finding a way past the barricade that for a few precious seconds they failed to notice his rush. Etse's first blow was good. His sword took one of the dead things in the neck, slicing almost all the way through. It was enough. The thing dropped to the floor of the cave, convulsing, blood splashing from the wound.

The other two monsters turned to engage him. Etse knew he was in trouble at once. The Gbohii didn't just rush in. One moved off to his right a bit, the other a little to his left. If he turned to face one, the other would have his back. Etse took a step away from the monsters. He had to get some distance to stop them from encircling him.

Then he took one step too many and his back brushed against cold stone.

The monsters saw he was trapped. Both went on the attack, moving forward at the same time with uncanny timing. They lunged at him with ferocious snarls. Etse raised his left arm, jamming his wrist into the neck of the one on his left. With his sword arm, he thrust at the other, but the blade sank into its chest – useless. Both of the monsters reached out to clutch at him. Etse could keep their teeth from his flesh, but not their hands away from his throat. The icy digits clamped down on his neck and took his breath.

"Have at them!"

Etse heard the yell but almost couldn't believe his ears. That was Agboko! The Gbohii seemed as surprised as Etse felt. They turned to face this new threat, leaving Etse gasping for breath. He sank to his knees, every breath painful but a blessed relief.

Agboko came rushing in, sword raised. Etse could tell that the man was badly hurt. Blood dripped from his armor. But Agboko still held his sword well, and as he ran forward to engage the monsters two other men joined him. They had only stout sticks for weapons, but they seemed unwilling to stay out of the fight.

Agboko closed quickly with the monsters. With a single thrust he stabbed upward through the jaw of the first one, slicing cleanly into its brain. The thing fell, but it trapped his sword. Agboko yanked on the blade, but it was stuck – he couldn't pull it free. He was helpless, and the other Gbohii closed fast. The two other men hammered blows down on the monster's head, but it never slowed. With single-minded attention, it closed its fingers around his shoulder, where they met resistance from his armor. But the grip let it pull him closer, into a deadly embrace. Viper-quick, it leaned in to tear into Agboko's neck, and red blood blossomed from the sudden wound. Agboko sagged as the thing fed on his flesh.

"No!" Etse shouted.

Etse forced himself back to his feet. Two steps brought him face-to-face with the Gbohii. It cast Agboko's bloody body to the cave floor. Then it snarled at Etse, Agboko's blood dripping from its teeth and down its chin.

"For Agboko," Etse said softly. Then his sword sang through the air. The note was not a glorious one; it was mournful.

The Gbohii were all dead. Etse went to Agboko's side. The two men who'd come out with him were already there, propping his head up. One of them held a cloth to the wound, but it was already drenched with blood. Etse watched the man's life leaving him with each breath.

"You came back," Agboko said. "Why would you come back?"

"We were never enemies," Etse replied. He pointed at the still bodies of the Gbohii. "Those are the enemy."

Agboko nodded. "Help them?" he asked. His eyes flicked quickly toward his people, the men and women he'd saved.

"I will," Etse said.

Then Agboko coughed, blood flecking his lips. His eyes grew very wide. And he died.

Etse got back to his feet, Agboko's blood staining his palm. In front of him stood the other two men who ran out with Agboko to rescue Etse from the Gbohii. Both of them looked lost, adrift.

"What do we do now?" one of them asked.

Etse saw movement down the tunnel behind them. There were people back there in the tunnel, where they had hidden behind a blockade of boxes and barrels. Their last stand, where they'd huddled in fear hoping for a miracle. Etse had tried to be that miracle, and he'd almost succeeded. But if it hadn't been for the dead man lying on the floor in front of him, he would've died in the attempt.

"I came back to save you. I'm not about to abandon you now," Etse said.

Everything he and Agboko had quarreled about earlier was still valid. The cave was a convenient hiding spot. It was no place to build a lasting home. Not even in these dark times. These people deserved something better. But how? Etse looked out over the people that he saved. They were potters, farmers, and sheepherders. They were regular men, women, and children. They weren't soldiers; that's why they hid when danger came. It's how they had survived this long.

But they might have to learn to become something more than what they had been if they wanted to continue in this new world. If there was one thing Etse was fairly confident about, it was his ability to teach novices how to fight. He'd helped Kwadwo train the men enough times. He could do it again.

The thought frightened him. Not the thought of teaching. That he thought he might even enjoy. It was the thought of being responsible for all these people that scared him even more than the

Gbohii. He'd never before been the one person responsible for everything before. There had always been someone else. His father. The Emperor. No matter how much responsibility Etse had been offered, there was always someone else there to give him orders. Someone else who shouldered the ultimate burden.

But here he was alone, and these people were looking to him for their very survival. If he failed there was no one else to ask for help or advice. It was all up to him.

"We can't stay here," Etse said. "Pack your things. We need to see to the dead, do what we can for the wounded, and then be on our way."

Etse could almost feel the ripple of anxiety flow through the people in front of him. They didn't want to go. They knew it wasn't safe here. There was no question that this place was not the sanctuary Agboko had claimed but they were afraid to leave it anyway. It was always easier to stick with what you knew, even after you learned it was wrong, than to risk your fate on the unknown.

"Once we leave this place," Etse said, "the first thing that we will do is look for weapons. You people are not victims! You're strong. And you will learn to be stronger."

"I'll get you spears and swords. And then I will teach you how to use them. Because whatever you were before the dead walked Asanteman," Etse said, his voice rising to carry down the passage, "from this day on you will be warriors. Knights, even. And together we will defend each other from this plague. Together we will be strong, and together we will do more than survive. We will prevail."

There was no cheering for Etse's words. The people he spoke to had no energy left for wild displays of emotion. But their faces had gone from terrified and helpless to grim and determined. They would follow him. They would learn to fight. Etse could see it in their eyes. And for now, that would be enough.

***

Sefadzi kept as still as she could, sitting in the tree. Off in the distance she thought she could hear the sounds of people screaming, but it might have been her imagination. She hoped Etse had arrived in time to warn the people in the cave, but she had a feeling he would not. They were too fast.

She shivered and wondered what tomorrow would look like. Maybe it would be sunny. She and Etse would be on their way, and find someplace nice, away from the dead things.

Something rustled in the leaves down below. Sefadzi froze, not wanting to give away her position. She watched, motionless, waiting to see the source of the sound.

Another rustle caught her attention, and her eyes scanned the forest floor below her. There! She spotted the source of the motion, a small figure hiding in the shadow of a tree a dozen paces from hers. Sefadzi watched the person carefully for a little longer. Then without warning, he darted from his hiding place and ran to another tree. He crouched there.

She could feel his fear from here. He wasn't a Gbohii, that much was sure. He didn't seem to be sick, either. Sefadzi worried that there might be more of the dead monsters lurking in the woods. If they found him, they'd kill him for sure. But if she revealed where she was, she might be in danger herself.

She decided to take a chance. "Boy!" she called out softly. She hoped her voice would carry far enough. It didn't seem to have, though. He wasn't responding to her.

"Boy!" she said again, a little louder. This time he did hear. He jerked his head around like he'd been slapped. He looked back and forth, trying to see her.

"Up here," she whispered, and risked a small wave.

Now he saw her and dashed to her tree.

"You're not one of them," he said. "Can I hide with you?"

Sefadzi nodded.

The boy didn't waste any more time. He wrapped his arms and legs around the tree trunk and started inching his way up. The bark must have been rubbing his arms raw, but he never stopped, and didn't complain either. He was panting by the time he reached the branch where Sefadzi was sitting.

His clothes were a mess, and he wasn't wearing any shoes. Instead, he wore cloth wraps to keep his feet safe. He was younger than she'd thought. Maybe the same age as she, give or take a bit. Twigs and bits of leaf clustered in his hair, which made him look a little funny. She stifled an inappropriate giggle. She didn't want to make him feel bad.

"Thanks for letting me come up," he said. "Don't wanna get eaten, and too dark to see the dead things."

"We need to stay quiet, and still," she whispered. "My name is Sefadzi. What's yours?"

"Amon," the boy said. He smiled.

Sefadzi liked his smile.

CHAPTER FORTY-EIGHT

Looking around, Kwadwo realized that he could place most of the men he saw here in that group. These were his auxiliaries, men he had trained to supplement the regular city guard in cases of emergency. Okere had ordered all the regular Takoradi guardsmen to Nicran. Most of them died there. These men weren't as well trained as the regular troops, but they knew what they were about. He felt his heart lift a little.

Of course, there was still the matter of all the families they'd brought with them. He couldn't fault the men for bringing their loved ones, but how in the hell was he supposed to get them all safely out of the city? And worse, feed them once they were out? It was going to be a logistics nightmare.

"How did you hear about this little get together?" he asked the man who'd stood up.

"From Lokko," he replied, nodding to another man.

"Lokko, you heard it from...?" Kwadwo asked.

"Ako," Lokko replied. "He said it was all right to tell a few people..."

Both men looked frightened, now. They weren't fools. They knew that these many people would be missed, even if they managed to get out of the city without being seen. Lugu would send her Haisetti after them for sure.

Ako came down the ladder then. He looked around, took in all the people in a single sweeping glance. Then his eyes came to rest on Kwadwo, standing there with arms crossed.

"Aw, shit," he said.

"I said you could invite a few trusted people. What the hell is this?" Kwadwo growled.

Ako scanned the room again, then cast his eyes down. At least the man had the grace to look abashed.

"We don't have time to argue about it now, Kwadwo," he said. "There's movement outside."

"Movement?"

"I think they're onto us," Ako said.

Kwadwo looked about the room. There were maybe twenty men present who he knew had training with weapons, and it looked like most of them had their spears with them. It wasn't going to be even close to enough. If Lugu had been tipped off about their meeting, she'd send an overwhelming force. She had the troops for it, now that the Haisetti were in Takoradi.

"How sure are you?" Kwadwo asked.

Ako opened his mouth to answer but was interrupted by the sound of splintering wood from somewhere upstairs.

"Pretty certain," Ako said grimly.

"Damn." That had to be the Haisetti, breaking in. It would take them a few minutes to find their way through the maze upstairs. But they didn't have long. Which meant there was only one way forward.

"We'll have to go out through the sewer," Kwadwo said. "All of us."

"Won't she know to guard the exit point?" Ako asked. He was sweating. With good reason. If Lugu caught them now, it was going to be ugly. Her favored method of dealing with people who gave her problems was becoming more infamous by the day.

"We'll have to chance it. Where's that sewer grate?" Kwadwo asked. "Quick, now!"

The people parted before him, and he followed the path they made to the spot. It was a steel grill that used to be bolted to the floor. The thing had been added to the warehouse years ago when the place above had been a fish market, to make cleaning easier. With mostly dry goods stored in the place now, it had been unused for years. Someone had already cut the bolts holding the iron grill in place. Kwadwo lifted it away and set it aside.

"I'll lead on the way out. I need to deal with the thing waiting for us down there," Kwadwo said. He saw some of the men shudder. None of them had faced a Gbohii before. He had, and the prospect of fighting another one wasn't pleasant, even if the thing was chained in place. He had some ideas about dealing with it, though.

"Ako, make sure everyone follows me in. Bring up the rear. See if you can slow them down a little."

"I'll do what I can," the big man replied.

"Don't get dead in the process," Kwadwo said. Then he turned and jumped down into the hole, splashing into the fetid water at the bottom. He took a few steps forward to clear the way for more men splashing down behind him. Ten of his reserve guardsmen plunged into the mess to help him clear the way out. Each of them carried a spear.

"Any of you know your way through this place?" Kwadwo said. His nose wrinkled. The tunnel was rank, the water sloshing about their legs foul. Someone passed down a torch from the room above, so at least they could see. But the men here all looked as lost as he felt.

Another splash. It was the young man who guided Kwadwo through the maze in the warehouse above. "I can lead you, me wura," the young man said.

"What's your name?"

"Odoi."

Kwadwo looked him over, still unsure whether he ought to be calling him a boy or a man. Still, he was doing a man's job tonight, no matter his age. And he'd known the warehouse well enough. Kwadwo hoped he knew these sewers just as well. Of course, if Lugu knew that there was an entrance to the sewers here, it wouldn't be hard for her to figure out where they'd have to exit. She could have a hundred men waiting outside the tunnel already. If she did, they were already lost.

"Lead on, Odoi," he said.

The boy slid past him to take point. More people were splashing down into the sewer tunnel now, as they tried to empty the room above. Kwadwo made ready to follow Odoi, but then heard someone call his name.

"Kwadwo!" It was Ako, still in the room above. "Best hurry, man. They've loosed Gbohii in the warehouse above. One of our men saw them come in and fled back to report. The things haven't found the trap door yet, but..."

But they would. More madness! If even one of those things escaped, it could ruin the entire city, just like Nicran. Lugu hadn't been there to watch that city fall, but she must know how dangerous this was.

Unless she truly didn't care how many of the people here died. Unless her purpose wasn't to rule here at all, and every living soul in Takoradi was already as dust to her. Kwadwo shuddered. He remembered how mad the woman was. It might just be that she was one who would be happy to watch the world burn around her.

"Follow as fast as you can, Ako. Don't engage them. Put out the lights and follow us as a rear guard."

Ako grunted acknowledgement.

"I mean it, man," Kwadwo called up. "I need you alive. We need to flee this field. There'll be another day for fighting."

He had to hope it would be enough. Ako was a good man, but he tended to fight when he really ought to withdraw. The other men knew him, trusted him, and would follow him – or Kwadwo would never have left him in charge of a retreat. It wasn't in the man's nature.

Kwadwo had other things to worry about. They had Gbohii behind them that they might avoid, if they moved fast enough. But there was another monster ahead that he had to slay, if they were to have any chance of escape. Gbohii to the rear, another to the front, and Lugu out there somewhere with her Haisetti. How the hell was he supposed to get all these people out of this mess alive?

CHAPTER FORTY-NINE

Kudowor bobbed along in the water, trying to keep his face above it. The current was damned strong out here in the middle of the river, and it was pitch dark out. He'd never have been able to see the others if they hadn't roped themselves together.

"I can't believe I let you talk me into this," he whispered to Musongola.

The other man grinned back at him, teeth white in the night, brilliant against his dark face. "It sounded to me like you wanted a piece of that asshole Rwamirama, after I gave you my report. Wasn't it you who wished he could burn the whole fort down around his ears?"

"Aane, well, that was before the whole getting wet part," Kudowor whispered back sharply.

"Hush," Tay-Natey murmured. "Sound carries at night, and we are not far now."

The hulking form of the island fortress was a black mark against the dimly lit sky. The night was overcast, the moon hidden behind the clouds and giving just enough illumination that they could make their way toward the target.

Targets, really. There were two. They wanted to recover Diata. And they wanted that ship Musongola had seen moored just offshore.

The down side? They were bobbing along in the current, wearing midnight blue clothes with faces painted indigo. They had their weapons carefully stowed into oiled leather to keep the water away. But no armor. They couldn't carry or wear armor so far through the water.

Worst yet, Rwamirama would almost certainly have his men on alert. It sounded to Kudowor like Musongola had been able to keep their secrets mostly hidden from Rwamirama. But he was a cautious, careful man, used to plans within plans. He was sure to have all his troops watching for trouble.

It would have been far better to wait a while, let him drop his guard again. But there simply wasn't time. They needed to keep moving. The Gbohii wave was still spreading out from Nicran, with more dead walking as they spread out, biting more victims. They'd reach this area soon enough, and scrounging off the land as their people had done so far would become impossible.

Without a ship, they'd never survive even the coastal sea. And while there might be more ships abandoned somewhere past the fort, that still left the problem of getting around the fort.

And then there was Diata. Musongola was obsessed with rescuing her. He was trying to keep it hidden and failing utterly. Kudowor wasn't sure whether he ought to be amused or worried. But either way, there was no way that he'd be content to leave without her.

"Magezi is almost to the ship," Tay-Natey whispered back to them.

Magezi was out front. There was at least fifty feet between him and the rest of the team. Tay-Natey was next, then Musongola, with Kudowor bringing up the rear. Everyone else was floating on the rafts, back well out of sight and moored to a rock. Waiting for them to give a signal – they planned for Tay-Natey to fire a flaming arrow into the sky.

There were so many things that could go wrong with the plan. There could be too many guards on the ship. Tay-Natey's bow could break. Musongola could be captured trying to rescue Diata.

He was tense as a pulled bowstring. But there was no help for it now. The die was cast.

"He's reached the ship," Tay-Natey said.

The current carried the rest of them closer and closer to the ship. Kudowor was sure that any moment now some guard was going to see them and call the alarm. He kept as still as he could, treading the cool water, trying not to raise more than the smallest ripples.

A tug on the rope, and then a harder one. Magezi was pulling them in. The coast must be clear. He tried not to sigh with relief.

A short while later, all four of them were nestled up against the ship's rudder, hidden from view. There was a bit more light here. Someone on board the ship had a lantern lit. That was a huge boon – the light would hurt the night vision of anyone on the vessel. Probably how they managed to get in without being spotted. The guards were more worried about Gbohii climbing up the anchor chain than they were about people swimming down the river.

No one said a word. Magezi braced himself between the hull and the rudder, fingers gripping both surfaces hard. He nodded sharply once. Musongola grabbed hold of the rudder's shaft and pulled himself up stepping on Magezi's shoulder. He jumped from there, catching the edge of the ship's rail with his fingers.

For a moment Kudowor thought Musongola was going to fall back into the river, his splash revealing all of them. But he hauled himself up instead and slid onto the stern of the ship.

The tail end of a rope dropped over the edge. Tay-Natey caught it before it plopped into the water. He grabbed hold and hauled himself upward, hand over hand.

Kudowor would be next to ascend. He steadied the tail of the rope for Tay-Natey while he made his way up. Tay-Natey vanished over the side. But before Kudowor could begin his own climb, he heard a yell from above. Then more shouts, and the sound of swords banging against swords. He lunged out of the water, climbing as fast as he could. They'd been spotted, and if the guards could sound the alarm – or if men on the shore saw the fighting – it was all over before they'd even started!

***

Musongola caught the first man's blade with his own, twisting his sword around his opponent's weapon. He continued the circling motion, then thrusted forward, hard. His sword went into the man's gut, slicing upward. He never had a chance to cry out. Musongola withdrew the blade and the body collapsed, blood gushing over the deck.

But he was too damned far from the second guard! The man was sprinting to a bell set on the mast. Musongola ran toward him, trying to catch up, but he'd never make it in time. Desperation fueled his legs, drove him on. If that man rung the bell, he'd never be able to get in and free Diata. And he wasn't going to be able to stop him.

An arrow flew past his ear and slammed into the guard's back. A second whizzed past, sliding into place a foot above the first. The guard dropped like his strings had been cut. Musongola turned. Tay-Natey already had a third arrow on his bowstring, just in case. But there was no more movement. It looked like two guards were all Rwamirama had spared for the ship.

"Well shot," Musongola whispered.

"I aim to please," Tay-Natey replied with a smirk.

Musongola groaned quietly, then went to help the others aboard. Kudowor was almost up already and just needed a quick hand over the rail. Magezi followed a moment later. Once they were all aboard, they gathered close to hold a whispered conference. They'd been over the plan before, but this was their last chance to hammer out any details before they put it into action.

"Tay-Natey, you still think you can get Musongola over their walls?" Kudowor asked.

"For sure," the bowman replied.

"And once you're in there, you sure you can get her out?" Kudowor prodded.

"I'll do my best," Musongola said. "Worst case, you'll have one hell of a diversion."

Kudowor reached out and clasped a hand over his shoulder. "Make it work. We can't afford to lose you."

Musongola climbed over the side of the ship, easing himself down the rope. Carefully, he slid back down into the cold water. He set off through the river, swimming his way to the rocky shore. He could hear Tay-Natey settle into the water behind him and begin to follow.

He appreciated Kudowor's concerns. Truly, he did. And he understood how deep a mess the man was in. He had few enough fighters as it was. Losing one warrior might be enough to doom his entire party to death. But Musongola couldn't worry about that, not right now. Diata was in danger – he knew damned well that Rwamirama would use her as a weapon and bargaining tool only as long as he needed her. Past that, he'd have no qualms handing her over to his men or simply slitting her throat. He was ruthless in his pursuit of efficiency.

He carefully avoided the docks, and the rocky beach near them. The little island was an odd one – and really, ideal for defense. Three sides of the rock were almost sheer drops of fifty feet from the top of the cliff, into the water, and from there into the depths. Only on the one side was there any sort of beach, and that was more piles of rock than anything else. The beach would be carefully watched, and they'd be picked off before they could ever reach the shore.

Instead, Musongola made for the sheer cliff right below the fort wall.

The stone was smooth from the flow of water over many years. Slimy with algae, slick with water – Musongola couldn't get a grip on anything. Tay-Natey had been right. There was no way he'd have been able to climb this thing.

"You owe me a drink," Tay-Natey whispered in his ear.

"Aane. You were right," he replied ruefully.

"My way is better," Tay-Natey said, chuckling softly.

"We'll see. You still have to shoot the arrow."

"You want me to shoot the arrow, you'll need to find me a spot to shoot it dry," Tay-Natey said.

The biggest challenge for this rescue had been keeping the damned bow and bowstring dry. A wet bow wouldn't fire. So the bow, along with the special arrow Tay-Natey made for the shot, were carefully wrapped in oiled leather to keep them as dry as possible. And the bowstring was stored in a bit of pig's intestine. It wasn't a perfect solution, but it kept the string safe while the man swam.

He needed someplace dry to restring his bow, though. Musongola ran his fingers over the cliff face, looking for a ridge or ledge. Finally, he found a small ledge – but it was two feet under the waterline. Reaching up, he could almost touch another small ledge above his head.

"Here," he whispered. "I'll boost you."

Tay-Natey looked dubious as Musongola made a cup with his hands. But he placed his foot and stepped from there to Musongola's shoulders. Musongola grimaced at the sudden weight, and felt his feet slip a bit on the rock. He reached out with his hands to steady himself again, and Tay-Natey wobbled in his perch.

"Keep steady!" Tay-Natey said.

Musongola saved his breath and worked at keeping his weight centered. Tay-Natey wobbled a bit. Then the tip of the bow was near Musongola's ear. He heard Tay-Natey grunt with effort –

that would be him stringing the bow. It was almost time. His pulse picked up the pace.

"Hold very still," Tay-Natey whispered.

The arrow was a special one. It lacked a regular arrowhead. Instead, Tay-Natey had placed a small metal hook on the end of the arrow and tied a rope to the steel. Musongola had to admit, he thought the resulting arrow looked too damned frail to support him. But Tay-Natey swore he had done this sort of thing before. And nobody else had any better ideas.

Worst case, the arrow would fail and they'd be stuck trying something even more stupid.

He heard Tay-Natey shoot the arrow and listened hard. A moment later, there was a clacking sound. Then all at once Tay-Natey's weight vanished from his shoulders. He looked up, remembering not to yell in surprise.

And there was Tay-Natey, rope in his hands, feet planted against the cliff.

"Looks like it will work," he said wryly.

"I still have to make it to the top," Musongola replied.

"That's two drinks you owe me, Musongola."

Musongola took the rope in his hands and placed his feet carefully. It would be a long climb. "I'll pay you when I get back."

"Be careful," Tay-Natey said more seriously.

Musongola didn't reply. He had already started working his way up the rope, which required all his focus. Somewhere up there was Diata. This rescue, impossible as it might seem, was her only chance of escape. Musongola steeled himself for what lay ahead.

CHAPTER FIFTY

Etse watched his people move into the farmyard with something that was closely approximating military precision. They weren't all that polished – not yet. But they'd come a long way in just two days. It helped that no one wanted to spend any more time in the caves than they had to. That gave them all the motivation he could have asked for. And he'd pushed them. Driven them. The group had precious few weapons, but they'd augmented their two swords – Etse's and the one Agboko had used – and handful of spears with a few fire-hardened wooden spears. They were useless against any sort of armored foe but against the Gbohii, they might just be enough to slow the things long enough for the swordsmen to take them down.

They were pretty sure a Gbohii lurked somewhere in the farmhouse. But Etse didn't think there was more than one. He hoped not, anyway. These people might be up to ambushing one of the things, but if there was more than one, he'd probably lose fighters. They weren't good enough to defend themselves against the lightning fast monsters, and Etse could only keep one of the things busy at a time.

There was no choice, though. They needed the food and other supplies they might find in the farm. And they had to begin making their way out of the hills, off to someplace safer. Takoradi seemed the best bet, as far as Etse was concerned. It would take them days to get there, though.

Jiagge and Kpeda led the rush to the farmhouse. They were brothers – or half-brothers, if Etse recalled right. Both of them carried true spears. Behind them jostled four other men bearing the wooden staves, one end sharpened to make a crude stabbing tip. With luck, they might find some more weapons soon. It wasn't unusual for an Asante to have a spear set about the house. These times were not without their dangers even before the Gbohii came.

"Uche, stay close with me," Etse said to the man beside him. Then he dashed forward to join the others at the farmhouse. He clinked as he jogged along – the armor was welcome, even if he feared he might never wash Agboko's blood from the tortoise shell shirt he'd worn when he died. It hadn't saved its last wearer from death, but Etse had already seen how effective armor was against the teeth of these things. Every small edge might help.

He reached the barn door with Uche still right at his side. So far, the man was doing well with his tutelage. None of the survivors from Agboko's camp had ever carried a sword before – but he needed to see every weapon in use. So he asked for volunteers and tested each one in duels with sticks. Uche had the strength and reflexes to become a decent swordsman. If he lived long enough.

Etse nodded, and Kpeda kicked the door open. Kpeda and his brother went into the room side by side, spears ahead of them. No monster greeted them just inside, so the two men stepped aside slightly to allow the next two spearmen in. Etse and Uche went in right after, leaving two spearmen outside to watch for trouble. The cottage wasn't large – a quick survey of the space showed that nothing lurked inside here for them.

"I could have sworn one was here," Etse muttered. There were all the signs. Bits of dead animal carcass scattered about in the yard. Flies were everywhere and a carrion smell emanated from the place. But if there had been one here, where was it now?

There was a yell from outside. Etse whirled and was back out the door before anyone else could move.

He cleared the doorway and went from the dim space of the house into dazzling sunlight. The Gbohii had found them – had found the two guards he'd left outside, anyway. They had used their spears well, both of them stabbing the thing just like he'd shown them. But he hadn't figured on the thing's strength, and even as he watched it brought an arm down in a hammer-like blow against one of the shafts, shattering it. It reached out with both claws to take the hapless man's head. Another step, and it would have him.

Etse moved just fast enough. He closed the gap with the thing, his sword licking out to take a hand off at the wrist. That got its attention and let the farmer-turned-spearman back up out of danger. Etse wanted to drive in against the thing, to cut it apart. He felt a furious anger at these monsters and wanted nothing but to break each one to bits with his sword.

But it wasn't enough to cut them down himself. He couldn't slay them all alone. He needed these men trained. So instead of cutting its head off himself, he took a step back.

"Take it," he told his men.

Kpeda and Jiagge charged at it, spears plunging into the Gbohii's belly. They spread out, their spears keeping it from rushing either of them. Both men panted with the effort and stress.

"Uche, the blow is yours," Etse said.

His student was shaking a little, but to his credit the man didn't hesitate. Three steps brought him within striking range of the monster. It seemed to know the danger and lunged at Uche. Again, Etse almost dashed at the thing, desperate to protect his people. But the only way he could ultimately protect them was by teaching them to fight for themselves. So he kept his place. This was Uche's show.

Uche swung the sword. The blow was too slow, and the Gbohii raised a hand to block. The arm bones snapped from the force, but the blow was diverted. It lunged at him again, and the spearmen could barely keep it off him this time.

"Best hurry. It wants to sink its teeth into you," Etse said. He kept his tone light, but he stayed on the balls of his feet, ready to rush in and help if he was needed.

Uche shouted a wordless battle cry and swung his sword again. This time, the blow was true, and the sword broke into the side of the thing's skull. Bone splintered and cracked. The sword blade bit into the monster's brain – and it died, crumpling to the ground. The man stood slack-jawed, staring at the monster he'd slain. Etse wondered if he'd looked like that when he killed his first one on the beach.

"Well done," Etse said, clapping him on the back. "Don't hesitate if your first swing misses next time, though."

"I won't," Uche replied.

Etse leaned down to pick up bits of the broken spear. That was going to be a problem. They needed weapons – good ones! Not makeshift sharpened staves. It was going to be hard enough getting home, without their weapons breaking every other day. Still, the men had done well. He looked them all over. No one bitten, and even the man whose spear broke held his ground fairly well. He'd been right in thinking that these people were not ready to face more than one of the things at a time.

Neither had he been, those first few fights. If they lived, these men would grow better at battling the things. Etse had ideas about training – some of the things he'd wanted to do with Okoth, back in Nicran. If only they'd had more time, back then! A battalion of men trained in techniques which worked well against the dead could perhaps have held that city.

Now the last Mikijen was dead. All that remained of Asanteman were scattered people trying to pick up pieces every bit as broken as the splinters of wood he held that had once been a spear.

They scouted the barn, to be sure there were no more Gbohii inside, but it was clear. Nothing was alive inside, although rotting, half eaten carcasses of a couple of the animals remained.

"Kpeda, go call everyone in," Etse said once the sweep was done. "The rest of us will start cleaning the more disgusting bits out of the barn."

There were groans at that. No one relished the idea of moving the decaying chunks of what had been sheep and cow. Etse smiled at the groans, though.

"Do you want Sefadzi to show up and take us to task for asking her to sleep in a barn full of dead animals?" he said, grinning.

The men smiled back. The girl was something of a mascot for their band of refugees. She floated through the crowd while they marched, passing a flower to one man, bringing water to a woman, staggering sometimes as she tried to carry a grown-up load of supplies. She was popular, and no one wanted to let the girl down. They set about their work.

Etse went back into the barn. It was crude, but it would keep them out of the weather and out of sight for the night. They'd need to be on their way again at first light, but traveling at night was too dangerous. It was bad enough when you could see the Gbohii at a distance and avoid the larger packs. But at night they could stumble into a band of the things before they realized the danger.

Better to hide through the night in places like this.

There was a hay loft in the barn, and the hay there was still dry and mostly free of mildew. The loft could only be reached by ladder. Pull the ladder up, and they'd have a little more security. Posting guards through the night would give them more.

Food was going to be an issue soon. Every farmhouse in Asanteman had some way to get fresh water nearby. But in the weeks since everything had gone to shit, food had become much harder to come by. It was too early for much in the way of harvest, and what there might have been was fast becoming overgrown from lack of care. Most of the animals and livestock were dead at the Gbohii's hands or had run into the hills. And stored food had often gone bad.

Etse's band numbered twenty three. Only four of those were children, which was both a blessing and a curse. The children took more care, could work less, needed more help, and were defenseless against the undead. So they could ill afford to have too many young ones with them for a trip like this. But it hurt Etse's heart to know that it was the children paying the highest price for this disaster. When he arrived at Agboko's caves, there had been eight children there. Of those, only two survived the attack. The other two children were Sefadzi – and her new friend, Amon. They seemed inseparable, ever since she'd found him in the woods and rescued him.

He was glad she had someone to play with. The girl was too quiet most of the time. There was always an oddness about her, like she was looking at the same things he was, but from a little different angle, somehow. He liked hearing her laugh, and Amon made her laugh.

He stood atop the hay, staring out the open window toward the west. Had Kwesi made for Takoradi, as Kwadwo said they planned? It seemed so damned far away, especially having to skirt the major cities along the path. They passed near two small towns, and both were full of Gbohii. He could only imagine the cities would be even worse. Was there anywhere left that might be safe? Sometimes he despaired of ever finding a way to get these people someplace they could call home.

"Where are you, father? Are you alive out there?" he asked aloud.

There was no answer from the evening wind.

CHAPTER FIFTY-ONE

Kwadwo sloshed through the sewer muck, following Odoi, the boy who'd led him through the warehouse. The youngster hadn't steered him wrong up above. Kwadwo hoped he knew these foul passages just as well. Somewhere not far ahead was a Gbohii. And not far behind them were the Gbohii that Lugu unleashed in the warehouse. The monsters hadn't found the trap door yet. He'd have heard the fighting begin if they had. But he knew that it was a matter of time, and not much of it.

He kept his breathing controlled as carefully as he could, because he could feel shivers running down his back, and it wasn't just from the cold water filling the bottom third of the sewer tunnels. He'd run into these things a few times already, and although he'd been lucky enough to survive the encounters so far, Kwadwo had a gut feeling that was only a matter of time. Eventually, he was going to be even the littlest bit unlucky, and a set of those terrible jaws would close on some tasty chunk of him...

Kwadwo shook himself, trying to break out of this dark mood. He didn't have time for it. Too damned many people counting on him, all of a sudden. He hadn't expected to see so many people show up tonight. Scores of Takoradi citizens – men, women, and children – trying to flee the city. And counting on him to show them the way out. To lead them, God help them all.

"Be ready," Kwadwo told the spearmen walking with him. "As soon as we see it, use your spears to pin it in place. I'll finish the thing."

They looked frightened. Lugu had shown off a couple of her pet Gbohii to the populace to cow them. It had worked. These people were terrified of the things. That was going to be a problem once they got outside. They'd have to face that fear more often than they would like.

He wished once again that Kwesi was here. The man would have known what to do. Would have taken charge and taken action. But Kwesi was dead by his mad daughter's hand. Etse was gone, lost in Nicran. Kudowor was God-knew-where, trying to keep the other Nicran refugees alive. Kwadwo felt like everything had flown apart, like all their carefully constructed lives were shattered and they were running around chasing pieces.

Up ahead, he heard the growl of a Gbohii. He motioned the spearmen to stillness and caught their young guide by the shoulder to stop him. The tunnel curved up ahead. The shade of the darkness just outside their torchlight had changed somewhat. Was that a blue tone he could see? The dim illumination of starlight?

He took three strides ahead, rounding the corner – and there it was, a black silhouette against the heavy iron grille. Beyond those metal bars – freedom! But only if they could get past the monster barring their way.

"Now, men!" Kwadwo said. The spearmen rushed forward, stabbing the thing with their weapons. It shrieked its rage, reaching for them with rotting claws. These were ordinary spears – no time to weld crossbars like Etse had suggested back in Nicran. But the Gbohii was chained to the sewer grate, keeping it from reaching the spearmen. All they needed to do was hold the thing in place so that Kwadwo's sword could do the rest.

He stepped forward to face the thing, dreading that it might have been someone he knew. He was spared that, at least. Kwadwo caught a glimpse of the thing's face, but it was no one he recognized. He heaved a sigh of relief mixed with sadness.

Even if it wasn't someone he knew, it had been a man once. Before the curse took him.

Best to end it. Kwadwo drew his sword and struck the thing's head off. It splashed into the muck and sank. He stabbed down where it had fallen, aware that even separated from the body, the head might still be dangerous if someone stumbled across it in the sewage. His first stab only bumped against the thing, but his second bit deep into the skull. He was confident the thing was dead. The body had already slumped down, hanging from its fetters on the iron rails.

"Stonecutters, you're needed now," Kwadwo called. No need for quiet now. If anyone were out there, they'd hear the masons cutting through the stone soon enough. The spearmen pulled back, giving the masons room to work. They went about the business quickly, chisels biting into the stone that held the heavy iron bars in place. No one wanted to stay in this tunnel with the dead thing any longer than they needed to. And everyone knew what was hunting for them in the warehouse above.

No sooner had Kwadwo had the thought than he heard shouts from somewhere up the passage behind them.

"Shit. With me!" he said to the spearmen and rushed back up the tunnel toward the place they'd entered the sewers from the warehouse. Ako would be trying to hold the space against the things. Kwadwo knew that the man had little chance of succeeding. Even one of those things might be more than they could handle. How many had Lugu unleashed?

People were fleeing down the watery passage as quickly as they could manage. They weren't going to get very far. Even as fast as the masons were working, it was going to take time to clear their path to freedom. Kwadwo grimaced. How to buy them the time they needed?

He reached the spot where he'd plunged into the sewer without seeing a single Gbohii – or the men he'd left behind as a rear guard. Where were they? He slowed down, more cautious. There were still oil lamps in the space above. He could see the flickering light they cast.

"Ako?" he called up, hoping the man was still alive.

"Aane," came the reply. Kwadwo almost sagged with relief.

"What the hell is going on up there?" Kwadwo asked.

Ako's face appeared over the hole from the cellar into the sewer. "It's a mess, Kwadwo. They're just outside the damned trap door. It's barred with a spear shaft for now, but it won't hold."

No, it wouldn't. Kwadwo remembered the things tearing apart the stout doors of the palace in Nicran. They'd make quick work of the trap door.

"Help me up," he said, reaching out a hand. Ako held out his own – just out of reach. Kwadwo jumped and managed to grab hold. With a grunt of effort, the big man pulled him up from the tunnel.

He looked around the room. Only five of the reserve guards had stayed with Ako. He must have sent the others down into the tunnel. Little was left in the room. All the refugees had packed light, bringing only what they could carry, and they'd taken it with them when they fled into the sewer. The trap door rattled and shook, and bits of the wood broke away as the Gbohii above clawed their way through. The only other thing in the room were the three oil lamps still left burning, and the big cask they were sitting on.

There was nothing they could use here. They'd have to retreat into the sewer and hope to fight the Gbohii in there, where at least they could use the narrow tunnels with their spears to keep the things at bay. It would have to be enough.

"Come on, let's grab the lanterns and make a run for it," Kwadwo said. He went over and picked one up, letting his hand rest on the barrel for a moment when he did. The barrel was heavy – full of something.

"Ako, what's in here?" he asked, unstopping the cork on the barrel. It was a water-tight cask, like one might use for ale. But the smell wafting from the open cork-hole wasn't a brew. It was oil.

An idea struck him. Desperate. Mad even. But these were mad times, and it might just work...!

Overhead, a large crack appeared in the trap door.

"All of you men, into the tunnel!" Kwadwo said. They moved to comply, and Ako went to follow them. "Oh, no. Not you, Ako." Kwadwo gave the man a wicked grin.

Ako groaned.

"I need you to help me with this barrel."

Kwadwo waited until the other men had fled the room. He put out two of the lanterns and carefully set the third up on a small stone ledge. Then he grabbed onto the side of the cask. Ako grabbed the other side.

"So, what are we doing with this?" Ako asked.

"Spilling it," Kwadwo replied, and pulled. Together, the two men heaved the heavy barrel over on its side. The top popped off, and thick oil poured across the floor. Some of it spilled down the hole into the sewer, but the stuff was fairly viscous. A thick layer spread quickly over the floor.

Above them came another loud crack, and a board came away from the trap door. A Gbohii arm reached through the opening. Growling and hissing noises spewed from the floor above as the things worried at the hole, making it bigger.

The sudden sound startled Ako. He tried to whirl, slipped on the oil, and fell into the stuff. He got back to his feet cautiously, his whole body glistening with oil.

"Damn it!" Ako said.

"Get out of here," Kwadwo said. "I mean to light this place up. I don't think you want to be too close to the flames, right now."

Ako shook his head. "I suppose not. But I'll wait just down the corridor for you." He turned and made his way to the sewer as quickly as he could manage on the slick floor. Kwadwo followed, even more cautious. Falling right now would be a disaster. He picked up the lantern as he went.

Above him, another board was torn out of the trap door. The hole they'd opened was big enough now, and one of the Gbohii jumped down. It hit the slick oil and lost its footing, smashing down against the stone floor.

No time to waste! Kwadwo grabbed the grate that had covered the sewer entrance in one hand, still holding the lantern in the other. He held the grate above his head and jumped down through the hole. The metal grate was bigger than the hole, and his fall stopped as soon as it hit the edge, leaving his legs dangling. The sudden stop jarred his other hand, though – the lamp slipped from his oily fingers and fell hissing into the ooze below him.

In the room above, three more Gbohii dropped down. They too slid around on the floor trying crazily to keep their balance, but for once their speed worked against them here. The faster they moved, the more they fell. The more they fell, the more covered with oil they became, which made it even harder for them to keep their feet beneath them.

Kwadwo hung, one hand on the grate above him. His boots were a few feet above the sewer muck. He stared upward. Without the lamp, he had no way of setting the room alight. He should drop down and run. He was about to do so when he heard a voice shout from down the tunnel.

"Me wura! I have a torch!"

It was Odoi! The boy was sloshing through the water toward Kwadwo. He reached Ako, and the big man grabbed the torch from him, plunging toward Kwadwo through the muck. He made much better time – his large body moved the water out of his way, plowing a path.

Kwadwo looked back up. A Gbohii was standing there, above the opening, slavering mouth open. He screamed.

The thing lunged down at his hand. Kwadwo was about to let go. Knew he had to let go or die. He had no choice...!

And then Ako placed the torch in his open hand.

Kwadwo thrust the flaming brand upward desperately. He stabbed it through a hole in the grate, and it set the oil alight all around the metal. The oil on his hand caught fire. Drips of liquid flame poured down like rivers of light from above.

The Gbohii had fallen on the slick floor. It was soaked with the stuff and caught the torch full in its face. It burst into flames, and Kwadwo saw it flee, engulfed, before he let go and dropped into the muck below him.

The water was blessedly cool on his scorched hand and where the fire had scorched his cheek. He rose to the surface, breathing hard. Bits of oil were alight on the surface of the sewer water, but most of the flames were contained in the room above. Kwadwo could hear the monsters scream, and the sound brought him a sense of vindictive joy.

"Come on. Time to be gone from here," Kwadwo said. The masons would be through the stone, soon. The fire above was intense enough that it was sure to set the warehouse above aflame. The distraction might just give them a chance to get out of Takoradi unseen if they hurried.

By the time they reached the grate, the masons were already done. Carefully, they lifted away the heavy iron bars. The sewage flowed from the pipe out into a small pool, and from there became a stream that flowed into a tributary of the Densu River. One by one, they helped each other step from the darkness out into starlight. It was a moonless night, which helped. And the walls seemed curiously lacking in guards. Lugu must have pulled most of her troops to help stop his escape. He could see the orange light from the fire even over the wall and heard the shouts and alarms of people running to help. A fire inside the city was dangerous. Whole blocks might burn if it wasn't controlled.

Ako led the first groups out of the sewer away from the walls, making west for the marshes. They might lose Lugu that way, hiding in the bogs and marshes west of the city for at least a while. Kwadwo stayed at the opening, helping more people through, until there was only one left.

"Odoi," he said. He smiled, and although it was too dark for the young man to see his face, he hoped that the expression came across in his tone. "You saved us all, tonight."

"You saved us, me wura. I only helped the little bit that I could," Odoi said.

"It was enough. More than enough." Kwadwo helped him down from the sewer, and the two set off to follow their band. They were refugees, now, without shelter in a world filled with monsters. But he had hope. He still had Kwesi's key. Whatever the legacy was, Kwadwo hoped it was worth all this trouble.

CHAPTER FIFTY-TWO

Kudowor reached over the side of the ship to help Tay-Natey back out of the water.

"Musongola made it?" Kudowor asked.

"Aane, he's inside the keep," Tay-Natey replied.

By his best guess, three hours had passed since he'd left the rest of the refugees behind on their makeshift island of rafts. Assuming they did as he'd instructed, they should have pulled up the rocks they'd been using as anchors and begun bobbing down the river some time ago. He hoped they would be able to steer well clear of the island. Rwamirama would have lookouts posted, watching for boats on the water. He had no doubt they'd send men after the rafts if they were seen.

Everything counted on timing. Musongola would be at the top of the fortress by now, waiting for their signal. He would give them a diversion and keep the fort's troops occupied. That would let the rafts drift through. And then Magezi, Tay-Natey, and Kudowor would take the ship around to pick up their people from the rafts, ideally rescuing Diata and Musongola at the same time.

"How did I let him talk me into this, again?" Kudowor grumbled. The plan was insane. They'd just drawn the anchor from the water, and the ship was beginning to drift a little in the current. Another minute, and the troops on the shore would notice. They needed to act before that.

Magezi laughed, a low rumble. "Because even if it fails, it works. Musongola will stir the pot up there. He might make it out with the woman. He might not. But even if he fails, he'll still give the rest of us the chance to make a break for it."

"The big man is right," Tay-Natey said somberly. "You think he is just doing this for the woman? He wants to save her, sure. But he is giving the rest of us a clear shot out of Rwamirama's trap."

Kudowor grimaced. "I hope he manages both missions, then. We can't afford to lose him."

Neither man replied, but Kudowor knew their minds. Either of them would die for Musongola. But neither of them had volunteered to take his place, because neither of them had a prayer of accomplishing what he was trying to do.

"Magezi, come help me with the sail. Tay-Natey, fire your arrow as soon as we're aloft." He set to climbing the mesh of rope rigging which ran from the sides of the boat up to where the mast met the yard. Damn, but it had been too long since he'd done this! His feet slipped on the ratlines in his haste to reach the top, but he caught himself and resumed his climb.

He was relieved to see that he beat Magezi to the top. At least he was still nimble enough to outrun a novice. He shook his head. Plenty of time to get back into practice soon, if everything went well tonight! As soon as his hands touched the yard, he heard the twang of Tay-Natey's bow below him. He looked over his shoulder to watch the arrow.

Tay-Natey had lit the thing from the lantern on the ship, so he was able to track it as it shot skyward. A hundred feet or more the arrow climbed, burning all the way up, before it arced over a little and began the long descent back toward the river. It splashed down a score of feet from the ship, hissing when it struck the water.

"That's woke everyone up for sure," Kudowor said. "Let's get these knots undone."

Carefully, he eased his way out along the yard – a wooden pole a dozen feet long to which the sail was tied. Knots all along the yard held the canvas in place, and each of them needed to be undone. He set about the work as quickly as he could.

They needed to be fast. He could hear the hue and cry on the island. Every soldier in the place would be up and moving soon. And the ship was drifting in the current – straight toward Rwamirama's fortress.

***

Making the top of the wall hadn't been hard for Musongola. He was a good climber, and although the rope had been thin and wet, he was fearful enough that the grappling hook would break or be discovered that he fairly flew up the wall. Once he reached the top, he pitched the arrow and rope back into the sea. He wished he could hold on to the rope, but it was too big, too bulky. He'd never be able to hide it.

Staying out of sight until Tay-Natey fired the signal arrow was much harder. The men on the wall were alert. They were Mikijen, and well trained. Say what you would about Rwamirama – he always maintained discipline well. Musongola managed to make it over the battlements without being spotted. But how to stay out of sight?

He saw quickly it wasn't going to be possible. Rwamirama had people posted at each corner, but he also had walking patrols marching around the battlements. One of those would catch him eventually if he stood still.

There was no place to hide. Which meant it was time to bluff, instead.

The next roaming patrol was about a hundred feet behind him. It would be where he stood, soon enough. But he was wearing Kiswalan clothing; he knew the signals and mannerisms of these men. How hard would it be to blend in with them? He started walking the wall, like he was on a roaming patrol himself.

There was a flaw with his plan. The other roving guards were pairs of men. He was alone. He had to hope that sometimes men would patrol or walk the walls at night alone. He passed the first corner tower, where two men sat on guard. One of them nodded to him as he walked by, and he nodded back. Musongola walked on trying to ignore the itching feeling that he felt between his shoulder blades. At least one of the men he just passed was armed with a bow. But no outcry was raised behind him. It was working!

He kept working his way around the walls, all the while examining the keep trying to see where Diata might be held. She had to be somewhere in the keep itself, but where?

Musongola rounded the second corner, passing a second tower, and realized with a start that the battlements didn't circle the keep entirely. On the back end, they came to an abrupt stop at the wall of the inner keep itself. A door allowed entrance – there must be a corridor inside which led to a similar door on the other side, so that the troops could access the battlements from either side of the inner keep.

He looked over his shoulder. There was no turning back. The patrol was still behind him. Had they picked up their pace? It seemed like they were much closer than they had been, the last time he looked. Had he aroused their suspicions?

He decided that his best chance would be to get into the keep itself. He might be able to lose himself in there somewhere. Damn it, how long did it take to swim back to the ship, anyway? Tay-Natey ought to be lighting that arrow already. Musongola was counting on that distraction every bit as much as Kudowor counted on the distraction he would provide in turn.

Musongola was almost to the door. Another few steps, and he'd be inside.

The door opened when he was still a spear-length away, a smiling Rwamirama waiting within.

Musongola's hand went to his sword hilt, but he heard the clatter of armor behind him. A quick glance over his shoulder showed the two guards, spears at the ready, only a few feet away. He pulled his hand away from his sword.

"When I got a report of a stranger up on our battlements, I knew it had to be you," Rwamirama said. "I'm impressed. This was quite a job, even for you."

"Not so much. Remember that time in Menu-Kash?" Musongola asked.

"Aane, there was that. How did you manage to get up here?" Rwamirama asked. "No, never mind. Better question: what am I supposed to do with you now?"

"Well, you have two prisoners, now," Musongola said, shifting the cloak off his shoulders a bit. "That ought to be better than one, when it comes to bargaining with Okere, right?"

"Right," Rwamirama scoffed. "Like I'd keep you around. Your ability to escape imprisonment is a legend even among my men, Musongola. You're a liability, not an asset."

That was when Musongola realized Rwamirama meant to kill him. It came as a shock, even knowing what the man had become, what he was doing. They'd campaigned side by side for years. He'd never really liked the taciturn Rwamirama, and had a feeling that was mutual, but they'd been comrades at arms... Somehow, he'd never really expected Rwamirama would order him slain. But he saw the order there, in the man's eyes. Another moment and he'd speak the words, and those spears behind him would plunge into his back.

Time to bluff. Stall. "I'd say you were right," Musongola said. "Except that I know something that you do not know..."

"And what would that be?"

At that moment, a flaming arrow shot skyward from the water. Everyone turned to look as the thing sped high into the air, higher even than the tallest tower of the fort.

Everyone except Musongola.

He pivoted to his left, sweeping his cloak up with his left arm. With his right, he drew his sword. The cloak whipped around the spears held by the startled guards behind him, pushing the deadly tips away. His sword was moving as he turned and sank deep into the belly of the closest man.

The soldier sank to his knees, gurgling blood.

Musongola whipped the sword back out before the man's knees struck stone. He whipped the sword over into a downward blow on the other guard. The man blocked desperately with the haft of his spear, but Musongola's sword cut the wood in half and kept going. The blade rang as it struck the man's helmet, and he crumpled.

Another pivot, to come back around and face Rwamirama – but the man was already gone. The door hung ajar, but no one was there.

All around, alarms were sounding. If things were proceeding according to plan, Kudowor would have the ship under sail by now, which ought to attract a fair bit of attention. It was up to him now to split that attention and confuse the enemy. He looked down at the men he'd already fought. Well, it was a good start.

He had to find Diata. Where would Rwamirama keep her? Musongola went into the fortress. There was a door down the hall, which ought to lead out to the battlements of the opposite wall. And there were two flights of stairs spiraling away from this level.

"Up or down?" he asked aloud. He peered down and heard the sound of armored boots climbing up the stone steps toward him.

"Up it is," he quipped. He raced up the steps, the enemy hot on his heels.

CHAPTER FIFTY-THREE

Etse woke to a sound he hadn't heard in a while: a cock crowing. The sound was a welcome one. They could all use a bit of meat. He rose quickly and went to the guard posted by the window. It was Kpeda's shift. The man remained alert, scanning the field, but he glanced over his shoulder as Etse approached.

"Good morning, Etse."

"Good morning. Are those chickens I'm hearing?" Etse asked.

"Aane. Several of them wandered into the yard this morning," Kpeda replied. He paused, licking his lips unconsciously. Then he said "Me wura, do you think we might...?"

"Oh, absolutely," Etse said with a smile.

A short while later they had four chickens roasting over a small fire. The cooking would delay their departure a bit, but it seemed worth the time. Even if they made good progress, they were still at least another long day's march from Takoradi, and who knew what they would find there? Some food would do these people good.

That also gave him time to finish scouting the farm. They found a few sacks, some clothes to replace worn bits, a water skin, and some other odds and ends. Anything they thought might be useful was gathered up and packed. Uche discovered a root cellar, and some of the food stored inside was still good to eat. The supplies they had were meager, but they might just be enough to see them through.

"Etse!"

He whirled to see who was calling his name with such alarm. Jiagge was up in the loft, on guard, and he was pointing into the distance.

"What is it?" Etse called up to him. If it were Gbohii, they'd have to move quickly to evade them.

"Riders!"

Riders? Etse climbed the ladder to the loft to see for himself. Sure enough, there they were. Six horsemen, wearing armor and carrying spears, trailing more kwapawnkah that had no riders. And they also had a host of people walking, although the walkers looked unarmed from this distance. The riders stayed in a circle around the outside of the pack afoot. Guarding them, it looked to Etse at first. But then one of the walkers stumbled and fell. A rider walked his kwapawnkah next to the fallen walker and stabbed down with his spear.

"God!" Jiagge exclaimed. "He killed the man!"

"Slavers," Etse said. "Collecting human booty and hauling it home with them."

They were headed straight for the farm, too. Straight for Etse and his people. Damn it all! He looked down at the cooking pit, where the chickens were roasting. You could probably see the smoke for miles. What had he been thinking?

He'd been thinking that his people were hungry, and that the Gbohii were unlikely to be drawn to the smoke. They hadn't seemed especially attracted to smoke or fire in Nicran, anyway. But he hadn't counted on the human predators.

Another few minutes and they'd be at the farm. He didn't have much time to prepare a welcome for them.

"Everyone with a weapon, with me!" he called out. "Everyone else, in the loft. We'll try to scare them off if we can."

People moved fast. There had been enough frightening things these last few days that no one hesitated when danger came.

Anyone who was in the habit of reacting too slowly was already dead.

"I'm going to go out to meet them," Etse told his fighters. "I want the rest of you to stay put. Defend the barn if they attack. Try to keep the rest of our people alive. Understand?"

They all looked a little lost, but they nodded. Etse swallowed hard. If he died, this whole band would fall apart. He could feel it. He was the glue that held them together. And that was a curse. Even death would not relieve the burden from his shoulders, because if he died, it would be the ultimate failure, the final disaster for the people he was trying to protect. They were not ready to survive on their own yet.

All those thoughts weighed on his mind, as he went out to meet the riders. These slavers might just run him down, pierce his body with spears, and kill all his people. But if they huddled in the barn, the riders could just burn the thing down around their ears. He had no choice but to face them.

At least this way, maybe he could make them a little afraid of him. He snapped up a spear. He had no shield, but with a spear and a sword, he'd look more impressive.

The riders halted just outside spear throwing distance. One hung back, watching their prisoners. The others trotted back and forth, wary, their eyes scanning the area around him. They were looking for more warriors, Etse realized. Only an idiot would go out on foot to face six armed riders alone. They figured he had backup somewhere. And he did – but they were so wet behind the ears that they'd be easy pickings for men like these.

The riders steered their kwapawnkah with reins, but Etse noticed that they kept trying to use their legs to command the mounts – without success. These men were used to warhorses, mounts trained to be steered with the legs so the hands were free to fight. The kwapawnkah, on the other hand, were common mounts, gazelles untrained for battle. Etse filed the information away.

The men's faces were painted with red and white streaks. Their skin was bronze-to-copper-brown, hair black and brown. Etse was fairly sure they were Haisetti, out of the northeast of Ki Khanga. Unusual to see them this far west unless they were part of a much larger raiding party. He stood his ground, playing the waiting game. Etse wanted them to react first. He was sweating a little as the sun warmed the air, and not all of the sweat was from the heat.

"Going to use your stick on us, Asante?" one of the riders called out.

Etse didn't reply.

"I started to believe you have no other warriors here with you. But we saw others here. Will none of them stand and fight with you?" the Haisetti asked.

"There are only six of you. It wouldn't be sporting," Etse replied.

The rider laughed. "Only six! Sporting? Ha!" He said something to the other riders in a language Etse didn't know. They all broke out in chuckles. One of them grinned at Etse and made a cutting motion across his throat.

"Amsalu there wants your skull, Asante. To add to his collection," the speaker said. "Should I let him have it?"

Etse managed a laugh. "He can try."

The speaker barked a few words, and the Haisetti he'd called Amsalu started his kwapawnkah into a trot. He rode off to the side a little, brought his spear forward, turned the kwapawnkah – and charged straight toward Etse!

The kwapawnkah went from a trot to a full gallop in just a few seconds. Etse had moments to react. The spear would be better here than the sword. Carefully, he hefted it overhand. Then he waited. He held the pose as the kwapawnkah thundered down toward him, held it as the enemy's spearpoint leveled at his chest.

He held it, thinking that while he had killed many of the dead, this would be the first living man he killed. What a tragic waste.

"Damn you, for making me do this," he said.

And he released the spear.

The Haisetti raised his shield to ward the weapon off, but Etse hadn't aimed for the man. The spear went into the kwapawnkah's neck, sharp blade coming out the other side. The beast screamed in pain. Its front end dropped like a puppet with cut strings, but the back hooves took another stride, and the tail end of the kwapawnkah flipped over the front. Somewhere in mid-flip, a man's terrified screams joined the kwapawnkah's cries. The kwapawnkah crashed to the earth only a few paces from Etse. It was still twitching, blood spouting from the terrible wound.

Etse was already moving again. The other Haisetti were stunned, but they wouldn't sit still long. He closed the gap between himself and the fallen warrior with long strides. The downed rider had been impaled on the spear head somewhere in the fall, and the shaft had broken off. His blood poured down his side from the wound; his teeth clenched as he held the broken end of the spear where it protruded from his belly.

Etse drew his sword and slashed downward with one easy stroke. The Haisetti's severed head rolled free to the ground.

Two of the other riders shouted war cries and spurred their kwapawnkah into action. They rode straight at Etse, their paths a V with him at the center. No time to waste thinking about the man he'd just killed. No time to think at all. Etse scooped up the dead Haisetti's spear with his left hand and ran straight at the nearest of the Haisetti riders. Just short of the rider, he planted the spear into the ground, holding it in place loosely with his toe.

A war kwapawnkah would have ridden him down. A kwapawnkah trained for war was trained to charge even when presented with long, sharp objects. But a common riding kwapawnkah would follow its instincts.

The kwapawnkah stopped dead in its tracks, spilling its rider into the dirt.

Etse stabbed down. The man tried to block with his shield, but these men seemed pitifully slow to Etse. After fighting Gbohii with their lightning reflexes, killing humans was almost pathetically easy. Etse sheathed his sword, grabbed the reins of the dead man's kwapawnkah and swung himself up into the saddle.

Four Haisetti left.

They all bore down on him, now. Four lances, from four different directions. Etse shook his head. If they'd coordinated their attack, they might have had him. He spurred his kwapawnkah into movement and sped at one of the riders. That one continued straight on at him, but the other three had to rein in their kwapawnkah, turn, and come at him from a new angle. It bought him time.

He stabbed out with the spear as his kwapawnkah closed with the other man's mount. His weapon took the man in the thigh, and he howled with pain. Etse blocked his counterstroke with the shaft of his spear. The man didn't slow his kwapawnkah down until he was over by his fellows.

"Enough!" That was the Haisetti who'd spoken before. "Enough games, Asante. Time to die."

Etse looked them over. Even the man he had wounded was still holding his spear level, ready to charge. They'd come at him together this time, as a wall of steel and kwapawnkah flesh. He was good, but his tortoise shell armor wouldn't stop their spears, and he couldn't block all of them. For a moment, he was frozen with fear. Then anger at the stupidity of it all washed over him. Men fighting men, when the dead walked and ate the living with impunity?

"You're fools, to be fighting the living," Etse said. "We have other enemies."

"We'll be alive. That is enough for today," the Haisetti replied.

"You've forgotten something, Haisetti," Etse said. He was looking past them now.

"Oh?"

Etse nodded. Then he kneed his kwapawnkah forward, leveling his spear at the Haisetti leader. These raiders were too full of blood lust – too angry, too lost in their battle rage. They'd forgotten where they were. They'd forgotten who else was there.

With a roar, their prisoners rushed at the Haisetti from behind. Some hung back and pelted them with rocks. Others came in close and grabbed at legs. Most of the prisoners were hobbled, their legs tied together with rope. But there were a lot of them, and what they lacked in weapons and skills they made up for in numbers and desperation. Two of the riders managed to get their kwapawnkah clear of the mass. Etse shifted his kwapawnkah slightly to the left and took one of those men under the ribs with his spear. The Haisetti tumbled from his mount to the ground, impaled.

Etse drew his sword and made for the other raider who'd broken free. It was the leader, the one doing all their speaking for them. He was brave – Etse had to give him that. Instead of running for it, he wheeled his kwapawnkah around and prepared to ride back into the mess to try to save his men. Etse respected him for that, but he couldn't let him succeed.

He brought his kwapawnkah directly in the path of the man's mount, driving his sword down at his head. The Haisetti parried the blow with his own sword.

"Damn you, Asante!" he said.

"You should have gone around," Etse replied, his voice cold. He brought his sword down in a series of strikes, the pattern designed to open the enemy's guard. The Haisetti saw what he was up to, though, and backed his kwapawnkah away from Etse's to avoid the killing blow. He was brave and good.

Etse had a spare moment to glance over his shoulder. The prisoners had already pulled the other two men from their mounts, and the Haisetti had disappeared under a mass of furious men and women. This battle was all but over. And Etse realized he didn't want any more deaths on his hands. This man wasn't the enemy. Not truly.

The Haisetti brought his kwapawnkah forward, stabbing at Etse's mount. Etse blocked the blow, and twisted his blade around the other man's, trying to whip it from his grasp. The raider held on to his weapon and swung again. Etse blocked, knocking the sword wide, and stabbed – stopping the tip of his sword only inches from the other man's face.

"I don't want to kill you, Haisetti," Etse said. "Ride away now, and I won't have to."

The man put up a brave face for several seconds, but Etse could see the chill certainty slip into his eyes. They'd exchanged sword blows for only a few moments, but that was more than enough for each of them to assess the other's skills. The Haisetti nodded, turned his kwapawnkah, and rode away into the west. He wondered for a moment why the man was heading west, instead of north. Etse needed to get these people west to Takoradi. He'd need to be extra cautious for the rest of the journey. He had no desire to run into that man again.

He dismounted, walking over to the mass of prisoners. Some of them were trying to help those wounded in the struggle with the Haisetti. Others simply sat on the ground, weeping or staring unseeing into the distance. It looked like most of them hadn't eaten or washed in days. The group was haggard. Etse had never seen a more desperate looking pile of humanity.

"Please..." one of them said as he approached. The man speaking dropped to his knees, clearly out of energy for anything more.

"I will help you," Etse said. "You're free from them, now."

"Please," the man said again in a half whisper. Then he fell forward onto his face, and Etse could see the gaping slash across his back where one of the Haisetti's short swords had opened him up to the bone.

"I need help!" Etse shouted to his people in the barn. "There are wounded out here!" People came pouring out of the barn at his call.

As he went to help the fallen prisoner, he looked down at a body, realizing with a start that it belonged to that first Haisetti who'd tried to ride him down. Etse felt his stomach churn. Who was he? Someone's father? Someone's son? The raider had been trying to kill him. He was just defending himself and his people. But that didn't make it any better, didn't make the pain of killing someone less. He supposed men like Kwadwo eventually got used to it, became inured to killing other men in battle. Etse wondered if he would ever feel that way.

He wondered if he wanted to, or if that would make him more like a Gbohii than a man.

CHAPTER FIFTY-FOUR

Lugu hissed in frustration. The warehouse was burning. How had the fire been set? The plan was perfect: block off all exits with her guards, send in some Gbohii, and let the monsters do all the work. Her guards could then dispatch the things, and she'd have the damned key. She was sure Kwadwo had the thing. And she was almost as sure that he was in that damned building.

"We have all the escape routes covered?" she asked.

"Aane, great lady." Her Haisetti were good warriors. They wouldn't let anyone out. Alive.

"I suppose all we can do is wait out the fire, and then sift through the ashes," she muttered.

Damn Kwesi and his legacy! Damn him for keeping it from her! It should have been hers, anyway. She was first born, and from what Okere said Etse was dead anyway. So she was Kwesi's only living heir. It was hers by right.

He hadn't ever meant for her to know about the place at all. But she'd been curious even as a child. She used to snoop in his office, and she saw the records of special shipments when he left them out on his desk, one day.

Kwesi had always been a canny man. He'd known for years that the Empire would eventually abandon Asanteman. He'd prepared against the time when the land would need to see to its own defense. Thus, the legacy.

When she saw those records as a child, the site was already an arsenal of prodigious size. Arms, armor, shields, and all manner of supplies. Kwesi had built a large enough stockpile to create a full army of heavily armed troops. And that was almost two decades ago. Lugu had no idea what he had added in all the years since. But she knew her father. He believed in building twice what you might only need once. She was sure he'd added still more.

But the place was locked away. The key was what she had travelled so far west to acquire. Without it, her birthright was beyond her grasp. And that bastard Kwadwo had stolen it from her!

She'd sift through every ash remaining from that building, to find the damned key. Hell, she'd burn down every building in the entire city if she had to. The world was on fire, and she liked it that way. But she wanted to have the tools to see things through to the end.

The warehouse was fully engulfed, now. She watched it burn. Lugu couldn't hear the screams of the people she knew must be trapped somewhere inside, so she contented herself with imagining them. The firelight flickered in her mad eyes, painting her lips and dark hair red.

"I'll burn it all, if I must," she whispered softly to herself.

***

It was dawn before they'd realized that no one had died inside the warehouse at all. The only bones they had uncovered were those of the Gbohii she'd sent in. Lugu had roused a large band from her fighting force to give chase.

She swore loud enough to startle her kwapawnkah. How far ahead had that bastard Kwadwo and his pack of dogs gotten? He'd had too big a head start. Escape through the sewers! She should have thought of it, but how was she to know that there was an entrance into the sewer system in that old warehouse? She'd been so sure that he was dead, buried under burnt timbers. But no – at first light, a guard on the wall reported the tracks.

Now she was out here riding after them in pursuit. She had a force of twenty mounted Haisetti with her, and another three score on foot. The rest of her force she'd left behind at Takoradi to keep the place under control.

"Are we gaining on them?" she called out.

"Aane, mootittii koo (*my queen*). They move too slowly. We'll have them before dusk."

Before dusk! Well, she could wait. She could be patient. And then she'd have Kwesi's key, and the legacy would be hers after all. With the armor and weapons Kwesi had stored away in Kamit coupled with her Haisetti army, she'd be the leader of perhaps the only major military force left in Ki Khanga.

They came to the crest of a tall hill from which she could see a long way into the distance. Was that them up ahead? She thought she saw movement, but it was hard to tell if it was Kwadwo's band or another herd of the dead at this distance. It was a goodly number, and the thought of that many Gbohii in one place made her shiver. That many dead would tear her men apart. She and her guard could evade the monsters on their mounts.

Though it would be a shame to lose the sixty men without mounts, she simply had more men than kwapawnkah.

One of her men whistled an alert, and she turned to see what was going on. A rider was closing on them from behind, coming fast from Takoradi. Someone riding at that speed had to be a messenger, and these days the messages almost always seemed to be ill news. She wondered if she should let this man live if he gave her bad news.

"The riders will wait here for his message. The rest of you go on ahead. I want Kwadwo's head on a pike," she said. Her men hastened to obey her.

They feared her and called her the Mootittii Halkanii (*Night Queen*). These people thought she was a hafuura (*malevolent spirit*) and believed she possessed magical powers. It was a delusion she'd worked to inspire fear and respect in them. In truth, she knew no magic. But she knew enough of how the world worked that she could make it seem that way to these simple people.

The rider was taking forever to get to her. Partway through the wait, she decided that she'd kill him for bad news, once he'd delivered the message. Making her wait was intolerable. And it would sow fear among her men.

Not that they weren't already terrified of her. Especially the men who knew of her newest pet project, and she was pretty sure that the rumor at least had spread to most of her Haisetti by now. She was quite hopeful about that effort, actually. It was more than just a diversion. In the end, it could prove as useful as the legacy itself in giving her the power she needed to rule.

Finally, the kwapawnkah and its rider approached the hill where she and her troops waited. The kwapawnkah was breathing hard as he brought it down to a canter coming up the hill, and finally to a walk coming to a stop in front of her. The Haisetti rider slid down from his shaking mount and knelt in front of her.

"Night queen, I bring news," he said.

"Rise," Lugu said, gesturing with her hand. "Aane, I know. Who comes to Takoradi?"

The man's eyes widened as he stood, and he made a gesture against evil spirits with his hand. Lugu managed not to laugh aloud, although she let her mockery show clearly on her face. How could these simpletons not see through what she did? Of course someone was coming to Takoradi. There were too many troops in the city for the cowed people there to revolt. And nothing else would cause a messenger to ride out to her with such urgency.

But this man heard her educated guess and chose to see it as evidence of her magical powers. Cold reason, interpreted by the blind as sorcery and divination. Pathetic, but such tricks maintained their respect for her – and through them, her power over others.

"It is Etse, Kwesi's son."

Lugu inhaled a sharp breath. "Are you sure?"

"Aane, my queen," the Haisetti said, ducking his head again as if to hide from her displeasure. "Gebisa's raiding party was attacked by Etse and his men. Only Gebisa himself escaped. Etse will be at Takoradi's walls before nightfall."

Her thoughts raced ahead of her. Okere lied then. Or was wrong. Either way, Etse had survived the debacle at Nicran. Somehow, he had gotten out by himself past a horde of the dead. That implied he was much more competent than Okere had given him credit for. Was he a tool she could use? Or an enemy to be slain?

It was hard for her to think clearly about Etse. She hadn't seen him since he was a child and she a young woman – shipped to Haiset to a husband she'd never met. She probed her feelings about the little boy who'd cried and clung to her when he found out she was leaving. She could never forgive her mother for marrying that bastard Kwesi, or for having a child by him. But at the same time, Etse was a sweet boy, and she could see so much of her mother in him that she found it hard to hate him.

It was confusing. Lugu wasn't used to having conflicted feelings about anything. She was used to knowing her own mind instantly and without hesitation.

Regardless, she needed to get back to Takoradi. She had to be there when he arrived. When she saw the man that crying child had become, she'd know what to do with him.

"We ride to Takoradi to meet my brother," she said. She regarded the messenger and reconsidered her plans to kill him. "You," she said to him, "Ride after the men in the hunting party and join them. I want Kwadwo brought to me by sunset. I want his head – and I want the key he carries. Fail to bring me either, and I'll feed you to my pets!"

"Aane, my queen," the man said. He mounted up and rode away without another word. Superstitious these people might be, but they were used to hard leaders and hard rules. It worked well for her.

"The rest of you, follow me," she said, kneeing her kwapawnkah into a canter. She rode for her city, her thoughts a swirling maelstrom of confused hate and love.

CHAPTER FIFTY-FIVE

Kwadwo saw the Haisetti in the distance and cursed. They'd done well to get so far away before the pursuit closed with them. He'd begun to hope that their luck might hold and perhaps they'd make the bogs northwest of Takoradi before the Haisetti could track them down. But that clearly wasn't going to happen.

He scanned the hilltop as kwapawnkah and men poured over the top. Some of the troops were mounted, the rest afoot. As he watched, the kwapawnkah stopped there. But the others kept coming. And they were moving fast, much faster than this hapless band of women and children could manage. He had twenty fighting men with spears, plus himself. It wasn't going to be enough, not against a force like that.

"Move faster!" he called. "They've seen us! Make for the marshes."

Everyone around him picked up the pace again. Men picked up children too small or too tired to keep up. Everyone raced across the moors. Kwadwo felt the ground squelch under his boots and felt glad. If they could make the swamps surrounding the Densu River up ahead, then they might be able to lose their pursuers. Not much further.

"Kwadwo!"

It was Ako, calling from up ahead. Kwadwo made his tired legs work a little harder and pounded up the hill to join the big man near the front of the party. He noticed as he was climbing the hill that people had all but stopped at the top, milling around.

"What's holding you up?" Kwadwo demanded. "They'll be on us soon if we don't make the marshes."

"That," Ako said, pointing.

Damn. Had all their luck vanished at once? There was a clear view all the way to the marshes – he could see where the hills stopped, and the swampy forest began. Kwadwo was still pretty sure they could lose their pursuers in the muck if they could just get in there safely.

But that was the trouble. Between his band and the safety of those trees was a wide swath of open space – a distance they'd need to cross if they were to escape the Haisetti. But just to the north was a pack of Gbohii, shambling south toward them. Kwadwo didn't think the things had actually seen his people yet. But they certainly would, as soon as they made a run for the marsh.

"What do we do, Kwadwo?" Odoi asked. The boy was following him around like a shadow.

Kwadwo looked back the way they had come, flinching when he saw the Haisetti coming at them. They'd picked up the pace, running across the moor with the long, rolling gait of soldiers used to traveling long distances at a fast pace. Those were hard men, well trained and used to combat. They'd rip his half trained recruits to pieces even at the best of times. And outnumbered three to one? His people would have no chance at all.

But out there against the Gbohii? There were only six of the things, but he'd seen them in action. His people might be able to take them down. But half of them would be dead by the time the battle was won. Or not dead, but bitten, which would be even worse.

They were all waiting for his orders. He was tired of this. Tired of being the man making all the decisions. The weight was wearing away at his soul.

There was really only one thing to do, this time. Behind them lay certain death. By forging ahead, they might live. They might even cross the moor before the Gbohii caught them and escape clean. But only if they hurried.

"We move," he said. "Quickly, everyone run for the marsh. I know it's a long way, but we must make this last run."

He looked back down the hill behind him, where most of his people were still struggling their way up the incline. "We're almost there. But we need to run for the marsh! Help your neighbor if they are too weak. Everyone together now. Run! Run like death itself chases at your heels!"

Because it is, he thought but did not say it aloud. It would not help.

They picked up the pace at his words, and soon even those trailing behind had reached the top, gasping for air only a moment before stumbling on their way back down the other side. Kwadwo followed, taking the last place in line. If it came down to battle against the Gbohii, he felt sure the rear was where they would strike, trying to cut down his weakest and slowest people. Ako fell in next to him, and Kwadwo grunted his appreciation for the company.

They ran, urging on the runners just ahead of them. The ones lagging this far back in the group were gasping for breath, panting with the effort of trying to keep up.

About halfway across the open area, the Gbohii spotted them. Their strange cries reached even across all that distance. The sound sent chills down Kwadwo's spine. He looked over at them, and all six had changed direction and pace. They loped toward his people, closing the gap with alarming speed.

"We're going to need to make a stand," Ako said between breaths.

"Aane. Soon," Kwadwo replied.

The first of his people reached the tree line, entering the bogs beyond. That would help them lose the Haisetti, but he had a feeling that wouldn't save them from the Gbohii. The things would hunt them wherever they went. It was going to be a fight to stop them, now.

He heard a yell off to his right – near enough to the Gbohii that he looked that way in alarm. It was Odoi! He must have reached the marsh with the fastest runners and then cut north through the trees. He stood there, unarmed, waving a long red sash and shouting at the Gbohii.

"What's he doing?" Ako muttered.

The Gbohii heard Odoi shouting and turned toward him. They saw the red – it was impossible to miss the bright color against the green and brown of the marsh and trees. Together, all six of them broke from their pursuit and went after the boy. Their loping strides carried them swiftly toward him – but he stood his ground, still waving the sash like a banner.

Kwadwo cursed and gave chase. He drew his sword as he ran, but in his heart he knew that there was no way he could get there in time. The monsters were too fast. They'd tear the boy apart long before he could arrive. Tears leaked from his eyes as he ran his heart out, desperately trying to close the gap. He was dimly aware that some of his spearmen had broken off from the main group and were running alongside and behind him.

He saw Odoi blanch, finally, as the Gbohii came within a stone's throw of where he stood. He fled then – too late, damn it! The boy would never get away from them in time now. Why had he waited there so long? Kwadwo watched in horror as the things closed in from behind Odoi while he sprinted toward a tree. He jumped, fingers catching a low hanging branch. He let his legs swing high and locked them around the same branch.

Beneath him the dead lunged, leaping toward him, fingers outstretched like claws. Their jaws snapped, ready to tear into the boy's flesh. He was too low! He'd never pull himself up before they got to him.

And then the lead Gbohii sank up to its knees in mud, stopping its forward progress cold. The one behind it smashed into it, sending it face-first into the muck. One after another, each of the Gbohii ran at the tree, trying to catch Odoi. And each became stuck fast in the thick mud around the base of the trunk.

All six of the monsters struggled in the thick marsh slime. They pushed at the mud. One flopped forward, reaching ahead, trying to pull itself out. Kwadwo could see that they wouldn't remain stuck for long. But he didn't need them to. He slowed to a walk and sheathed his sword.

"Give me your spear," he said to the man walking beside him. He took the stout shaft in his hand, flipped it around so it was pointed down, and stabbed at the one trying to scrabble its way out of the mud. The spear went into the thing's skull, and it died.

The rest of the Gbohii went wild at that, working hard to get themselves free. But the spearmen had the idea now. They came forward, careful to stay out of range of the Gbohii's reaching claws and stabbed down with their spears. Some missed. But where one spear missed a head and pinned a shoulder instead, another spear quickly stabbed down and killed the pinioned monster. In less than a minute, all six were dead. And without a single human casualty.

"Odoi," Kwadwo rasped, barely able to find his voice. He'd run his throat ragged trying to get here in time. "That was one of the bravest things I have ever seen."

The young man swung down from the tree, landing carefully on a large, exposed root. He must have run up that root to avoid the mud pit. If he'd slipped, Odoi would have been stuck in the mud – and all six Gbohii would still have fallen into the trap, but the boy would have been in there with them.

Odoi ducked his head, blushing at the praise.

"And if you ever do anything like that again," Kwadwo went on, "I'll…" He stopped there. What was he supposed to do? The young man was too old to threaten to tan his hide.

Ako sensed his thoughts and laughed. "You'll do what, you old fart?" He clapped Odoi on the back, almost knocking him over. "The boy has spunk. We need more men like him."

"We do indeed," Kwadwo said. "And we need to be on our way. No time to rest on our victory here. The Gbohii are not our only enemies."

The Haisetti would not be far behind them. Best to lose themselves in the bog and hope the enemy couldn't track them there.

CHAPTER FIFTY-SIX

Musongola took the steps two at a time. Rwamirama must have gone down to get more men. His enemy was a cautious sort – and although they'd never fought, Musongola was pretty confident he could beat Rwamirama in a straight up fight. But stack enough guards on his side, and he'd win without any hazard to himself. That was how Rwamirama liked it – winning without risk.

Musongola didn't feel like it was worth winning unless he had at least a little skin in the game. He'd been called reckless before, and impetuous. But really, he just knew he was good at what he did. There weren't many men who could stand against him.

He flew up the stairs, sword drawn, and hit the top almost before he realized it. There were two men with their own swords drawn waiting for him, and he ducked to avoid one of their blades, parrying the other with his own.

He swept the blocked sword in a circle, his sword biting into the man's wrist. The guard dropped his weapon with a yelp and backed away. That left the other – who was swinging again. There was no way to duck this blow, so Musongola dropped into a roll instead, rising back to his feet. His sword was moving even before he had his balance back.

There was no time for subtlety here. He hammered blows down on the guard, who desperately tried to ward off the attacks. Each of his blows drew the man's sword a little further from his body. And then there was the opening – Musongola saw it, took it, and thrust his sword through the man's belly.

The man clutched at the wound, his face going ashen as Musongola withdrew his blade. Without a word, the guard toppled sideways into the stairwell, landing with a thud on the steps below.

"Murderer!" the other guard cried. He'd recovered his sword and rushed in to avenge his friend. Musongola parried the first two blows and then took off the soldier's head in a sweeping arc of his sword.

Disgust rocked him. What a waste. He'd killed four of these men – good men, Mikijen. Aane, they'd been ready to kill him, and he didn't regret having slain them first. But he boiled with anger at the man who'd made this all necessary. The Gbohii were a grave threat. Musongola had seen the mainland as they sailed from Kiswala. Nearly all life had been picked clean from those lands. No sign of human civilization remained at all. Just packs of Gbohii killing anything they came across.

All men and women everywhere were in danger of being wiped from Ki Khanga by those Cleave-spawn and their plague. But Rwamirama would rather fight over scraps than work together?

Damn the man.

Dealing with Rwamirama would have to happen another day, though. Today, he needed to get the hell out of there. He could hear the tromp of boots coming up the stairs again. They'd be here soon enough, and even he couldn't fight an entire army alone.

"Diata!" he shouted. "Are you near?"

"Musongola?"

He almost chuckled at the disbelief in her voice. She sounded like she was just behind that door. That locked door, he amended. The men he just killed must have been posted here to guard her. One of them probably had the key, but frankly he didn't have the time to search them, and the door was only wooden planks.

"Stand back!" he said.

With a loud battle cry, he hammered his foot against the door, smashing it against where the lock held the thing closed. The wood gave a loud crack, but didn't break. He brought his foot down on it again, and again, with a loud cracking sound.

The guards were almost up the stairs. He had no time for this! He ran at the door, smashing his shoulder into the thing – and this time, the wood split at the lock, and the door burst inward.

Diata was standing just inside the doorway. They'd taken her armor from her and found her a gown from somewhere. It was a cheap thing – something they stole from some peasant, no doubt. But he wasn't used to seeing her in women's clothing at all, and it took him a moment to stop staring.

By the time he had, her cheeks were beet red, and she was tapping her foot.

"Is this a rescue, or did you just come here to ogle me?" she snapped.

Musongola recovered as quickly as he could, smiling broadly at her. "A rescue, I assure you."

He saw her eyes widen and whirled, just in time to face off against the first of Rwamirama's soldiers to make it up the stairs. He parried the man's attack and struck back. Musongola rained lightning blows down against the soldier, whose eyes got very wide, very fast. He retreated swiftly toward the stairs. Musongola followed, pressing his advantage.

And then Diata swung a sword, taking the man in the thigh where his armor wouldn't protect him. He cried out, clutching the wounded leg with his free hand, and backed down the stairs. Musongola could see more guards coming up behind him – many more. Even with Diata fighting too, he doubted they could hold the stairs long against so many.

"Where'd you find a sword?" he asked.

"The man you beheaded seemed to have dropped it," she replied. "I didn't think he would need it anymore. Come with me!"

She turned and ran down a hallway, away from her cell. Musongola cursed – he didn't want to lose the advantage of the stair top, but he didn't want to leave her alone again, either. He followed.

At the end of the hallway was another short spiral stair. Diata was already climbing the steps and throwing back a bolt to a trap door. She flung the door upward, and wind swept down the stairs past them.

"The roof?" he asked.

"Rwamirama took me up here after I was captured. Threatened to toss me off," she replied.

The roof was clear of battlements – just a large square stone surface, flat except for the flagstones that paved it. From here you could see for miles in every direction, but Rwamirama hadn't placed a guard. It would have been an uncomfortable place to stay long – the wind whirled swiftly at this height, and with no walls, not even rails, the edges seemed treacherous and close.

Men were coming up the stairs. Musongola slammed the trap door back into place, but they'd tear it apart soon enough.

"Now what?" he said. They were out of space to run, and there was nowhere to hide.

"Do you trust me?" she asked.

He didn't hesitate. "Aane."

"Sheathe your sword," she said. He did.

Then she grabbed his arm and ran toward the edge of the roof. Almost, he balked and stopped their run. Was she mad? They were a good height up – forty feet at least. They'd both die from a fall like that.

But he'd told her that he trusted her. So he let her lead them over the edge. And then they were out in the middle of the air.

Falling fast.

Stone sweeping by his vision in a blur.

Then Musongola's back collided with something – but it wasn't stone, like he'd thought it would be. They'd fallen into a huge pile of hay! They sank deep into the stuff, but it broke their fall.

"How?" he sputtered, picking bits of hay from his mouth.

"Saw it when Rwamirama threatened to throw me off," she gasped, trying to get her breath back. "They've been gathering it from the local farms, fodder for their kwapawnkah."

"They have kwapawnkah here?" Musongola asked.

She pointed, still struggling to her feet. "Over there. I had to toss my sword when we jumped. Did you see where it landed?"

"No time!" he replied. There were guards on the roof now, shouting and waving their arms. They didn't seem interested in taking the same shortcut down, but they were pointing and yelling. Other soldiers would be on them soon enough. The fort was crawling like a kicked anthill.

"Come on!" he said, dashing toward the stable.

He drew his blade again while he sprinted the short distance to the stable. One kick served to smash down the door, startling the two men inside saddling kwapawnkah. One of the two was just a stable hand and ran for it. The other was one of Rwamirama's men, already armed and armored. The man tried to draw his sword, but Musongola cut him down without breaking his stride.

They'd already saddled one kwapawnkah and were starting on another. From the commotion outside, Musongola wasn't sure he and Diata had time to finish saddling the second. Riding double would have to do. He bounded up into the saddle and reached down his arm to her.

"Grab on!"

She took his hand without hesitation, and he hoisted her up behind him. Then he kneed the kwapawnkah into action. He felt Diata wrap her arms tight around his waist, and for a moment found himself wishing they were not fleeing for their lives right now. The scent of her skin so close made him feel flushed. What the hell was with all these feelings? He'd never been so addled over a woman before.

The kwapawnkah left the stables behind at a canter, and the fresh air helped to clear his head. Rwamirama's men had assembled a troop in the courtyard, over a score of soldiers massed and ready to march out to the boats. In the narrow confines of the river, those boats might be able to chase down the sailing ship. But only if they got to the boats.

The gates were opening to let those men out. Musongola spurred his kwapawnkah to a gallop and rode straight at the rear of the assembled men.

"Hold on tight," he said to Diata.

A few of the soldiers in the rear of the formation looked over their shoulders when they heard the pounding of hoofbeats behind them. The smart ones parted for him. One damned fool stood his ground and tried to raise his shield. He went down under the kwapawnkah's hooves.

From the second rank on, most of the men had no time to even realize what was happening. The kwapawnkah drove through the middle of their formation, Musongola's sword cleaving deadly arcs with each swing. Men fell, wounded or dead, and the formation shattered.

All at once they were through and flying out the doors. The kwapawnkah pounded along the rocky shore. There was only one way off this island – across the pontoon bridge. Musongola made for it, trying to knee every ounce of speed from the kwapawnkah that he could.

They reached the bridge, and there he had to slow. It was nothing more than a row of small rafts, each lashed to the next. There were small gaps between the wood, and they tilted as weight was applied to them. The kwapawnkah could easily slip, and fall. Musongola cursed, but he had to let their mount return to a canter.

An arrow hit the wood in front of them with a thunk. He looked back over his shoulder – archers lined the wall now, loosing arrows down on them. Another hit, right next to the kwapawnkah. It whinnied and shied away from the spot, and the pontoon tilted. The kwapawnkah fell over the side but it caught its balance, planting its feet firmly and snorting.

More arrows came down, and these ones didn't miss the kwapawnkah now that it stood still. One struck its rump, another its neck. The beast tried to sprint away from whatever had stung its hind end, but blood from the neck wound splashed across the wood beneath its feet. It stumbled and fell.

Musongola saw the fall coming and rolled clear, hauling Diata with him. More arrows stabbed down around them. He looked wildly around for cover – and there wasn't anything. Two more arrows hit the dying kwapawnkah, which tried to cry out from the pain. The sound came out more like a gurgle, and the animal died.

It was the best cover they had. Musongola tucked Diata up tight against the kwapawnkah's body and rolled in close behind her. More and more arrows whistled in around them. They were more or less safe here – the body gave them enough cover that it would be almost impossible to hit them. But they were trapped. Soon, men would storm from the keep and take them.

Musongola desperately went over options. He had to keep Diata alive somehow. He must! There had to be some way… Perhaps if he could pitch her over the side, and distract the enemy while she escaped? If he timed it right, she could flee while he engaged the troops when they came down the bridge.

Then Diata rested a hand on his arm. "It's all right, Musongola," she said. "Thank you for trying. I'd rather die free than be that one's toy, anyway."

Another volley of arrows slammed in around them and then…the shots stopped. Musongola spared a glance up, expecting to see men charging toward them. And there were men – but they were still back on the shore, trying to find cover among the rocks. As he watched, an arrow took one of them in the throat, and he fell dying to the ground.

Who was shooting at them?

Musongola looked back over his shoulder, toward the shore, and almost shouted in relief.

It was Kudowor and the others, in the ship! They must have come about, and now they were sailing the ship through the gap between the island and the shore. Tay-Natey was on the ship's rail, firing arrows as quickly as he could draw his string – which was damned fast. The man wasn't missing many shots, either. His bow was strong enough that it was making the archers atop the wall keep their heads down and pinning the soldiers behind the rocks on the shore as well.

Musongola's eyes widened as he realized where the ship was sailing. It was coming between the island and shore – which meant it would smash right through the floating bridge!

"Come on!" he shouted, standing up and pulling Diata's hand. She followed him, and they sprinted across the rocking pontoons toward where the ship would break through.

"Run!" Tay-Natey shouted from the deck. The ship was close now. And Musongola could see they weren't going to make it. The bow crashed into the wood rafts, breaking them into tinder. Shattered boards spiraled off in all directions, and the bridge just started to come apart.

The impact threw Musongola into the water. He came up sputtering, looking for Diata. There! She was hanging on to one of the pontoons.

The ship was sailing away! It was picking up speed. There was no way he could swim to the thing, and certainly no way

Diata could. The dress would weigh her down and she'd sink to the bottom.

Then an arrow flashed into the boards a foot from Diata's hand. It had a rope tied to the end. Diata dashed forward, grabbing the rope and tying it to the corner of the pontoon with a quick knot. Then she turned to Musongola.

"Grab my hand!" she said.

He reached.

The rope grew taut. The wood creaked under the strain, but Diata's knot held and the pontoon started to move. His fingers brushed hers, barely touching. The pontoon began to pull away from him, dragged along behind the ship. He lunged, reaching one last time.

Diata's hand locked around his wrist. He wrapped his fingers around hers. The smile she spared him was a better reward than anything else he could imagine.

They sped away behind the ship, leaving the fort behind.

CHAPTER FIFTY-SEVEN

Etse plodded on, leading one of the remaining kwapawnkah through the trees. They'd only managed to save two of the Haisetti' kwapawnkah. The others were dead or too badly injured during the fight. The wounded or dead animals were quickly slaughtered and cooked. The size of Etse's band had more than tripled overnight after they rescued the prisoners from their Haisetti captors. There was plenty of water, but with three times as many mouths to feed, they needed every scrap of food.

They'd lost part of the day in the barn, letting those newly rescued rest a while. That had cost them every scrap of food they had. But only a single Gbohii wandered by – which Etse dispatched with the help of his men. And they learned good news from those they rescued. The band was much closer to Takoradi than Etse had thought. They were less than a day's march away, so they set out despite the late hour. Etse's hope was that they would arrive before dusk.

But now the sun was setting, and although he knew Takoradi was not far, he worried they might not make it before dark after all. He knew these forests – they were thin, which was good. It let them see a decent way, so they could avoid ambush. But it was hard to say how many miles were left before they reached the city gates.

He glanced back at the kwapawnkah. Sefadzi was falling asleep there, lulled by the rolling gait of the animal's plodding footsteps. Behind her rode her friend, the boy Amon. He was still awake – alert eyes watching the sides of the road. Etse knew the boy must have had a run-in with one of the Gbohii at some point. He could see it in his eyes; in the way he was hyper-vigilant.

Etse sighed, looking away. It was sad to see that in a child. But perhaps it was a survival trait, these days. They were all going to have to change, to survive in this new world. They were going to need to become harder, stronger.

There was a scuffling sound from the rear of the group. Etse handed off the reins to Jiagge.

"Uche, with me," he said. The other man fell in alongside him, and together they set off to see what was going on.

Etse's band had gone from twenty three to seventy-four people with the defeat of the Haisetti slavers. The new folks outnumbered his people from the cave, and he wasn't sure what to make of all of them. Still, it was his people trusted with weapons. His men out on the perimeter, watching for danger. He felt more secure knowing that.

He wished that the group would stay a little tighter, though. Such a large band meant they were spread out far more than he'd like.

The tail end of the line was made up of stragglers – people too weak to move quickly, or just too tired of fighting, and near giving up. There was little he could do for most of those people. There was no cure for the desolation many of them felt, their worlds shattered and destroyed. Some people were able to pick themselves back up and keep going. Others…not so much.

Kpeda was there, urging them to move more quickly. He still had his spear, but there was blood on the tip, and he was breathing hard.

"Etse!" he said. "Thank god."

"What's going on?" Etse asked.

"They're coming – back there," Kpeda said, waving his arm in the direction the group had come from. "Following us."

"Who, man?"

"The dead… They're coming, Etse. I killed one of them, but there were so many. All I could do was run. I think I lost them in the woods, but they're coming."

They'd managed to avoid bands of the things so far. It wasn't hard to kill one or two of them, although he was impressed that Kpeda had managed to slay one by himself. Still, they had enough men with spears, and a few with swords. They'd added the weapons taken from dead Haisetti to their stock of arms and armor, which left them a bit better off than they had been. A small band of Gbohii should be something they could tackle. But…

"How many were there?" Etse asked.

"I don't know," Kpeda said, starting to shake.

That didn't sound good.

"Can you estimate at least?" Uche asked. "You must be able to at least give us a guess."

Kpeda just stood there, miserably shaking his head. "No. There were too many."

Etse felt his heart sink, his gut churn. He looked around – they were still surrounded by trees. Wherever the Gbohii were, they were still far enough away he couldn't hear them. But if there was a big pack nearby, they'd follow the scent of a large group of humans easily enough. There was nothing he could do to hide their trail from the dead. Etse spotted one fairly tall tree and walked over to it. With a grunt of effort, he jumped up and grabbed hold of the lowest branch.

It was a struggle to get his body up the tree. He still had armor on. Some days he wondered if he would ever take the stuff off again. His hands were scraped and raw from the bark before he broke through the tree line into open sky. From there he could see miles in every direction.

The first thing he saw was the end of the forest – the huge swath of cleared farmland just beyond – and there, on a hilltop, the walls of Takoradi. Banners flew in the breeze above the city.

It looked just like he remembered, and the sight brought tears to his eyes. He was at long last almost home again.

Then he turned back the way they'd come, and hope turned to ash. The forest was thin here – thin enough that he could see the monsters loping after them. Kpeda was not wrong. Even from his treetop vantage point Etse couldn't begin to count the monsters as they came. It was like a sea tide was coming in, pouring through the trees, flooding around them. The things were not running, just rolling in as inexorably as the ocean.

Etse descended again as quickly as he dared. As soon as he hit the ground, he turned to his men. Uche must have gathered a few of the other armed troops while he was climbing, because now he had ten men there, ready to fight.

Uche saw his face and blanched. "That bad?"

"Worse," Etse replied. "It looks almost like what I saw in Nicran. Thousands of the things. Maybe ten thousand, I don't know."

"We can't stand against that!" Uche said.

"No, we can't. We need to run," Etse replied. "We'll make for Takoradi. It's not far."

"These people can't run much longer." Uche sounded dubious.

"They'll move," Kpeda said. "Once they know what's coming, they'll move."

"Spread the word. We'll make it," Etse said. They had to. Worse than death waited for them, otherwise. "Guard the rear until I return."

He jogged forward again, back to Sefadzi. The girl was awake now, those sharp eyes tracking him as he came closer.

"What's wrong?" she asked.

"How do you always know?" Etse returned.

"It's all over your face," she answered. "Gbohii?"

"Aane. Too many to fight. We need to run for it."

Etse raised his voice a bit to carry to everyone nearby. "We need to pick up the pace. Takoradi is not far – a few miles due west of here. Follow the setting sun. But a horde of Gbohii is behind us. Hundreds of them, all headed this way. We must make the walls of Takoradi before they reach us."

He didn't need to say anything more. Every one of these people knew what was on the line. The pace picked up. Nobody bolted, which impressed him. But they were all moving along faster.

A woman stumbled beside Etse, and he leaned over to help her back to her feet. She smiled in response and hurried on her way.

"What do you need me to do, Etse?" Jiagge asked. His hand was locked around his spear, and his lips were a line etched with barely restrained terror.

"Get Sefadzi and Amon to Takoradi safely," Etse replied. "I will have to be everywhere at once for a little while. I need someone I can trust to see them through. Can you do that?"

Etse could see his words give the man heart.

"I will," Jiagge replied.

"Good man," he replied. But when he turned to go, he felt a small hand on his shoulder. He looked up to see Sefadzi's serious face staring down at him.

"Be careful," she said.

"I will," he replied, smiling at her with a confidence he wished he really felt. The dead behind them were too near. It was going to be a close thing, whether they reached the walls in time or not.

He hurried to the rear of the group again, where he and his men worked tirelessly to keep the slowest of the party moving. By the time they broke from the woods, Kpeda was carrying one old man who'd twisted an ankle. Everyone was exhausted, but they were, finally, out in the open again. Safety was within sight. Cross those fields, climb that hill, and they'd arrive.

The Gbohii had been here, that much was certain. Most of the farms looked deserted. A few had a fortified look about them, with spikes driven into the soil, and low walls erected. Etse shook his head at those, hoping the owners had already abandoned them for the somewhat surer safety of Takoradi. The horde of Gbohii coming this way would wash over those buildings, bounding over their pitiful defenses and shredding anyone still inside. He wanted to go and warn those people – at least one farmhouse had smoke coming from the chimney. But he didn't have time, not if he was to save the men and women counting on him here.

They made it to the base of the hill before the Gbohii horde broke from the trees. Uche was the first to look back and see them.

"Daarila," he gasped. Then he shouted at the top of his lungs "Run!"

Etse looked. It was as bad as he feared. The things boiled out of the wood line in a mass, more and more pouring from the trees. So many came that it seemed like there was no end to them. And they weren't loping along anymore – they were running, racing at his party with preternatural speed.

"Run for the city!" he shouted, joining others in urging the group on. "Run!"

Then he followed his own advice, pumping his legs hard to climb the steep hill. Once he hit the road, it was easier going. The paving bricks made the run easier. Someone fell in front of him. Etse slowed to help him back to his feet and then ran on.

The gates were near. Etse could see some of his people had already made it and were milling about in front of them. What was going on? Why weren't they going inside?

The gates were closed.

Atop the walls, guards shouted down at his people. The panicked people screamed back, begging for mercy, begging for the gates to be opened. Etse reached the gates. Behind him he saw the

Gbohii reach the farms, tearing through them. That might distract them for a moment, but it wouldn't last. They needed sanctuary.

"Open these gates!" he shouted up at the guards on the wall. "I am Etse, son of Kwesi. Open the gates for these people at once!"

There seemed to be a buzz up atop the wall, and for a moment Etse thought they were opening the gates for him. But no – they remained closed.

He looked down the hill again. All his people had reached the top now; everyone gathered around the gates. Some were screaming, others crying. At the base of the hill, death boiled upward toward them. He had led these people to this end. That knowledge was bitter. He drew his sword and went to the rear of the formation.

Perhaps they would all die here. But he'd be damned if he was going to fall without a fight!

Etse heard a blade coming from its sheath next to him and looked over. Uche grinned a toothy smile. "What, think I would miss all the excitement?"

Then Kpeda joined their line, and Jiagge. Etse raised his eyebrows at Jiagge.

"I got them safe to the wall, me wura," Jiagge replied. "I can do no more for them. I would stand with you."

Etse nodded his assent.

More of the men joined their ranks, until they had a short line of spears and swords aimed down the hill. It wouldn't be long now.

"You men are my mu onimuonyamfoah (*knights*)," Etse said. "Each of you is as brave as any man I have ever known. I am honored to stand with you today."

The fighters roared back in response and set their spears.

"Come quickly! Come this way!" a woman's voice called over the din.

Etse spared a glance back over his shoulder to see who was shouting. It was a dark haired woman, dressed in white, standing atop the wall. She was beckoning to them. And beneath her – the doors were opening! Etse almost sagged with relief.

His people started pouring through the gates into the city. They were going to make it. It was going to be close, but they were going to make it! He didn't know who the woman was, or why the gates were suddenly opening, but he didn't have time to second-guess their good fortune.

"Hold your ground, men," Etse said. "Fall back in good order – we need to make sure everyone gets in safely!" As a group, the line of warriors began backing toward the gates.

And then they were all through. Etse held his position in front of the gates, sword drawn and ready, until they shut with a booming sound, men setting the heavy wooden beam into place. Beyond the doors, he heard the iron portcullis slam down. They were safe. The Gbohii would have a hard time getting through that!

He sagged to his knees, almost dropping his sword. They had made it.

He was home.

CHAPTER FIFTY-EIGHT

Kwadwo slogged through the muddy water, boots squelching with the stuff. His sword was sheathed. Instead, he carried a long staff with both hands, as did most of the people with him. The stick had two purposes. Ideally, it let him find the ways that were safer, and less deep, so that he didn't end up in one of the pits of deep mud that were abominably common here.

The other purpose was to keep his balance when he slipped in the slimy stuff. Which happened frequently. He was covered with slime, enough to make him wonder if he'd ever come clean again.

On the plus side, they hadn't seen a single Gbohii since coming into this mess. Either they knew better than to go wandering about swamps – which probably made them more sensible than he felt, right about then – or they were getting stuck in the mire near the eastern edge of the marshes, and not making it this far in.

He could tell they were getting closer to the river. There were deep pools of water between the trees, now. Somewhere ahead, the trees would stop entirely, and they'd have reached the Densu. At least the marsh was confined to this side of the river. The other side ought to be farmland. From there, a day's ride on a ship ought to get them to Kamit. And then he could see what Kwesi had left them. He still wore the key around his neck, hidden under his shirt. Kamit was an island that Gbohii probably couldn't get to, but it they did, it was a place they could help fortify and defend. They needed that, badly.

But right now what he needed most was to know where those Haisetti were. He hoped they were lost, wandering aimlessly in the mire. But in his gut he knew better. Lugu wouldn't let them give up that easily, and they were skilled enough to follow the trail Kwadwo's people were blazing. It simply wasn't possible to pass through a mess like this swamp without leaving some traces. He looked around. Up ahead a bit, there was a particularly tall tree.

"Odoi," Kwadwo called. "You up to some more climbing?"

"As long as it doesn't involve dead things trying to eat me, sure," he replied.

"I need to see if we can spot our pursuers."

"Say no more," Odoi replied, eyeing the same tree Kwadwo had thought most likely to serve as a good lookout perch. "I'll need a boost though."

Ako shambled over. "I'll get the boy up there."

"Without throwing me, please?" Odoi said with a grin.

Ako growled back at the young man, but the smile playing behind his thick beard showed his true feelings. Kwadwo was glad indeed to see them getting on so well. Both had been instrumental in getting them all this far. He needed people like them: men and women able to think fast on their feet, and able to get things done in moments so dire that most would simply fall apart.

A few minutes later Odoi was scrambling up the tree. It was a tall one, making its neighbors look stunted in comparison. It had sunk deep roots into a small island here, surrounded by water but with plenty of rich earth to protect it. Most of the trees around here had to deal with floods every wet season, but Kwadwo thought that big old tree might stay dry most years.

It seemed like the young man was gone for a long time. Kwadwo had Ako lead the party onward – no sense waiting in one place, and he could catch up easily enough once Odoi was back down. Finally, he heard the breaking of branches that signaled his descent. With a grunt, Odoi swung down to the lowest branch and dropped from there to the ground.

"There's good news and bad news, me wura," Odoi said. He seemed somber. Kwadwo had a feeling the news was mostly bad.

"We're close to the river," he went on. "I could see Ako and the others – he and the other people up front are almost there."

"Well, that's good news," Kwadwo said. "And? Are the Haisetti still behind us?" He figured that had to be the bad news. But if they could get to the river, swim or barge their way across, they could lose themselves easily on the other side. It was all wilderness over there, dotted by small settlements. And the deeper you went into the west, the more hilly and rugged the terrain became. He was almost certain they could lose the enemy out there. Eventually, the Haisetti would have to give up.

"The Haisetti are back there, and it looks like they still have our trail," Odoi said. "It doesn't look like they're gaining on us too quickly. But we haven't lost them, either. They're just a bit north and east of us. That's not the worst of it, though."

Odoi paused for breath, wincing at the thought of whatever it was he'd seen. Kwadwo knew there was only one thing out there that could be worse than the damned Haisetti.

"Gbohii?" Kwadwo asked. "Where?"

"Across the river, me wura. It's… Too many of them to count. There must have been a village nearby or something, because they're all over the shore. Little clusters of a few here and there, but no matter where we crossed as far as I could see, we'd run into some of them."

"And then the noise of the battle would draw others," Kwadwo said.

Odoi nodded.

"Walk with me," Kwadwo said. "We need to catch up with the others before they reach the river."

The easiest solution would be to just build rafts, and drift down the river to the sea. Simple, safe. Even this far upriver, the Densu was deep enough that they could stay in the middle and be safe from the dead. The problem was that building rafts would take time – time he doubted the Haisetti would give them. They'd never complete the rafts before the Haisetti fell upon them.

Too many Haisetti to fight. Too many of the dead to fight. And not enough time to run the safe way. The only way forward was to continue on foot and hope they could stay ahead of the Haisetti. And with the river before them, and the Haisetti to their north, the only way to go was south along the riverbank.

Which took them dangerously close to Takoradi. Damned if he didn't feel like he was being herded. This had the feel of a trap's jaws closing. And there was nothing he could do but keep going, and hope an opportunity arose to turn the tables on their pursuers.

CHAPTER FIFTY-NINE

Etse followed the woman in white up the hill toward his home. Behind him trailed his people – most of them still half shocked with the realization that they were not about to die after all. Behind them, soldiers took the walls. Etse noted that some of the soldiers were Asante, and others were Haisetti. Was this woman responsible for the raiders he'd fought?

"You must all be exhausted after such a terrible journey," she said. "Come to the palace. We will get you food, drink, and rest."

She seemed friendly enough. And it did Etse's heart good to see his home still intact! He'd been half afraid that Takoradi would be another burned and dead city by the time he got there, but it had held.

He stepped up his pace a little to come alongside the woman. One of her guards bristled, but she stilled him with a gesture and cocked her head at Etse questioningly.

"My lady, I thank you for your hospitality," Etse said. He half wanted to add 'in my home,' but there was no sense being rude. "I must ask: have you seen my father, Kwesi Panin? He was making for Takoradi, and I hoped to meet him here."

"No one by that name has announced himself to me," she replied. "But you are welcome to wait here for him. You are Etse Panin, then? That would make this your home more than mine!" she said, gesturing at the palace house ahead of them.

"I confess a longing to see my own bed again," Etse said with a laugh. "But I suspect that I have you and your men to thank for having a home to come back to at all."

"Likely so," she said. "We both have tales for the other, I am sure. But they can wait until you are clean and have good food and drink in front of you." She clapped her hands, and a score of Haisetti servants came forward to guide them in. A woman took Etse by the hand, gesturing with her other hand for him to follow her.

"A bath first," the woman in white said, wrinkling her nose. "I will see that a feast is ready for you when you are done."

The servant led Etse into his father's house. The thought of a warm bath made him sigh with pleasure. It was such a relief to be home, and safe, even if it was only for the moment. He realized with a start that he hadn't even gotten his benefactor's name. A sure sign of how worn out he was. He'd have to ask at dinner.

***

The bath had been exquisite, although Etse had found himself forced to shoo the servant out of his room while he bathed. He had the feeling that she was all too willing to help him with more than getting clean, and though the thought wasn't at all unpleasant, he found himself worried about his people. He wanted to get back to them – ensure things were well, that they were safe and being cared for. He sighed, shaking his head ruefully. This was what responsibility did for you. It made you into an old man before your time.

Etse went to where he'd left his clothes in a pile on his bedroom floor – his bedroom! It still seemed like a dream – but they were gone. Someone had hauled them away. Hopefully to be thrown out. They were pretty badly mangled.

No matter, though. It looked like someone had been using his room in his absence, but most of his clothes were still here. He wasn't sure how he felt about someone else having been here. Who had been sleeping in his bed? Were they even now off somewhere, wearing some of his clothes? It felt odd, intrusive, and the thoughts jangled with his emotions. But he had a hard time faulting the strange women and her people. Things were falling apart. People were doing what they had to do to survive. And these people had kept Takoradi alive. Without them, Etse and all his band would be dead right now.

He looked over his old wardrobe, shaking his head. He remembered wearing most of those clothes, remembered buying or commissioning most of them. How young the man who'd done those things seemed to him now! He ran his hands over silks, and embroidered finery. Trash now. Useless to him. He fished about until he found a clean white linen tunic and leather trousers, then dressed quickly. The boots he'd been wearing for his journey were worn, but still serviceable. They were comfortable, worn in from so many miles walked.

His hand reached automatically for his armor. Being without armor was like asking for death, out there. But he thought it might annoy his host if he came to dinner dressed for battle. Better to leave it here for now. His sword, though – that he belted around his waist. Only a fool went anywhere unarmed these days.

As ready as he could be, he opened the door to leave his room. A guard stood outside, a Haisetti dressed in ringed-leather armor with a sword belted to his side. Etse's eyes narrowed in suspicion, but the guard snapped to attention as soon as he saw Etse emerge.

"I am to bring you to the queen," the Haisetti said.

"Very well," Etse replied. "Lead on." A queen, was she? Etse wondered again who she was. He knew so damned little about the people of Haiset. He wished again that his father was there. Kwesi would know who she was, he had no doubt.

The guard led him through the palace to his father's largest banquet hall. The space was rarely used when Kwesi was in residence, but it clearly had seen much more use since. Etse stepped through the open double doors into a room brilliantly lit by torches and lanterns. Tables were set throughout the room, heavily laden with food. It looked like all of his people were in here, and most of them were already making short work of the meal and drink. Most of them hadn't eaten this well since the Gbohii came, and it showed in how heavily laden their plates were now.

"My queen," the Haisetti guard came up next to Etse and called out in a booming voice, "I present to you King Etse of the Asante."

Etse blinked, confused. Where had this confusion come from? His father was a king, not him. It was certainly never a title he'd ever thought about applying to himself, and he flushed with embarrassment. What would his people think?

But he looked around at their faces, and none of them were angry. Most broke from their repast for a moment to slap their hand on their knee.

"Hail, Etse!" came the call from the room. Then, louder, "Hail, Etse!"

He flushed again.

From the table at the far side of the room, the woman in white beckoned to him, smiling. He made his way across the hall to her table.

"Welcome, Etse, to my table. Please, sit," she said, gesturing to the chair beside her.

He went to the chair and made ready to sit but paused. "My lady, you have my thanks for our rescue, and for such care. But I am sorry – I do not even know your name."

She laughed, a tinkling sound. "I have not said? My apologies, then. I am Luganan."

He sat beside her.

"Your sister was long a friend of mine," she said.

Etse sucked in his breath. Lugu! He hadn't seen her since…too long ago. Too far in the past to remember her. He had only the vaguest of recollections of his sister, sent away when he was barely more than a toddler. He knew she'd been sent to Haiset to wed a Haisetti wura, but his father refused to speak of her.

"How is Lugu?" he asked.

Luganan's face fell. "Dead, Etse. She died of an illness some years ago. I thought you would have known. Didn't your father tell you of her passing?"

"No, he kept the news from me," Etse said. Anger sparked at the thought. The man had always been about his damned secrets. Etse was about done with that. They were going to have words when he found his father at last.

"I'm so sorry," she said. "I didn't mean to bring you pain."

"I haven't seen her since I was practically a baby," he said. "But she was my sister. I wish I had known her better. Come to that, you probably knew her much better than I did, if you were her friend."

She sipped her wine, then said "I did. But there will be time for that later. For now, eat, drink and rest. Your people are safe here. You have brought them home."

He settled back into his chair, picked up his cup, and drank a long gulp. It wasn't wine after all, he realized, but a very strong beer. The stuff tasted amazing. How long since he'd been able to relax? To really let down his guard? He sipped again and felt some of his tensions slipping away.

"So how did you come to be here?" he asked.

"I am a queen among my people," she said.

"The Haisetti?"

"You Asante call us that, yes. Our name for ourselves is just 'the People,' in our own tongue. We heard the Kiswalan emperor was here and came to see him."

Not strange. Many smaller rulers and lords had flocked to Nicran once word of Okere's presence got out. Oddly, Luganan looked Asante herself to Etse's eyes. But then, he hadn't seen many Haisetti, either. Which reminded him…

"I met some Haisetti raiders, on the road," he said. "Was it possible they were your people?"

She grimaced. "Some of my people did not take well to holing up in this city after the monsters walked the land. They wanted to race for home. I've had a few small bands of deserters. You might have run into one."

It made sense. He wasn't sure why they'd gone to such trouble to collect prisoners if their objective was to return to Haiset, but who was he to guess at the thoughts of men in the madness the world had come to? Doubtless their motives were clear in their own heads.

The night blurred to Etse's tired mind. At first, he resisted drinking too much. He was in the habit of keeping his guard up, and even the familiar feel of his childhood home around him didn't completely set him at his ease. But Luganan's servants kept refilling his goblet for him. Out there before him were all his people. They were warm. They were well fed. Their laughter made his heart glad. He'd brought them through; past all the evil the world could muster. At last, they were safe.

Etse yawned, long and loud. He blushed furiously. "I'm so sorry, my lady."

"No, it's me that ought to apologize," she replied. "I've been keeping you here chatting, and after all you've been through. You all need warm beds and rest."

Etse looked out over the banquet room. Some of his people were already asleep, drifted off right at the tables. Others were still talking among one another, but the laughter had died down, and even the hardiest seemed bleary-eyed.

"I think we would all appreciate that, my lady."

She rose and clapped her hands. "Please help our new guests to the accommodations I have prepared," she said. Guards and servants alike stepped forward and began helping the exhausted revelers up from their tables.

"My thanks," Etse said. He pushed back his chair and struggled to rise. He got to his feet, but a wave of dizziness struck. He had to reach down to grasp hold of the table with both hands to avoid falling.

"I've kept you up far too late," Luganan said, taking his elbow in her hand.

"I fear I've simply indulged in too much of your beer," Etse replied. "I notice you have not been so afflicted."

She ducked her head. "I tend to not drink too much."

"You're probably wiser than I am," Etse said.

"Come," she said. "Let's get you back to your room."

Etse would have protested, but he found his legs were wobbly enough that a little help might be needed, after all. And besides, Luganan was beautiful, kind, and helpful. How long had it been since he'd had a beautiful woman on his arm? Too long. And if he was technically more on her arm than she was on his, that was a thing he could live with. As they walked, her scent filled his nose. She wrapped her left arm about his waist and clung to his right arm with her right hand.

"I am a bit embarrassed to be in such a state," Etse said. How much of that beer had he drunk? He didn't recall drinking enough to make him drunk, but then he couldn't tell for certain, because he'd never emptied the cup more than halfway before it was filled again. He suddenly got the feeling he'd had far more of the stuff than he'd intended.

"I am glad to be able to help you," she replied. Was her hand stroking his hip? No, that must be his drunken imagination. They were at his door, at last. She opened the door, helped him inside. He made his way across the room to his bed with at least some semblance of grace and sat down heavily. The room wasn't spinning, at least. He'd gotten that drunk a few times in the past. Never a good thing.

"My lady, thank you for the escort," Etse said with as much dignity as he could muster under the circumstances. "I apologize for having made it necessary."

She came to stand next to him. Sitting as he was, she was taller than he, and she reached down to stroke his cheek. Her nails left trails of fire behind them. Etse gasped at the sensation.

"No apology is needed, Etse," she said softly. She touched her other hand to his other cheek, cradling his face in her fingers for a moment. Etse looked up into her eyes. He could see a passion there that matched his own. Perhaps even exceeded his own. Her hands drifted down his neck, sliding over his shoulders.

Then all at once she released him. Like she'd made a decision, both of her hands went to the neck of her dress, and undid a clasp which must have held the entire dress together. The weight of the silk bore it swiftly to the floor and left her standing naked in the moonlight. She was achingly beautiful. Etse found he could barely breathe, seeing her so. She reached down, her bare chest coming tantalizingly close to his face, and grasped the bottom hem of his tunic, pulling it up and over his head.

As soon as the garment was out of the way she leaned forward into him, pressing her body against his, hands and mouth seeking him out. He pulled her closer, exploring her mouth with his. He fell backwards onto the bed, bearing her with him. Her fingers were working at his trousers, sliding them down over his hips so that he could feel the whole of her body against his.

CHAPTER SIXTY

Kwadwo led his people out of the trees and into the open moor again. The ground rose here, and the bogs they'd been slogging through for all these hours were behind them now. At least those damned Haisetti would have to get through the rest of the bog to reach them. He was sure they were still back there, tracking them.

He made the top of the hill, panting a bit from the climb. Off in the distance to the east was Takoradi – which they had to give wide berth. North were the Haisetti still chasing them. To the west was the river and the sea, and although he couldn't see them anymore in the twilight, he was fairly sure that the Gbohii on the far side of the river were still walking south. They'd been blocking the way across all day.

And to the south? Well, if they could slip by Takoradi and get far enough south, they might lose their pursuers there. That was the plan right now, anyway.

"A sail!" Odoi said.

Kwadwo looked out over the river but saw nothing. "Are you sure?" The boy had already demonstrated keen vision, but a sail, out there, at night?

"I saw the moonlight gleam off a sail, just for a moment. Out there," he said, pointing to the south. That would be somewhere out near where the Densu became a bay. There could well be a river-ship out there. But would it be friend, foe, or neither?

In the end, it didn't really matter. There was only one route left they could take: south. They had no choice. Even if they were running straight into the hands of sea raiders, it couldn't be worse than falling into Lugu's hands again.

"Keep an eye out for it. Tell me if you see anything out there again," Kwadwo said. "Everyone keep moving! We're not safe here."

They needed no urging. They all knew that the best they could expect from the Haisetti was death, and the worst would be significantly worse. But even if their will was strong, their bodies were somewhat less so. The Haisetti troops chasing them were soldiers. They lacked the discipline of the Mikijen or Asanteman guard, but they didn't lack in courage or hardiness. Kwadwo's people simply didn't have the fitness to outrun those fighters, not forever. And their strength was flagging.

It would take a miracle to get them clear. And Kwadwo didn't see any miracles in the making.

CHAPTER SIXTY-ONE

Etse woke with a start. Some noise had awoken him, but he wasn't quite sure what it was, at first. His head was aching, but he didn't let it slow him. His hand went for his sword, still tucked beside the bed. Etse's fingers found the weapon and pulled it closer without drawing it. Then he sat up in his bed, casting the sheet off his naked body. Where was Luganan? She'd certainly been there when he fell asleep! He smiled at the memory. She must have left after he dozed off.

He cast his gaze around the room, searching for anything amiss. As his sweep passed the door, he saw it open just wide enough to admit a man in dark clothes. The stranger silently slid the door shut again behind him.

"Can I help you?" Etse asked.

The man whirled, his face flashing briefly through the moonlight as he turned. Etse had only the briefest of glimpses, but he knew those features. It was the Haisetti he had fought just the other day. The one he had allowed to escape. Now the man came to repay that kindness by killing him in his sleep? Anger seeped into Etse's veins.

"No," the man replied. "You are the bane of my existence, Etse Panin. You cannot help me. Your coming here has destroyed my life. But I am here to help you."

The man knelt on the floor before Etse's bed, presenting his sheathed sword to Etse with both hands.

"Why?" Etse asked. He was suddenly confused. A man coming to kill him, he understood. But it was hard to parse the logic in the man's seemingly contradictory statements. He took the sword, still trying to discern in what spirit it had been offered.

"You spared my life. Now I must help you in kind," the man replied. He rose from his kneeling position. "But we must be away swiftly. The danger is very close."

Danger? What danger? He stood, casting about for clothing. "Are my people at risk?"

The Haisetti sighed. "Your people are even now being fed to the Gnaw Maws or are being bitten by them to enlarge the Night Queen's menagerie."

"Gnaw Maws?" Etse said confused. "Gbohii?"

"Call them what you wish. But Cleave-spawn they be."

"And Luganan…the Night Queen?" It didn't make sense. She wouldn't hurt his people, not after hosting them so well. And why would anyone intentionally create more of the creatures? "I don't believe you."

"Not Luganan. Lugu, daughter of Nai. She gave you a false name, you see?"

Etse sank back onto his bed, all the strength gone from his limbs. If what the man said was true, then he had led his people into a horrible trap, and his own half-sister had… His eyes flickered to the bed they'd just shared, and he cringed inside.

"Show me," he said, throwing his tunic and tortoise-shell armor over his shoulders.

"We should flee, while we still can," the Haisetti warned.

"Show me!" Etse repeated.

"Very well. But you will not like what you see."

Etse angrily belted on his sword, slid into his boots, and followed the man out of his room through the darkened hallway. What was the truth here? Someone was lying to him, that much was certain. Etse's gut clenched, seeing a still lump of shadow ahead. It was a guard at the far end of the hall, dead in a pool of blood. Etse raised an eyebrow at that. This Haisetti had risked much coming to him with his warning. Or perhaps he sought to kill Etse and then blame the guard's death on him.

Together they silently slipped out a back door from the palace house. The moon still lit the land, casting everything in a pale blue color. Even from here, Etse heard the sounds of the Gbohii outside the walls. There must be hundreds of the things out there, growling and scraping at the stonework.

They went down the hill, away from the palace toward the warehouse district of town. Etse remained tightly aware of every motion his guide made. This might, after all, just be a ploy to get him outside the palace and slay him. But he was harder to kill than most, and...if the man was telling the truth, then Etse was the only chance his people had at survival.

The growling sounds of the Gbohii still carried easily on the night air. If anything, they sounded much nearer down here. Off to his left, down an alley, Etse saw the ruins of a large warehouse, gutted by fire. Something caught his eye out that way, something moving. But when he looked again it was gone. He brought his full attention back to the Haisetti.

"Around the corner is another warehouse. This one has been converted to store darker things. What you need to see are the heads resting on spears, on either side of the door," the Haisetti whispered. "You will want to rush in. If you do, they will kill you."

Etse narrowed his eyes. "Why not just tell me what's there?"

The man just shook his head. "No. You wanted to see. You need to see."

Etse braced himself, coming to the corner of the building so he could cast a quick glance. He checked where the Haisetti stood – several feet away, arms crossed. And Etse still had the man's sword, tucked into his belt. Feeling safer, he ventured a look.

It seemed like an ordinary warehouse. Except this one was clearly busy, even at night. Two guards stood outside the front door, and torches lit the area. The light was enough to see the two heads, mounted on spears just as his guide had claimed. One of the heads caught his attention immediately, because it was still moving. Snarling, jaws gnashing – it was Okere's head, animated as a Gbohii.

Etse brought his gaze to the other head, then, and his vision went wet with sudden tears. After coming all this way, no reunion after all? His father had been an immortal, unbending, unyielding part of him all his life. And now his head decorated a spike in this bitch queen's madhouse. At least his head was still in death. That was a small mercy.

He staggered back from the corner, his mind reeling. Silent sobs escaped his lips, each one a struggle to keep quiet. And then he heard screams from the building behind the heads, the scream of someone in mortal agony.

Etse's arm snapped out and caught the Haisetti by the front of his collar. "They're killing my people in there right now, aren't they?" he snarled. "Were you going to tell me?"

The man clutched at Etse's fingers but couldn't pry them open. "What good would it do for you to die too? At least live, to avenge them!"

"I'd rather live and save them. Or die trying."

"Why?" the man asked him. His eyes seemed desperate to Etse, like this answer had real meaning to him.

"Because they are my people," Etse replied, releasing the man. "And because evil men – and women – only thrive if there are no good people to oppose them." He turned to go.

"Wait," the Haisetti said. "I will help you. Two swords would be better than one, yes?"

Etse turned back to the man. "Can I trust you?"

"For tonight? Aane. I want this evil ended, too."

"Good enough for me," Etse said. It would have to be. If his people were to have any hope of surviving, he needed any edge he could find. He handed the man back his sword. "If we're to fight together, what's your name?"

"Gebisa," the Haisetti replied.

"Well, Gebisa... let's finish this." Etse took long strides around the corner, picking up his pace to a full run. One of the startled guards gave a yell that Etse cut off halfway through by cleaving through his neck. Gebisa stabbed the other in the gut with his short sword, clapping a hand over the dying man's mouth and stabbing upward into his heart. The battle was only seconds old, and two enemies were slain.

"There will be more inside," Gebisa said.

"Good," Etse replied, his mouth a hard line. He gave a shout and kicked the door. The jamb splintered, sending bits of wood flying into the room beyond, and then he was inside.

The space was a scene out of nightmare. Most of the warehouse was taken up by two large pens. One was filled with people – Etse's people, damn it! Or what was left of them, anyway. The other pen was filled with Gbohii, each one chained to the concrete floor. The Gbohii were all devouring something – someone – inside their pen. Another person Etse had failed to save. Another person he was too late for.

In the middle of the room were six armed Haisetti soldiers. Two of them were even now holding someone else, sticking his arm through the bars into the Gbohii's pen. It was Kpeda, and he was screaming.

"Kpeda! No!" Etse flew across the room, his sword a splinter of light. Two of the soldiers moved to stop him. He stabbed one in the throat. While he withdrew his blade, the other tried to slash at him, but he took a step closer to his attacker and slapped his forearm with an open hand, foiling the attack. Then he kicked down, shattering the man's leg. The man dropped to the floor, screaming.

The two men holding Kpeda had let him go, but not before he'd got a bloody wound on his right hand. Etse's soul went cold then. All four men rushed him, swords drawn, and he wove his blade against all four. One fell, his gut opened up, hands clutching his belly. Then another went down as Gebisa joined the battle and stabbed him under his armpit. The last two didn't stand a chance. Etse sent his sword around into a fast butterfly arc that ran its course through both their necks.

The headless bodies fell to the cold floor.

Without hesitating for even a second, Etse took swift steps to Kpeda's side. The man lay on the floor, his eyes streaming with tears, his wounded hand clutched to his chest – showing the deadly bite he'd already received.

"Do you want to live?" Etse asked, his voice like cold iron.

"Aane!" Kpeda replied, desperation and fear making his words tremble.

Etse took his hand and laid it out on the stone floor. He stripped the belt from his waist, and wrapped it around Kpeda's upper arm, just as he'd seen Kwesi's surgeons do long ago. But where those surgeons had been too late to save their patient, perhaps Kpeda could still be saved if the hand was removed before the corruption spread.

"Gebisa?" he asked. The man took his meaning at once and came to hold the hand. Kpeda saw what he was about as soon as he raised his sword to strike. His breaths turned into pants, his voice a whimper, but to his credit he didn't cry out for Etse to stop. Etse wasn't sure what he would have done if he had – probably struck anyway.

His sword swung down and clove the hand from the body. Kpeda was screaming again, and Etse couldn't blame the man. He could taste his own tears, mixing with his sweat and dripping down his face. Swiftly, he applied cloth to the wound and put pressure on it.

"I need one of the torches," Etse said.

"Here," said a small voice next to him.

After his world had been broken into so many small pieces tonight, he never thought he'd smile so easily again – but hearing that voice again brought one to his lips easily. "Sefadzi." He turned to give the child a hug.

"Don't burn yourself," she said, hugging him back. She was holding a torch, and he took it from her. First he put the flame out. Then he took the warm pitch from the base of the torch and spread it over the stump of Kpeda's wrist. That caused Kpeda to pass out completely, but it also stopped the bleeding and let Etse wrap the wound better.

"Will he live?" Uche asked.

Etse stood back up and clasped his friend's hand. "I don't know. No man has survived a bite, but I know of no one who's had the wounded limb severed so soon after being bitten before. He has a chance."

The rest of Etse's people had freed themselves, once the guards keeping them in the cell were slain. There were only eighteen left.

"They took the bitten someplace else, after they were bitten. To 'set' they said," Uche shuddered. "I don't know where, though."

Etse looked at Gebisa, but the Haisetti shook his head.

"They'll be back soon though, for the next batch. More guards. We should be gone by then," Uche went on.

"Aane. You – and anyone else trained with weapons – arm yourselves from these dead men. There's two more swords and ringed-leather coats on dead men outside the door, too. Let's get ready to be off."

He tried to sound commanding and it seemed to have worked, since everyone bustled about, carrying out his orders. But the fact was he had no idea what to do next. He was in the middle of an enemy controlled city filled with hundreds of Haisetti soldiers. And even if he somehow got outside the walls, the city was surrounded by hundreds of howling Gbohii. Maybe he could raise the city? Get them to fight back? They might just do that, for Kwesi's son. Unless Lugu had them completely cowed.

"Um, Etse?" Jiagge whispered. "I think we have a problem."

"Just one?" Etse said, a small smile playing at the corner of his mouth.

"No, seriously. I went outside to get the gear from those dead guards, and…just look."

Etse frowned but went to see what he was talking about. He peeked outside, looking about. Movement caught his eye almost at once, from the ruined building down the street that he had spied earlier. His eyes grew wide, watching as Gbohii after Gbohii climbed up out of the ruins and strode out into the night. There seemed to be no end to them – just an ongoing stream of monsters.

CHAPTER SIXTY-TWO

"Eda save us," Gebisa whispered.

"Those aren't Lugu's creatures, then?" Etse asked.

"No. Your father's man escaped with a few followers, and Lugu burned the building down trying to kill them. She had men set a stone across the sewer tunnel, but the things must have moved it."

More dizzying news. The city was filling up with Gbohii, but… "My father's man – Kwadwo is alive?" It had to be Kwadwo. Etse was tired of the dribs and drabs of information. "When we get a moment, Gebisa, I want the full story."

Gebisa laughed. "And I'll want yours. Everyone thought you dead. Your sister about shit herself when she found out otherwise."

Etse peeked outside again. The Gbohii were spreading out as they emerged. None of them were coming this way yet, but that wouldn't last forever. Takoradi was doomed. That much was certain. Any hope he had of trying to rouse the city against Lugu was shattered. Most of those people out there, asleep in their beds tonight, would be horribly dead by morning. Escape was the only chance for survival, now. Save who you can and run. He did some mental math. Etse knew the walls well. The monsters were coming out of the sewers at a constant rate, which meant they must be packed in down there. That probably meant they were swarming into the hole outside, which ought to be spotted by the guards on the wall before long. It would also mean less Gbohii running around in the open out there. Every Gbohii that went into Takoradi right now made the space around the city more passable.

"Gebisa, how many kwapawnkah in the stables?" Etse asked.

"I don't know – forty? Maybe fifty?"

"That will do," Etse said. "Jiagge, Uche, with Gebisa and I. I want two people assisting Kpeda." He was back on his feet, but his face was pale and sweat-streaked. "We're making for the stables by the front gate. Once we get there, we grab kwapawnkah, and we're out of here. Be careful – Gbohii are loose in the city."

"Let's go!" Etse finished and stepped outside.

Gebisa was close behind him and whispered. "You didn't explain how you plan to get the gate open, once you have those kwapawnkah."

"I'll figure that out when we get there," Etse replied.

"I'll wait to be astounded."

Sefadzi overheard Gebisa and stuck out her tongue at him. Gebisa responded by sticking his tongue out at her, which made her giggle. Etse wanted to smile, but he was too wired with adrenaline. He couldn't let his attention lapse even a moment or people might die. People were going to die tonight, no matter what he did. He'd save who he could, but there would be an ocean of blood running through the streets of his home city tonight, and inside his heart was shattering. He knew if he stopped to think about it for more than a moment, he'd break down in tears. There would be time for the living to shed tears later, but first they needed to stay alive.

His band moved swiftly down back streets. No one was about. The guards were sleeping, or up on the walls. The townsfolk were all abed – but Etse knew that would change any moment. Already there must be several scores of Gbohii within the city, with more entering every minute. He was stunned that no one had sounded an alarm yet.

And then it came – screams, from near the warehouses they'd just left. High, piercing screams, suddenly cut off. Horns sounded a moment later from the wall top, answered by more horns from the other walls.

"They know they're in trouble now," Etse said. "Will they try to fight the things? Defend the town?"

Gebisa shook his head. "Your father had an escape tunnel built into your palace. Those horns are an alarm telling every Haisetti in the city to get their asses up there or be left behind."

Etse grimaced. "She's not even going to try to defend these people?"

"Against that? Would you?"

Etse gave him a look.

"Dammit to the Cleave, man. I guess maybe you would. And probably kill them all, too."

"With several hundred trained soldiers at my back? Aane," Etse said.

They reached the stables and paused in a pool of shadow across the courtyard. The stables were close to the gates – just inside the main gate to the city wall. Two Haisetti guards stood outside the stable, although it looked to Etse like they'd all abandoned the wall itself. They seemed nervous, their eyes darting at shadows. They knew what was coming. Inside the building, others were gathering up kwapawnkah. As he watched, one Haisetti took a string of kwapawnkah, already saddled and ready to ride up the hill toward the palace.

"As soon as the next one comes out, we move," Etse said.

"Why wait?" asked Jiagge.

"Why not let them saddle our mounts for us?" Etse said with a grin.

They didn't have long to wait. A few moments later, a Haisetti left the building leading a train of six kwapawnkah. He nodded to the guards and was about to start up the hill after the other man.

Without saying a word, Etse got to his feet. The guards saw him at once. The Haisetti with the kwapawnkah stopped, and backed the beasts into the stable again, vanishing from sight. Both guards waved spears angrily at Etse, saying something to him he couldn't really understand.

One of them threw his spear.

Etse sidestepped and cut it in half with his sword.

He'd already closed half the distance by then, so he launched himself into a sprint. The second spear flashed through the air toward where he had been, but he was already someplace else. The men tried to draw their swords to face him. One didn't even manage to get his weapon free from its scabbard before Etse's blade tore his throat out. The other tried to duel Etse – but he had no idea what sort of swordsman he was facing, and Etse wasn't in the mood to give gentle lessons. He cut the man down without a word.

"Anyone inside who wants to live, run now, out the back way," he called out. There were no doors big enough for kwapawnkah out the back. Etse heard hasty scuffling inside, and then nothing. He kicked the front door down, sweeping inside, his sword up in a guard position. But no one remained inside – the Haisetti had taken his words seriously and fled. Good enough. He had more need to get his people out of this trap than to pursue vengeance – today. There would be another day for that.

"Quickly, saddle enough kwapawnkah for everyone," Etse said. "We don't have much time." The Haisetti still outnumbered them more than ten to one. And the Gbohii would be swarming over this part of the city any time now.

"We'll need to open the gate," Gebisa warned.

"I know. Uche, up to a challenge?" Etse said.

"Every day with you brings new challenges, me wura," he said, smiling. "What are we doing?"

"Follow me," Etse said.

It would take the others a few minutes to saddle enough kwapawnkah for everyone to have a mount. With the kwapawnkah, they might hope to burst through the Gbohii outside and outrun the things. That left them a little time to get up into the gatehouse and raise the portcullis. The timing on that last would be tricky indeed. Etse snagged one of the already saddled kwapawnkah and went outside with it, Gebisa and Uche following close behind.

He strode out to the gate in plain sight. As he walked, he scanned the walls carefully for troops – but there was no one there. The Haisetti had all retreated to his father's palace. Gebisa was right. They planned to withdraw, abandon all the people here. Much as Etse himself was doing. The thought made him wince.

Etse looked back over his shoulder. Some small fires were already burning, and he could hear screams of terror on the night air. Death had come to Takoradi, and he doubted anyone would be left alive inside the city by morning. Still, he wished he could take this kwapawnkah and ride into the town, cutting down every Gbohii he could find, for as long as he could until they ended him in turn. Only the responsibility he felt to save these people stayed him from doing just that. He tied the kwapawnkah to a post at the base of the wall. She was one of his father's warhorses. A fine mount, trained for battle and unlikely to startle. He brushed her mane appreciatively.

They climbed the stone steps up to the top of the wall. From there, they could raise the portcullis that blocked their exit – and blocked the Gbohii from coming in, too. Etse was afraid that the area outside the gate would be packed with the things. But when he reached the top of the wall, he was relieved to see they were scattered and wandering aimlessly – and nowhere near as numerous as he had feared. There must be far more Gbohii coming into the city that he'd guessed.

As if summoned by the thought, he spotted one of the things loping down the battlements toward them. It snarled and moaned as it came, gnashing teeth.

Uche didn't hesitate. He stabbed out with his spear, taking the thing under the ribs at an angle to its approach. That stopped it cold for a moment, and before it could turn and run down the spear shaft toward Uche, Etse's blade took off its head.

"Well done," Etse said. "There will be more. Keep an eye out."

"Etse, there are more," Gebisa murmured, pointing the other way.

Etse turned and saw a band of the things coming down the battlements on the other side of the gatehouse. Six of the monsters. He ran into the building and threw himself against the door on the far side before they could reach it. With a grunt, he slammed down the bar across the door. Two inches of stout mahogany ought to keep the door shut for at least a little while.

And there was the portcullis mechanism. Easy to operate. Remove the block, throw the lever, and the thing would rise.

"Uche, get back down there and get everyone on kwapawnkah in the yard just outside the gate," Etse said. "Once they're there, I'll throw the lever and follow as quickly as I can."

"I'm on my way," Uche replied, and vanished back down the stairs.

Beside him, the Gbohii were pounding on the door, but it should hold for the few minutes they would need. Etse stepped back outside to watch for more of the monsters. He knew they'd be coming soon enough.

But no more of the things arrived before Uche led a kwapawnkah out from the stable. He looked carefully around the yard for danger, saw Etse up on the wall and sketched a short salute. Sure that the way was as safe as it could be, he mounted his kwapawnkah and led the others out of the stables. Soon all of

Etse's people were mounted, waiting outside the gate. It was as good a moment as it would be. Even Kpeda was mounted double behind someone else – was that Sefadzi? Etse watched anxiously as Jiagge lifted the stout bar from the gate and opened the doors as softly as he could. But only the very nearest Gbohii were attracted to the movement – three of the things coming to claw at the portcullis. Not enough to be a real threat.

A hissing sound was Etse's first warning that something was terribly wrong. Then a swarm of the monsters boiled forth from the center of the town, hissing and burbling as they came running out toward the tasty lure of soft human and antelope flesh assembled.

CHAPTER SIXTY-THREE

Kwadwo thought this ridge would be as likely a place as they would find. He and his people hadn't gotten as far south as he'd hoped, and the Haisetti were already closing on them fast. He looked back over his shoulder and in the distance he could see the moonlight glinting off their spear tips. Off in the distance to the east, he could easily spot the lights of torches on the Takoradi walls. They'd gone so damned far. To be back almost where they started their escape was maddening.

This spot seemed good enough. Look as he might, he couldn't see any Gbohii nearby. The ground was high enough that the enemy would be coming uphill at them – a small edge, but anything would help. And the land was clear here, so no one was going to be sneaking up on anyone. It would be a stand up battle. Against trained soldiers who outnumbered his armed men better than two to one. Kwadwo shook his head, trying to fend off fears that this was just going to be a slaughter.

"We'll make our stand here," he said, loud enough for his voice to carry to all who were with him.

Ako came up alongside him and placed a hand on his shoulder. "Are you sure?" the big man whispered. "I could hang back with a few of the men, buy the rest of you some time…"

Kwadwo turned to face him fully. The silverback-like man had been one of the best of his trainees, and even now he demonstrated why Kwadwo had enjoyed his company so much. He never gave up. And he always volunteered for whatever job was worst or most dangerous. It was a habit that was going to get him killed, sooner or later. Kwadwo would rather put it off as long as he could.

"Together, we might just win. Or at least kill enough of them to break the rest. They're far from home now. Strangers in a land that is strange to them. We have a fighting chance. Together," Kwadwo said.

"Together, then," Ako replied. He looked dubious about Kwadwo's hopeful words but seemed willing enough to accept the orders anyway.

The spearmen arrayed themselves in a long file, facing down the hill. On the other side of the hill waited all of their non-combatants. Most of those had grabbed something to defend themselves with, even if it was only a stout bit of wood. If push came to shove – and it likely would – they'd all fight. There was nothing to lose by trying. The fate of capture was likely much worse than death.

"It's going to be a long wait, men," Kwadwo said. He plopped his bottom down on a tuft of soft grass. "Might as well rest while we wait for them. Let them be the ones all worn out and us fresh, eh?"

Odoi came over and sat down next to him. He was playing with something with his hands, and Kwadwo peeked to see what he was about, but it was just a handful of stones.

"That ship is still out there, you know," Odoi said.

"Is it?" Kwadwo replied.

"Aane, and closer now."

"We can't wait for it, Odoi. We don't know if it's a potential ally or another enemy," Kwadwo said.

Odoi shrugged. "Oh, I know that," he said. "But after we win, it might be worth checking out."

"Aane boy," Kwadwo said. "After." If there was an after. The odds were not looking good for them, but he didn't want to spoil the boy's faith in their victory.

The line of men was nervous enough that their laughter sounded almost like giggles to Kwadwo's ears. It wouldn't do. Morale might make or break this fight. He'd have to find a way to rally them, just before the Haisetti actually made their move.

Time passed, and the Haisetti kept up their steady jog, chewing up those last miles. Kwadwo lounged on the ground pretty much as long as he could, the image of nonchalance. He chatted with the men. A few boys went through their line with flasks of water, and he made sure everyone drank plenty and had a small bite of food. They'd need the hydration, and the energy. Then the Haisetti were rolling their way down the next hill over – still a goodly distance away, maybe a thousand feet. He stood up then and started brushing dirt from his legs.

"What's the boy up to?" Ako grumbled.

Kwadwo snapped his head around. Odoi had left the group, wandered down the hill a bit. He stood about ten feet away from them now, sideways to the oncoming Haisetti, as if he was waiting for something. The enemy was still over two hundred feet away. When they reached about two hundred feet, by Kwadwo's best guess, the boy dropped a bit of leather and rope from his hand and began to spin the tool in circles.

A sling! That was why he'd been playing with the rocks. "You any good with that, Odoi?" Kwadwo asked.

"Aane."

Just that one word. No boasting – but then, he wasn't a boastful young man. He had proven himself to be effective and smart, time and again. "Aim well, then," Kwadwo said.

Odoi didn't reply. He just kept spinning the sling, whirling it faster and faster.

When the Haisetti were about one hundred and fifty feet away, he released. The stone whistled through the air and slammed into one of the Haisetti. Kwadwo could tell when it hit because the man simply stopped running in mid-stride and fell to the ground. All of the Haisetti hesitated for a moment, some going back for their fallen man while others plainly urged their fellows onward. The ones checking the victim quickly left him where he lay and joined the others, running full tilt now.

Odoi had already fitted a new stone to his sling before the first hit its mark. By the time the Haisetti got themselves together and organized again, his second stone was in the air, a third twirling. The second stone bounced off a Haisetti's leg. Kwadwo could see the man limping, falling behind the others. Clearly injured but still dangerous. The third stone sang out and hit one of the Haisetti as they started to climb the hill toward them. Kwadwo could see the damage this time as it smashed into the front of the man's skull, shattering bone. The injured Haisetti fell over backwards and didn't move again.

But the others were still coming fast. And Odoi was holding his ground, trying to get off one more shot. Kwadwo could see by the set of the young man's face that he wasn't going anywhere. He'd hold his ground until the last moment and take down every enemy that he could.

"He's not going to get back to us," Kwadwo whispered under his breath. He could see it play out in his mind – the boy would never make it back to their line before he was overrun and gutted by angry Haisetti.

"If any of you can't take out as many Haisetti as that boy, you're not half the men I think you are!" Kwadwo yelled. "With me!"

Then he rushed down the hill, hoping like hell that his men were following close behind him. He reached Odoi – passed him by, even as the young man fired off one more shot. He didn't have a chance to see where that stone impacted though, because he was too busy fending off spears with his sword.

But then Ako's huge sword clove the attacker to his left nearly in half. And spears bristled next to him, fending off the enemy.

Still more of his people charged forward with clubs. Men and women alike, they rushed in to stop the wave of attackers cold. Another stone zinged by over Kwadwo's head, finding its mark on a Haisetti shoulder two ranks back, so Odoi was safe. For the moment at least.

There were over fifty Haisetti, though. All of them battle hardened and furious. Kwadwo felt himself having to back up a step as they surged forward against his line. And then another. A woman tried to block a Haisetti spear but was stabbed in the belly instead. Her screams were terrible, and worse, there was really nothing anyone could do to help her as they were forced to back up even further up the hill, leaving her behind to be stabbed repeatedly by the enemy until her screams cut off.

They were fighting as hard as they could. But Kwadwo could feel the pulse of the battle, and his people were losing.

CHAPTER SIXTY-FOUR

The Gbohii ran in, howling their glee at such easy prey waiting for them.

"Go. Save them! I've got the portcullis," Gebisa said.

Etse had just one moment to consider the action. If he trusted Gebisa, and the man failed to do as he said, then all of his people were doomed. But if he went for the portcullis instead, the Gbohii would fall on them before he could stop the things, and they'd be just as dead. Trusting Gebisa was the only chance any of them had. He just had to hope the man was worthy of that trust.

He took the steps five at a time coming down, leaping from the last landing into the saddle of the kwapawnkah he'd left there, slashing down with his sword to cut the rope free. The kwapawnkah was startled by his sudden appearance but quickly settled herself. He kneed her into a gallop and moved to intercept the monsters.

"Go, as soon as Gebisa opens the portcullis!" he shouted. Then he was past his people and riding down toward the monsters. It was like a dream, in a way. He'd gone over this death in his mind more than once. Riding into battle against a horde of the things, wearing mail, sword free in his hand. His sword slashed down and took one of the things in the head. His mare's hooves slashed down another. He caught a third on the backswing. But there were too many of them. And just like in the dream, they slowed his progress enough that soon he was surrounded by biting, gurgling honhommawne.

Spears pierced the Gbohii on other side of his saddle. Then more spears, and more flashing hooves, a line of horsemen smashing into the monsters like a wave and plowing them under. Etse was stunned. He'd charged fully expecting to die, but suddenly there were no enemies within weapon reach. He could see scores more of the things coming their way, but for the moment they were free and clear.

"Come on, Etse!" Uche shouted. He and his men had already wheeled their mounts. Etse did the same, and they rushed for the portcullis. It was still down.

Etse glanced over his shoulder. They had a few moments until the next wave of the dead crashed down and buried them all. "Gebisa!" he shouted.

Then the portcullis was rising, rattling and clacking into the air. All their kwapawnkah charged, armed men leading the way to clear a path. Etse held off just a moment longer, just inside the gate. Where was Gebisa? He couldn't wait – the Gbohii were swarming up the street even now. They'd be all over him any second.

He heard a yell from the wall above, and Gebisa barreled out of the gatehouse, running like all the honhommawne of hell were chasing him. Which was pretty much what was happening. The six Gbohii Etse had barricaded on the other side of the door were hot on his heels.

"Jump!" Etse shouted.

Gebisa heard him. The man hit the edge of the stairs with the monsters close behind and gaining fast. He leapt. Etse tracked his arc through the air, guessed where he would land, and started his kwapawnkah in that direction. There was no time to grab another kwapawnkah – Gbohii were sweeping down on them from all directions now. It was leave or die!

Gebisa hit the ground feet first, but tucked gracefully into a roll, turning over one shoulder before coming up to his feet again.

Etse was already there, reaching out a hand to the man. Each man grasped the other's wrist, and with a bound he was in the saddle behind Etse.

"Go, go, go!" Gebisa shouted.

Etse needed no urging. He kneed his kwapawnkah into a gallop, racing through the gate into the night air, and freedom. Behind him, at least a score of the Gbohii howled and gave chase, but even riding double they couldn't keep up with his kwapawnkah. Ahead were his people, still riding west away from Takoradi. They'd slowed to a canter, allowing Etse to close the distance.

"We won't be able to go far, riding double," Gebisa warned.

"Would you have preferred I leave you behind?" Etse asked him, a smile quirking at the corner of his mouth. Was the man always this grumpy? It reminded him of Kwadwo, a little. The thought brought a pang to his heart. Gebisa said Kwadwo had escaped – or someone Etse guessed was Kwadwo, anyway. But where was he? How the hell was he supposed to find him out there in all of the mess the world was in?

But he knew he must find Kwadwo somehow. And any of the rest of his people that he could. When he could. For the moment, he had to get these people someplace safe. That meant as far from Takoradi – and his sister – as he could manage.

"We were hoping you'd join us," Jiagge quipped as Etse came up alongside the rest of the party. Etse chuckled. Jiagge had been one of the first to take up the call of 'King Etse,' back in the banquet hall. He knew now that had just been Lugu buttering him up so that he would lower his guard. Damn the woman! And himself, for that matter. He should have known better than to fall for pretty words.

Even if he'd managed to stay more alert, it might not have saved anyone else. But it was galling that he'd been so completely duped. And then she'd come to his bed…! He blushed scarlet, grateful that no one could see his face well in the pale moonlight.

"There's something going on up ahead," Uche said.

Etse brought his full attention forward. They'd been racing pretty much straight toward the river. From there, Etse had the idea to turn south, and make for some of the fishing villages dotting the coast where the Densu River met the sea. But Uche was right. There was a clash of some sort up ahead, on a hillside near the riverbank. Even from this far, Etse could see the flash of steel on both sides. So it was men against men, and not Gbohii.

Which probably meant one of the sides was Lugu's people. He gritted his teeth. Etse was loathe to leave anyone to face her troops without assistance, but his people had already been through so much…

"Anyone up to another little skirmish before bed?" Etse asked aloud. He had to ask. He'd already failed them – he had no right to command them. "One of the groups fighting up ahead are bound to be more Haisetti."

"We owe them," Jiagge growled.

"For our dead," Uche agreed.

"For my hand," Kpeda spat out, pain lancing every word.

"Then it's agreed," Etse said. Over his shoulder, his voice pitched not to carry, Etse spoke to Gebisa. "You don't have to be a part of this. I'll drop you off. You can make for home. You've more than repaid any debt you owed me."

Gebisa looked back over his shoulder, his eyes filled with sorrow. "We are a proud people, fallen to ruin because of that woman. You might be the one man I have seen capable of defeating her cunning, Etse – mostly because you think with your heart. No, I'll stay with you."

"Not out of debt to me anymore, then?"

"No," Gebisa replied. "Out of a debt to myself."

The ride became wordless at that point. Everyone with weapons formed a wedge at the front of their formation. The few of their party who were unarmed, like Kpeda and Sefadzi, fell back a few paces. They'd stay clear of the fighting.

The night air was crisp as it flew by. The moon cast enough light to see the battle unfold ahead of them, now. The force higher on the hill was retreating with casualties, but they were making their foe fight hard for every footstep gained up the hill. The force on the lower side of the slope were the Haisetti, who grossly outnumbered the other group.

Time to even the odds.

"The bottom group are the Haisetti!" Etse shouted to his fighters. "We'll swing downhill and hit them from the rear."

The Haisetti must have seen them coming long before they reacted, but they did nothing. Etse could only assume they thought his force was reinforcements, coming from Takoradi to aid them. It was a logical guess. But as his force swung into place below them, it was also fatal. His kwapawnkah couldn't maintain a full charge up the hill into the rear of the Haisetti troops – but they were still going very fast. The Haisetti realized their danger at last and tried to turn, but it was too little – and far too late.

CHAPTER SIXTY-FIVE

Kwadwo saw the riders and despaired for a moment. They were already losing; five of his people bled on the ground, dead or dying. And they were running out of ground to give way. Soon they'd reach the top of the hill. Then the Haisetti would use their superior numbers to envelop his people. Once surrounded, they'd have no chance at all.

And now this – a group of cavalry, there to finish things off even more surely. He gritted his teeth. He'd take many of them with him before he fell. That was all he could hope for now.

And then he heard something that shattered his desperation in an instant.

The leader of the horsemen – the man riding point in their wedge – shouted out "For Asanteman! With me!"

Kwadwo couldn't believe his ears.

It was Etse.

The Haisetti Kwadwo was fighting looked over his shoulder at the shout. Almost mechanically, he used the moment of distraction to stab the Haisetti in the throat. Blood fountained around his sword. The Haisetti sank to the ground. Kwadwo watched as the horsemen smashed into the rear of the Haisetti like a tidal wave, men vanishing under the flashing hooves, bodies hacked down by their swords or impaled on their lances.

How the hell could Etse still be alive? Kwadwo had seen him fall! Seen him lay there, broken on the stone ledge. No one could have survived that, let alone fought his way out of Nicran by himself after.

And yet there was no mistaking that voice. It was deeper, more commanding than Kwadwo recalled. He wondered what the young man had been through on his journey here, to give his voice that blend of steel and fire. He wiped his face, realizing with a start that the wetness there was from tears, not blood.

The battle was over in minutes. Between the crush of Kwadwo's people pushing hard from the top and the destruction the horsemen wreaked, the Haisetti had no stomach for much fighting. They broke with a third of their force still on their feet – about twenty men. The remnant fled for Takoradi.

"Shall we pursue, me wura?" asked a man on horseback. Kwadwo was about to answer out of habit but realized quickly that the man was speaking to Etse.

"No need," Etse replied. "They're headed right into a pack of dozens of Gbohii – the ones who were chasing us. They're dead men. They just don't know it yet."

Then Etse saw him. Their eyes met. Kwadwo could see the depths of the young man's grief in those eyes – how much this journey had cost him was written on his face. But as soon as he recognized Kwadwo, Etse's eyes lit up. He jumped down from his kwapawnkah and raced to Kwadwo's side. Once there, though, he hesitated a moment. Kwadwo wondered what he was seeing in his face, what secret pains he was revealing to the young man even now.

They'd all been through so much.

Kwadwo broke the impasse, reaching out to embrace Etse.

"You're alive," Kwadwo said. "Daarila, how did you survive?"

Etse stepped back and smiled. "It'll be a long tale, and we don't have time right now." As if on cue, they heard men screaming from somewhere east of them. Screaming in fear, in pain, screaming for mercy.

“That will be the Gbohii chasing us,” Etse said. “We need to get out of here, fast.”

“And how do we do that, your majesty?” asked a man beside Etse.

“Majesty?” Kwadwo asked, cocking an eyebrow.

“Very long story,” Etse demurred. “Gebisa – meet Kwadwo. Kwadwo, Gebisa. You’ll like each other.”

Etse strode to the hilltop, scratching his chin. Kwadwo and Gebisa followed him up. Kwadwo wasn’t sure how they were going to escape the oncoming horde of monsters, but he had no doubt it would be interesting.

CHAPTER SIXTY-SIX

The wind whipped Etse's hair into his face, and he brushed away a few strands that stuck there. He was bone weary, but this was no time to show it. Looking around, he could see that Kwadwo's people were wiped out. How long had then been fleeing before they were forced to turn and face their Haisetti pursuers? Long enough to exhaust them all. If that wasn't enough, they had wounded as well as dead. Etse's party had escaped the fight with no serious injuries except to their kwapawnkah. His people were unused to mounted combat, and the kwapawnkah had not been trained for fighting. Nine of their eighteen mounts were dead or badly wounded enough that they would not survive the night. That left nine kwapawnkah for about three score people.

He looked east. Somewhere out there on the dark moor was a horde of monsters. He could hear some of the noise of their last victims even now. The Haisetti who'd fled hadn't gotten very far. Which meant the Gbohii would be on them soon.

North was a marsh. They might lose themselves in there for a while. South was more open land. No escape from the Gbohii that way. And west?

To the west, Etse swore he saw a sail, out there in the Densu.

"Is that a ship out there?" he asked aloud.

"Aane, me wura," said a young man standing at his right arm. "I've been watching it. It's been coming closer to shore all night."

"Have you tried to signal it?" Etse asked Kwadwo.

"No. How would we signal it without drawing the Haisetti or Gbohii down on us?" Kwadwo asked.

"The Haisetti aren't an issue anymore. And the Gbohii don't seem all that attracted to fire. Let's try," Etse said. He cupped his hands to his mouth and called "Everyone grab any wood you can find and bring it here!"

Etse knelt in the grass. It was about knee high here, where it hadn't been trampled down. But at the base he found what he was looking for – tufts of dried out grass down near the dirt, a layer that would catch fire quickly and easily. He gathered up several big handfuls of the stuff as quickly as he could.

"Gebisa, keep watch to the east. They're coming. We need warning before they attack," Etse said.

Gebisa nodded and went off to stand guard.

A little work with flint and steel, and they had a small flame burning. It was a weak thing, though. There wasn't enough wood here to make a really noticeable blaze. Etse picked up a stout stick that one of Kwadwo's people had been using for a cudgel. Then he tore off a chunk of his shirt, wrapping it tightly around the stick, and thrusting the makeshift torch into the fire. Once it was burning, he pulled it out and went to the west side of the hill.

"They might not be friendly," Kwadwo said, following him. "They could be slavers from Kongo. Or more Haisetti. Or any other number of potential foes."

Etse looked him in the eye. "You have a better plan?"

Kwadwo shrugged. "Not really."

"Then we do this," Etse replied.

He set about carving letters in the air, written in fire. HELP, he wrote. He repeated the statement, the torch already beginning to gutter out. The boy who said he'd been watching the ship came running up with another lit torch just as his guttered out.

Etse took the torch. "Thank you. What's your name, young man?"

"Odoi, me wura."

"You must have been an incredible boon for Kwadwo," Etse said.

"He has been," Kwadwo agreed. Odoi blushed.

Etse resumed his skywriting.

"The ship turned, me wura," Odoi said. "It's coming this way."

"But are they coming to help us?" Kwadwo asked aloud.

"If they are, good. If they are not…? Then we take their ship away from them and feed them to the monsters," Etse growled. "Either way, we should head to the shore and make ready."

Etse left nine of his men behind on the hilltop, under Uche's command. One for each of their remaining kwapawnkah. "Skirmish with any Gbohii you see leading the pack," Etse said. "But flee the moment you see a larger group, retreat to rejoin us. Understand?"

"Aane, me wura," Uche replied. Gebisa nodded behind him. Etse was sending the more experienced man along, too. Uche would be in command. But Gebisa would make sure that his people got back in one piece.

The rest of them began the short march to the shore. It wasn't far. A twenty minute walk brought them there, even dragging litters for two of Kwadwo's more badly wounded people. Etse offered Kpeda a litter, but he refused. He walked with the rest of them, face stiff with pain, his stump clutched to his chest.

A short way down the river was a small jetty, rocks piled atop one another to make a strong pier. It was about ten feet wide and reached out thirty feet into the water. By the end, the water was deep enough that the Gbohii would be hard pressed to climb the rock pile and reach them. It would do.

"We'll fight from here, if we need to," Etse said. "Pack the young and injured furthest out into the river and kill the things as they come across the rocks."

"It might work," Kwadwo said, rubbing his chin. "But we won't hold against a large force."

Odoi broke in. "My lords, the ship has dropped anchor, and it's sending out a little boat."

The ship was near now. Not within bowshot, but close enough that Etse could make out the individuals moving about on the deck. And yes, they were sending over a rowboat. He counted eight people on board.

"We might not need to fight, if those people will carry us away from here," Etse said. He had hopes that they might. The people on the ship could see the shore as well as Etse could see them. They had a rough idea of the numbers. But they had sent over only eight. Was that because they were friendly, and hoping to help? Or because they considered those eight expendable, and would take the ship away if their rowboat crew was attacked?

Nothing to do but wait as the boat splashed its way across the water toward them.

Before the boat arrived, Etse's nine riders came over the hill toward them. They were moving fast, but not at a full gallop. The kwapawnkah were panting but not broken. Etse guessed that they'd run into trouble – but how much time did they have before trouble came calling?

"What's the report?" he called out.

"About fifty Gbohii, all coming this way. Fifty now – we picked off three before coming back. A few that had gotten away from the others. But the rest are moving in a pretty tight pack."

"How long do we have?" Kwadwo asked, giving voice to the question everyone was wondering.

"Ten minutes? Maybe fifteen?" Gebisa said. Still atop his kwapawnkah, he looked at the jetty. "A good spot. Not so good for the kwapawnkah, though. They'll break a leg on those rocks."

Etse turned back toward the little boat still coming their way. A lot depended on what those people had in mind. Were they coming to help? To fight? What were they up to? He judged they were close enough for his voice to reach. Time to find out.

CHAPTER SIXTY-SEVEN

"Hail the boat!" Etse called out, cupping his hands to his mouth. "We could use some help here, if you're willing."

There seemed to be some commotion on the boat for a moment, then someone shouted back, "Etse?"

"Musongola?" Etse asked. He looked at Kwadwo, who just shrugged and shook his head. Clearly Musongola hadn't escaped Nicran with Kwesi and Kwadwo, then. How had he gotten out, and then travelled all the way here? Etse grinned a little. How had any of them, for that matter? Each of their tales was probably like something out of a song.

"Musongola, we've got big trouble here. We could use some help," Etse said. The boat was close enough for him to make out shapes now. Each person on board was wearing armor and bearing weapons. Most had spears and swords, but one bore a powerful bow.

"Dead trouble or living trouble?" Musongola asked. "Aane, we've had some of each, too." He was sitting in the prow of the rowboat and tossed a line toward the shore.

"We'll have to compare notes later," Etse said. He caught the rope and started pulling the boat in toward the rocky pier. "But right now, about fifty Gbohii coming this way."

Musongola jumped to the shore and clasped Etse's arm. He looked the same as he had when Etse had last seen him: full armor, wearing a big grin, sandy hair a bit disheveled. How the hell had the man managed to come through everything thrown at him and still have the same smile? Etse wasn't sure if he should roll his eyes or grin back. He chose the latter.

"It is good to see you," Etse said. "The ship – yours?"

"Kudowor's," Musongola replied.

"He did it," Kwadwo breathed. "Kwesi put him in charge of the refugees when we made for Takoradi."

"He led us here, well enough," Musongola said.

Etse assessed the boat. If they had two people rowing, they could perhaps carry another ten people back per trip. It was going to take a lot of trips to get everyone aboard the ship. He looked east and saw the first Gbohii boiling over the hill. In another minute the horde would be all over them. He looked around at the people huddled on the rocks, and out at the ship, so close and yet so far. They could swim for it. Most of them might even make it. But many would not.

Everyone was looking at Etse. For whatever reason, they were all waiting for his decision. He took a deep breath. No matter how he decided, people were going to die here today.

Better they die on their feet.

"Musongola, I can't ask you for help, but…" Etse started.

Musongola cut in, saying "Of course you can. My sword is yours. Ask."

"Then let's get the injured and the children on the boat. Send them to the ship. The rest of you," he went on, raising his voice. "It looks like we have one more battle before we get to rest. Raise your spears!"

He strode back toward the shore a bit, stopping on the edge of where the water was deep enough to prevent the Gbohii from easily flanking them. No, he wanted the things coming at them where they could be seen. And they were coming fast – dozens of fiends running at them with clashing jaws and howling noises.

Etse drew his sword.

On both sides of him, more men stepped up. Musongola drew his blade on Etse's right. Kwadwo stepped up on his left. Spearmen came to join their line. Etse looked behind him and saw more men forming up into ragged rows. Mostly armed with spears, they'd be able to fight through the front line, pinning the monsters with their weapons. Back further still, he saw Odoi spinning a sling. It might not stop one of the Gbohii – but then again, if the young man was a good enough shot to hit their heads, it might. Beside him a thin bearded man was stringing a powerful bow. He'd come with Musongola.

"Your bowman any good with that thing?" Etse asked.

"Beyond good," Musongola replied. He was breathing hard, each breath tight between his teeth.

Etse could feel the tension mounting in his arms and shoulders. It was always worst in these moments just before the clash. The things were twenty feet away now and coming fast. An arrow flew over their head and pinned one in the eye. A sling stone took another in the forehead and it went crashing to the ground. Then another arrow took one down. The men cheered, seeing the enemy falling.

"I do think they're competing with each other," Etse muttered.

"Good," Kwadwo said.

The first Gbohii were on them before they could say more. Etse lost track of everything but the movement of his blade. He wove a wall of sharp steel around him. Musongola hacked the head from one monster that came too close to grappling with Etse, and Etse stabbed another in the eye with his sword. Off to the right, he saw a great axe cleaving through the monsters, hacking bits of them off. He shook his head. These men needed more training. The axe should be so much more effective than that – but the Gbohii didn't care if they lose hands or arms.

The spears pinned the monsters, but poorly. None of these spears had crossbars, so the Gbohii were able to pull themselves down the spear toward the hapless spearman. Etse saw one get close enough to grab the screaming spear holder by the shoulders, mouth open wide to bite his face. His sword clove the thing's head from its shoulders only just in time. But the thing's arms still held the man fast as it tumbled sideways into the water. The man sank beneath the surface and didn't come back up.

The front line was tiring. "Next rank, advance!" Etse shouted. He ducked back, narrowly avoiding a claw. One of the spearmen behind him took his place, pinning the thing. Etse took another step back, panting. Kwadwo was wincing in pain, backing away from the line. He didn't seem to be bleeding, but he was holding his shoulder.

"Are you all right?" Etse asked him.

"Aane, but I've torn something in my shoulder," Kwadwo replied.

Etse winced. Kwadwo was a good fighter, but he was also old for his profession, and he'd been running and fighting hard for a long time now. It wasn't shocking that he was wearing down.

"I saw Gbohii in the water. Stay back and guard our bowman and slinger," Etse said. The pair were still firing as rapidly as they could find targets. Etse wouldn't be surprised if they'd already reached the double digits each in kills.

Kwadwo nodded, too weary to argue.

Etse shook himself and prepared to re-enter the fight. It looked like the line of the enemy was thinning, but his left flank was falling apart. The Gbohii were thick enough there that they'd pulled themselves close to the spearmen. Before Etse could get there, two of the monsters tore chunks out of the men fighting them. He raced to help before the line broke apart completely.

He picked up a spear someone had dropped to the rocks and threw it. The weapon broke through the front of a Gbohii's skull and the monster dropped like a felled tree. Then he was in their midst. His sword sliced through the neck of one Gbohii. His backswing took the leg from another, and it toppled into the dark water. Etse was screaming a long, unending battle cry now. He was dimly aware of the men fighting alongside him as he pushed harder, advancing against the monsters, pushing them back, driving the things before him. He would chase them all down, kill every last one of the things, and…

…then suddenly there were none of them left.

Etse stood, panting, looking about him for more foes. But there were none. He'd slain the last of the monsters they faced here. Behind him on the stone levy, men wept in relief, or pain, or both. Etse wasn't sure how he felt himself. He was still alive. It was almost a surprise. The enemy was dead, but this was a tiny skirmish and there was so much left to do. The work ahead felt daunting – crushing him with the weight of it all.

But there was Musongola, standing there with his armor gleaming in the moonlight. And beyond him, Kwadwo – solid and patient as ever. On the boat was Kudowor. And there were others he'd met on the road – or that these close companions had brought. Each had shown their mettle in this battle. And he knew they'd support him through what was to come ahead.

It was not enough to merely survive. He'd seen the answer here tonight. If they worked together, they could retake their home from the monsters that plagued it. He turned back to the assembled people, all of them still basking in the rush that followed a battle – for the survivors.

"Let's get our wounded out to Kudowor's ship. We'll have to bring the surviving kwapawnkah if we can, too," Etse said. "We'll need them." And more mounts as well. Cavalry would be effective against the things. So would archers – he'd seen how devastating Tay-Natey and Odoi were tonight.

People started moving, but before they got far, Etse went on. "We've won a mighty battle here, tonight. We held the ground against the real foe – the Gbohii. It's a first step. A battle won."

He strode into their midst. "It's just a beginning, though. We will defeat this enemy. We will destroy this foe. We will roll back this evil plague into the sea and wash it from our shores."

People were nodding now. Etse could feel his words bolstering their confidence, feeding into the post-battle euphoria. Later, they'd feel less sure. But he would lay what foundation he could right now.

"Asanteman is ours! It belongs to the living – not the dead," Etse said.

"For Asanteman!" Musongola called.

"For the living!" Kwadwo joined in.

"For King Etse!" Uche shouted. "May he lead us to victory!"

More of the people assembled took up that last call. Etse didn't even try to stop them, not this time. He caught Musongola's eye and saw the raised eyebrows. He gave a little shrug in return. The people needed a leader, needed someone to shoulder the burdens ahead. Etse hated the job. He would turn it down in half a heartbeat if anyone else would do it. But who? His father was dead. Kwadwo was old, and too cautious. Musongola simply didn't know these people well enough. There was no one else.

So he smiled back at his people, as they buffeted his back and bestowed what they thought was a great honor. He managed not to grimace at the weight of the invisible crown they placed on his head. He would be their leader – their king, if that's what they wanted to call him. At least until he died, or they found someone better.

"To the ship, then!" Etse called. "We have much to do."

CHAPTER SIXTY-EIGHT

Lugu stopped her kwapawnkah, taking a moment to stare back over her shoulder at the ruins of Takoradi burning in the distance. Thousands had died in the fires and slaughter there. They were an acceptable loss, but it was annoying. The city had been a decent place to build her power from. Now she would have to start anew.

Security against the dead was a problem. They could climb, tear through almost any block, and even rip aside things like the huge stone she'd had her man lever into place to cover the sewer opening. The world could be hers for the taking, but that would do her little good if she couldn't control the monsters that had given her this chance at greatness.

"My queen, we must keep moving," one of her riders called out to her. "The dead still hunt out there in the dark."

She nodded absently. The Gbohii were mostly still busy eating Takoradi. There were a few bands out there, and she had no doubt that some might be following her army. She'd escaped with most of her force, hundreds of men. It was easy to follow such a troop, but she was confident they could slay any small packs of Gbohii they ran into. Worst case, she and her mounted troops could outrun any larger groups.

She was furious over losing the key, and Kwesi's legacy. It was still out there somewhere. With the damnable luck Etse seemed to have, he might have already run into Kwadwo and recovered the key for himself. He would gain access to the stores and weapons that she ought to have. Half of her wanted to give chase, but she would have to ride north a long way to cross the

Densu safely, and if Etse reached Kamit before her she'd have to besiege him at a fortress with huge stockpiles of food inside – and Gbohii stalking the country outside. The thought made her shiver.

A sniffling noise from behind her brought her mind back to her present plans. Not all had been lost from the disaster at Takoradi. She reached behind her to pat the boy riding double on her kwapawnkah gently on his head. He was perhaps even more valuable than they key had been. Her fool of a brother had him and let the child slip through his fingers. Etse had probably never even noticed how important the boy was.

"Hush now, Amon," Lugu said. "You will be safe with me."

"I miss Sefadzi," Amon whispered into her back.

"Perhaps we can re-unite you with her, in time," Lugu said. "But first we must keep you safe."

She'd inspected each of Etse's people personally, of course. It had been easy to spot the crescent moon shaped scars on the boy's leg. He'd been bitten – and lived. She had only a little while to talk with the boy, and he'd told her a wild tale about being sick in Nicran, and an old woman with a magic cup who had cured him.

It was a story she would never have believed, except that he was living proof a cure existed. The plague could be stopped. The bite did not need to be fatal.

That was power, more than any other power in the world – the ability to save or condemn those who had been bitten. Who knew, perhaps even the power to reverse the curse on those who had become Gbohii, or a means to control the monsters and use them as a weapon?

She would use the boy to find this power.

Once she had it, all her enemies would pay.

ABOUT THE AUTHOR

Balogun is Master Instructor and Technical Director of the *Afrikan Martial Arts Institute* and the founder and owner of Roaring Lions Productions, which creates works of non-fiction, fiction, screenplays, audio plays and films.
He is the author of more than forty non-fiction and fiction books, contributing co-editor of three anthologies: *Ki: Khanga: The Anthology*, *Steamfunk* and *Dieselfunk* and contributing editor of the *Rococoa* anthology and *Black Power: The Superhero Anthology*.
He is creator of the *Steamfunkateers Role Playing Game*, the comedic martial arts role playing game, *The Ice Cold RPG*, the

horror RPGs *4EV4 Friends* and *The Haunting of Truth High* and the revolutionary role playing game *Stick It to The Man!*. Finally, Balogun is the Director and Fight Choreographer of the feature film, *A Single Link*, and the short films, *Forward Motion, Rite of Passage: Initiation* and *The Dentist of Westminster*; co-author of the award winning screenplay, *Ngolo*; co-creator of *Ki Khanga: The Sword and Soul Role-Playing Game*, creator of the comic book series *Jagunjagun Lewa* and co-creator of the comic book series, *Ngolo*.

www.ingramcontent.com/pod-product-compliance
Lightning Source LLC
Chambersburg PA
CBHW061521050726
47503CB00015B/2304